Gift of *Sydney*

Also by D. MANNING RICHARDS

Destiny in Sydney

Gift of
Sydney

An epic novel of the struggle to forge the
multicultural, world-class city of Sydney, Australia

D. MANNING RICHARDS

**ARIES
BOOKS**

ARIES BOOKS

ARIES BOOKS - Fiction
Washington, DC, USA
www.AriesBooks.com

This book is a work of fiction. The characters are products of the
author's imagination or are used fictitiously, and any resemblance
to real persons, living or dead, is entirely coincidental. The portrayal
of well-known historical personages, however, are based on
recorded history.

Cataloging-in-Publication Data:
Richards, D. Manning, 1942-
Richards, D. Manning. *Gift of Sydney: An Epic Novel of the Struggle to
Forge the Multicultural, World-Class City of Sydney, Australia*.
Washington, DC, USA: Aries Books, 2014.
1. Historical family saga fiction. 2. Sydney, Australia. 3. Multiculturalism

ISBN 978-0-9845410-3-4

Dedicated to Judy
My wife, with grateful thanks for her early research,
writing of first draft narratives, constructive review
comments throughout numerous drafts, and for
her enthusiastic support and encouragement.

CONTENTS

AUTHOR'S NOTE

Gift of Sydney is the second in the series of novels about Sydney, Australia. It begins where the first novel, *Destiny in Sydney,* ended in 1902. If, for some reason, you are only interested in the more recent history of Sydney and Australia from 1903, then go ahead and read this novel. Otherwise, I strongly recommend that you read *Destiny in Sydney* first to provide context for this second novel and to increase your enjoyment of it.

Those who have read *Destiny in Sydney* will be surprised to see that this second novel covers the period from 1903 to 1981, instead of through the 2000 Sydney Summer Olympics, as I had original-ly intended. The reason for this shortening of the years covered is that readers of *Destiny in Sydney* have told me that they hesitated buying the novel because of its intimidating thickness and the time required to read nearly 500 pages. Well, *Gift of Sydney* would have been considerably longer through the year 2000, so I decided to write a third and final novel in my Sydney series at a later date.

The portraits of public personages, who appear in *Gift of Sydney* under their real names, are offered as accurate. Whenever possible, I used their own words taken from public records, history books, bi-ographies, and recorded interviews. In dialogue scenes with fiction-al characters, however, personage's quotations were sometimes used from different dates to create a flow of dialogue that fairly repre-sented what the person would have said about the issues of the day.

As in *Destiny in Sydney*, some of my characters use racist, re-ligiously biased, and sexist terms that were common at the time. It would be misleading and inaccurate if they were not to do so. I tried not to be gratuitous in their use. Although you will find these malicious and vilifying words and phrases hard to take, I hope you will agree that they help to illustrate the bigotry that existed up to and through the civil rights years, until a more enlightened period began in the 1970s. Also for the purposes of verisimilitude, my characters do a good deal of swearing, especially soldiers fighting in the two world wars, but I can find no way around their use to realistically express the horrors of war.

I gave a disproportionate number of pages to dramatize the story of the Sydney Opera House. It is, after all, *the* iconic building of Sydney and Australia and is World Heritage listed alongside other architectural treasures such as the Taj Mahal, Notre-Dame Cathedral, Pyramids at Giza, and Vatican City. Its construction, however, was a fiasco. Its mismanagement and escalating cost were factors in toppling the state government. The breakup of the close relationship of architect Jørn Utzon and structural engineer Ove Arup was poignant and tragic. By telling the story of Jørn Utzon's forced withdrawal from the Opera House project, I have taken on one of the most controversial and still contentious issues in the history of Sydney. Of course, because it was such a drama, I could not possibly avoid it.

As I did in *Destiny in Sydney*, I appended a Fact or Fiction? section by chapter and provided a list of my primary sources in Acknowledgments and Sources. My website www.dmanningrichards. com may be visited for additional information.

Before I write the third and last Sydney novel, I will write two historical novels that have nothing to do with Sydney: *Paris in Ruins: A novel of passion and the French Résistance* about the years before and following the "Battle for Paris" in 1944, and *The Kentucky Faith Healer* about a charismatic preacher from 1945 to 1966.

PROLOGUE

In the prequel *Destiny in Sydney,* the First Fleet transporting British convicts arrived in 1788 in the place that would later become Sydney, Australia. Convicts provided the forced labor to establish Sydney Cove, a brutal, dehumanizing penal settlement from which few would return home to Britain. Fictional Scottish marine Lieutenant Nathaniel Armstrong made a heedless decision to marry an Irish convict he loved, Moira O'Keeffe, to start a family. Their Scot-Irish family rose from modest beginnings to become one of the wealthiest, politically astute, and respected families in Sydney. By 1902, Eleanor Armstrong Norman had become a well-known philanthropist, supporter of Aboriginal people, suffragette, and chairman of the venerable Norman Builders. Her nephew Thomas Armstrong had advanced to presidency of the company, the largest real estate developer in Sydney. Her first cousin once removed Samuel Armstrong had achieved eminence as the New South Wales treasurer of the Progressive Party with aspirations to become the premier of New South Wales.

The indigenous Eora coastal people were devastated by the white invasion of their country. Some tried to fight the invaders, like the warriors Pemulwuy and his son Tedbury, while Bennelong, Bungaree, and others attempted to fit in. But all to no avail. Within the first five years of white settlement in Sydney Cove, a wave of European diseases—smallpox, typhoid, typhus, influenza, measles, and chicken pox—killed seventy percent or more of the native people. Most of those remaining had their land and water appropriated and were driven away through violence and starvation. By 1902, two-thirds of the estimated 9,000 Aborigines remaining in New

South Wales lived on government reserves and stations or Christian missions. The Aborigines in Sydney numbered in the hundreds, eking out a meager existence. A starving, four-year-old indigenous girl was found by a young drover and taken to an orphanage in Bathurst, New South Wales, where she was given the name Baranga. She would begin the Hudson family line of Aborigines who work to improve the lot of indigenous people.

In 1853, three Fong brothers from Canton, China, traveled to Australia during the gold rush hoping to strike it rich and return home wealthy men. As sojourners, they did not try to fit in. White gold diggers objected to the large number of Chinese diggers and their foreignness. Sing-woo Fong was murdered by a gang of ruffians, and his brother Ho-teng, feeling responsible, died despondent in an opium den. In 1902, the third brother, Min-chin Fong, prospered as a market gardener. The Immigration Restriction Act, known as the White Australia Policy, was the first act of Parliament following Australia's federation in 1901. It expressed Parliament's intention to make Australia an outpost of the white British race in Asia/Oceania, encourage the Chinese to leave Australia, and keep out all undesirable immigrants. Against the odds, Ming-chin decided to stay with the hope that his grandchildren would be accepted as part of a future multicultural society.

So *Gift of Sydney* begins in 1903 in Sydney, an international port and a striving metropolis with a population approaching 500,000. In many ways, the city is a more desirable place to live than most cities in the mother country, especially for those who value a healthier climate, recreation, better opportunities, and greater freedoms.

But there are also problems. Australians are not sure of themselves on the world stage and feel a self-consciousness about their "convict stain." There remains a vexing "Aboriginal problem" to deal with. Asiatic and Oceanic peoples are pressing to immigrate to Australia where they are not welcome. And Britain, Australia's principal trading partner and protector, is 15,000 miles away on the other side of the world.

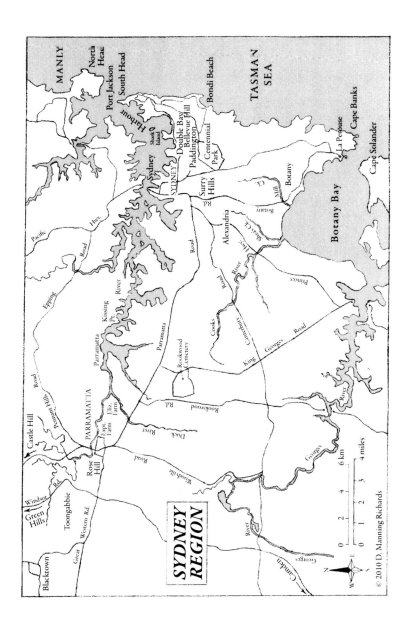

SYDNEY REGION

© 2010 D. Manning Richards

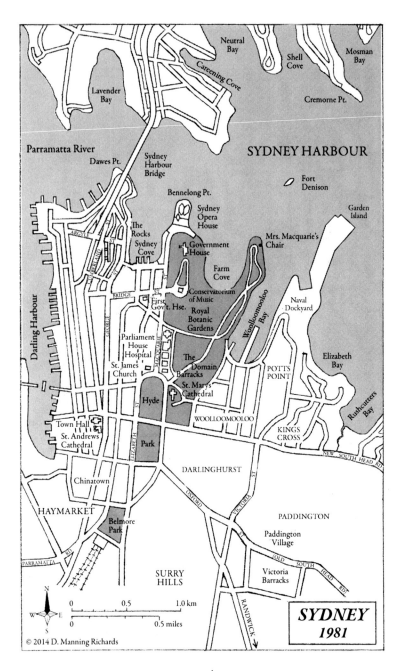

Neutral Bay

Shell Cove

Mosman Bay

Careening Cove

Lavender Bay

Cremorne Pt.

Parramatta River

SYDNEY HARBOUR

Dawes Pt.

Sydney Harbour Bridge

Fort Denison

Bennelong Pt.

The Rocks

Sydney Opera House

Garden Island

ARGYLE ST

Sydney Cove

Government House

Mrs. Macquarie's Chair

Farm Cove

CUMBERLAND ST

BRIDGE

First Gov't. Hse.

Conservatorium of Music

Naval Dockyard

Darling Harbour

GEORGE ST

Royal Botanic Gardens

Woolloomooloo Bay

Parliament House

Hospital

MACQUARIE ST

POTTS POINT

Elizabeth Bay

St. James Church

The Domain

Barracks

St. Mary's Cathedral

WOOLLOOMOOLOO

Rushcutters Bay

Hyde

Town Hall

St. Andrews Cathedral

ELIZABETH ST

Park

KINGS CROSS

NEW SOUTH HEAD RD

Chinatown

DARLINGHURST

HAYMARKET

Belmore Park

OXFORD ST

VICTORIA ST

PADDINGTON

Paddington Village

PARRAMATTA RD

SURRY HILLS

Victoria Barracks

OLD SOUTH HEAD RD

RANDWICK

N
W E
S

0   0.5   1.0 km

0   0.5 miles

SYDNEY 1981

© 2014 D. Manning Richards

Gift of Sydney

"Australian multiculturalism is a unique achievement. Australia may have stumbled into the multicultural epoch. We were a nation comparatively small in size and insular in outlook. But within a period of time that is short in historical perspective, Australia has been enlarged in capacities, talents and outlook by millions of men and women from every corner of the globe."

—Malcolm Fraser, Australian Prime Minister
from multiculturalism address 1981

Chapter 1

Convict Stain

"**I'm very upset.** I never suspected anyone in my family of being a crook—suddenly I have two." Eleanor Armstrong paused after writing this line in her diary, wondering whether to continue writing about the disturbing facts she had discovered during the past month, February 1903. Compulsion overcame caution, and she wrote on:

> My high regard for our Armstrong family has plummeted because of what I've found about my beloved grandmother, Moira Armstrong, and my cousin's son Samuel, whom I had great hopes for as a leader following in Duncan's footsteps. Unlike Duncan, however, who was honest and tried to do what he thought was best for Australia, Samuel is doing what is best for Samuel. If the accusations are true, and I fear they are, he is a charmingly venal politician who is corrupting others in Parliament and government service.
>
> As a retirement project, I decided in February to finally look through the two boxes and sea chest containing my father's notebooks, letters, and voluminous papers. I thought if nothing else, I might learn more about our family lineage.

What I found were disturbing references to my grandmother's background that did not fit well with what my father had told us: He said his father, Nathaniel Armstrong, a marine lieutenant on the First Fleet, had sent for his wife, Moira, after he was settled. She was presumed to be an adventuresome, independent, young woman who came out by herself.

The date of my father's birth was the first thing I noticed; it wasn't consistent. I found reference to my grandmother being born and raised in Ireland, not Scotland. A letter from a distant Armstrong relative answering my father's letter, said that they would not welcome a visit because of the 'soiling' of the Armstrong name. There were other disturbing anomalies and then I found a tightly folded Warrant of Emancipation for Moira O'Keeffe. She had been convicted of robbery and sentenced to seven years' transportation to Australia. I couldn't believe it: my grandmother was an exile! I'm still dumbstruck and don't know what to do with this vexing discovery. I even considered burning the warrant, but couldn't bring myself to do it; probably the same reason Father folded it so tightly and tucked it away, out of sight and mind.

A week later, Eleanor told Samuel about what she had found.

"*Birthstain*, that's what it is! Dammit, Aunt Eleanor, how long have you known this, and do others on your side of the family know?"

"Calm down, Samuel, it isn't the end of the world."

"Not for you—you're retired. But I have . . . or *had*, a chance to become premier of New South Wales. I also have a position in society to maintain, to say nothing of my financial relationships. This cannot get out."

"It won't."

"Who else knows?"

"I expect no one else knows. I found it in my father's papers a week ago."

"You haven't told Priscilla or Thomas?—she was supposed to

be such a grand lady; it's hard to believe. How did you come across it; are you sure?"

"Please, Samuel, one question at a time. There's no doubt about it: I've found her Warrant of Emancipation. I'm as shocked as you are. I haven't told anyone. I'm only telling you because of the situation you're in."

"This will not help 'my situation' if it gets out. I want you to destroy that warrant. The press would love to get hold of it to smear me. I wish you hadn't told me. I don't need to know this."

"Do you think you can still be elected to lead the Progressive Party?"

"Oh please . . . I can forget that now, can't I? What with *The Sydney Morning Herald's* unsubstantiated allegations and now this skeleton in the cupboard."

"Do you want to know why she was transported?"

"No, I *don't* want to know anything more about it, thank you very much. Knowing we have a convict in the family is quite enough."

"Is there any truth in the corruption allegations regarding the Sydney Electric Light Authority?"

He looked at her askance. "Really Eleanor . . . what kind of question is that? . . . coming from you. That's almost naive, not an adjective I'd ever expect using for you."

Her questioning gaze remained unchanged.

"Look, Eleanor, you ran your own business. Was everything you did one hundred percent ethical? . . . See here, they're fishing, looking for dirt. It's all absolute rubbish."

"Well, I thought you should know."

"Because you don't like my politics, and didn't like Dad's either. That's it, isn't it? Putting the last nail in my coffin, are you?"

"No, that wasn't my agenda, Samuel."

"What the hell is your agenda then?"

"If you seek to become premier, it's bound to come out. You needed to know. What are you going to do?"

"I don't know. I'll have to give up treasurer, that's for sure. If that doesn't quiet things down, I don't know what I'll do. I'll have to resign if it goes much further. It's the only way I can recoup some semblance of integrity. I don't *have* to be in politics, but I do have to make a living."

* * *

A gentle voice whispered "Baranga."

It was Molly the Aboriginal kitchen helper who had become the protector of the little, sickly, indigenous girl in the Benevolent Foundation Orphanage in Bathurst. Molly continued to call her Baranga, even though the matron had given her the name Daisy.

Molly sat down on the edge of the bed, and they embraced. In whispers, they talked about their day and what they were looking forward to. When Baranga giggled loudly, Molly raised her forefinger to her lips and hushed "Ssshh." They had talked as long as they dared. The skinny little girl reached out for the warmth of Molly's fleshy arms around her.

"I call ya Baranga forever, cos that bin yer name," she whispered. "Molly and Baranga got no *wiyanga*," mother. "I *wiyanga* ta this little one." Molly softly sang a song while gently rocking the little girl to sleep.

When Baranga awoke in the middle of the night, Molly was gone. Although such visits were infrequent, Baranga listened intently every night for her before falling to sleep. When an opportunity presented itself, Baranga would steal into the kitchen for a short visit with Molly to share a thought or ask a question. Molly often gave her a taste of the meal being prepared. Daisy could rely on an encouraging word, a warm smile, and an affectionate hug before scampering off, reassured and exhilarated.

One day while Molly was scouring a pot in the kitchen and humming away, the matron came in unexpectedly. "Molly," commanded the matron, "come with me." Molly wiped her hands and uneasily followed the matron to her office. The matron told her to sit down and then scolded:

"I'm on to your tricks, Molly. Don't think you can fool me." Molly stared at a spot on the floor between her feet. "I want no more of your secret night visits to Daisy or extra food in the kitchen, and no more speaking your gibberish to her. We speak *only* English here! Your duties are in the *kitchen*, not with any of the orphans—is that understood?"

"Yes, ma'am."

"You may go."

Sobbing, Molly rushed down the stark white hallway and threw herself onto her cot.

The matron also called Baranga into her office and ordered her to stay away from Molly. Still, Baranga and Molly shared a meaningful smile now and then and an occasional furtive embrace. Several months later, Baranga was summoned to the matron's office.

"I consider you six years old now, Daisy, so I'm transferring you to the Warrawindra Aboriginal Station."

On the morning of her departure, Baranga's heart ached as she sneaked into the kitchen. Seeing Molly alone, Baranga cried out as she ran to her and draped her arms around Molly's legs, laying her head against her apron. Molly looked around nervously before bending down on one knee to embrace and kiss her. Their tears ran freely knowing they would never see each other again. Molly said, "Yer me piccaninny always, Baranga."

"*Daisy!*" the matron's voice came from down the hallway. "You'd better not be in the kitchen!"

Molly looked frightened. She kissed Baranga one last time and said, "Go this way quick." Molly sprung back to the kitchen sink and smiled at the matron as she entered.

The matron found Daisy in the sleeping quarters and took her to a horse-drawn wagon waiting outside. An Aboriginal man stood next to the wagon.

"Daisy, you've seen Harvey, our groundskeeper, before. He'll take you to Warrawindra Station." She handed him a bag. "Here's your lunch." And then a brown envelope. "This contains Daisy's papers and a list of items for you to bring back from Warrawindra. The station superintendent, John Gabbett, should have the items ready for you." She helped Daisy up onto the seat of the open wagon. "You're a dear little girl, Daisy, be good and study hard, and you'll be all right. Go along now, Harvey."

Daisy had seen the kindly old groundskeeper many times. He always had a warm, friendly smile for the children, and had even shared a greeting now and then with Daisy. There were few men at the orphanage, and he had become something of a father figure to her. They had ridden for only a few minutes when Daisy asked, "Where we goin'?"

"Warrawindra Aboriginal Station."

"Where t'at?"

"We go fair way west." Seeing that her inquisitive face looked perplexed, he added with a smile. "Ya see. The mission good place fer little girl like ya ta grow up in."

Daisy turned her attention to the passing sights. As they left the settlement and entered the bush, Daisy began to feel strangely at home. She let her legs swing freely with the rocking of the wagon. They passed by paddocks with grazing sheep too numerous to count.

Arriving in a country town, Daisy's eyes widened, and she murmured "Oooh" in amazement. There were so many people and big buildings. So much … of everything. She looked up at Harvey, sharing her astonishment. He smiled and nodded, appreciating her excitement. She stared off again, bedazzled, and not knowing where to look first.

Two boys playing alongside the road were rolling a hoop along. Daisy's arms moved involuntarily as she imaged herself flicking the stick to roll the hoop. She stared at three girls with long golden hair the color and brightness of the sun and yearned for a beautiful, pastel-colored dress like they were wearing. In wonderment, she gaped at the lifelike dolls they were playing with. An elegant lady with an impossibly tiny waist and a gorgeous high-collared, lacy blouse came out of a house with a man. They climbed into the shiny black carriage with gold engravings.

After the wagon rolled out of town, Daisy tugged on Harvey's sleeve.

"Me hungry."

"Me too."

A short while later, Harvey drove the wagon off the road and down a slight grade to sheoak trees beside a creek. Daisy climbed down and immediately scampered off.

"Don't go too far orf," he said.

Harvey collected dry twigs and started a fire to boil the billy for tea. Seeing Daisy returning, he mischievously peered into the bag containing their lunch. Daisy sat down next to him and anxiously eyed the bag.

"Hmm, guess what we got fer tucker?" Harvey said as he shook the bag as if something alive was in it.

She leaned closer, eyes widening. The bag seemed to move on its own. Taking out a piece of cooked mutton, Harvey said, "Oh, live goanna, gotta kill it."

Daisy giggled. "T'at silly. T'at not alive."

Harvey cut a piece and passed it to her in a wedge of damper bread.

Daisy looked at it and took a bite. "Mmmm, goanna. Me like it."

They looked at each other and broke out laughing.

After lunch they resumed their trip. The uncomfortable bouncy wagon seat exhausted Daisy. She climbed into the back of the wagon, wrapped herself in a canvas cover, and dozed off intermittently. Just before dusk, Harvey woke her to tell her they were approaching Warrawindra Station. They rode by a fenced cultivated field toward a line of buildings and turned through a gate into a large central courtyard.

Daisy didn't like the look of the place. It wasn't pretty. Shabby unpainted wood cottages lined opposite sides of the central dirt courtyard with an imposing brick building at the end. There were no trees or grass. Groups of Aborigines sat on stoops in front of their cottages. A few waved at Harvey, although they did not look happy. Their plain clothes were dirty and torn and a layer of dust seemed to cover the buildings, wagons, and even the people.

As they rode up to the brick building, surrounded by a wide white-painted veranda, a neatly dressed heavyset white woman came out to meet them. Unsmiling, she said hello to Harvey and helped Daisy down from the wagon. Apprehensive, Daisy ran around the wagon to Harvey and took hold of his coat with one hand.

"Don't be afraid of the nice lady, Daisy, ya'll like it 'ere." He took her hand and led her to the woman. "This 'ere Mrs. Gabbett. 'Ere's the envelope 'bout Daisy, missus."

She smiled at Daisy. "Hello . . . aren't you a cute little thing." Reaching down, she took hold of her hand and led her up the steps. At the top, Daisy turned, smiled, and waved to Harvey, a final good-bye to the only person in the world with whom she had any connection.

He returned a broad smile and waved back.

"G'bye, Daisy."

* * *

The Sydney Electric Light Authority held a lavish event on July 9, 1904, in the Ultimo Power Station. Samuel Armstrong was one of the honored guests present when the Lady Mayoress threw the switch that turned on the electric lights replacing gas illumination in the central business district of Sydney.

Having resigned from government and left politics, Samuel attended as a private businessman. His resignation satisfied his accusers and removed him from the headlines. Eleanor kept their secret by telling no one else that Moira had been a convict.

Two attendees were talking when Samuel Armstrong walked by. "What do you think of our illustrious treasurer resigning his post?"

"I know all about that bugger. I reckon he had his hand in the till—he'd steal stamp money from his poor blind mother."

Samuel's duplicitous involvement with the Sydney Electric Light Authority had forced his resignation. As treasurer, he had orchestrated a lucrative noncompetitive tender for Glebe Electric Wire Company to manufacture and supply all the electric transmission wire required by the city. An investigation contended he was one of the principal owners of the company, whose involvement constituted a conflict of interest. Samuel successfully defended himself by proving he had no interest in the company, although he held a personal promissory note for a large loan to a friend, who happened to be the president of Glebe Electric Wire Company.

With the press no longer interested in him, Samuel accepted the president's shares in Glebe Electric Wire Company as payment of the promissory note and became both its majority owner and chief executive.

His first order of business was to build a larger and more ef-
ficient manufacturing plant. The facility in Glebe was running at
capacity to supply wire to Sydney. Hemmed in on all sides, there
was no room for expansion. The future was electrification of the
suburbs, and Samuel wanted those contracts as well.

In Alexandria, Samuel's real estate agent found an ideal site for
his new factory that met the requirements of approximately fifteen
acres, a central location, and inexpensive land. The landowner William Starkey was willing to sell for the price offered but explained
that there was a problem with the lease. Fong Min-chin leased the
low-lying land along Shea's Creek for market gardening. The agent
and Starkey agreed to let Samuel Armstrong deal directly with Mr.
Fong to solve the lease problem.

The next day, the real estate agent met with Samuel and his solicitor to plan a strategy.

"The landlord, Starkey, said the dumb Chow doesn't have a solicitor," the agent said. "He's let Starkey's solicitor prepare all of the
leases he's signed over the years."

Samuel's solicitor visited Fong Min-chin unannounced and
gave him a lease termination order. Later the same day, the solicitor
met with Samuel.

"Did you show him exactly where the termination clause is
written in his lease requiring only sixty-days notice?" Samuel asked.

"Yes. And the Chinaman immediately started to berate himself
for not buying the land himself. He said he knew the land could
be sold out from under him, but thought the wet, low-lying land
would be good for only market gardening. I utterly intimidated
him when I showed him your plans to pipe the stream, fill it over,
and build an eight-acre factory."

"Did he say *anything* about the other lease?" Samuel asked,
squeezing the chair arm.

"No, and *I didn't* say a word about it. He—"

"Did he say anything about having a solicitor?"

"No. I offered him my services, for when he relocates, and he
took my card without saying he has one."

Samuel settled back in his office chair. "Good. But if he gets

a solicitor, he'll figure it out; it sticks out like dog's balls. Well . . .
you've given him notice, so we'll just have to wait and see if we have
a problem. He won't catch it himself; most of them don't read English worth a damn. I expect we'll be just fine, and he'll be gone by
mid-September.

* * *

It was ten o'clock in the evening, past Daisy's usual bedtime at Warrawindra Station; even so, she sat quietly in a corner of the bedroom listening intently to the big kids talk. She had been assigned
to Aboriginal parents who occupied a cottage with only one child,
Billy. Her foster parents treated her lovingly, and Billy had become
her "big brother."

"How old you?" Billy asked.

"Fourteen," Mabel answered. "How old you?"

"Fifteen, same as Louisa. But me sixteen birthday in two weeks."

Billy was Louisa's boyfriend. She and Mabel had sneaked out of
the girls' dormitory through loose wood slats of the building wall
after the nine o'clock lockdown. Louisa had done it before. They intended to sneak back in during the night when everyone, including
the dormitory matron, was asleep.

Girls who turned twelve were forced to live in the girls' dormitory to avoid "immoral influences" and to be trained for domestic service. Boys lived with their parents and worked in the fields,
learning to be farm laborers. Louisa's and Billy's families occupied
adjacent cottages. The parents expected the two young ones to marry someday.

"How old you, sweetie?" Mabel asked Daisy.

"She don't know," Louisa said.

"Do *too*. I bin six when I come 'ere . . ." Daisy looked at her
fingers. "Seven now."

Mabel screwed up her face. "You little one—don't look seven."

"She not seven. She don't know 'er birthday," Billy said.

"No birthday!" Mabel said. "Why that, sweetie?"

"No one tell me," Daisy answered.

"She adopted," Louisa said.

"Ah ... sad ... Hey, ya can use mine!" Mabel said with a huge smile. "4 September. You seven an' me fifteen. We 'ave big birthday party."

"*Wahoo!*" Billy said slapping his leg. "Good idea. We do big proper party fer little sister. First one. Whaddya think, Louisa?"

"Yeah, proper dinkum birthday!"

"With *presents*?" Daisy asked. "Never git presents."

"Yep, we make 'em fer ya," Billy said. "Whaddya think, Louisa?"

"I dunno ... ma'be me not 'ere. Matron say ma'be they send me out ta service soon."

"Ya tell 'em ta go ta buggery!" Billy said.

"I can't, Billy. I 'ave ta go. They give me family the boot, if I don't."

"Blasted boss an' 'is bitch wife," Billy said.

Billy's mother came unexpectedly into the bedroom. "Boss Gabbett comin' this way. Ya two girls hide up in the roof, quick-quick."

The tall, burly, white station superintendent sauntered up to the group of blacks talking among themselves on their front steps and, without a greeting, said to Louisa's father and mother:

"Look, I'm gettin' right tired of havin' to chase down your Louisa. She and another girl mucked up slats of the girls' dormitory wall, which I had to fix. So they won't be sneakin' back in there tonight. Tell her to report to me in the morning for a caning. And just so ya know, Louisa's training is over, and she'll be sent out to service next week." He turned abruptly and walked back toward his house.

As the superintendent had warned, Louisa was sent off to service five days later. Her assignment seemed promising though, because she was sent to work for "a rich doctor's family." A month later, a letter arrived at the station addressed to Louisa's parents (and Billy.) One of the Aboriginal girls who assisted Mrs. Gabbett in the office saw the letter from Louisa and said:

"Billy, ya got letter comin' from yer girlfrin' Louisa."

At Warrawindra Station, it was the responsibility of Mrs. Gabbett as matron to read all incoming mail, including residents' personal mail. The Aborigines Protection Board policy directed station superintendents to exert prudent postal inspection and censorship for the purposes of order, security, government business

confidentiality, and to remove troublesome and offensive information. Mrs. Gabbett would cut out any part of a personal letter that
she considered inappropriate before delivering the altered mail to
the addressee.

Billy anxiously waited two days and then went to the office and
asked Mrs. Gabbett for his mail.

"It wasn't addressed to you, Billy," Mrs. Gabbett said. "It was
addressed to her parents; your name was in parentheses. But that's
not the point, really. After reading it, my husband and I decided
it wasn't appropriate to give it to her parents. It was unnecessarily
critical of her employer and the Aborigines Protection Board, told
where she was assigned, and mentioned her misconduct with you.
There wasn't much letter left to give to her parents" (then she lied),
"so we destroyed it."

"Ya *bitch*, ya *can't* read an' destroy other people's mail!"

"*What!* You *get your arse* out of 'ere, young man, before I get mad!"

Entering the office, Superintendent Gabbett heard the end of
what his angry wife had just said. "*What's* goin' on 'ere?"

Billy said, "I got letter from Louisa—"

"Yeah, I got it right here, *mate*." He took it out of his shirt
pocket. "Seems you and Louisa have been havin' a right good time
together that could get ya thrown off the station. Yer lucky she's
gone, and I can overlook it now."

"Give me the letter," Billy said.

"Can't do that."

Billy walked toward the superintendent and reached for the
letter. Gabbett held it away from him and strong-armed him away.
"Ya can't have it, boy." Half a foot taller than Billy, the superintendent easily fended him off and then pushed him violently away,
laughing as he did it.

"Now don't get yer knickers in a twist, Jacko," he said and then
guffawed.

Angry, Billy rushed in, fists flying, connecting with the side of
Gabbett's face. The superintendent picked him up around the waist
and deposited him at the top of the veranda steps. Billy tripped
backwards down the steps and landed on his backside in the dirt.

He jumped up and fuming and fumbling withdrew a pocketknife. Finally opening it, he pointed it at Gabbett.

"I *want* that fuckin' letter. It mine, an' I wan' it."

Mrs. Gabbett had been screaming since the start of the fight, arousing the community to the confrontation. She retreated inside when Billy threatened her husband with the knife.

"Yer little knife don't worry me, but it does piss me off," Gabbett said. To the crowd forming in front of the station office, he said, "For threatening me with a knife, I'm expelling him from the station. Billy, if you don't put it away, I'll have the police arrest you. Now put it away and git the hell off the station."

Hearing angry voices, Daisy was drawn to the commotion.

"I ain't leavin' till ya give me the letter, ya bastard!"

For the crowd's benefit more than Billy's, Gabbett said, "I won't give it to you, but I'll read the part about you—ya lovesick puppy. 'Show this to Billy so he know I miss him. I want to go to the riverbank again and start our family.' That's inappropriate conduct, Billy, and grounds for rejection from the station. *Blimey!* She's propositioning you in the letter."

"Ya go ta buggery!" Billy said and spat at him. His spittle landed on the steps.

"That's part of the reason why we couldn't give the letter to Louisa's parents," Gabbett said loudly. "So now that ya heard the part about you, Billy, ya can collect yer things and git the hell off the station."

"Where Louisa?"

"Can't tell you that. It's government business."

"Does it say in the letter?"

Without waiting for the superintendent's answer, Billy rushed up the steps and reached for the letter while jamming his knife into him.

"*Ahhh SHHIIT!*" Gabbett cried out, reeling back in horror.

His wife screamed and stepped out holding a shotgun.

BAM.

Billy flew backwards off the veranda and landed on his back.

Mrs. Gabbett dropped the shotgun and collapsed.

The crowd, including Daisy, rushed to Billy's aid. She recoiled at the horrible, bloody disfigurement of Billy's head.

Devastated, Daisy turned away and walked back to her house in a daze, crawled under her bed, and curled herself into a fetal position. Billy's parents, her foster parents, found her there that night, mute and staring into the distance. They carried her to Dr. Bayer, who had been called from the nearby town of Barmora to treat Gabbett. He examined Daisy.

"Don't worry," Dr. Bayer said. "She's seen a terrible thing and is in shock. She's young and resilient though. Make sure she eats, drinks enough water, and gets plenty of rest. In a few days, she'll come out of it. I'll check her progress on Saturday."

Because Billy had attacked Superintendent Gabbett and grievously wounded him, the police did not charge Mrs. Gabbett, who had acted in her husband's defense. After a short service, Billy was buried in the blacks' cemetery.

*   *   *

Min-chin had not been himself for over a month. His wife Lumgum had learned over their years of marriage to bear his bad-tempered moods while he worked through his business problems. So she was surprised when he said they had to sit down and talk about a crisis at his market garden.

Min-chin came right out with it: "Mr. Starkey has sold my land, and I have to leave by September 14. I should have bought it when I had the chance, regardless of its high price! I should have ensured my family's and our son's future."

Lum-gum sat across from him at the kitchen table. She reached over and laid her hand on his. "Don't blame yourself, Min-chin; all's not lost. We have money saved. You can rent other land to farm."

"It will take a long time to find suitable land, prepare the soil, plant, and produce a profitable crop. We will spend most of our savings by then. I'm sixty, an old man. We will lose everything we've accomplished in twenty-three years of hard work."

"We won't lose our son. Wing-yuen is a young man who can help you get started somewhere else."

"Wing-yuen is still in school and shows no interest in market gardening. We will have to return to China, I think . . . where we can live cheaply."

While they talked, Wing-yuen listened from upstairs. He became concerned when he heard his father say that they would be forced to return to China. He came downstairs and addressed his parents.

"Father and Mother, forgive me for listening. May I ask if you have lost your lease to your market garden, Father."

"Yes, Son, I am ashamed to tell you. The land has been sold and the new owner will start construction of a factory there. I have been given 60-days notice. There is nothing I can do."

"How can they do that to you, Father? You have leased this land for a very long time."

"There is a termination provision in my lease that says if the owner Mr. Starkey sells his land the new owner can terminate my lease. I never expected the land to sell at the high price Mr. Starkey has demanded."

Wing-yuen saw the lease lying on the table and pointed to it. "Could you show me where it says you can be ordered off your leased land, Father?"

"I have no patience for this now, Wing-yuen. Your mother and I have much to decide."

"Please, Father, I want to help if I can. I can read English better than you."

"*Bai!*" For pity's sake. "Here's the lease, find it yourself, and leave us alone!"

They returned to their discussion. Wing-yuen took the lease up to his room. An hour later, he returned and took a seat at the kitchen table with them.

Min-chin asked, "You found the part that allows the termination of the lease, *kwa*?"—right?

"Yes, Father, but—"

"Then you see that I have no choice?"

"Yes, but you rent fifteen acres, don't you?"

"*Yes,*" Min-chin said impatiently.

"The lease is for only thirteen acres."

"*No* . . . it isn't! I know it say thirteen acres on the front, but if you had read more carefully, you would have seen that there is an attachment for the other two acres."

"I saw reference to it, Father, except it wasn't attached."

"I have the attachment in my office. All the same conditions apply."

"Why weren't the two acres simply combined into the same lease with the other thirteen acres?"

"Because I leased them first, from Catherine Starkey, Mr. Starkey's sister."

"Maybe the termination clause doesn't apply to her two acres, Father."

"*I told you!*—all the same conditions apply. What does it matter? What can I do with two acres when I have to vacate the other thirteen?"

"May I respectfully suggest, Father, that you talk to your friend Kwong Tang about this. He seems very smart about such matters."

"No, you may not tell your father what to do . . . when you are only sixteen and still a student! You do not show proper respect. Kwong Tang is not so smart about such matters, his business is doing poorly."

The next day at his office, Min-chin read the attachment to the lease and was confused by its legal terms and provisions. He called Kwong Tang and explained his predicament. Concerned, Tang said Min-chin could come over to his office later in the afternoon.

Tang read the main lease and the attachment.

"The main lease references the two-acre attachment and says it runs 'conterminous' with the larger thirteen-acres lease. Conterminous, though, can simply mean the two leases have the same lease periods. It doesn't say specifically that the termination clause applies."

"That's what I thought," Min-chin said, not understanding Tang's point but beginning to feel hopeful.

"Although the two owners are brother and sister, a case can be made that they wanted different lease specifics, for whatever reasons. Where are these two acres located relative to the fifteen acres you lease?"

"In the center. I expanded outward from there."

"How many years do you have remaining on your lease?"

"Almost one and a half years."

"You said the new owner wants to start construction of a factory next month. What kind of factory?"

"I can't remember." Min-chin scratched his head. "I was so upset. I didn't look closely at his plans. Something about producing wire . . . 'transmission' wire, I think."

"*Transmission* wire! . . . the new owner must be Samuel Armstrong—I went to his wedding. He's won a huge contract with Sydney Electric Light Authority to provide all the electric transmission cable to light the entire city. *Ho-wan pangyau!*" Fortunate friend! "Your problems are over. The gods have blessed you for your virtuous life. You are about to become a rich man."

To an incredulous Min-chin, Tang explained that because the attachment to Min-chin's main lease was unclear, the termination clause's application to the two acres could be contested in a court of law. The factory could not be built while the matter was litigated because the contested two acres occupied the center of the site. Tang then recommended an aggressive white solicitor to represent Min-chin.

Samuel Armstrong knew he could not afford a lengthy delay to litigate, still he feigned willingness to go to court. Although, after a few weeks of posturing, he allowed his solicitor to negotiate a buyout of Min-chin's lease on the original two acres for £800—four times Min-chin's highest annual earnings. Indeed, Kwong Tang was right: Min-chin would soon be a rich man.

After Min-chin had the buyout payment in his bank, he held a celebratory dinner to honor his son Wing-yuen, who first raised the possibility of a way out, and Kwong Tang, his longtime advisor, for his sage advice. Near the end of the celebration, Min-chin took Kwong Tang aside.

"What can I do for you, Tang-*Gaausi*, wise teacher for over twenty years?"

"Ah, this humbled man thanks you for your kind inquiry. I have need of a friend, Min-chin. You know I have not recovered from the 1890s depression. I have been unable to raise the funds necessary to renovate my store and upgrade my stock. I'm afraid I've become the 'vulgar man' in the proverb: 'A gentleman makes demands on himself; a vulgar man makes demands on others.' This pitiful businessman is in urgent need of a loan of about £150."

Bowing, Min-chin said, "It would be my honor, Esteemed Counselor."

"Thank you, Min-chin. You have made a poor old man very happy. Teach your smart son the ways of business, so he will never be poor—for as the Ancients said: 'With money, a dragon; without money, a worm.'"

With the remainder of the buyout money, Min-chin looked for land to purchase that would ensure the prosperity of his son and family. He and Wing-yuen found eight acres of reasonably priced marshland along Mill Creek north of the small village of Botany. Once drained, the land would possess the nutrients and nearby water source necessary for their market garden. It had one drawback though; it was twice as far, four and a half miles, from the Belmore Park Market as their old Alexandria garden.

It took two and a half years to produce the first crop of marketable fruits and vegetables. By this time, nineteen-year-old Wing-yuen was his father's indispensable right hand.

"We should buy a house in Botany, Father, where we can live close to our market garden," Wing-yuen said.

"Your mother and I do not want to leave Surry Hills where we have lived since our marriage and raised you," Min-chin said.

"Our neighborhood has been destroyed by the construction of Wentworth Avenue serving the new Central Railway Station," Wing-yuen said. "In Botany, you can buy a house with enough land around it so Mother can have a flower garden, and you can build a small temple to our ancestors. It would be an easy walk to our market garden and eliminate our long trip every day."

"You are right, Son, the trip every day has become tiring for me. Even so, I do not wish to move away from my friends. Dixon and Sussex Street are the center of my life. I want to spend more time counseling at the Sun Wei Tong, meeting with my friends in restaurants, and going with your mother to Chinese shops. We do not speak English as well as you and would not feel comfortable in Botany. I will manage our vendors and run our stall at the Belmore Park Market. You can improve the shed on our land and manage the Botany garden."

"That would be a hardship for me to be away from you and Mother for most of the week."

"Those are not hardships, my son. You have no appreciation of how easy our life is now. Soon all the produce markets will be relocated to Paddy's Market that is under construction. It will be a boon to our Chinese community. The new market will be connected by railway to Darling Harbour. This will be very good for us."

"Maybe not, Father, the new market could bring in imported fruits and vegetables that may undercut our prices."

"That is a good thought, my son, but who will provide these fruits and vegetables to compete with us? The whites do not have the skill or desire to dirty their hands at market gardening. The White Australia Policy has eliminated Chinese immigration. The number of Chinese in Sydney has fallen to less than 3,500. Our market garden business has little competition. We Chinese grow most of the produce the whites eat. I am not concerned about imported competition; instead, I see an opportunity to export to other places through Darling Harbour. Our business should grow threefold."

* * *

After witnessing the violent death of her "big brother" Billy, Daisy lay listless in bed and vomited most of the food her foster parents fed to her. They continued to follow Dr. Bayer's advice, even though she either could not or would not cooperate. Within a month, she looked like a skeleton. Dr. Bayer became increasingly concerned as her health declined. He did not know that she had been in the same mental condition at the age of four when found emaciated and alone in the bush.

Dr. Bayer was the Medical Officer of the Warrawindra Aboriginal Station employed by the Aborigines Protection Board to provide emergency medical care and to visit at least once a month to attend to the general medical needs of its ninety-four Aboriginal residents.

After Dr. Bayer visited Daisy, he talked to Percy Hopkins, the new station superintendent who had replaced the dismissed Gabbetts.

"My prognosis is that Daisy's condition is psychological rather than physiological. Some form of mental illnesses; however, I don't know what kind."

"Are there different kinds of mental illness?"

"Yes."

"Well, we can't treat her here for *that*," Superintendent Hopkins said. "Can the hospital in Bathurst treat her?"

"It may accept her. But . . . she's a full-blood Aborigine. I fear that she will not receive the attention necessary to save her life. Most likely, she'll continue to waste away and die. Within a month, I should think."

"So there's nothing to be done?"

"I'm a student of Viennese Dr. Sigmund Freud's work. Have you heard of him?"

"No—a European doctor?"

"Yes. He wrote *Studies on Hysteria* and, in 1899, *The Interpretation of Dreams*. He writes that he has cured patients with her condition through hypnosis. Daisy is repressing her brother's death causing emotional stress within her mind, which makes her sick."

"So she wants to die because her brother died?"

"No, she doesn't *want* to die; that's the end product of her mental condition. Rather, she doesn't want to deal with the vision of her brother's violent death, so her traumatized mind shuts down and her health declines."

"What can be done about that?"

"Well, there are techniques. Her parents say she has dreams, and they can hear names, places, and her crying out—"

"Excuse me for interrupting, Doctor, but those aren't her parents and Billy wasn't her real brother; they're her foster parents. We know very little about her background."

"Hmm. That's interesting. There may be some conflict there

too . . . Well, about dreams. They can be listened to and analyz-
ed and repressed events can be discovered. There are techniques.
For instance, a hypnotized patient can be encouraged to cough out
pent-up secrets that are causing the psychological problems, then
you can discuss them with the patient out in the open."

"Oh, my word," Hopkins said, "have you done that with other
patients?"

"No, though it's something that makes sense to me, and I'd like
to try it. Unfortunately, it takes time and attention that I can't provide here. She would have to live with my wife and me."

"That's very good of you, Doctor. But I'm a bit surprised that you'd
be willing to put yourself out like that. Would your wife approve?"

"I've already asked Erika. We agreed that if there was no improvement this visit, I would ask you and her parents to release Daisy to me. The way her health is deteriorating, I give myself less than
a 50-50 chance of saving her. But I feel it's her best and last hope."

Daisy's foster parents released her to the doctor's care. He reported at his next monthly visit that she was improving. At the following monthly visit, he met again with Superintendent Hopkins.

"She's a lovely, sensitive child and is going to be fine. I'll bring
Daisy back my next visit. Erika's going to miss her; I'll tell you that.
It's been a fascinating and enthralling process for me as a doctor.
It all happened exactly as I had hoped it would. I listened to her
dreams, which gave me questions to ask her under hypnosis. The
poor child has suffered horrific losses in her few years. She saw her
mother and father, and perhaps brothers and sisters, murdered, and
then it happened again with her foster brother."

"Pitiful. It shows the mind can only take so much, eh?" Hopkins said.

"I took her through healing discussions of what had happened,
told her it wasn't her fault, and she responded like a blossoming
flower. It's so gratifying for me, I must say."

When Dr. Bayer returned Daisy to her foster parents in Warrawindra Station, she was eating and drinking normally again and
had regained most of her weight.

* * *

Daisy's growing-up years from age seven to twelve were happy. Her foster parents loved her and took care of her. She developed friendships and did well in school. Having celebrated her twelfth birthday on September 4, 1910, the matron placed her in the girls' dormitory to begin domestic training. 1910, however, was a year of radical changes for Daisy and the station.

The station was being dramatically affected by the Aborigines Protection Act 1909 that had narrowed the definition of Aborigine to exclude those of "admixture of Aboriginal blood." The objective of the act was to drive "lighter-caste" Aborigines off the government's stations, reserves, and missions and into the white community to promote the board's assimilation policy and reduce costs. The act gave the Aborigines Protection Board power "to assume full control and custody of any neglected Aboriginal child and to apprentice them between the ages of 14 and 18 years."

Fair complexioned Aboriginal children were being removed from their indigenous families and sent to children's institutions. Older children, some as young as thirteen, were sent out to service: girls to learn domestic service on the job and boys as apprentice farm hands.

The act provided funds for improvement and expansion of Warrawindra Aboriginal Station. Construction began on an additional girls' dormitory. The new and existing dormitories were renamed the Warrawindra Girls' Training Home. The Aborigines Protection Board provided new training equipment, including a cooking stove, clothes wringer, laundry stove for hot water, sewing machines, and housekeeping manuals.

An additional one hundred acres were burned and cleared for farming to train more boys. Five new cottages, a butcher shop, and a tool and storage shed were erected.

Daisy was largely unaffected by these changes. She had developed into a quiet, studious girl, who applied herself to her domestic service studies and applications. After two years in the Girls' Training Home, she was considered a star student. The matron, Amy Hopkins, called her into her office on December 18, 1912.

"You've been ready for your first domestic service assignment for a while now, Daisy. We've held off, though, because we wanted to send you to an exceptional family. Well, we have a request from a well-to-do, respected family in Sydney, the Armstrongs. You will start there after the first of the year.

"It's a small family, only the two parents and their son. They have a married butler and maid couple, so you'll be under their guidance. You will be paid sixpence a week, part of which the Aborigines Protection Board will save for you in a trust fund until you've successfully complete your apprenticeship at age twenty-one."

The matron smiled. "Being 'in service' is a noble and respected career, Daisy, and one to which many white people aspire. It can lead to a lifelong career. You should consider yourself fortunate."

"Yes, madam, I do," Daisy said, believing she was about to make a place for herself in the world.

"I advise you to remember what you've learned and to maintain your pleasant manner, punctuality, and neatness. These are attributes which will serve you well in the future. I'm sure you will be a great success."

* * *

On January 5, 1913, as Samuel Armstrong was preparing to leave the house, his wife Ellen said, "Oh, I almost forgot to remind you that the new Aboriginal maid starts today."

"Where's she coming from?"

"The Warrawindra Girls' Training Home west of Bathurst."

"I certainly hope she's better than the last one."

"I hope so too. I just don't understand what happened to Angela. She started out so well and showed such promise."

Ellen had followed the example of her husband's cousin's wife, Caroline Armstrong, who altruistically had taken on two domestics from Warrawindra. Both Aboriginal girls had worked out well. Fourteen-year-old Angela had started out well too, only to worsen in six months into a brooding, sullen, and overweight girl."

"I'd best be going." Samuel put on his coat and hat. "Christo-

pher will be finished by now, and I don't want to miss the first race."
He gave her a perfunctory kiss on the cheek and went out the door.

Samuel drove to the stables in Centennial Park, but Christopher was not waiting. He parked and walked toward the stables breathing in the pungent smell of horses.

How I love horses and riding . . . freedom, nothing better.

Not finding Christopher in the stable, he walked out to the practice ring. There he saw his twenty-year-old son astride Payton approaching the last hurdle. Christopher waved, and then horse and rider made a powerful jump over the hurdle, easily clearing the bar. The landing was solid and confident. Samuel marveled at the sheer beauty of it and his son's oneness with the horse.

A natural rider, Samuel thought proudly. What a handsome, robust young man he's become . . . unusually sure of himself; nevertheless, I wish he'd go back to Sydney Uni to continue his education.

"Hello, Father," Christopher said as he dismounted from his dapple gray mare with a flourish. "Sorry to keep you waiting. Payton seemed a little hesitant the last go around. I wanted to give her another chance . . . restore her confidence. I think she'll be fully trained for the Royal Easter Show." Samuel nodded while he stroked Payton's head. Together they walked to the stable and handed Payton over to the stable boy.

While driving to Randwick Racecourse, Samuel said, "I'd like you to think about returning to Sydney Uni, Christopher, if you won't work with me. You're wasting your time working part-time as a copy boy."

"I'm not a flamin' copy boy, Dad, I'm a copywriter and sometimes I write drafts that are put into the newspaper."

"Not under your name. They're rewritten by a reporter who gets the credit."

"I'll be a reporter soon."

"There's no future in it, Christopher."

"Sure there is. I can become an editor like Uncle Curtis."

"Still no money in it. He and Priscilla live in that little Paddo terrace house and are worth nothing. But if you want to become an editor, you'll do it a lot faster with a university degree in English."

"I guess that's right, Dad. Give me some time. I'll think about it."

Arriving at the raccourse, Samuel drove past the carriage paddock where horses were tied and carriages parked, and slowed at the car parking area looking for a prominent spot to park his imported American Model-T Ford. He wanted it to be noticed among the mostly British and European models.

As they left the car, Christopher patted the bonnet. "She's a beaut, Dad."

They took their places among the well-dressed, upper-class wagerers in the box seats.

Christopher greeted a friend, "G'day, Harry. Feelin' lucky ta day, mate?" and mingled with his father's colleagues. "Mr. McDougall, you're looking quite smart in that new hat, if I may say so." He offered his hand and said, "Mr. Wayne, pleasure to see you again, sir."

Christopher fancied himself "the grand manipulator of the human race," who through his handsome appearance, intelligence, and natural charm and grace could fashion any situation to his own advantage. With mates he was a carefree, irresponsible, frolic-loving "larker" who used entertaining and earthy slang below his class. Adults were manipulated with feigned respect. Older women readily succumbed to his compliments. It was with women around his age, however, that he turned up the charm full throttle with the intent to seduce them.

Father and son walked over to talk to a group of elderly gentlemen. Samuel asked, "Mr. Wayne, will I see you at the naval ceremony tomorrow to celebrate the arrival of Australian Navy's first two warships, *Parramatta* and *Yarra*?"

"Indeed, I wouldn't miss it," responded Mr. Wayne, a political crony of Samuel's father Duncan. "It's a shame your father didn't live to see this."

"Yes. He was a strong advocate of building our own navy."

"I, for one, certainly will feel much safer with our own ships to protect us," Mr. McDougall said.

"Two warships won't deter any aggressive nation that means us harm, I fear." Mr. Snelling said.

"It's a start," Samuel said.

"I'm not sure that we shouldn't just save our money and rely on the British Fleet," Mr. Snelling said.

"Britain is a long way off," Samuel said.

Christopher nodded respectfully to indicate he was listening to every word, although his eyes and mind were on a group of young ladies four rows below. He excused himself. Approaching them from behind, he said, "I wonder if this group of beautiful ladies will say hello to me."

Turning at the sound of his familiar voice, the girls exclaimed, almost in unison: "Chrissie" and "Christopher."

"Mmm … my, Mary," he said warmly to the least attractive one, "you're lookin' particularly lovely today."

Mary smiled demurely, while others tried to hide their disappointment at not being singled out.

"How do I look, Chrissie?" Helen asked.

Christopher did not have a chance to respond because it was loudly announced "The horses are on the track! Make your bets!"

Everyone turned for a better look at the horses passing by in review.

"I don't know what horse to bet on. Which horse do you girls like?" Christopher asked, drawing attention back to himself.

They began vying, pointing and exclaiming the names of their favorites.

"By a Nose is the one!" Mary said and then giggled.

"No, no, One Chance will win!" another said.

Helen said, "I have a winning ticket here for Lady Lane!"

"I'm going with Helen's 'Lady Lane'!" Christopher declared and unexpectedly planted a playful kiss on her cheek. Before she could react, he said, "That's for good luck!—for both of us!" He rushed up the steps saying, "I'm off to bet on Lady Lane!"

Christopher returned and sat with the four girls for three more races and then excused himself and rejoined his father. He winked at Harry and felt the envy of the older men, including his father.

On their way home, Samuel and Christopher discussed their wins and losses, and the horses. "Diamond Jewel in the fifth paid seven to one for me. Wasn't she a beautiful filly?" Samuel said.

"How 'bout those fillies I was with four rows down?" Christopher asked. He looked at his father and gave him a man-to-man wink of the eye. "That Helen Jenson is a filly I'd like to corral."

"You have a way with the ladies, all right, Christopher. Too bad you can't make a living at that," Samuel said, not unkindly. "But see here, we're getting another native maid today. I'd just as well not bother, but your mother wants to try again. How about doing me a big favor and leave this one alone." Samuel turned to look at his son to see his reaction.

Christopher gave him a look of revulsion without saying anything.

"I'm not a fool you know; I was a young man once. I don't want you wasting your overwhelming charm on our black help. So don't create problems for your mother and me."

Christopher knew when to keep his mouth shut. If he said anything there would be a discussion. He was pretty sure his father was guessing and continued to look straight ahead, hoping his father's warning would satisfy him.

Ellen was in the parlor talking to the new Aboriginal maid when they entered the house. She was short, thin, and dressed in a maid's black uniform with white collar and cuffs and a crisp white apron. Samuel was perturbed: she was much darker than he had expected.

Greeting her two men too cheerfully, Ellen said, "Hello, my darlings. This is our new maid Daisy." She gestured with her hand. "Daisy, this is the master of the house: my husband, Mr. Samuel Armstrong, and our son, Christopher."

Daisy curtseyed with an appropriate downcast gaze. With a trembling, unsure voice, she said the words she had been trained to say to the man of the house: "Pleased to be of service, sir."

"We are happy to have you with us, Daisy," Samuel said. "We've been at the races."

"Did you enjoy yourselves?" Ellen asked.

"Bonzer!" Christopher said. "I won handsomely." With a playful glint in his eye, he said, "Now I can buy you that diamond necklace you've always wanted, Mum!"

"You can give it to me for my birthday," Ellen teased back.

Seeing a look in Samuel's eyes, Ellen said, "Christopher, why don't you talk to Daisy for a minute while I talk to your father." She led Samuel into the library and closed the door behind them to speak privately. "What is it?"

"She looks like a full-blood Aborigine, for Chrissake, Ellen."

"I-I know. I didn't know what to do—"

"Why the hell did you accept her? Do I have—"

"—give me a chance, and I'll tell you!" Ellen angrily responded.

An embarrassed Daisy stood frozen in place; her eyes fixed on the floor. She could hear the parents arguing and their son, Christopher, was looking her over. He towered over her, six foot one inch tall next to her five foot three inches. He estimated her age at thirteen or fourteen and quickly assessed that she was inexperienced and afraid of him.

Samuel stormed ahead. "You know I wasn't anxious to have another dark half-breed; this one's even darker, looks like a full blood to me!"

"Well, I was upset too when Miss Ames brought her in. I was going to reject her straightaway, but Miss Ames anticipated my dissatisfaction and implored me to accept her. She has over two-years training and was the school's top student!"

Ellen tried to sound confident and in control, while cursing herself for letting that clever Miss Ames convince her to take Daisy.

"I could see how smart she is right away, and so pretty and sweet. She seems cheerful and positive—eager to work—and much brighter than Angela was. I liked her after talking to her for a while, and I think you will too. Remember, we're doing this to look altruistic."

"I don't give a rat's arse about looking altruistic to Eleanor's side of the family or anyone else. She's your idea and your problem. If she doesn't work out, I don't want another one in this house."

Feeling extremely ill at ease and not knowing what to say or do, Daisy curtsied. "Can I git a glass of water fer ya, Mr. Armstrong?"

Enjoying his feeling of control, Christopher didn't answer. He decided that she was not quite a woman yet, a bit thin . . . but pretty, if "prettiness" could be attributed to an Aboriginal girl. Finally, in a friendly tone of voice, he said:

"Is this your first placement, Daisy?"

"Yes, Mr. Armstrong."

"Don't call me that, Daisy. That's my father. I'm just a few years older than you. Call me Christopher."

She didn't know what to say. It did not seem right to call him by his first name.

"How old are you?"

"Fourteen, sir."

"Do you like our house?"

"Oh, yes sir, it so big an' beautiful!" She raised her eyes from the floor for a fraction of a second to look up at Christopher before lowering them again and curtseying, for no other reason than nervousness. She stood motionless, petrified, praying for his mother to open the library door. She wanted to move away from the intense stare of this handsome but intimidating man. No man had ever stared at her like this before. She didn't like it.

As the library door opened and Ellen and Samuel emerged, Christopher said, "Nice to talk to you, Daisy, I'm sure you're gonna like it here."

The first week at the Armstrongs went very well for Daisy. Ensconced in her own private room in the basement, she lay in bed and happily relived her first week's "successes."

I had tea, jus' fer me, with Mr. an' Mrs. Buffrey, the butler an' maid, in their small 'ouse next to the main 'ouse; I rode in a proper carriage fer the first time; I saw streets lighted by electric lights that Mr. Armstrong said he did, an' Mrs. Armstrong said I'm doin' very good.

Suddenly, her thoughts were interrupted by a soft knock on her door. She sat up in bed, but before she could answer or get out of bed, the door swung open. Christopher walked in, carrying a piece of cake on a plate. She gaped at him, while a flood of emotions rushed over her—fright, embarrassment, and confusion. With a big smile, he pulled a chair over and sat down next to her. She pulled the covers up around her neck.

"I'd like to congratulate you on your first week's work, Daisy. You've really done well, and Mother and Father are very pleased. I am too. So I brought you this piece of cake to celebrate. I hope you like it."

He placed it on her side table, along with a fork he produced from his pocket with a dramatic slight of hand that made her giggle. He gave her a reassuring smile, stood, turned, and slipped silently out the door. She let her arms down and relaxed. Emotionally exhausted and too excited to eat, she stared at the cake for a few minutes before falling asleep with a smile on her face.

* * *

The ocean temperature at Bondi Beach was warm in late February, perfect for avid bodysurfers like Nigel Armstrong and his mates to surf the waves. They called their group The Wave Masters and contested who could catch the largest wave to carry him farthest into shore. Nigel, the fifteen-year-old son of Peter Armstrong, treaded water with his friends, waiting for the right wave. He let a large one go by and used the swell of the next to choose a wave to surf. The beautiful crescent-shaped beach of Bondi was in clear view. People dotted the beach, enjoying the sparkling clear day. Nigel's group of mates had been drawn north by the crosscurrent. He could no longer see their girl friends sitting on several blankets placed together on the beach and hoped someone was keeping an eye on his surfboard. There were only a few other homemade surfboards on Bondi Beach.

Nigel was proud of his nine-foot-long board, which he had made out of a solid plank of sugar pine. It was modeled on a board used by the Hawaiian Olympic swimmer Duke Kahanamoku, who was staying at Freshwater Beach and giving demonstrations of how to surfboard. Duke had shown him and others how to execute a "turtle roll" to get a large board through the waves. Nigel had been practicing the maneuver, but it was an exhausting technique. He was getting better at it and had even made it through the large waves several times. He was practicing riding in on his knees, but had not yet tried standing up, for fear of losing hold of the board and having to return to the beach to retrieve it.

Nigel thought that he should bodysurf in to see if his cousin Christopher had arrived yet. He had told him about his surfboard, and Chris said he would come down to the beach in the early afternoon to watch him ride it.

"*Wooo-eee!*" cried out Lester, Nigel's mate.

Nigel swiveled his head to look out to sea. There was a large building wave coming at them.

"*Bonzer!*" Nigel yelled, and started swimming as fast as he could. He felt the wave building behind him and its tremendous force trying to drag him backwards... he swam faster... the wave's spumy crest formed around him... faster, faster... he was over the top of the wave now... faster still, faster, faster... HE CAUGHT IT! Feeling a huge adrenaline rush he *swooped* down the front of the wave using his extended arms as a rudder to prevent the monster from passing over him, pulling him under, and devouring him.

"*Wooo-eee!*" Nigel screamed, although he could not hear his voice above the roar of the wave.

As the wave dissipated in the shallows, Nigel scrambled quickly to his feet and gave his head a jaunty toss, flipping his long hair from his face. He looked for Lester and was pleased to see him five yards behind. Chest out and grinning broadly, Lester ran toward him laughing and deliberately knocked into him. They both fell with uproarious laughter.

"Nigo!" Christopher shouted. "*Nigel!*"

Nigel heard his cousin's yell. He stood up and saw him sixty yards away at the water's edge. He waved and yelled back, "*Chris, hi.*" He and Lester walked toward Christopher sharing the fine points of their death-defying experience.

Christopher said, "Where's that surfing board you've been telling me about, mate? Why aren't you using it?"

"It's up the beach with the girls. I was bodysurfin' with my mates, Chris."

"Nigel, *you've* got a girlfriend?" Christopher said in a mocking, incredulous tone.

"Nah, they're just friends, mate."

Several of their girls friends were wearing cossies—black, short-sleeved, bathing costumes with knee-length breeches—and frolicking in the water. Seeing Nigel, Lester, and a tall, blond-haired, cute fellow approaching, the girls regrouped at the blankets. As Christopher was introduced, he allowed his eyes to roam with abandonment over Nigel's young girl friends while thanking god that Catholic Archbishop Kelly had not been successful in preventing mixed-gender bathing and outlawing clinging cossies as indecent.

"This is my surfboard, Chris," Nigel said.

"It's *twice* as big as you, mate. Can you lift it?" Christopher joked and the girls laughed.

"No worries." Nigel picked up one end of the board, worked his way to the middle and lifted it. He balanced it horizontally, and with a cheery "Here goes!" walked toward the water, struggling to make it look effortless. The board was awkward to carry and weighed over sixty pounds. Nigel strained to carry it into water deep enough to float it. Pushing the board, he went through the first few low waves, then dropped onto it and swam it forward. He knew all eyes were on him and wanted to do well. He formed an image of himself with his knees bent, left leg and arm forward, arms extended for balance, as he valiantly rode his trusty board (standing for the first time) to shore with everyone on the beach looking at him with mouths agape in astonishment—master of the surf!

Nigel paddled over increasingly larger waves. From shore it appeared that each larger wave would upend him. Seeing the waves were now too large to paddle over, Nigel repositioned himself in the middle of the board and firmly gripped its rails. As the wave grew large in front of him, he flipped the board over on top of himself and hung below it to act as a sea anchor. The force of the building wave tried to yank the board out of his grip, so he pulled down hard to keep it from breaking away. When the wave broke over the board, he thrust its nose forward to punch through the wave. The board now pulled him forward as it came through the wave. Nigel flipped the board back over and pulled himself aboard, smiling to himself that he had just completed a perfect turtle roll.

He had to do the roll three more times before he broke through the breakers into an area of calm swells. Nigel raised himself up and waved to his friends on the beach. He felt triumphant that he had made it through the waves without making a fool of himself, though he was exhausted by the effort. He rested with his legs dangling over the sides. An odd sensation swept over him. He felt very much alone and vulnerable without his mates around him.

A large building wave showed itself. Nigel lay face down on the board and paddled vigorously, but his timing was off. He missed the wave, lost his balance, and fell into the water while holding onto the board with one arm. He paused in the water to catch his breath. *Brruuusshh*. Something large brushed his leg—*Jeez a shark!* Nigel violently kicked with his feet and propelled himself up and onto the board. He lay face down with his arms at his sides and legs bent above his buttocks and scanned the water. There was a suspicious swirl in the water immediately ahead but no fin. Was he being spooked by the story he had heard so many times about his relative Alistair Norman who had been killed by a shark?

Hearing a wave surging up behind him, he looked behind and paddled frantically. Fearing the wave was going to pass him by, he dug in deeper and swam harder. He caught it! He surfed down the front of the wave lying on the board and rode it all the way in. His heart still pounding wildly, he looked around for a second before he got off the board into two feet of water. He brushed the hair from his eyes and turned to see Lester running up.

"Why didn't you try to stand up?" Lester said and then saw the fright in Nigel's face. "Hey, what's wrong, mate? You look like you've seen a ghost."

"I think a shark brushed my leg," Nigel said. "*Something* big did!"

Lester knew that his mate did not scare easily. "Bugger me dead!"

"I'm not going out again today."

Lester helped Nigel carry the board up the beach. Nigel saw Christopher sitting among the girls with everyone seemingly having a good time. He was disappointed that none of them seemed to care about his surfboard ride. Unexpectedly, Christopher said, "Nigo! Great ride, mate! We all saw you ride it all the way in."

Nigel and Lester plopped down together at the edge of the group. Nigel was too embarrassed to tell them his shark story. The girls were all laughing, anyway, while Christopher dramatically described a motion picture show he had seen. Nigel admired Christopher's congenial, fun-loving personality and easy way with girls.

It's due to his good looks, Nigel thought to himself. He doesn't have my ruddy complexion, ugly red hair, and damn freckles. He's not sunburned and grossly peeling all summer. The lucky bugger is over six feet tall, and I'm only five foot six. A bloke like me doesn't stand a chance with the sheilas. Reluctantly, his mind told him that there was something else Christopher had. Nigel thought about it for a moment, trying to identify what "it" was, but concluded that whatever "it" was, he didn't have "it."

A little later, Nigel, Lester, and three of the girls said their goodbyes to Christopher, Bronwyn, and Gladys, who decided to stay a bit longer. Nigel and Lester carried Nigel's board to Charlie's Storage Shed, and the group changed their swimming costumes in dressing booths. They all took the tram home to Bellevue Hill.

Showing obvious attention to Bronwyn, Christopher wished that Gladys would leave. He suggested that they find a shop and share a snack of fish and chips that he would pay for. Gladys tagged along. While eating and drinking, he talked primarily to Bronwyn, hoping that Gladys would become aggravated or embarrassed and leave. It resulted in them both saying they had to go home for dinner. Frustrated, he told them that he had a delightful afternoon and hoped he would see them again soon.

He went to a Bondi pub. After three middies of beer, he joined three gents who needed a fourth to play a bit of darts. While playing, he ate some pub food for dinner. A little drunk and still feeling frustrated, he arrived home at nine-thirty with thoughts of Daisy. The house was quiet. His parents were at a function and weren't expected back until midnight. He walked through the house to make sure the butler and his wife were gone.

Unlike his treatment of Angela, he felt he had been very considerate of Daisy. He actually liked Daisy's innocent, sweet disposition. From time to time, when the spirit moved him, he had popped into her room to talk or give her some little present, just to soften her up. Over the weeks, he had become a kind of friend to her. Hell, he thought, her only friend. He had taken his time and gone step by step, preparing for this evening.

He rummaged in the kitchen and found her favorite biscuit and made a pot of tea. Placing these of a tray, he headed for her room. She knew it was him from the sound of his walk down the stairs and his amusing signature rap on her door.

"Come in," she said.

Affecting a jovial attitude and carrying the tray upright in one hand like a waiter, Christopher announced:

"Your favorite biscuits and Indian tea, m'lady, if you please."

Daisy tittered. She sat up in bed, placed her pillow behind her back, and leaned against the headboard. He pulled her side table alongside the bed and placed the tray on it.

"How was your day, Daisy?" he asked, pulling a chair over to sit down.

She told him what had happened over the past three days since they had last talked. He told her about the beach and Nigel's surfboard, saying he would take her to see the beach soon before summer ended. After they finished the biscuits and tea, Christopher moved the side table and sat down on the bed next to her. He lowered his head to kiss her. She gasped and put her head down, so he kissed the top of her head.

Standing up, he started to undress.

"Oh *no!*" Daisy said, and rolled away from him and pulled the sheet over her head. "No, Christopher, don't do that . . . *please!*"

While he was taking off his clothing, he said, "I really like you, Daisy, and I think you like me too. This is what adults do when they like each other. There's nothing to be afraid of or ashamed of."

Taking hold of the sheet he gave it a little tug. "I can't *see* you. I know you're under there." Then he pulled the sheet away from her. She remained turned away from him with her head in her hands. Taking hold of one of her wrists and then the other, he turned her toward him. He intended to kiss her, but her eyes were closed.

"Haven't you ever kissed a bloke, Daisy? I want to kiss you; you're so cute and sweet."

"No, master Christopher, it ain't right."

He pulled her toward him and tried to kiss her on the lips, but ended up on her cheek as she moved her head sideways.

When he straddled her, she opened her eyes and pushed against his chest. He pulled up her nightgown and lay on top of her. He tried to kiss her again. She rolled her head away.

"Please, Christopher, I don't want ta. I'm scared!"

He smiled at her and removed strands of hair from over one eye. "There's nothing to be afraid of, Daisy. I'll be gentle, and you'll like it; you'll see."

He felt around between her legs and entered her gently.

"*No, no, don't!*" Daisy squirmed under him, but it was hopeless.

She thought to scream; however, she was more afraid of losing her apprenticeship than what was happening. If she screamed, people would find out that she had let him into her room many times to visit. A million confused thoughts passed through her mind as she endured the pain and excitement of her first sexual experience.

The next day, Daisy had to force herself to concentrate on her duties and suppress the unfamiliar emotions that had been unleashed—excitement, fear, embarrassment, confusion. As she absentmindedly dusted the furniture in the foyer, she asked herself: What does it mean? Does he really like me? Will he want to do that again? She heard someone coming down the front stairs in rapid steps and looked up to see Christopher.

"Good morning, Daisy," a chipper Christopher said and winked at her.

A smile formed involuntarily, and she quickly turned away, wondering what to make of it all, what to do?

* * *

Thomas adjusted the pillow behind Eleanor's back. "Better?" he asked.

"Yes, thank you, Thomas."

Eleanor was seventy-eight and had been living with her nephew Thomas and his wife Caroline for two years. He could tell when she was uncomfortable and knew what aches and pains were himself at sixty-nine.

Normally, Eleanor hated to be fussed over, but today she appreciated it; her back was giving her considerable discomfort. Now comfortable, she reached for her tea cup.

The senior officers of Norman Builders were having their annual strategic planning meeting at Thomas's house. It had become something of a tradition to meet on or around June 1 of each year. This was Eleanor's opportunity to impart her substantial market knowledge to help set the course of the company for the coming financial year. She had let it be known that she would soon retire as chairman in favor of Thomas, which would allow his forty-five-year-old son Peter to become managing partner.

"I'd like us to consider the pros and cons of buying land in our designated federal capital city, Canberra," Thomas said. "The American chap who won the city planning competition, Walter Burley Griffin, has proposed a simple yet elegant plan with a strong city center, a university, well-defined neighborhoods, lakes, curving streets, and parks. It would be a terrific place to buy land before it becomes too expensive."

"Do you have a sense that the project is sure to go ahead?" Peter asked.

"It appears to have the support it needs," Thomas said.

"I'm wary of investing in land with such an uncertain lead time," Eleanor said. "There are many detractors who say the remote, barren region cannot possibly attract the projected population of twenty thousand residents in twenty years. These cities starting from nothing always take longer to realize than anyone expects. Take William Gilbert Smith's master plan for Manly resort as an example. It took so long that he finally gave up and returned to England."

Eleanor sipped her tea, and Thomas reached for another biscuit, both pondering the options.

Senior executive Robert Spencer said, "What about north of the city? The Labor government has appointed John Bradfield the engineer-in-charge of the Sydney Harbour Bridge construction project. It's to start in . . . what? . . . a few years. The cleared land in The Rocks has provided the southern approach to the bridge. Goodness knows, northsiders are overloading the ferries crossing the harbor."

"Well . . . I think you're right, Robert, northside builders are certainly busy meeting the demand for large Federation-style houses and Arts and Crafts homes," Thomas said. "Although, it won't take off until the bridge is a reality, and really, will the bridge *ever* be built?"

Eleanor thought how she liked the modern architectural styles with their asymmetrical layouts, rambling roof lines, playful chimneys, and special features: bay windows, nooks and crannies, stained glass, fretwork, and ornate plasterwork, often bearing Australian motifs such as waratahs and kangaroos. Terrace houses, which she and Alistair had pioneered in Paddington and now dominated the city suburbs would always hold a special place in her heart, but they were no longer in fashion.

Peter nodded in agreement and decided it was time to bring up the location that had dominated his thoughts since Nigel became obsessed with surfing. "Norman Builders has made much of its reputation in Manly, due to its beach resort community. Why not develop close to home in another emerging beach community—Bondi Beach? We could do a hotel and shops, and, of course, houses. There's the tram . . . and the beach is attracting vacationers."

"I see a new attitude toward sea bathing," Thomas said.

"You mean cossies a woman can wear into the water without drowning?" Eleanor said, shaking her head and grinning. "Those ridiculously heavy, neck-to-knee, bathing costumes."

"And those ridiculous bathing boxes," Thomas said, chuckling.

After the reminiscing died down, Peter said, "Bondi is underdeveloped and land prices are still reasonable."

Eleanor nodded thoughtfully. "I like it, Peter," she said. "A luxury hotel might be just the thing . . . Yes, I like it."

*   *   *

Ellen Armstrong could not believe it was happening again. Daisy had been a joy for her first five months; unfortunately, everything changed during the past month. Ellen felt she had no choice but to confront her.

"I just do not understand you, Daisy. You have a good position here, and you've been doing so well. What's happened over the past month? You've become despondent and difficult. You sleep in and don't follow direction from me or the Buffreys." Ellen searched her own conscience, to assure herself that she had done nothing wrong.

"Have I mistreated you in any way?"

Fidgeting with her apron, Daisy shifted uncomfortably and shook her head no.

"Well, I don't know what else to do. Mr. and Mrs. Buffrey don't either. I'm thinking of sending you back. Do you have anything to say for yourself?" Ellen stared at Daisy.

Feeling the oppressive glare of the mistress on her, Daisy found herself unable to speak and continued to fuss with her apron.

"For goodness sake, *leave* your apron alone, Daisy. *Look* at me. If you have nothing to say, then I'll have no choice but to ask Miss Ames to come for you. Is that what you *want?*"

Daisy finally found the courage to speak, almost inaudibly. "Master Christopher . . . he . . . uh . . ."

"What?" Ellen did not like hearing her son's name mentioned, and said impatiently "*Speak up!*"

"Christopher . . . he . . . give me baby."

"*What!*" Ellen jumped to her feet. "I never—*how dare you!* My son would *never* touch a black person!"

Daisy wanted to tell her more: How Christopher had become enraged when he saw that she was pregnant and blamed her. How he told her she had to leave—go back to her parents to have the baby. How he had offered her money to leave. How disappointed she was with him and did not know what to do.

Ellen, in tears, blurted out, "Go to your room. I'm calling Miss Ames. *Get out of my sight!*"

Crying, Daisy ran down the stairs to her room, where she pushed a chair against the door. She undressed, got into bed, and pulled the covers over her head. The next day, a carriage called for her.

Miss Ames of the Aborigines Protection Board helped Daisy pack her things and place her two bags into the carriage. Daisy had not seen Christopher for a week. He did not show up to say goodbye. As they rode in the carriage, Miss Ames said:

"I'm taking you to a nice place to live until you have your baby, Daisy, the La Perouse Aborigines Mission. You'll be in a house with three other women in your condition. There are over one hundred Aboriginal people living there permanently. We've built new houses and there's a lovely beach on Botany Bay. We should be there in about an hour."

On November 21, 1913, fifteen-year-old Daisy gave birth to a healthy baby boy. She gave him the name Harvey after the grandfatherly Aboriginal groundskeeper who had been kind to her at the Benevolent Foundation Orphanage in Bathurst.

On June 28, 1914, Superintendent Groom asked Daisy to come to his office. Miss Ames was there and another woman, Mrs. Mitchell, from the Children's Relief Board.

"I'm very happy to tell you," Miss Ames said, "that your request to return to domestic service has been approved. We've found the *perfect* family for you in Orange. It's a respectable family of five with *three daughters*. They are anxious to have you start as soon as possible."

"Thank you *so* much, Miss Ames," Daisy said.

"You are most welcome, although we have to address your unwed situation first. I'm afraid that after trying my best, I've determined that no respectable Christian family will accept an unwed mother with a half-caste child."

Mrs. Mitchell jumped in. "You're only a child yourself, aren't you, dear?—only fifteen, I understand. You'll want to marry in the future, I imagine."

Superintendent Groom said, "You want your child to have an education and a Christian upbringing, I assume. Well, of course you do: all parents want the best for their children."

"Give up, Harvey?" Daisy asked, digesting what they were saying.

"Oh no, you'll be able to see him, of course," Mrs. Mitchell said. "We would take excellent care of him, so you can complete your apprenticeship with the fine family Miss Ames has found for you. You shouldn't say anything to them, however, about being an unwed mother or having a child. This will give you the fresh start you need."

"I need some time ta think about this," Daisy said.

"I wish I could give you some time," Miss Ames said. "But the family in Orange wants to know today if you've accepted the position with them or not. There's another well-qualified maid they are considering."

Superintendent Groom said, "As you know, Daisy, the house you are staying in for unwed mothers is overcrowded. Please take this gracious opportunity for you and your son, or I may be forced to turn you out."

Mrs. Mitchell said, "I came to this meeting under the impression this wonderful opportunity would be readily taken. We are offering to take care of your son until you are twenty one, dear. It's your only chance to start anew after your mistake." She produced a document that she quickly explained to Daisy.

Confused and having no one to turn to for advice, Daisy signed the document in the place directed.

They all walked together to her house and waited for Daisy to gather Harvey's things. When Harvey sensed the stress in the group, he began to whimper. Daisy turned to pick him up, but Mrs. Mitchell quickly gathered him up in a blanket and held him close, comforting him. He squirmed and then settled down looking at Daisy. She moved toward Harvey, but Superintendent Groom stepped between them and ushered everyone out the door and toward a waiting car.

"Noo, noo, " Daisy said mournfully.

Miss Ames put her arm around her. "There, there, Daisy, it'll be fine."

Mrs. Mitchell adjusted the blanket around the baby. "It's for the best, and best for the baby, dearie, really. We will let you know where you can visit him."

With tears rolling down her cheeks, Daisy said in a weak quivering voice, "H-his name is Harvey."

Mrs. Mitchell, who was bending to get into a car, stopped and turned. "What did you say, dear?"

"His name is Harvey."

"Yes, I know." Then she and Harvey were gone.

Two days later, Daisy left for her new assignment with the family in Orange, New South Wales.

She was never contacted by the Children's Relief Board.

Chapter 2

The War to End War

On June 28, 1914, the same day that Daisy gave up her baby Harvey, the First World War was triggered by the assassination of Archduke Franz Ferdinand of Austria and his wife Sophie by a Bosnian Serb nationalist in Sarajevo. When Germany invaded neutral Belgium, Britain declared war on Germany on August 4. Australia's Prime Minister Andrew Fisher immediately pledged full support for Britain "to the last man and the last shilling" and called for volunteers. Australians greeted the news with great enthusiasm, like the rest of the world, expecting the exciting conflict to be over by Christmas. Within weeks, all of the great powers of Europe were at war.

Christopher volunteered for the First Light Horse Regiment. In his uniform, he visited Nigel and found Lester there.

"*Chris*, you look great, mate! I heard you enlisted," Nigel said, shaking Christopher's hand at the door of his house.

"My brother signed up too," Lester said from behind Nigel. "Three weeks ago at Victoria Barracks, right after war was declared." As Christopher walked into the foyer, Lester said, "You look like a real soldier, Chris."

"Thanks, Lester. I heard the Light Horse was training in Rosebery, so I went down there to see if they'd take me. I passed their riding test easily, and two days later, I passed their shooting test at Malabar Rifle Range."

"When will you be leaving?" Nigel asked.

"I don't know. I have to complete my training first. We new recruits have to learn a lot of things that the Light Horse militia already knows."

"What's the *Light Horse*? Is that the cavalry?" Lester asked.

"No, we're different. We don't charge the enemy with a sword and lance like the regular cavalry. We're called the Light Horse because we pack light and move fast on our horses behind enemy lines to do reconnaissance work and harass them. We all have to be expert riflemen, who can hit a target up to a half a mile away."

"*Half a mile!* Really?" Lester said.

"Yeah, I'm learning to do that. So we can harass the enemy and then ride away before their artillery can shell us."

"What kinda gun do you shoot?" Nigel asked.

"A .303 Lee Enfield rifle. I've shot the same rifles before with Dad at his shooting club. I qualified for the Light Horse by hitting stationary targets at hundred-yard intervals up to four hundred yards, nearly a quarter of a mile. Beyond that I didn't do real well. I have to learn to hit moving targets up to five hundred yards away, or they'll discharge me. A lot of the militia blokes are bonzer marksmen. They're from the country—bushmen—who can shoot a runnin' kangaroo at five hundred yards or more."

"How come they're training here?" Nigel asked.

"Our old sergeant said militias from all over New South Wales are being assembled here to form the regiment. We'll sail from the overseas wharf in Sydney Cove. The sergeant said he rode in the Boer War! They're accepting only a few new recruits, so I was really lucky."

"What did your parents say when you told them?" Lester asked.

"My mum cried, of course, but Dad said he was proud of me. He said we promised England an initial expeditionary force of twenty thousand volunteers, and he's proud I'm going to be one of them. I'm going to be a 'Six-Bob-a-Day Tourist,' as they say. They're paying me six bob a day to see the world!"

"I'd like to go fight the Germans," said Lester.

"How old are you, Lester?" Christopher asked.

"Seventeen."

"You'll have to wait until you're eighteen, mate, or get your father's consent."

"I've been thinking about asking him. Would you enlist with me, Nigo?"

"My father would never give his permission. He'd want me to finish school first. We'll be eighteen after graduation and can sign up then, Lester."

"It could be *over* by then, Nigel," Lester said. "It'll take months to be trained and transported. I'm going to ask my dad."

"The Light Horse sounds exciting—fighting behind enemy lines," Nigel said. "You'll have to write to tell us what it's like."

"I'll try to, Nigo, though I'm going to be pretty busy with something special."

"What's that?"

"Um . . . I haven't told anyone yet. I'll let you know after I get it started."

"What is it?—you can't say somethin' like that an' then not tell your mates," Lester said.

"Yeah, it's not fair dinkum to keep a secret from your cousin," Nigel said. "Whisper it to me."

"It's only an idea of mine. I'm going to keep a journal of my Light Horse adventures and get it published when I come home."

"A diary," Nigel said. "Great idea!"

"No, not a bleedin' *diary!* That's something a girl keeps! I'm going to write a professional *journal* to record the adventures of the Light Horse, its campaigns, strategies, successes, and the killing and dying of war. Also about the fun times and the sights I see. If it's any good, I'll be as famous as Ned Kelly!"

* * *

Christopher's training lasted only seven weeks. Additional training would be given on board the ship during the voyage and in England. On October 19, 1914, the first contingent of the Australian

Imperial Force marched down the streets of Sydney to embark for war. Thousands of well-wishers lined the route, cheering, clapping, waving enthusiastically, blowing kisses, and dabbing tears. Christopher rode with the 480 troopers and 25 officers of the First Light Horse Regiment. He proudly saluted the Armstrongs, from both sides of the family, who sat together on a second-story balcony overlooking the parade.

Samuel yelled loud enough for Christopher to hear "*I'm proud of you, Son. Give 'em hell!*"

Christopher chose a place along the starboard rail of the SS *Star of Victoria* in hope of seeing his house as the ship passed through Sydney Harbour. It was a beautiful day. The sky was laced with white wispy clouds, and a fresh spring wind blew in from the ocean. Tugboats maneuvered the large troop ship out of Sydney Cove. While passing by Fort Denison, he could see the tower, gun batteries, and barracks better than ever before. A myriad of pleasure boats, harbor ferries, and military vessels, blowing horns and ringing bells, escorted the ship past Rushcutters Bay, Double Bay, and Rose Bay. Christopher could make out the part of the hill where his house sat but could not see the house itself through the trees. The ship passed by Vaucluse Bay and Watsons Bay. He marveled at the smooth ride through the large swells between the looming South and North Heads as the ship entered the Tasman Sea. He relaxed and began dreaming about the adventures ahead.

Australian troop transports from Melbourne joined the line of Sydney ships traveling to King George Sound, south of Perth, Western Australia, where they anchored to await other ships. Two days later, ten transports carrying New Zealand troops arrived, escorted by four warships, including ally Japan's cruiser *Ibuki*. A convoy of forty ships was formed and left Australia on November 1 bound for England by way of the Suez Canal.

On their way to England, Britain declared war on Turkey after it joined the Central Powers. The British War Cabinet redirected the Australasian troops to Cairo to strengthen the British garrison there against a possible Turkish attack from Palestine, part of the once vast Ottoman Empire.

In Cairo, three months after leaving Sydney, Christopher wrote his first letter to Nigel. Settling back into his chair, Christopher read the letter to himself:

Dear Nigo,   Jan. 21, 1915

I wanted to send you a photograph of a belly dancer, but the postmaster wouldn't allow a "half-naked lady" to be sent through the post. Too bad for you, mate. These sheilas dance by moving their hips and bellies around in a sexy way. Nothing like it at home.

Made some good mates on the trip here. We climbed the Great Pyramid, rode camels, saw the Sphinx, and have sampled all the delights of Cairo. You wouldn't much like the people here. They live like animals and are very poor. We travel in groups, because they are always crowding around you trying to sell you something, act as your guide, or snatch your wallet. The dirty nigger kids are the worst, real pains in the arse.

We lost only a few horses on the trip over, but they are fit enough now to go on mounted exercises. I've become a crack shot. Also I like hand-to-hand fighting and bayonet training, so much so, that I'm called "Killer" (which I suggested myself).

Started my journal the second day on the boat. Only write in it when I have something interesting to tell. Don't know when we will see action or where we will be sent.

Please keep all my letters to you. I've asked everyone I write to keep my letters, so I can use them to write my "war memoirs" when I come home. Thanks, Nigo.

Your cousin,
Chris

After months of training, the troopers grew anxious for action. Following dinner, Christopher and a group of his mates sat together on their bunks doing various chores while discussing where they were likely to be sent. Christopher was writing in his journal.

"Chrissie, do you think the Anzacs will join the British and French on Lemnos Island to attack Constantinople?" asked Joey Miller, a nineteen year old from the country town of Tibooburra.

"I doubt it. The British navy couldn't fight its way up the Dardenelles Strait last month, so a direct attack on Constantinople isn't likely. I reckon any attack will have to be overland." Christopher focused on Joey's eye and laughed. "Damn, Joey, that shiner of yours has more colors in it than the rainbow."

"Supposed to, it's healin'. Whatcha writing in your journal this time?"

"About how you earned your shiner."

"Now that was a good time," Joey said. "But I didn't have as much fun as you, Killer. I can't believe you screwed that Gyppo whore in front of everyone while the whorehouse was burning down around us."

"He was all over her like a rash," Trevor said.

"And she had a face like a horse too," Joey said.

"Hey, mate, ya don't look at the mantelpiece when yer stokin' the fire," Christopher said.

"Good-oh!" Joey laughed along with everyone else. "So read to us what you're writin'."

"Wait a minute, let me finish this paragraph." Christopher finished and then read to the group what he had written:

"Apr. 4th–Battle of the Wazzir: We've been in our first battle and lived to laugh about it. On leave with two of my mates on April 2, we joined some Aussie infantry lads' grog-on celebrating their orders to ship out to the British base on the island of Lemnos. Seems the infantry will be attacking the Turks soon. We decided to go with them to 'the Wazzir,' the red-light district, for a proper send off. Problem was, the brothels must have heard about the deployment because they raised their prices for their girls and swill. Evidently the bastards saw this as their last chance to fleece us, and they meant to do it royally by charging us as much as double for their whores who have given many of us the clap. Pushing and fighting broke out when their strong-arm guards tried to throw us out.

"We left, but heard on the street that an Anzac had been knifed by a nigger guard at a whorehouse down the street. We all ran down there, kicked their arses in good, and ransacked the place. There were over a hundred of us now and our numbers just kept growing. We threw brothel beds, mattresses, furniture, and clothing into the street and someone set fire to it. The fire spread to a bar and then to the whorehouse we were in. We got out of there. It was now a full-fledged riot with all the grog you could drink. Whores were running everywhere with lads grabbing and jumping on them."

Out of the blue, Trevor asked, "How'd ya get to know so much about women, Killer?"

"I might ask you the same question, Trev. How'd ya get to know so much about sheep?"

The group broke out in a spontaneous roar of laughter. Trevor jumped from his bunk as if to attack Christopher, who jokingly put up his fists. The two sparred playfully. Between fake blows, Trevor said, "C'mon, Killer. Howja learn so much about the sheilas?"

"I got nookie from our Abo maids for years before you even noticed women have tits, mate. I probably have a little half-breed running around in the bush somewhere. Now let me finish our Battle of the Wazzir." He returned to writing in his journal:

The Egyptian fire brigade came barreling down the narrow street and hit some of our fellows. We knocked the Gyppo firemen about for that and cut their fire hoses. I noticed about then that there were as many En Zeds (New Zealanders) in the street as Aussies. The Anzacs (Australian and New Zealand Army Corps), as we are now called, were having a grand time getting revenge for the way we'd been treated.

A number of mounted British military police showed up, shot their revolvers into the air, but quickly turned tail when they realized we were too many for them. With most of the brothels emptied, we got mad drunk and did what we wanted. With my leave over I had to return to camp, although the riot went on through the night and into the next day.

Rumors of an Allied landing, on April 25 in Turkey, circulated throughout the Light Horse camp. Several days later, wounded arrived at the camp hospital amid talk of heavy casualties. The wounded said that the Allies had secured a tenuous hold on a stretch of beach on the Gallipoli peninsula. The Turks held the high ground. On May 6, the First Light Horse Regiment received orders to ship out without their horses.

Six days later, Christopher found a burrow to sit in and hurriedly wrote down his first impressions of war:

May 12th–Gallipoli: Landed at dawn. Under fire for first time! Our landing boats were fired upon but no casualties. High range of steep dark hills cut by dry gullies with low scrubby bush. Beach under fire from snipers, desultory machine-gun fire, and occasional artillery shells. British and French at Cape Helles, 10 miles south at entrance to Dardanelles strait. Saw line of covered dead.

Afternoon–Poor bloke killed 100 feet from me by artillery shell and two of his mates wounded. We're ordered to Pope's Hill Post on the front line.

May 13th–Pope's Hill Post: We're in a support trench set into side of hill just below the front trenches. We had steep 400 ft. climb under fire to Pope's sitting on crest of hill, half a mile inland. Johnny Turk was using timed artillery shells that exploded above us and threw out a hail of shrapnel. Two or three hit on way up, none seriously. Situation here is that enemy is right in front of Pope's in parallel trenches stepping up the hill. To left, enemy holds high ground up to elev. 900 ft. or more. To the right are our posts, Quinn's, Courtney's, and Steele's, in a broken line along the crest of hill, Turk trenches opposite in some places as close as 30 feet away. Sounds of rifle fire, machine-gun bursts, and explosions are constant. Smell of dead pretty bad. We replace front line tomorrow. Not looking forward to it.

May 18th–Reserve Valley: Resting in sheltered valley below Pope's. Feeling much better now after delousing my clothes. Four days on front line, three killed and seven wounded. We shoot at Turks, and they at us. Johnno is game, often sneaking into his front trench only feet away and lobbing a grenade into our trench and then scurrying away before we can return the favor. We take turns sleeping, most can't, but I can. Don't know why.

The front line is a wretched place. The trench is a cemetery because we are forced to surface bury our dead beneath duckboards and in the parapet walls, so legs and arms stick out here and there. Terrible. Maggots fall onto you, getting into everything, even our food. Trench infested with crawling lice and fleas that get into your hair, socks, and underclothes. Drives you crazy with itching. Flies are a terrible nuisance, and huge rats have plenty to eat. Some of the lads can't take it and go a bit mad. I don't let it get to me. It's only for a few days.

Night of 15th: Forgot to include: We supported the Second Light Horse at Quinn's who were ordered out into no-man's-land to cut Jacko's communication lines. Poor bastards were found out and with no cover 45 were killed or wounded in seconds.

May 24th–Pope's: I'm supposed to be in ready position (but all's quiet, so I'm writing). Amazing, unbelievable sight in front of me—smiling Johnny Turks greeting our lads and exchanging cigarettes!!! They're burying their dead.

However, I'm ahead of myself. I want to write about my life or death battle on 19th that shook me up a bit. Killed two Turks in hand-to-hand fighting who got into our trench. Evening of 18th, expecting an attack, the big-heads moved us back up to reinforce Pope's. After midnight, shelling and machine-gun fire all down the line told us the stunt was on. At about 4 a.m., Jacko came at us shouting '*Allah!*' and blowing his trumpets in two separate waves that our rapid fire and Maxim machine guns mowed down. About two hours later, a third wave came right into our post—70 to 80 Turks. I got one in the throat with my bayonet as he jumped in and the other with my knife as we fought. He wouldn't die, so I had to keep sticking him. I had his blood all over me and didn't know how I felt about it. Now I know it was him or me and that's just the way it is. No worries.

Johnno was granted an eight-hour ceasefire to bury his thousands of dead. Something had to be done. It was bad before, but now the nauseating stench from rotting corpses that have been lying in the hot sun for five days is almost unbearable. Even I can't eat and hold it down.

After the failed Turkish offensive of May 19, the front settled into a stalemate. In late July, Christopher was caught in the open by a screaming shrapnel shell. Flattening himself to the ground, he was hit in the back and right leg. In great pain, he was taken face down on a stretcher to Anzac Cove's dressing station and then sent out to a hospital ship to undergo surgery to remove a large piece of shrapnel lodged between two ribs. While he was convalescing, the First Light Horse Regiment took part in a massive offensive to wrest control of the peninsula heights from the Turkish army.

From his cot on the deck of the hospital ship, Christopher had a front row view of the entire offensive, which began on August 6. In the afternoon, the Allied forces in the south attacked the Turkish positions at Cape Helles and Lone Pine beginning a diversionary "right hook" operation to draw Turkish forces from the north to the south. In the late evening, the Australians attacked from southern Steele's Post to complete the "right hook." Following Steele's attack, the New Zealanders began the primary "left hook" operation in the north. The objective of their night attack was to overrun the Turkish reserves on the key heights of the Sari Bair Range by early morning. They would then be in position to support a breakout in the center of the line by Pope's, Quinn's, and Courtney's Posts. To provide the additional troops required to fight a sustained battle to the north, once the breakout was achieved, a large British force began to land during the night at Suvla Bay north of Anzac Cove.

At 5:00 a.m. in the morning of August 7, the New Zealanders were still fighting their way up the gullies and lower ridges of the Sari Bair Range and were in no way able to support a breakout from the center of the Allied line. Nevertheless, the attack from the center was ordered as planned. The futile attacks by the Australians at The Nek, resulting in their slaughter, effectively ended the overly ambitious offensive.

Released for combat on August 15, Christopher returned to Pope's Hill Post with a group of replacements. The first thing he realized was the large number of new faces. He found Joey Miller and one other digger mate, Trevor Baldwin.

"You were lucky to miss the stunt, Chrissie," Joey said. "The heads fucked up royal. We had at least a hundred fifty casualties out of the two hundred who made the charge."

"Ah, bloody hell," Christopher said.

"Sarge McGregor and Gibson copped it," Joey continued. "Major Reid, Captain Cox, and Lieutenant Nettleton were all killed, and B squadron was nearly wiped out."

With baffled incredulity, Christopher slowly said, "Fuck—a—*duck!* I don't believe this."

"I was in C squadron held in reserve. Trev here was one of the few to make it back uninjured."

"I was with Glasgow's group," Trevor said. "We cleared the first two trenches with bayonets and grenades, then bunched the Turks into the end of the third row near the top—lost a lot of mates gettin' there an' couldn't go no farther. We blocked off the trench with sandbags and bodies and tried to hold on there while the battle developed, taking furious fire and grenades from above. Saw our poor diggers on The Nek being cut to pieces, and not being able to hold on any longer, got the hell out of there."

Several months later, Christopher wrote Nigel abroad the SS *Ionian* as it steamed toward Alexandria, Egypt:

Dear Nigo,   Dec. 22, 1915

I'm on a ship heading back to Egypt. We evacuated Anzac Cove two days ago. The British and French will follow from Cape Helles. Remarkable that we were able to slip out at night without Jacko getting wind of it, or maybe they just let us go. I don't know.

Johnny Turk turned out to be a dinkum fighter, no doubt about it. He fought fair and hard. They never gave way and were a fanatical lot. Probably because they were defending their country. They didn't start the war, and we don't feel any hate toward them.

We were greatly outnumbered. We probably never had a chance with them holding the high ground from the start. I hated to slink out leaving our dead diggers without a proper burial on foreign soil, but it's over now. We did our duty and can be proud that we fought them to a draw. Can't say as much for our pommy commanders or the British chaps at Sulva Bay and Cape Helles. If we had more Anzacs we could have broken through.

I hope this reaches you before you ship out, or you may not receive it for months. You should be close to finishing your basic training at Holsworthy. How do you and Lester like the army? Wouldn't it be bonzer if we could meet up in Cairo? I don't know where we will be sent next, except I hope it's on our horses as Light Horsemen rather than the blooming infantry—oops, no offense intended, cousin.

I've completely healed from my shrapnel wounds. Funnily enough, after all the fighting I've been in, and although I admit that I was scared a few times, I somehow knew I'd come through it all right.

Good luck,
Christopher

* * *

Just four months after Christopher and the Anzacs were evacuated from Gallipoli, a spontaneous and overwhelming public demand forced the prime minister to name April 25 "Anzac Day" to commemorate the date the Anzacs landed at Gallipoli. The fifteen-year-old nation of only five million was appalled by the bloodshed of its first major military campaign and united in grief. The eight-month campaign had made casualties of half of the fifty thousand Australians who served in Gallipoli and killed nearly eight thousand.

On April 25, 1916, the parents of Christopher and Nigel walked along Macquarie Street on their way to view the first Anzac Day parade. The street was adorned with a profusion of flags, bunting, and garlands of flowers. Stopping at a decorated stand, operated by nurses in neat gray and red uniforms, they donated to the Soldiers' Support Fund and received contributor pins.

"We received a letter from Nigel a few days ago," Peter said. "He looked for Christopher in Cairo, but the First Light Horse was not there, and he couldn't find out where they had been sent."

Samuel sighed. "It would be a shame if our boys weren't able to meet up. Christopher's last letter was from a place in the desert west of the Nile River, which he wasn't at liberty to name. I read we're fighting Senussi tribesmen from Libya who have sided with the Turks. He could be there."

They found a place to observe the parade in front of the statue of Robert Burns, the Scottish poet, near St. Mary's gate to The Domain. An army band led the parade of dignitaries, nurses, and four thousand returned soldiers, some seriously injured. After the parade had passed, the Armstrongs walked into The Domain and chose a place to sit in front of the high dais erected for the speakers.

They laid blankets on the lawn, opened their picnic baskets, and took out a lunch to share.

"Christopher writes such interesting letters," Ellen said. "He's such a good writer! I think it comes from his keen interest in reading. You know he's keeping a journal that he hopes to get published when he returns?"

"How wonderful," Anne said. "I wish Nigel would write more often."

"I'd like to see Christopher make something of himself as a writer," Samuel added. "He's shown no interest in business."

Peter said, "Speaking of business, my board approved replacing Norman Builders with the name Armstrong Development Company to more accurately reflect our business these days."

Samuel gave a wry grin. "Eleanor must have rolled in her grave when you changed the name of the company she started in the 1860s."

"Actually, her husband Alistair Norman, a builder, started the company in 1850," Peter corrected. "After he was killed by a shark in Double Bay, Eleanor ran the company."

"That's right, I'd forgotten that after all these years. It doesn't diminish what an astute businesswoman Eleanor was . . . one of a kind, an exceptional woman, I must say."

"You're not forgetting Mary Reiby are you Samuel?" Anne said. "Another remarkable businesswoman. I remember Eleanor saying that Mary Reiby was a better businesswoman than herself and did it while raising *seven* children without a husband!"

They all knew that Mary Reiby was a former convict. Anne had committed an indecorum: polite company did not discuss convicts if it could be avoided.

Samuel took a newspaper out of the picnic basket and opened it. "Let me read to you an article that I think you'll find positively inspirational." He turned pages looking for it. "Ah, here it is.

"The king sent this heartfelt message: 'I heartily congratulate you on the splendid conduct and bravery displayed by the Australian troops in the operation at the Dardanelles. They proved themselves worthy sons of the empire.' " He thumbed to another section.

"The *Herald*'s editorial refers to Gallipoli as Australia's 'baptism of blood' equal in importance to federation." Turning to another article, he said, "Listen to what the Anglican archbishop said, 'Before the war Australia was looked upon as a distant settlement in the southern seas, but now we are known as a real part of the empire.' Marvelous and fitting, don't you think? I'm proud that *our* Christopher had a part in it!"

"I'm proud of our boys too, Samuel, and of Christopher's part in Gallipoli," Peter said, "so please don't get me wrong, but don't you think this is all a bit much? I mean . . . the campaign was a failure, wasn't it?"

"It wasn't a *failure*, they fought to a draw—*my word!*" Samuel said. "Christopher said the Anzacs never had a chance to win from the start and shouldn't have been landed where they were. It was all bloody Winston Churchill's fault. As First Lord of the Admiralty, he came up with the ill-conceived plan to attack the Dardanelles. That's why he was dismissed from the government and is now serving on the western front as a common officer. Our gallant boys fought to a draw against insurmountable odds in the most difficult of conditions. I'd say we should be proud of what they did."

"I am proud, Samuel," Peter said contritely. "Allow me to propose a toast to the safe return of our sons, to our stalwart Anzacs, the king, the empire, and Anzac Day."

"Hear, hear!" Samuel said.

Years later, April 25 would be formally enshrined as the national memorial day to commemorate military service in all of Australia's wars while retaining a special emotional link to Gallipoli.

*   *   *

Nigel's and Lester's Fifth Division arrived in Marseilles on June 13, 1916, and proceeded by train to Amiens, France, twenty miles from the Western Front. The front was locked in a war of attrition that measured success in yards.

Two years earlier, the Kaiser's Imperial German Army had marched through neutral Belgium to attack France. After the battles of movement ceased, the opposing armies became bogged down along the Western Front in a stalemate of trench warfare. In 1916, the Allies planned a summer offensive to break through the fortified German line near the Somme River. One of the main purposes of the breakthrough was to relieve pressure on the French at Verdun. The first day of the offensive, July 1, was the worst day of losses in British military history. By the end of the day, there were 57,500 British casualties, nearly half of the 120,000 men thrown into the assault. The Germans sustained only 8,000 casualties. Such a massive offensive into machine guns and artillery was never repeated, although smaller scale attacks under different names continued, all later known as the Battle of the Somme.

On July 18, west of the remnants of Fromelles village, Nigel and Lester were bivouacked with their company around a destroyed farmhouse. The soldiers were called together and the company commander stood on a flatbed truck to address them.

"Men, before first light tomorrow morning, our company will relieve British troops in the center of the Fromelles line. In the late afternoon, following an intense bombardment of the German line, our battalion will attack across three hundred yards of no-man's-land. The British Sixty-first Division will be on our right flank. I want us to show the British what we Australians are made of. Let's make ourselves proud by accepting nothing less than success. Go to bed early tonight and get a good night's sleep. God bless you and good luck."

The next day, the bombardment of the German line began at five o'clock in the afternoon. An hour later, upon hearing the shrill sound of whistles up and down the line, Nigel and Lester went over the top with their company, walked through openings in the bands of barbed wire, and moved forward at double time. They shared reassuring glances. A distant *rat-tat-tat-tat-tat-tat-tat* of a single German machine gun quickly built into a roar as other machine guns joined in. Men started to fall. A man screamed out in pain near them.

Jeez, Nigel thought, men are already being shot. The German line seemed far away. The enemy's artillery opened up with shells that sent huge geysers of earth high into the air ahead of them. Soil, stones, and debris rained down. A human leg hit the ground in front of them. Whistled commands told them to run forward. Hunched over, Nigel ran with his head and shoulders lowered, his left shoulder leading into the maelstrom, eyes looking forward beneath the brim of his steel helmet.

Bullets zipped by. I'm going to be hit any moment—please, not in the head. Multiple screams—everyone's being hit—Jesus, Mother of God . . . where's Lester? Nigel looked around and saw Lester a bit behind him. Nigel jumped over a downed man. The ground exploded into a barrier of dirt in front of him. Can't run through this!

He jumped into a bomb crater and buried his head. Lester followed. Dirt and stones rained down. A shell burst threw a soldier through the air onto Lester. Nigel scooted over to them on his knees. The left side of the soldier was missing spewing blood onto Lester. The soldier looked at Nigel and mouthed "Help me" and then died.

"*Stretcher-bearer, stretcher-bearer!*" a horrified Lester was yelling as Nigel shook him to point out the man was dead. They drew away from the body. Another soldier jumped into the crater with them. The sound of battle was deafening.

They had been trained to keep moving toward the objective no matter what, stop for no one; stretcher-bearers would follow to mend the fallen. Nigel looked at Lester. They crawled out of the crater together and ran forward.

Keep close to Lester! . . . run together . . . we'll get through this . . . slap of something on my face—blinding flash—ear-piercing roar.

Nigel landed on his back upside down with his feet extending out of a crater. He sensed the ground quivering and siding away from him. Slowly, he regained consciousness.

Am I dead? Hold on . . . can hear something . . . far off . . . is this what death feels like? Floating . . . not so bad. I can see blue . . . clouds . . . I'm dazed. I should try to get up . . . in a second . . . ears ringing. I'm not dead. Hope nothing's broken . . . mouth full of dirt . . . *cough, spit* . . . acrid smell of cordite fumes.

Gradually, Nigel came around, the ringing in his ears lessening.

He rotated his body and slide down to the bottom of the crater. Moving his head, he looked around for Lester. The sound of battle was less. He was alone.

I should look for Lester . . . in a minute.

He sensed more activity and saw soldiers running by.

Must be a second wave.

Nigel raised himself up onto a bent arm and looked himself over, then pushed himself up to lean against the side of the crater. Two soldiers jumped into the crater, looked at him, and continued on. He was in one piece. His rifle was gone. Raising himself, Nigel peeked over the edge of the crater. There were bodies nearby. He sensed there was less machine-gun fire. Bent over, he crawled out of the crater and staggered around looking at bodies for Lester. He picked up a working rifle with its bayonet attached and stumbled forward. There were several soldiers running fifty yards ahead of him.

We must have taken the enemy trench. . . . almost there. Loud shrapnel burst above . . . still shelling us . . . through German wire . . . keep going . . . trench.

Nigel jumped into the trench and landed on the stomach of a German lying at its bottom. The impact forced a "Oooph" from him. He thrust his bayonet into the German's chest before seeing that half his forehead was gone. Nigel quickly looked right and left to take in the grotesque chaos of the trench, a carnage more horrifying than anything he could imagine. Transfixed, he looked at bodies in all manner of convoluted positions, piled one on top of another, amid a shambles of rifles, machine guns, upturned duckboards, fallen sandbags, shovels, and battle refuse filling half the height of the trench. The mass of bodies, covered in mud, dirt, and blood, made German indistinguishable from Australian. There was some movement in the mass and pitiful groans. Several Australian soldiers were stepping their way through the bodies at the far end of the trench. Nigel decided to follow them.

A voice from behind suddenly screamed into his ear, startling him, "*Get yer goddamn-fuckin'-arse goin', ya dumb son-of-a-bitch, this ain't bloody motherfuckin' Kings Cross!*"

Nigel turned to see a sergeant. "Where to, Sergeant?"

"Move yer arse aside and follow me through this lot!"

They scrambled through the front trench and around its protective zigzag and walked a distance past two other Australian soldiers and turned right into a communication trench leading uphill toward the second trench row. At its entrance, the sergeant stopped, looked left and right and turned around.

"Youse first five go right as far as youse can. Youse behind 'em follow me to the left." He grabbed Nigel by the shoulder and pushed him right. "*Move!*"

Nigel led the four behind him toward the sounds of fighting further along the trench. He could not see the fighting because of a zigzag in the trench further ahead. Nigel approached a corporal at the zigzag who said, "Keep goin', mate." Twenty men or more were gathered together. A lieutenant was organizing a defense at the next zigzag in the trench. He pointed at Nigel's group and said:

"You five go back a bit and man the parapet. Prepare for a counterattack from over the top. Collect grenades from the dead! Go!"

Nigel and the others looked at the sandbags along the parapet that were being pulverized by German machine-gun fire from the next trench line up the slope. He could make out the distinct sound of Australian Lewis machine guns responding. Keeping their heads down, Nigel's group collected grenades from dead Australians and Germans and handed them out to soldiers already sitting on the parapet platform. No one seemed interested in looking over the parapet to exchange fire with the German machine guns.

Then mysteriously, the German machine gun fire let up and became intermittent. The lieutenant looked over the parapet and said, "Prepare for a counterattack." But nothing happened.

It was getting dark, and Nigel realized he was hungry. He found an apple in his pack and ate it quickly. The lieutenant said loud enough so most could hear: "We will hold here until we are reinforced. Pass it along."

German artillery began shelling them. Everyone jumped from the parapet platform to the bottom of the trench. Explosions sounded up and down the first two German trench lines occupied by the Australians. A part of the trench wall caved in burying some of the men. Nigel and others dug them out quickly enough to save all but one. British artillery dueled with the German artillery. Hours passed.

Around eleven o'clock, the German shelling stopped. An hour later, just as Nigel rested his head against the parapet wall to get some sleep, sounds of combat suddenly erupted from the first trench. When the second trench came under fire, they realized that the Germans had flanked them, and they were encircled! German flares arched into the night sky illuminating the battle. Nigel picked out movement to shoot at but did not pull the trigger for fear they were Australians.

Grenades started to fall in and around their trench. A grenade cleared the parapet and bounced off Nigel's shoulder. He yelled "*Grenade!*" to the man below. He threw a sandbag over it and jumped away. There was a muffled explosion.

The Germans were attacking from both the east and west. The Australians were being forced toward the center of the second trench where Nigel was. A team with a Lewis machine gun entered their area of the trench and set the gun up. A captain took over command from the lieutenant. There were fifty or more soldiers in their part of the trench now, many of them wounded. The Lewis machine gun was a godsend. The Germans were repulsed again and again by fire, grenades, and bayonets. Then everything quieted at four o'clock.

The captain and lieutenant met and then walked among the men telling them what they had decided. If they fought in the morning, they would be overrun and everyone, including the wounded, would be killed. Better for the able bodied to breakout under the cover of darkness and the wounded to wave white flags of surrender. Anyone who wanted to surrender could do so with the wounded. Nigel decided to escape rather than surrender.

The breakout plan was to follow the captain quietly over the top carrying a grenade in each hand and rush across the thirty yards to drop them into the first trench. The explosions would create chaos and allow an escape into no-man's-land to seek the shelter of craters. The captain ordered those escaping to remove anything that would make noise and to darken their faces and arms with dirt.

The twenty or so men who opted to breakout formed a line along the parapet platform with the captain in the middle. When he rose to go over the parapet, the others followed.

The line of men sprinted for the front trench and were nearly there when the first sentry shots sounded. Nigel threw one of his grenades forward into the trench and dropped the second one in as he jumped over it. Individual shots rang out and an escaping soldier in front of him stumbled and fell. Flares ignited lighting the area. Nigel saw a break in the barbed wire and ran through it and dove into a shallow crater as a German machine gun opened up. The captain thumped down beside him. Machine guns concentrated their fire on men caught in the barbed wire and out in the open. When the flares went out, Nigel jumped up and made it to a deeper crater before additional flares ignited. Between flares, he ran crater to crater. Bullets were hissing by and striking the ground around him. As the light of dawn increased, the captain plunked down beside him in a crater.

Australian soldiers in the first trench on their side of no-man's-land were following the progress of the breakout soldiers while pouring fire into the German first trench. The captain and Nigel saw that they were only sixty or so yards from the Australian trench. They studied the thicket of wire in front of the trench for breaks and chose the best route. Jumping out of the crater, they dashed for the Australian trench. Nigel raced ahead through an opening in the wire and dove over the parapet somersaulting into outstretched arms. Between congratulations, he heard the screams of the captain. Nigel climbed up onto the parapet platform and looked out.

The captain was some fifteen yards away, shot through the leg, screaming in pain and frustration as he crawled desperately toward the Australian trench, bullets kicking up dust around him. Before anyone could stop him, Nigel went over the parapet and ran to the captain. He grabbed his wrists and dragged him toward the trench. A bullet knocked Nigel's left leg out from under him. Several soldiers went over the parapet and pulled them both to safety.

A tourniquet was tied around Nigel's leg. He was placed into a stretcher and taken to a treatment dugout along with the captain. They were placed beside each other in the waiting area.

Nigel saw that the captain had been shot in the upper part of his right leg.

The captain smiled. "We made it, mate." His voice was raspy and weak. "What's your name?"

"Nigel, sir."

"I'm Billy Seaton—*owwh!* What's your last name, Nigel?"

"Armstrong."

"Thanks for saving my life, Nigel Armstrong."

The doctor cut away the captain's pant leg and said "E-o-r" to his assistants. As Seaton was lifted, he grimaced and let out a quiet "Ahh" and then saluted Nigel.

Four months later, from a hospital in London, Nigel wrote Christopher:

Dear Chrissie,   Oct. 17, 1916

I apologize for not writing for a while, but you know I'm not much for writing. I see from your last letter that you know I lost the lower part of my left leg and that Lester was killed at Fromelles. I couldn't believe this all happened in our first battle. I didn't feel sorry for myself too long living amongst so many poor fellows much worse off than me. I've been fitted with an artificial leg and foot. I'm lucky to have my knee which should allow me to walk almost normal and maybe even surfboard when I return to Bondi Beach.

The big news is that I got the Distinguished Conduct Metal for "conspicuous bravery." This is nice; however, I hope to use it to become a pilot with the Australian Flying Corps! A mate here who was a pilot says I can fly with my crook leg, no problem. I don't want to go home after only one battle. I wouldn't feel right about it. Soldiers' Aid and my pilot mate are going to help me apply for flight school. You are the first I've written about this, so don't tell anyone in our families until I find out if they will accept me or not.

Compared to Gallipoli, your letters about the Sinai

Desert sound like you really enjoy fighting on horseback. I know you didn't like fighting as an infantryman in Gallipoli. Seems like you have great trooper mates. I am glad you are happy under Aussie Gen. Chauvel and proud of the part the Light Horse played in the victory at Romani.

I got a letter from home last week that said everyone is fine and in good health. I think this war is going to grind on for a while, so don't take any unnecessary chances.

Your cousin,
Nigo

* * *

Min-chin had correctly predicted that Paddy's Market would increase the number of buyers of Chinese gardening produce. In response to the greater demand, Wing-yuen purchased more acreage and increased production through the use of farm machinery, better fertilizers, and improved farming methods. Min-chin, at seventy-two years, was happy with his son's management of the family business and pleased to be able to work fewer hours. One afternoon, after discussing business with his father, Wing-yuen changed the subject.

"Father, may I ask if the matchmaker has found a wife for me yet?"

"It should be soon, Son, please continue to be patient."

"I'm twenty-eight, Father, it's been over a year since you employed the matchmaker. I would like to start a family to give you and mother grandchildren."

"I will meet with the go-between to see what he has for us."

Looking at the floor, Wing-yuen said, "I've found a Chinese woman I would like to marry."

Min-chin calmed himself knowing he had failed his son by not finding a wife for him after a year of trying.

"Who is she?"

"Her name is Xiao Kui ... she works in Paddy's Market. I have talked to her. She is very pretty and sweet and nice to talk to. I think she is fifteen or sixteen years old."

"Is that a Yao name?"

"I don't know, Father, I don't know her well enough to ask."

"What does she do at Paddy's Market? Is her father a merchant?—I don't know any Xiao."

"She works for the management . . . sweeping floors."

"This is not possible," Min-chin said shaking his head. "I am disappointed that you would consider such a woman."

"Father, I would like you to see her. She is very pretty and has many suitors."

"Whether she is pretty or not has nothing to do with it! I have seen her and know who you are talking about now. Her mother is a white Australian, a *kwai-lo!* Her father is Yao and a laborer. *I forbid it!* This is ridiculous to even talk about."

"We are all Chinese here, Father. Some Yao, Hakka, and other minorities have done very well in Australia. The old animosities have no place here in Australia—we are all considered the same here—as despised Chinese!"

"I understand your frustration, Wing-yuen. I think the go-between is very close to arranging a betrothal from the Sun Wei District. He told me he expects to receive final approval from the immigration people any day now."

"That isn't going to happen, Father. You should save your money. I have looked into it. The matchmaker doesn't know what he is doing. Even naturalized Chinese are having little success in sponsoring the entry of their relatives. You missed your opportunity to become a naturalized citizen, and now it's not possible. It's all changed since you were betrothed to Mother. It's not possible to immigrate here anymore."

"When the go-between told me that the immigration people were being difficult, I told him to look for an appropriate wife in Sydney as well."

"There are very few full-blood Chinese girls in Sydney, Father, probably less than one hundred, and only a few of them would meet your requirements. You should tell him to consider mixed-blood Chinese girls—or he'll never find a wife for me."

"I'll instruct him to look in Melbourne too."

"I've been very patient, Father, but now I want your approval to choose my own wife—a half-breed, if I must. The ancestors should realize that adjustments have to be made when Chinese live in foreign lands. I'm afraid you are more concerned with a loss of face than my happiness!"

"You don't understand, Wing-yuen. I *can't* allow this; *it's impossible!* It is my responsibility to keep the Fong line pure. I cannot be the first in five centuries of Fongs to pollute our blood line. The ancestors would curse me for all time. How would I explain it to my Elder Brother Sing-woo? I would be cast out, and my name removed from the revered ancestor tablets. If I said yes to what you ask, I would be tormented in my sleep and my days haunted. You would be the first elder son to disobey his father in a thousand years, bringing disgrace upon yourself and on me for raising such a son."

"Please, Father, that's old thinking. I do not really want an arranged marriage. I would like to choose a wife I like."

"Our *old ways* are better than those you are learning in this country."

"You'll never change, Father, but I understand both your ways and the new ways. A Chinese proverb I've heard you and your friend Kwong Tang say many times 'Only the wisest and the stupidest never change' is—"

"Don't be disrespectful! You have always been a good son, and I ask only for more time. Now that I know how strongly you feel, I will double my efforts. You have always followed my advice and must continue to do so. Remember that the masters also said, 'Of all the myriad virtues, filial piety is the first.' You must trust me and give me more time to find a suitable wife that will bring honor to our family, you, and the Fong name."

Wing-yuen agreed to be patient for a while longer. Five months later, Min-chin announced that he had found a suitable Cantonese woman in Melbourne. Breaking tradition, Wing-yuen demanded to meet her before the match was finalized. He found his seventeen-year-old intended wife, Sek-leih, to be attractive and sweet. Following her graduation from school, they were married in an elaborate and traditional wedding ceremony.

* * *

After a week reconnoitering enemy territory, Christopher returned to base camp and found that he had received a letter from Nigel. He read the letter again and again while writing him back. It was a pleasure to express his admiration for Nigel's fortitude and his extraordinary achievement of being accepted for pilot training. He also enjoyed writing about the successes of the Light Horse against Turkish forces; however, he felt shame as he wrote lies about himself:

Dear Nigo,   Aug. 17, 1917

How's the pilot? Now when I see an aeroplane soaring, I'll think of you. If I didn't love the Light Horse, I'd try to become a pilot too. You make it sound so great. Many Light Horse blokes have become pilots. I admire your spunk for not taking 'No' for an answer. I'm not surprised that the boofheads took one look at your artificial leg and stamped your application "Medically unfit!" No bloody consideration for the quality of the man! They didn't take into account that they were dealing with an Armstrong!

Your letters are too short, by the way. You have to write me more than "We decided to petition King George V and were amazed when five weeks later my application was approved for transfer to the Australian Flying Corps." There must be more to it than that! I'll probably have to wait to talk to you in person to get the whole story, but good on you. You must be more than halfway through your training by now, since you hope to finish by the end of the year. Write me back as soon as you get this letter to tell me how your training is going.

Because I'm an old hand at this game now, the heads tried again to promote me to corporal, over our fifteen troopers. I told them to shove it again. I'm not interested in making the military my life and don't want to order my mates around. They follow me already because I know what I'm doing The only problem is when we get a difficult dickhead corporal, like the one we are saddled with now.

We have pushed the Turks out of the Sinai back to their thirty-mile defensive line in Palestine running from Gaza directly east to the town of Beersheba. East of Beersheba is a rocky, and some say, impassable desert. Our advance has been protected by the British navy on the west and the Arab Revolt in Arabia to the east. Rumor has it that the Arabs are led by a British intelligence officer, named Lawrence, who took the port of Akaba last month. Not much is known about him other than he's taught them how to blow up trains to keep the Turks from flanking us. We are stalled here until our new general Allenby comes up with his plan to break through.

When we arrived back at base camp yesterday, we found that the thieving Bedouins had sneaked past our guards at night and nicked many of our personal belongings. I lost clothes, a jeweled dagger, and an extra blanket. Thank god they didn't steal my journals. I hate those niggers. They cut the throats of the wounded, dig up the dead for anything valuable, act as guides for us and spies for the Turks, and pinch anything they can get their hands on.

Poor Curly Beckles, my best cobber, died this morning. We brought him back shot through a lung. He was a true-blue, decent sort. I keep vowing not to make any more chums, but I can't seem to keep it.

I know I have asked you before, but please keep all of my letters, so I can use the information in them after the war. Thanks.

All the best,
Chrissie

Eight days earlier, in preparation for Allenby's upcoming offensive, Christopher's 15-man section crossed into enemy-held desert to reconnoiter Turkish positions and to capture Bedouin spies, who might report the movements of Allied forces. Through his field glasses, Christopher spotted figures hidden among rocks on the crest of a distant hill.

"What do you think, Curly?" Christopher said, handing his field glasses to his mate. "I make out three of them, Turk lookouts or Bedouins."

After watching the furtive figures for a minute, Curly agreed. "I see the three, can't tell what they're doing, but it doesn't look right. Could be a trap, Chrissie. I'm guessin' you want us to go see, right?"

Christopher cautiously led his section along a wadi in a round-about way to the hill. They came unexpectedly upon a small band of Bedouins who seemed distressed by their sudden appearance. The four Bedouin men in the band held their rifles level and pointed at Christopher's section until he ordered his men to point their weapons at them. The four Bedouins then lowered their rifles, and Christopher's men took the band into custody.

Because they were carrying marked up maps, Christopher made the decision to take the band of four men, five women, and four children back to the regimental base camp for interrogation and internment until the offensive began. When the group camped at an oasis for the night, the Bedouin men were placed under guard with their arms tied. The women and children were permitted to camp nearby under guard.

After a dinner of bully beef, biscuits, dates, and hot tea, the troopers sat around talking.

"I'm glad we found this oasis, or we'd be up a gumtree with this lot," a trooper said. "I was near out of water and flamin' thirsty."

"No worries, now," another said. "We'll be able to make base tomorrow before nightfall, I reckon."

"I remember once when I thought I would die from thirst," said Curly. "We had lost our way in the Sinai in a three-day dust storm and were out of water. Tell the story about Sergeant Radnage and his peaches, Chrissie."

"No, you tell it, Curly. It's your yarn."

"No, you tell it better than me," Curly said. "Go ahead and tell it, ya bugger."

"All right," Christopher said. "Radnage was one mean bastard. He didn't care about anyone but himself."

"Killed at Bir el Abd, wasn't he?" asked one of the troopers.

"Yeah," Christopher said. "Anyway, we were sitting around like this, tryin' to figure what to do, and Radnage's rummaging around in his haversack and suddenly lets out a yelp: '*Ooo*, lookee wot I 'ave 'ere.' He's looking at us with that malevolent smirk of his.

"The bloody fool has found a tin of peaches in the bottom of his sack he's forgotten about. He opens the tin and starts sloppin' it down, slice by slice, right in front of us. Never so much as an offer to anyone else—takin' pleasure in us suffering. Someone asked him for a slice, and he says, 'There's too bleedin' many of youse, I wouldn't 'ave nothin' left for meself' and goes right on gulping. Finished, he throws the tin away, and then gets this odd look on his face and starts turning green. The tin had spoiled in his pack. He starts moaning and then pukes out every last peach slice, fine as can be, on the sand in front of us. We all burst out laughing, and Curly here says, 'Who asked for a slice? Now ya can have the whole bloomin' lot!'"

While everyone was laughing, Christopher excused himself. "I'm going to check the prisoners. You boys have a nice nighty-night."

The next evening back at base camp, Christopher was ordered to report immediately to the regimental headquarters. He was shown into the lieutenant colonel's office.

Without any preliminaries the lieutenant colonel said, "One of the Bedouin mothers you brought in says you raped her daughter."

"You can't believe those niggers, sir," Christopher said.

"Do you want me to convene a hearing to ask your men, under oath, if any of them heard or saw anything to corroborate this woman's accusations?"

"Rather not, sir."

"Well . . . why'd you do it, corporal?"

"I was trying to get information out of her, sir."

"*That's utter rot!*—you don't understand her gibberish. For the last time, why'd you do it?"

"The opportunity presented itself, sir. . . . been in the desert a long time, sir."

"You are a corporal in command of a section—what were you thinking! I'm knocking you back in rank and pay. It's not just because of the rape—you're self-indulgent, show no self-control, do damn well what you please, and are a poor example to the men. *We don't rape internees for Chrissakes!* My goodness, man, where's your morality! I should bring you up on charges, but you're an experienced man we need for the offensive. *Stand at attention when I talk to you!* You have no respect for rank or yourself. I'm transferring you out of my command to the Twelfth Light Horse Regiment. Turn in your stripes to my adjutant in the morning. You're getting off easy here. If I hear of you getting out of line over there, I promise you: I'll bring you up on charges. Dismissed."

* * *

General Allenby's offensive began on October 27 with a land and sea bombardment of Gaza, followed by a feint toward Gaza by the XXI Corps infantry intended to draw Turkish forces from Beersheba, the planned main breakthrough point to occur four days later. In complete secrecy, during the dark of night on October 30, Lieutenant General Chauvel, the first Australian to command a corps, led the Desert Mounted Corps in a wide arc toward Beersheba. The plan was to attack at dawn.

Chauvel held the Australian Mounted Division in reserve. The XX Corps infantry attacked at dawn on October 31 from the west. The battle for Beersheba raged on into the afternoon. Then Chauvel received intelligence that there were no barbed-wire fields or anti-cavalry pits protecting the Turkish trenches southeast of town. Evidently, the Turkish generals believed that any attack from that direction would be suicidal because there was no cover for four miles of open downhill ground. With the infantry attack going badly, Chauvel decided on a desperate Light Horse charge across the open ground with the dual objectives of taking the town and securing its wells to provide water to the troops and horses. If the charge was repulsed, the Desert Mounted Corps would be forced to withdraw to an oasis miles away. The Australian Mounted Division was ordered by Chauvel to assemble behind a ridge hidden from view in Beersheba.

Christopher described the charge in his journal:

<u>Oct. 31st</u>–<u>Charge at Beersheba</u>: We were held in reserve in a dry wadi most of the day. We could hear the sounds of battle and wondered why we had not been called forward to engage Johnny Turk. In the late afternoon, we were ordered to assemble beneath a low ridgeline out of sight of the town. We were lined up side by side, each horse-man separated from the next by five yards, which made wide rows by squadron. I was in the second row. Looking back at the three or four rows behind me was a pretty impressive sight. The rows were separated by a few hundred yards. Word was passed down the line that the stunt was to secure the wells in town.

I had caught glimpses of the town and it looked far away across open terrain, a killing field for artillery. Looking around, I thought how the terrain reminded me of our outback. For the first time since Gallipoli, it passed through my mind that I might not see home again. For the charge, our rifles were slung over our backs; however, many of us held our long bayonets as weapons. We were all nervously yelling, laughing, swearing, and shouting like giddy schoolboys, warning Abdul that his day had come. All to bolster our courage and resolve.

A general advance was ordered, and the first row went over the ridgeline. As we in the second row went over it, I saw clearly the lushness of Beersheba sitting in the valley between hills; the white dome and minaret of its mosque catching the golden glow of the setting sun. It was too far off to see Johnno's trenches. I felt sure we were going to have high casualties. Out of the blue, Tennyson's poem "The Charge of the Light Brigade" came into my mind (I'm not sure I can write this right):

Theirs not to reason why,
Theirs but to do and die:
Into the valley of Death
Rode the six hundred.

We were in a steady trot when Jacko's artillery opened up with shrapnel shells hitting the first row, beginning the slaughter I expected. Horses and men began to tumble in front of me and then in my row. The charge order was given then and very shortly we outpaced Jacko's ability to time the bursts over us, although the rows behind me may have copped it. But my row had a jolly Sunday afternoon ride downhill for awhile.

Unable to get his artillery right, Abdul opened up with his machine guns too early, maybe two miles out. Abdul couldn't get that range right either. Within a mile of his trenches, the air was literally whistling a merry tune with his bullets, but mostly overhead. I kept my head down next to Taboo's hoping that would save me. Again, I think we were moving so fast downhill that Jacko couldn't correct his sights to our ever changing range and was shooting over us, at least over my row. We could see their trenches clearly now and were riding at a mad gallop, screaming our lungs out to release the excitement, with our bayonets pointed in their direction like swords. I was amazed that so many of us had made it to their trenches.

I gripped my razor-sharp bayonet tightly knowing what it can do to a man (I've used it to butcher meat and even to chop wood). After jumping over the first trench, I sliced a running Turk across the neck taking off a good part of his head. (Later, I found him dead where I struck him.) I jumped the second trench without incident and dismounted with my section to attack from the rear. I could hear the battle behind me meaning others had orders to ride into Beersheba to secure the wells. After a short fight, Jacko saw the game was up and started to surrender. I quickly collected a willing group of nine.

After the battle, I looked Taboo over and was pleased to see he was untouched. I nonchalantly ran my hand down through his tail and panicked when it came out all bloody. He had a nice piece of rump sliced off, probably from a vertical piece of shrapnel, though he'll be all right. It was a magnificent charge (and grand fun) that deserves to go into the history books.

The Desert Mounted Corps rode northward from Beersheba, skirting the Turkish artillery emplacements guarding the passes through the Judean Hills, and moved out onto the Philistine Plain. The Turkish Eighth Army at Gaza fearing encirclement retreated north along the coastal plain. Fighting both rearguard and side-guard defenses, the Turkish forces valiantly fought their way north to Jaffa and Jerusalem. Jaffa fell first to the Desert Mounted Corps, and Jerusalem was taken by the infantry without a fight when the enemy retreated north toward Damascus. On December 11, 1917, Allenby triumphantly walked into the holy city of Jerusalem to accept the city's ceremonial surrender.

*   *   *

Nigel couldn't sleep and was perspiring heavily. He'd almost been killed today.

I shouldn't have been daydreaming. The beauty of the billowing clouds, the serenity of the day had lulled me into a daydream. On a joyride. *Stupid. Idiotic. Careless.*

... out of the sun from behind me. *Classic.*

He rolled over and reshaped the pillow beneath his head. Closing his eyes, he demanded himself to settle down and go to sleep.

I tried everything, every trick I know: snap turns, rolls, twisting loop, sideslips, stalls—he followed every maneuver with lightning speed. Unbelievable. Couldn't shake him. Great pilot. Smart. I wonder if he was someone we know—had to be an ace. Can't believe I wasn't hit. Thirty-two bullet holes. Good Lord, I was lucky. No worries, so let's go to sleep.

... had me dead to rights. God, I felt the heat of bullets ripping through the aeroplane. *Pop-pop-pop-pop-pop-pop-pop* just waiting for the searing pain, again. This time in the head or back. Just like a clay pigeon. A pigeon. Dumb luck. Can't believe the engine wasn't hit—or the gas tank! I was outmatched. Goodnight, that's it . . . lights out. I'm going to be exhausted tomorrow.

... shouldn't have gotten separated from the others. Should've probably headed back. I'm not as good as I thought. Let that be a lesson. Stupid to fly alone in hope of finding the others. Sitting duck. Deserved to die. What if there had been two or three of them! I'd be dead now. Jesus. Stupid arse, just lucky this time. God, my nerves are shot. I've got to get some rest; it'll be light soon.

... saved by a little cloud—the only one near us. I guessed right that he wouldn't follow me in but slow and stay high and behind. Didn't expect me to become a duelist. My only chance. Him or me. Only way to have *any* chance. Zoom arc climb at full throttle, half-roll and there he was right in front of me. Felt great to have a chance. He was brave, didn't flinch. Fearless. Almost a head-on collision. Missed him by inches. *Knew* I got him when he jerked back. Slight angle down when he let go of the stick.

Twist power dive and poured it into him—*tat-tat-tat-tat-tat-tat-tat*—just to make sure. He pitched drunkenly and started a nosedive, engine on fire, no fluttering or wobbling, engine roaring, must've fallen forward on controls, straight dive into a field. Our side. Another confirmed kill. I was bloody lucky this time. Have to fly smarter. Let me sleep now, please.

Nigel wrote Christopher about his fourth confirmed kill, describing how lucky he was to survive the better pilot. He then paused in writing his letter and thought that Christopher would be interested in the Americans, for his journal, and the first fully mechanized attack on the Western Front:

> Now I have something for your journal. It should note that the "green" Yanks gained the respect of Aussies in the battle of Hamel. We call them "Sammy" for their Uncle Sam. Four American companies were placed under the

command of Aussie Gen. Monash to gain battle experience. From what I hear, Sammy showed fighting ability and is likely to be a pretty good fighter. Sammy evidently wanted to do well because they were fighting on their July 4th Independence Day. Knowing how you like poems, this one was printed in the AIF magazine *Aussie*:

"FROM AUSSIE TO SAMMY:

Say, how do, old cobber, give us yer mitt!
Pleased to meet you I certainly am.
We can now pull together in doing our bit,
Said the Aussie to proud Uncle Sam.
We've both got some stars on our banners, you know,
And I guess that our blood's the same hue,
And the old Southern Cross shining below
Sends a warm greeting ray out to you."

Monash carried out a brilliantly coordinated mechanized battle. Infantry, tanks, artillery, and our flying corps all worked well together to overrun Hamel in less than two hours. First our aeroplanes bombed Hamel, then the artillery laid down a barrage including smoke to hide the advancing tanks, followed then by the infantry. We dropped supplies and intelligence from the air to the advancing machine gunners.

I was very encouraged by this battle. I hope that we have seen the last of suicidal infantry frontal attacks into machine-gun emplacements. With the American build-up here, and your success in the Holy Land, I'm beginning to think the Allies can win the war this year. It would be wonderful to return to Sydney next year. We will have so much to talk about when we meet again.

Sincerely,
Nigo

* * *

After Jerusalem was taken, several regiments under Allenby were shipped to the Western Front in France, leaving him without reinforcements. From June through August 1918, sufficient replacements from Australia, New Zealand, South Africa, and India arrived to renew his offensive against the Turkish army.

In August, Mustafa Kemal the hero of Gallipoli, later known as Ataturk and the father of the Republic of Turkey, was appointed commander of the Turkish Seventh Army, standing between Jerusalem and Damascus. This time the Allies had a better chance to defeat their nemesis, who led a beaten and demoralized army.

Allenby made it appear that the big push north would be up the Jordan Valley under the command of New Zealander General Chaytor. The Arab irregular army under Prince Faisal, advised by British Colonel T. E. Lawrence (Lawrence of Arabia) participated in this deception by attacking the important railway junction at Deraa on Allenby's eastern flank. Secretly, Allenby had moved the bulk of his troops north of Jaffa where they maintained a discreet presence among groves of olive and citrus trees preparing for the main thrust up the coastal plain of Palestine. A coordinated attack from September 19 to 21 pierced the twenty-five-mile-long Turkish front at Megiddo. The Allies pursued the Turkish army relentlessly, preventing any chance for regrouping, pushing them north past the Sea of Galilee and across the Jordan River and onward to the outskirts of Damascus. Late in the evening of September 30, Christopher's Light Horse regiment established camp on a plateau overlooking the verdant valley of Damascus. In just twelve days, they had fought continuously across nearly 150 miles of mountains and deserts. The "Great Ride" would be noted in history books as an extraordinary feat.

As the exhausted horsemen prepared to lie down to sleep, the earth suddenly shook with violent explosions lighting up the sky. The Turkish army was blowing up its ammunition dumps near the city. From the plateau, Christopher and his mates had a clear view of the fireworks. Christopher was surprised to see a blue Rolls-Royce below them on Damascus Road. It stopped at the checkpoint across the road.

"Stan, Bert, look at that armored Rolls at the checkpoint," Christopher said.

The car passed through the checkpoint and drove into their camp. A British officer and three Arabs stepped out of the car. Two of the Arabs walked behind the car and urinated on the ground.

"Ah, bloody filthy niggers, don't they know we got latrines fer that?" Bert said.

A group of Light Horse officers walked over to the Rolls-Royce, and a crowd began to gather. A buzz of voices passed around the news that Lawrence of Arabia had come in the Rolls.

"He's that secret-duty intelligence bloke who's been leadin' the Arabs an' blowin' up Abdul's trains, isn't he?" Bert asked.

"Yeah," Stan said.

"Let's have a little look-see," Christopher said.

Walking down the slope, they met their section corporal, Rory, coming from the gathering.

"Corp," Stan said, "is one of them Lawrence of Arabia?"

"Yeah, the one in the white robe, dressed like Gad Almighty," Rory said. "But youse can't go over there."

"Get stuffed, Rory," Christopher said. They continued toward the building crowd.

Officer were waving men off as they approached. "You men go on back. Nothing to see here. Get some sleep . . . go on now. Break it up."

Christopher and his mates paused. The two Arabs were arranging their tarps to sleep on the ground, and Lawrence was crawling into the back seat of the Rolls.

On their way back, Christopher said, "I'll see ya back there. I gotta hit the dunny and drain the dragon."

"Now don't be jerkin' the gherkin in there," Bert said.

Christopher laughed. "We'll see."

When reveille sounded early the next morning, the Rolls was gone. After breakfast, Rory called his twelve-man section together.

"Most of the Light Horse has been ordered ta move fast this mornin' to encircle Damascus an' blockade its gates to prevent any more Johnny Turks from escaping. But we, and a few other sections, have a special reconnoitering job ta do. Intelligence say Mustafa Kemal and the Turkish high command snuck out of the city last night and are probably heading north. We're to check out the road to Homs to see if he took that one. If we find them, we are to report their location, not engage.

"It's a risky stunt, but I know youse are up to it. Jacko's goin' ta have a rearguard defense, and ya know what that means. 'Specially if he's protectin' his high command. In other words, they're goin' ta be layin' fer us.

"Over the past two weeks, you men have given me one hundred percent. I want ta thank youse. No section head could ask for more. Now I have ta ask—"

"Ah, pull yer head in," Christopher interrupted.

"This is fer the newies, not you old hands," Rory said.

"Stop havin' yerself on!" Bert said.

"I need to organize the—" Rory started to say.

Christopher interrupted. "You couldn't organize a fart in a baked bean factory."

There was a thunderous outburst of laughter from everyone.

Angry, Rory took a step toward Christopher, raised his fist and shook it at him. "How d'ya like yer eggs done, *mate?*"

"Scrambled, like yer fuckin' brains, Corporal," Christopher retorted.

"Git rooted," Rory said, giving him the finger.

"Always tryin'," Christopher said.

Rory started toward Christopher.

Laughing, Stan stepped in between them. "C'mon . . . no blue, *enough.*"

Later, as they saddled their horses, Stan said, "Rory's a bloody pain in the arse."

"Yeah, he's like a rider with boils on his arse," Christopher said. "But he's smart enough to let me run this section . . ."

As they rode out of camp, Christopher, as if nothing had happened, rode up beside Rory and said, "What's the plan?"

"Ride up the north road until we scout out their column. Gotta better one?"

"Did you look at the map?"

"Yes, I looked at the bloody map. I know where the fuck we're goin'."

"Then you know that Homs Road runs along a valley with hills on both sides. If Mustafa Kemal is up that road, they'll place a number of sacrificial pickets at defensible spots in the hills on both sides of the road for miles. They'll allow us to ride far enough in and then start picking us off. Receiving fire from both sides, that valley will be our graveyard."

"So what's your plan?"

"Avoid the pickets. Ride fast up the parallel valley on the west side to get ahead of Abdul. Then move east and up the hill to observe Homs Road, waiting for Kemal or his pickets to show up. That way, if we haven't gone fast enough and far enough north and run into their pickets, it will be head-on rather than copping it from two sides.

They pulled out a map and agreed to follow Christopher's plan.

Riding fast up the parallel valley, they stopped only once to water their horses and eat a quick lunch. At four o'clock, they turned east, figuring they should be ahead of the slow moving Turkish high command, if it was on Homs Road at all. At the base of the hill, Rory and Christopher took out their field glasses and searched the top of the hill for pickets. Although the hill was largely devoid of trees, except for a few pines here and there, there were plenty of boulders and knee-high brown grass and shrub growth to conceal oneself. Seeing no pickets, they rode up the slope in single file, well apart, to lessen their group target. The first four horsemen were Bert leading the way, followed by Christopher, Rory, and Stan.

Halfway up the slope, Christopher said, "Bert, I just saw movement at two o'clock, to the left of that big boulder. See anything?"

"No, mate."

Rory heard part of what Christopher had said. "Two o'clock?"

"Yeah," Christopher said.

Their section stopped while Rory raised his field glasses and focused on the hilltop four hundred yards ahead.

"*Shit!* They're up there, boys; the game's up! Let's give Jacko a run for his money!"

As soon as they turned their horses, a chorus of shots rang out. The horsemen quickly dispersed across the slope to create only individual targets and rode madly downhill. The *zip, zip, zip* sound of bullets sped by and sand spurted in front of them. To Christopher's ears, it sounded like only four or five riflemen were shooting at them. The sounds of their individual shots echoed down the valley. Christopher passed Rory and as he rode past Stan he was laughing loudly. The exhilaration of being under fire always excited him into laughter. Stan angrily looked at him not seeing the humor of their situation. Christopher's powerful horse, Taboo, gained on the horses ahead.

"*OOHFF!*" Christopher suddenly exclaimed.

"Shit. *Shit!* I'm hit. *I'M HIT!*" Christopher yelled out. Looking down, he confirmed the worst. "*Oh fuck!*"

Stan galloped to his side.

"*Ah, ahh, ahhh. Stan, I'm shot through the fuckin' stomach, mate!*" Christopher was swaying from side to side trying to stay in the saddle.

"Stay on, Chrissie, stay on. I've got you, ol' mate, hold on."

"*Ahh, ooh, oooh, ahhh, oh god, owww*, I'm shot through the fuckin' gut, Stan."

Rory rode up on the other side of Christopher.

"Rory, grab his reins," Stan said. "Let go of the reins, Chrissie. I got ya, hold on. Wadi comin' up, mate, hold on. Almost there." Bullets zipped by as they rode down the steep slope of the dry watercourse.

Ooohhh, ahh. Christopher fell into outstretched arms and was lowered to the dry, sandy streambed. Troopers placed themselves along the top of the slope to defend their position if necessary.

"Taboo's hit low down on his neck," Christopher said.

Rory said, "Just *cut* his shirt open, Stan!"

"Jus' grazed him, Chrissie," Bert said looking at Taboo. "He'll be orright."

"You take him, Stan," Christopher said. "*Ahhhhh*, Christ . . . he's better than that nag you're riding."

"You'll be all right, Chrissie. We'll patch ya up, mate," Stan said.

"I'm buggered, Stan. After all—"

"Give me another compress, goddammit," Rory said. "Get that morph injection into him. We're goin' to patch ya up, mate."

"Ah, fuck you, Rory. *Cough, ooow, ahhhh.* I'm coughing up fuckin' blood, shot in the gut . . . forget it. *Ahh, ooww.* Fuckin' bleedin' to death inside. Seen it a thousand times. *Ahhrrrgg, cooough, ahh, ooh god.* Sorry, Rory—yer all right, mate. Sorry I buggered ya."

"That's orright, mate."

"This was fun till now . . . don't ya think? Wipe that shit off my face will ya, doesn't smell too good. *Oh, ah.* Thanks. Did you think—"

"Could ya jus' shut the fuck up—for once, Chrissie," Stan said. "I'm workin' here, fer Chrissake. *Rory*, apply pressure, ya dumb arse. *Goddammit—push it in! Stop the blood!*"

"Ah, *ahhhh, AHHHRRRGG!*" Christopher screamed.

". . . been a bloody glorious ride . . . Get me a blanket, Bert, will ya? *OWww, gaaa, cough, ahh*—Jesus . . . Ohhhhhh. . . . what a fucking mess . . ."

"Here's a blanket," Bert said.

"Forget the blanket," Rory said.

". . . hardly a pulse. . . . I think that's it. . . . *Chrissie?* . . . still no pulse," Stan said.

"Gotta have blood ta have a pulse," Bert said. "Dammit, Chrissie . . . I'm goin' ta miss yer bullocky."

*　*　*

On October 1, the day that Christopher died, his son Harvey lost a father he never knew; a father who had not known or cared that he existed. Harvey's mother Daisy, having received no word of where her baby had been taken by the Children's Relief Board, had adjusted to a new life without him. Nearly five, Harvey was alone in the world.

Harvey had arrived at the Aboriginal Children's Home at Bomamulla, sixty miles south of Sydney, with only his given name noted in his file. He was assigned the next surname on the list, Hudson. The home raised Aboriginal infants and children until puberty. Funded both by the Children's Relief Board and the Christian

Charities Fellowship, its custodians shared a mission of mercy and religious instruction for their young charges. The home sat on twenty-four acres of land with a stunning view down a valley to the Tasman Sea, providing a cloistered existence for the children.

Harvey sat at his desk staring out the window, wishing he was outside running, jumping, and playing. He was not paying attention to the twelve-foot-long blackboard, where the teacher was placing on the wide chalk tray various hardback pictures of white people eating in a dining room, playing croquet in front of a house, working at office desks, reading to one another, frolicking at a child's birthday party, praying in church pews, and riding horses. Directly beneath these pictures, sitting on the floor and leaning against the wall, was another set of hardback pictures of groups of Aborigines. These pictures showed practically naked Aborigines in various group activities, such as eating around a camp fire, relaxing in the dirt in front of a humpy, playing stick games, drinking, fighting, begging, and stealing.

The teacher clapped her hands together—*clap, clap*—to get their attention. "Let's start our lessons now, children. Sit up straight!"

She proceeded to draw the differences between the pictures of the whites and Aborigines. She presented the whites as civilized, hygienic, moral, productive, responsible, and religious in contrast to the Aborigines who she represented as uncivilized, dirty, immoral, lazy, crime-ridden, irresponsible, and godless.

"Sally, do people who steal from others go to heaven?" the teacher asked.

"No, ma'm."

Pointing at Harvey, she asked, "Harvey, when you grow up, would you like to work on a sheep station and ride a horse or beg and steal?"

"Ride a horse," Harvey answered.

And so the lesson went until lunchtime. While the children walked to the lunchroom in twos, Harvey thought to himself how fortunate he was to be a lighter skin tone than the boy next to him.

* * *

A wry grin formed on Peter's face as he turned his attention from his son Nigel to his son's girlfriend Wilhelmina.

"So, are we to understand, Wilhelmina, after knowing my reticent son for four months, that he has never told you *how* he lost his leg in the war?"

"I assumed he lost it . . . somehow—flying?"

"And I expect that he told you nothing of his medals?" Peter asked her as his smile turned mischievous. "Am I right?"

"Really, Father," Nigel said. "Is this necessary?"

"I'm curious now, Nigel, allow Miss Volbrecht to answer . . ."

"Yes . . . I mean, *no*, he hasn't told me anything about earning medals."

"Well allow me, since you may never hear it from him. The two are connected you see. He received the Distinguished Conduct Medal for carrying an officer to safety from no-man's-land. Unfortunately, that's when he was shot in the lower leg, which he later lost to gangrene. Because he could no longer serve in the infantry, he became an aeroplane pilot through the intervention of King George V."

"Hold it there, Dad. We wrote King George, but I don't know that he did anything. However, a month later, I *was* accepted to pilot training. So go on if you must play the role of the proud Father," Nigel said.

"That's right, I am a proud Father, so be it."

"And proud Mother," Anne said.

"Yes," Peter said. "Where was I? . . . then he received the Distinguished Flying Cross for his nine victories in the air, making him an Australian ace pilot. There, I kept it short, Nigel. Now do you have anything to add?"

"No."

"I thought not, although I'm happy to boast a little about my son to his girlfriend."

Nigel looked at Samuel and Ellen who were seated across from him at the table. "If anyone deserved medals it would be Christopher for all the battles he was in over three and a half years. Willa, my cousin Chris served in the Light Horse and fought at Gallipoli and in Palestine. He was killed near Damascus. Uncle Samuel, have you found Chrissie's journals yet?"

"No. We've written to no avail," Samuel answered.

"Please accept my condolences, Mrs. and Mr. Armstrong," Wilhelmina said.

"Thank you, dear," Ellen replied. "We do have Christopher's letters, which are a comfort."

After the dinner, the women retired to the veranda, and Peter, Samuel, and Nigel went into the den.

"Seems our prime minister, The Little Digger, did a good job for us at the Paris Peace Conference, what with obtaining the League of Nation's mandate for German-held territory in our sphere," Samuel said.

"Yes," Peter agreed. "We got everything south of the Equator: the Bismarck Archipelago, New Britain, and German New Guinea. I feel much safer knowing that the front door to Australia is in our hands, backed up by England's navy."

"Japs didn't like it much, I understand," Samuel said.

"I think Prime Minister Hughes offended them on another issue, Uncle Samuel," Nigel said.

"Are you referring to the Japanese proposal to include a racial equality clause into the covenant of the League of Nations?"

"Yes," Nigel said.

"That was a blatant attack on our White Australia Policy, and Hughes saw it for what it was and put a stop to it. Hughes said that the League's endorsement of our White Australia Policy was perhaps his greatest achievement at the peace conference, and I agree."

Sensing Samuel's irritation, Peter stepped in. "Nigel, many people think the Japanese have designs on our underpopulated country. Evidently, they introduced the racial equality clause just to embarrass us. I doubt that they are concerned with our exclusionary immigration policy because few Japanese immigrate here, unlike the Chinese."

"They are both being kept out now by our White Australia Policy," Nigel said. "But that wasn't the issue."

"However, that's the purpose of the policy," Samuel said. "I agree with Hughes that we have a right to let in those we want—whites, who speak our language and share our values. Asians can't assimilate. It just makes good sense to keep them out."

Once again, it was his uncle's cocksure manner that aggravated Nigel into a full response.

"Look, I agree with the need for our White Australia Policy, living so near Asia. That really wasn't the issue. Hughes went *overboard* on the Japanese's mild racial equality proposal. I was in London and Paris when this was being debated and heard firsthand how Hughes was ridiculed by the Europeans. His vitriolic anti-Japanese language in Paris offended our allies, imperiled the Anglo-Japanese alliance, and made Australia an adversary of Japan. He wouldn't accept even the mildest proposed language. A mild equality clause wouldn't have prevented us from restricting immigration. I just hope we will not rue the day we insulted the Japanese."

Chapter 3

The Great Depression

At ten in the morning, Nigel walked out of the ocean at Bondi Beach carrying his surfboard under his arm, crossed the wide sand beach, and headed for the new bathing pavilion. As he walked across the tile floor, the custom-made rubber sock over his prosthetic left foot made a sound—*squish, squish, squish*—that announced he was in the gentlemen's change room. Heads turned.

"Nigo, hi, mate!" several fellow surfers greeted the Bondi surfing personality.

"Did ya have a good session, mate?" one surfer asked.

"Bonzer, mate." Nigel lowered the rubber band around the top of the sock and worked the sock off his prosthetic foot. After showering, he dressed with a white shirt, tie, and business suit and jauntily bid the others a "G'day."

He headed for work at a block of flats under construction by Armstrong Development Company, where he was the project manager. Walking along Campbell Parade, the main street running parallel to the beach, Nigel noticed a new For Sale sign on a large commercial building. He stepped back to examine the tawdry but well-located building, two buildings from the corner. Contemplating the possibility of buying all the buildings encompassing the corner, he examined the facades of the next two buildings and walked around the corner. Engrossed, he failed to notice his wife Wilhelmina walking toward him pushing a pram.

"I declare, Nigel," Wilhelmina said when almost beside him. "We could have walked right past you, and you wouldn't have noticed." She added teasingly, "I'm happy though that you missed those three beauties just ahead of us."

Playing along, Nigel swiveled his head to look at the three teenage girls crossing the street on their way to the beach. Turning back to her, he mischievously grinned and said, "Too young for me, I prefer my pretty wife." He kissed Wilhelmina on her cheek and then reached into the pram.

"I thought you'd be at work by now," Wilhelmina said.

"I am at work, love. The building around the corner has gone up for sale." He lifted the red-cheeked baby out of the pram and cooed, "Looook at you. How's daddy's little Archie?"

"What would you do with it?" Wilhelmina asked.

"The company has been thinking for years that Bondi needs a new first-class hotel, even better than our Corso hotel in Manly. They put it off during the war. What better location than the corner of Campbell Parade and Curlewis Street? We could buy this property to start our assemblage of the corner. I'm going to talk to Dad about it."

"There are already a couple good hotels. Would another one be successful?"

"I'm thinking of a large, luxury hotel with around 40 rooms, Willa. Sydneysiders don't realize what we have here. I've seen the beaches in Europe, England, and Egypt—Bondi's got them all beat. We have one of the best beaches in the whole world and no really first-class hotel. With a great hotel, I think Bondi Beach can grow into an international beach community, especially with the new electrified tram line. He gave Archibald a kiss on the cheek and placed him back into the pram.

"I have to go, love. Be careful at the beach . . . the waves are treacherous today. If you go in, be sure to swim between the flags. I'll be home around five-thirty." He kissed her. "Bye."

Peter agreed that Nigel could work with an agent to buy the

building as the first property toward assembling the corner for a future hotel. By the end of the week, Nigel had negotiated a purchase price and a month later the property was purchased. Within a year and a half, working through several real estate agents, the Armstrong Development Company was able to purchase or obtain options to purchase the four properties comprising a developable corner lot.

The preparation and approval of plans, arranging financing, and clearing the site took three years. In September 1927, the Armstrong Development Company finally began construction of a first-class hotel, The Hotel Bondi. Over the four and a half-year development process, Peter and Nigel watched with satisfaction the growth of a beach culture that was transforming Bondi Beach into a tourist mecca.

At the end of the second year of construction in September 1929, Peter and Nigel held a progress meeting with John Winton, chief banker with Sydney Fidelity Bank, who was financing the construction, and the hotel architect E. Lindsay Thompson. The meeting was uneventful and near its end digressed into a discussion of the Sydney Harbour Bridge, which had been under construction for six years. Public interest in the bridge had increased greatly since the construction of the bridge arches began in April 1929. In September the partially constructed southern arch extended much further out over the harbor than the northern arch.

The banker Winton asked, "The southern arched arm looks precarious. Is it supposed to look like that, Lindsay?"

"It does look rather precarious, doesn't it, but it's not in danger of falling into the harbor. You see, the top two chords of the arched arm are secured to a huge continuous steel cable that is looped through a horseshoe-shaped tunnel dug through solid rock behind each arched arm. The southern arched arm is actually five structurally framed steel boxes connected together. Each box has two chords at the top and two at the bottom and a diagonal steel member across each side. If you think these five boxes extending out over the harbor look precarious, just wait until there are fourteen boxes from either side of the harbor before they are joined."

"The big question is..." Nigel said with a dramatic pause, "will the two half arches meet perfectly, so they can be permanently attached?"

"That's certainly a concern," the architect agreed. "Yet before then, I'm worried about the extended arms resisting lateral pressure. A freak cyclonic storm from the ocean could exert enough side wind load to make the extended arms start swaying and twisting until they fall apart or sideways into the harbor."

Peter asked, "What's the construction method, Lindsay? I see a crane at the end of each arm."

"They're called *creeping* cranes, Peter, because each crane sits across the top two chords of the arch and creeps along, building each of the fourteen boxes in turn."

"How is that possible?" asked banker Winton.

"Well, the crane picks up steel off a barge in the harbor, builds a structural box, completes tracks for itself on the two top chords of the new box, and then creeps out onto it to build the next box. The bridge will be the longest steel arch bridge in the world at 1,650 feet when it's completed."

"Tell me if I'm right, Lindsay," Peter said. "The passageway for cars and trains will be hung from the completed steel arches above: a six-lane roadway in the center, a railway along either side of the roadway, and a pedestrian walk on either edge."

"I believe you're right, Peter," Lindsay said. "At its highest point, the bridge will be 440 feet above the harbor."

"I happen to know that's about the height of the Great Pyramid of Egypt ... because I climbed every foot of it," Nigel said.

"Well, I must say, the engineering of the bridge is a wonder to me," the banker said. "Before we adjourn, I'd like to cover one more business point. I'm sure you've all read that Australia's commodity prices, especially wool and wheat, have fallen steadily since 1926, especially so in the past year. This decline in export revenue, if it continues, portends a number of future financial problems, such as higher interest rates for bank and federal government borrowing, difficulty in securing loans, trade irregularities, and higher unemployment. No one knows the future, and I'm certainly not overly concerned right now; nevertheless, one needs to think about the cost of things not getting out of hand. With the cost of the hotel a bit over budget, I'd advise that it be brought back to budget soon and some thought given to cost savings—just to be on the safe side. You wouldn't want to have to ask the bank for additional funds to complete the hotel."

* * *

Lum-gum, Min-chin's wife for forty-eight years, died in 1931. Two months after her death, Min-chin finally agreed to leave his small house in Surry Hills and move in with Wing-yuen's family in Botany, which now included Sam Kee, eleven, and his five-year-old-sister, Lin Yee. Most of Min-chin's friends had passed away, and with his wife gone, he had turned cantankerous and eccentric. The only times he seemed his old self was when Wing-yuen discussed business with him.

On Saturday, March 12, 1932, Min-chin had arisen at ten rather than his usual eleven o'clock, and went for a walk to clear his head before his lunch meeting with Wing-yuen. The Great Depression was in one of its worst years. Nationwide unemployment was close to thirty percent. Bankruptcies, unemployment, evictions, and inadequate public relief had created a large homeless population seeking refuge and food. The unemployed homeless, living in a slum of tents in The Domain, had been evicted. The police moved them to government land along the north side of Botany Bay near La Perouse Aborigines Mission. Their shantytowns became known as Frog Hollow, Hill 60 after a hill in Gallipoli, and Happy Valley.

"The thievery has gotten even worse in the past month, Father," Wing-yuen said. "Before our crops have even ripened, the thieves from the shantytowns and Aboriginal mission steal most of it at night. Last week, one of our guards was knocked unconscious and badly injured by them. They unashamedly come even during the day sometimes. I've added barbed wire to the fence, as you suggested, but it makes no difference. I don't know what more I can do."

"You must get the police to arrest them, Wing-yuen. We pay taxes. The police must be forced to patrol our fields."

"I have been to the police station many times, Father, and have talked to our councilman. The police have chased them out of our fields several times, but won't agree to stay, and won't patrol at night when the thieves come in large groups to rob us. The police have told me that if our guards injure any of them, I will be held responsible."

"Will you have anything to take to Paddy's Market this month?"

"Almost nothing, Father. We are working for the homeless and black thieves now. I am paying our workers from our savings."

"Times have never been this bad," Min-chin said. "We should stop planting and sack workers that we do not need. . . . It cannot last much longer."

"I don't know. I think it may get worse. We may be forced to sell some of our land to live."

"No, do not think of such foolishness. You won't get a good price during the depression. The land has always sustained us. You must think of another way, Wing-yuen."

Sek-leih knocked on the door of the sitting parlor and brought them in their tea. Sam Kee followed his mother through the door and rushed to his father's side.

"Do not bother your father with that now, Sam Kee," Sek-leih said.

"But I haveta," Sam Kee said anxiously. "Can we go to the opening of the Sydney Harbour Bridge next Saturday, Father, please, please. Everyone in my school is going."

"I'm sorry, Son, I have to work," Wing-yuen said.

"I *have* to go! You take me, Grandfather. You can show me where you lived in The Rocks when you came from the goldfields."

"Don't bother your granddaddy," Wing-yuen said.

"But I *have to go!* All my friends are going and will be talking about it on Monday, and I will be left out again. There's going to be a parade, floats, and people in all kinds of costumes. The bridge is high, and I want to look down at the ferries. *Please, please*, Father, please Grandfather, please, *I have to go!*

"All right, Sam Kee," Wing-yuen said with a fatherly smile, "if it's *that* important to you, we will go."

Sam Kee threw his arms around his father and hugged him. "*Thank you, thank you*, Father. Will you go too, Granddaddy? You promised to show me where you and your brothers lived in The Rocks."

"Your Granddaddy is too old to walk across the bridge, Son."

Min-chin angrily looked at Wing-yuen. "I take long walks *everyday*. I am not too old to show my grandson where I and my brothers lived when we first came to this city. You say people will be dressed in all kinds of costumes, Sam Kee?"

"Our teacher said there would be Scottish men wearing skirts, black people in white paint, soldiers in uniforms . . . rugby teams, marching bands—and all kinds of floats and—"

"I will wear my gift from Kwong Tang, given to me the year he died," Min-chin said with finality, pointing at a multicolor embroidered silk robe hanging on a stand, displayed as a work of art.

"No, Father, you don't want to do that," Wing-yuen said. "You would be laughed at. We do not want to draw attention to ourselves."

"It is a *lung-pou*, dragon robe. I want to wear it before I die. It would honor Kwong Tang and my homeland. It is suitable for such a gay occasion where people are dressed in their national clothing."

Wing-yuen tried to reason with his father. "We honor Kwong Tang enough by displaying it honorably. A commoner should not wear such a fine robe in public."

"*Bai!* You are ashamed of your heritage! The *kwai-lo* know nothing of our culture. They should see the beauty of this robe. It is very expensive for someone of high birth to wear to the imperial court. I am not concerned if they laugh. It will show their ignorance. I will not go if I cannot honor Kwong Tang and our people!"

Wing-yuen saw the determination on his father's face. He took a fresh look at the robe.

It really is a beautiful Manchu robe, he thought, with delicate detailing. Gold thread embroidery, proclaiming heavenly glory. Made of the finest silk. A background color of blue with highlights of emperor's yellow, red for happiness and good luck, and green for harmony. Marvelous dragons, animals, waves, mountains, clouds, lucky signs, and Buddhist and Taoist motifs sewn in harmonious patterns. It wraps across the chest and closes on the right side beneath the underarm. Long tubular sleeves ending in horsehoof cuffs. A skirt with slits to facilitate horse riding and terminating above the ground for easy walking. Its straight, vertical cut with a fitted neck-band will look good on Father, who has lost weight recently. Sek-leih can make any necessary adjustments and help him dress.

Thinking that his father was right and the dragon robe de-served to be worn, Wing-yuen threw care to the wind.

"Very well, Father, I hope you will not be disappointed."

* * *

Nigel sat in his office thinking he had made a terrible mistake in pushing his father to build The Hotel Bondi. Construction had been rushed in 1931 to open the hotel before Christmas, the start of the swimming season. Initially, the occupancy rate for the hotel's thirty-nine rooms was good but then dropped below sixty percent. They had opened a world-class tourist hotel at the worst possible time, during the world-wide Great Depression.

He had not been able to reduce the escalating construction cost of the hotel. After the bank refused to advance additional funds, Armstrong Development Company was forced to use its own mon-ey to complete the opulent interior finishes. Debt service and hotel expenses were consuming all of the company's monthly revenue. The bank threatened to foreclose if so much as one interest payment was missed. At this point, Armstrong Development Company was trying to find a financial partner who would help weather the storm. Regrettably, no person or institution was willing to take the risk.

The tea lady stood at Nigel's door trying to get his attention without speaking out.

"Oh, good afternoon, Betty, the regular please, white and a lit-tle sugar," Nigel said.

His father Peter walked in with his tea as Betty pushed her cart on to the next office. "The blooming English cricket team is ruining the game with this bodyline assault, don't you think?"

"I think it's unsportsmanlike, but there's no rule against it, Dad. The batsman has always defended the wicket, as well as him-self, with his bat. This has all come about because of Don Bradman's sensational scoring."

"Yes, that's exactly why the Brits have come up with this ploy. They can't bowl fairly to a man who scored 452 not out in 415 minutes. You know I saw Bradman set that record at the Sydney Cricket Ground. Bloody good show it was too."

"The English are achieving their objective. Bradman's scoring average is way down."

"Well, this bowling at the batsman has got to stop. Why, their fast bowlers are putting our players into the hospital! My word, if one of our players is hit in the heart or head and is killed, this will seriously upset our friendly relations with England. I reckon we should try to have England thrown out of the Imperial Cricket Conference."

"Not very likely, Dad, but I agree that bodyline bowling should be disallowed. By the way, do you and Mum want to go with us to the opening of the Sydney Harbour Bridge this Saturday?"

"Yes, if it's a beaut day, although not if it looks like rain."

"I'm going to take Archie, regardless. He wants to use his new box camera that we gave him for his birthday. I'm kind of looking forward to the pageantry of the whole thing myself. Remember how we celebrated when the two arches of the bridge were joined?"

"I was getting ready to go to bed when horns and bells throughout the city started making a terrible clatter," Peter said. "Everyone knew what it meant immediately and came out of their houses banging on pots and pans and blowing all manner of noisemakers."

"Archie wanted to go down to the bridge right then and there. He couldn't fall asleep for hours," Nigel said.

Three days later, Nigel and Archibald walked on the closed roadway leading to the Sydney Harbour Bridge. Over 750,000 people gathered in Sydney's streets at the southern entrance to the bridge awaiting its official opening by the New South Wales Premier Jack Lang. Lang, a Labor party leader, had defaulted on loan payments to the state's creditors, including British banks. By opening the bridge himself, he was ignoring protocol and snubbing the British-appointed governor.

Before the premier could cut the ribbon stretched across the bridge opening, Captain Francis de Groot, on horseback and dressed in his military uniform, unexpectedly rode forward and slashed the ribbon with his sword shouting: "On behalf of the decent and loyal citizens of New South Wales, I declare this bridge open."

De Groot, a member of the ultra-conservative, paramilitary New Guard organization, thought Premier Lang was a treasonous radical socialist. He was arrested and taken away in a paddy wagon to a psychiatric hospital.

The ceremonial ribbon was tied together again and, without further delay, cut by Premier Lang. With horns blaring from the land and from boats in the harbor, a group of officials led the surge of people onto the bridge.

A long line of floats, military units, community groups, public service organizations, and musical bands began a parade across the bridge. Nine-year-old Archibald was overwhelmed by the sheer number of photo opportunities. He took several photographs of a float of Captain Cook's ship *Endeavour*. Nigel pointed out a navy destroyer in the harbor, which Archibald photographed.

A musical group from La Perouse Aborigines Mission calling themselves the Gum Leaf Band provided lively entertainment as they led a group of Aborigines across the bridge.

Archibald looked around to see what to photograph next. "I'm going to take a picture of those blackies," he said, pointing at the Gum Leaf Band.

"Call them Aborigines, Archie," Nigel said. "Take as many pictures as you like, I have plenty of film. Take a few photos of the Bondi Lifesavers' float that's behind them."

Heads turned skyward toward the roar of Royal Australian Air Force planes, which flew close to the top of the arch, thrilling the crowd.

Archibald took pictures of the harbor full of colorful boats and ships and then snapped a photo of his father in the crowd with the city behind. At about the same time, they both saw a curious sight. A large group of people had formed around a very old, foreign-looking man in a spectacular robe. Bent over with a pronounced humped back, he leaned on a gnarled wood walking stick with a polished brass handle. His bright eyes were set off by a brilliant white, long mustache that combined with a long, thin beard. He had a proud, stately countenance and looked pleased with the attention. Women were closely examining his fine silk robe. People were taking pictures, including a photographer with professional equipment who demanded that people stand aside for a clear, uncluttered photograph.

"Can I take a picture of him too, Dad?" Archibald asked.

"Ask him if you may, Archie."

"I don't want to. Will you ask him?"

Nigel noticed another Chinese man, dressed in western clothes, holding the hand of a young Chinese boy. Taking hold of Archibald's hand, Nigel approached the man.

"Pardon me, sir, might that be your father?"

"Yes he is," Wing-yuen said.

"Would you mind if my son took a few picture of him? His robe is simply stunning."

"Why thank you. I'll tell Dad you said that, thank you. Yes, of course, your son can take as many pictures as he likes; my father would be very pleased."

"I presume this exquisite robe is worn for special occasions in China?" Nigel asked.

"Yes. My father told me that men of high birth would wear such a robe to the imperial court."

Wing-yuen thought how wrong he had been to tell his father that he would be laughed at. Perhaps his father was right, he should be more proud of his heritage. Once again, he had underestimated his father.

As Nigel and Wing-yuen talked, Archibald and Sam Kee were discussing Archibald's camera. Archibald, a bit younger than Sam Kee, was explaining the workings of his camera with great authority. He permitted Sam Kee to look through the viewfinder at his grandfather and snap the shutter to take a picture. Their fathers smiled at each other and their sons.

Archibald took two more pictures of Min-chin. Then Nigel took a picture of Archibald and Sam Kee standing next to Min-chin.

Nigel made a slight bow to Min-chin. "Thank you, sir."

Min-chin smiled a wide grin and nodded with a delighted look on his face. Nigel and Wing-yuen bid each other goodbye, and Nigel and Archibald continued their walk across the bridge.

"What kind of person was that old man, Dad?" Archibald asked. "He looked kinda funny."

"Different . . . not funny, Archie. He's a Chinaman, from the country of China."

*   *   *

Following his Sunday morning service, young Reverend Bonner stood on the porch of his Methodist church located next to the Murraroo Aborigines Mission and two miles from the town of Gura in New South Wales. The reverend was shaking the hand of each member of his mostly Aboriginal congregation while he bid them goodbye. Looking down the line of parishioners to the end, he was pleased that Harvey Hudson was not yet in line. Good, he thought, he's probably going to be one of the last to leave again.

Harvey sat in a pew enjoying the sublime vision of bright morning sunlight streaming through the single, small, stained-glass window behind the pulpit. It showed the Sermon on the Mount with Jesus preaching to the multitude as angels looked down from white clouds above. He believed in Jesus's message of salvation and felt a sense of fellowship in church. It was a good church with hymn books, piano, and an enthusiastic preacher who gave stirring sermons. Reluctantly, Harvey rose to join the dwindling line of parishioners waiting to leave.

"Thank you for attending, Mr. Hudson," the reverend said as he shook his hand. "May I have a word with you?" Pointing toward the last pew, he asked, "Would you mind sitting down over there for a moment, Harvey, while I say goodbye to the last few?"

Harvey stood dumbfounded: what could the preacher want, and how did he know his full name?

"It will only take a minute, if you wouldn't mind terribly."

Harvey nodded and said, "Uh-huh." He stepped back into the church and sat down in the last pew next to the center aisle. Several minutes later, Reverend Bonner walked into the church, and Harvey jumped to his feet.

"I enjoyed your deep baritone singing again this morning, Harvey. Where did you learn to sing so beautifully?"

Too ill at ease to meet the pastor's eyes, he looked at his chest. "Sunday school . . . an' church," he said in a low, soft voice the pastor could not hear well.

"Did you say choir?"

"Didn't have no choir," Harvey said in a barely audible whisper while moving back a half-step.

Harvey's shy, defensive demeanor told the minister to go slowly, if he hoped to receive the answer he wanted.

"I understand you live in the fringe camp outside the mission."

Harvey wondered what this was all about, then thought he was about to be told not to return. "Yes, Reveren'."

"As you know, I'm the new pastor here. You've attended every one of my Sunday services, I believe, over the past six weeks."

He continued to look at the preacher's chest as if was being reprimanded.

Not getting an answer, the reverend asked, "Haven't you?"

"Yes, Reveren'."

"Please, Harvey, let's sit down for a minute. We haven't had a chance to talk, and I like to know something about every one of my parishioners. This is my first parish. I'm from Melbourne, and I must admit I didn't know any Aborigines there; so I want to learn more about my congregation. Do you mind if we talk for a few minutes? It would really help my ministry."

"Orright."

"How old are you?"

"Twenty-one."

"Twenty-one! I'm only five years older than you, twenty-six. Are you married?"

"*Ha*, no sir," Harvey said, smiling for the first time.

"You know my wife plays the piano for our hymns?"

"Yes, Reveren'."

"She's pregnant with our first . . . . Where's your family?"

"Don't have none. I'm a orphan."

"Oh . . . You grew up in an orphanage then?"

"Yes sir."

"Where?"

"Bomamulla Children's Home an' later in Methodist mission in Danedine."

"Do you know why you were orphaned?"

"No. Bomamulla matron told me they gimme up 'cause I was a little halfie—they didn't want me. She mussa been right 'cause they never come ta visit me or anythin'. Ma'be they was killed . . . don't know. But no worries, 'cause I like the orphanage."

"What did you like about it?"

"Sports . . . swimmin' in the bay, cookouts, playin an' such. Goin' ta church an' singin' too."

Bonner's wife entered the church carrying two glasses of lemonade. Harvey stood, and the pastor did too.

"I thought you might like some refreshments," she said, handing each a glass.

"Oh how nice, thank you, dearest. You know Mr. Hudson, Patricia."

Patricia was drying her wet hands in her apron and smiled at Harvey. "I certainly hear your divine voice, Mr. Hudson, when we sing the hymns. Very inspiring."

"Thank ya, missus." Harvey's stood transfixed with his head down looking at the glass of lemonade, which he held with both hands. He had not taken a drink yet.

"Well, I have cooking to attend to," Patricia said. "So nice to have met you, Mr. Hudson."

Harvey nodded his head, his eyes still on his glass of lemonade.

"It's a beautiful morning, Harvey, let's go outside and sit on the steps, shall we?"

Embarrassed and overwhelmed, he wanted to find some way to excuse himself. They sat on the top step and enjoyed their drinks without speaking. Bonner decided that the time was ripe to get to the point.

"Patricia enjoys playing the piano for our hymns and has noticed that your voice leads the congregation. She is forming a choir and would like you to join."

Harvey wanted to run; however, he had a half-full glass of lemonade in his hand. He didn't know what to say to the reverend.

"Would you like that, Harvey?"

He shook his head no, too self-conscious to make eye contact with the pastor.

"Well, will you think about it?"

Harvey felt relieved he didn't have to say anything. He nodded that he would.

"Do you think you'll stay around here?"

"Don't know."

"When did you leave the Danedine Mission?"

"After fifth grade. They sent me ta Young as apprentice ta do orchard work."

"What did that involve?"

"Prunin' trees, sucker cuttin', weedin', pickin' fruit. Left there when I got out of orphanage system . . . been takin' care of meself since."

"With this economic depression and your living in the fringe camp, do you mind if I ask how you take care of yourself?"

Harvey took a quick look at the face of the pastor. He could see he was sincerely interested. Being proud of how he had learned to live independent of the government's Aboriginal system, he didn't mind answering the questions of this likeable young preacher.

"I didn't know where I was goin' when I left Young, didn't know me way aroun'. I jus' went out on the road carryin' me swag. I was lost for a while. I ate fruits an' veg'ables from the fields and found good tucker in the council tips."

The reverend could not hide a look of disgust at the image of eating from a pile of garbage and rubbish. Seeing the look of horror on his face, Harvey felt compelled to explain.

"There's plenty of good grub in council tips before it turns crook. Even poor whites eat off tips now, 'cause of the depression. The co-ops dump oranges jus' 'cause of bruises, bakers throw away good bread an' pies, an' schools toss packed sandwiches that ain't ate. Later, I learn from the old natives 'bout bush tucker and how ta hunt."

"What kind of bush tucker is there?" Bonner asked.

"There's plenty, once ya git ta know where ta look an' how ta git it. I learn animal signs and how ta track and throw a *boondy*, a throwing stick, ta kill wallabies, rabbits, goannas, parrots, an' cockatoos. A big rock will work jus' as good. Possums are a good feed an' so are witchetty grubs. In the streams there's yabbies, mussels, an' turtle eggs. For sweets, there's wild bee honey, yams, lillypilly berries, an' quandong fruit. I learn all this from old blackfellas. Plenty of wild tucker, no worries. They show me how ta make a humpy from things in the tip."

"If you don't work and you're not on the dole, how do you buy clothes and other necessities without money?"

"Ya have ta do seasonal work fer cash in yer hand. All I need is tea, sugar, jam, lollies, an' flour ta make Johnny-cakes damper. I git old clothes from the missions. I earn money cleanin' up in the shearing sheds when it's sheep-shearin' time. I go ta Griffith durin' grape-pickin' season an' back ta Young ta pick cherries, tomatoes, peas, an' beans. From early December right through May ya got plenty of fruit. Nearly all year round ya got oranges, an' in winter there's carrots an' beetroot."

Having finished their lemonade, Reverend Bonner said, "Thank you for this little talk, Harvey. It was very helpful, and I appreciate getting to know you better. Please think about joining the choir. Mrs. Sweeney and Miss Beverly have already accepted, but we need a baritone voice like yours. You will think about it, won't you?"

"Yes, Reveren'."

As they shook hands goodbye, Reverend Bonner said, "Well, have a nice day, Harvey, and may the Lord be with you."

Harvey walked down the steps and then had a worrying thought.

"Reverend...?"

Bonner was at the church entrance and turned when he heard Harvey's questioning voice. "Yes, Harvey?"

"If I don't join the choir... can I still go ta church?"

"Oh my word, of course you may, Harvey, please don't be concerned. We want your wonderful voice in the congregation even if you don't join the choir. See you next Sunday, Harvey."

At twenty-one, Harvey Hudson had grown into a strapping man: five feet eleven inches tall, straight-backed, square-shouldered, narrow-waisted, muscular arms and legs, and with the easy walk of a natural athlete. Although quiet and shy, he nevertheless carried himself in a way that said he could take care of himself if threatened.

On Saturday morning, before the heat of the day, Harvey joined other Aboriginal men for rugby league practice. The coach was a large, burly white man who they called Coach Foster when he was on the playing field, but Superintendent or Boss Foster everywhere else on Murraroo Aborigines Mission, which he managed.

Coach Foster called his players together. "Good news. The Aborigines Protection Board has approved our playing other mission and station teams." The team members whooped and clapped in celebration. "Our first contest is against Brangel on Saturday the eleventh. I've decided that I like Peterson's name for the team: the Murraroo All Blacks. What do ya think of that?" Nodding heads and numerous "Yeahs" meant the name was accepted.

"Before we practice . . . some things. You lot need to improve yer tackling. Not you heavy forwards who naturally use yer weight when you tackle, but you smaller backs who are still grabbing with yer hands, like girls. You won't bring a big man down with yer hands; ya have to use yer body weight. The only heavy hitter in the back pack is Heavy, that's why I'm switchin' him from wing to fullback."

There were a few snickers that Coach Foster decided to ignore.

"He uses his whole weight by hitting with his shoulder and driving with his legs. He hits like a larger man. I want ya ta watch Heavy now." There were a few more snickers. "Willie, take this ball up the field and try ta run pass Heavy."

Taking the ball, Willie ran up the field a ways and turned to face Harvey.

"Stop that bloody snickering. Now get serious you lot and watch how Heavy does it."

Using a stiff arm defense, Willie tried to run by Harvey, but he hit him hard and took him down.

"See how Heavy—I mean *Harvey*," Foster said, realizing his mistake. "Have I been callin' ya Heavy right along, Harvey?"

The players burst out laughing, some falling onto their sides laughing.

"Yeah, Coach," Harvey said, smiling.

From that day on, Harvey had the nickname "Heavy" among his mates.

Following practice, Foster took Harvey aside. "The rules are ya have ta live on the mission to play on the team. I want you to move into the single men's dormitory."

"I'd like ta play fer the team, Coach Foster," Harvey said in a low voice while looking at the ground, "but I don't want ta live on the mission."

"Why not?"

"Like ta live on me own. Don't want ta live under no rules. I have me own humpy in the fringe camp. Can ya tell 'em I live on the mission?"

"You mean lie and break the rules—no! Look, you don't want to live in the fringe camp, Harvey, constantly being harassed by the police and told to move on. I can get you rugby shoes, so you won't have to play in yer bare feet."

"I'll think about it, Mr. Foster," Harvey said and turned to walk away.

Foster touched him lightly on the shoulder. "Wait, Harvey . . . the team needs ya. We want to do well, see. You have the ability to be our top scorer. Whatever problems you have with living on the mission, I can solve them for ya."

"Ma'be I can sleep in the dorm an' spend me days on me own?"

"No, I can't allow that. Everyone has ta do their work assignments for their rations, except the old and the sick."

Harvey grimaced. "I'll think 'bout it, boss."

"Look here, Harvey, I like you—ya don't want to go against the system." Frustrated, Boss Foster decided to lean on him a bit. "Ya know the police can arrest ya for vagrancy outside the mission?"

Disgusted, Harvey looked at Boss Foster.

"I always carry money in me pocket, so I can't be vagged, boss." Harvey turned and started to walk quickly away.

"Well, you think about my offer, Harvey!"

Without looking back, Harvey murmured, "Orright."

"I want yer answer by next Saturday's practice!"

Harvey walked away conflicted. He wanted to play for the team but didn't want to live in a white man's institution again. He decided to avoid the issue by staying away from Boss Foster and the mission for a while, to let things cool off.

A month later, after the Murraroo All Blacks had lost badly to the Brangel Brumbies, the fringe camp was raided by the police, and Harvey was arrested.

Superintendent Foster visited Reverend Bonner and told him that Harvey Hudson was in Gura's jail and had a hearing coming up. He asked if Bonner would be willing to vouch for his good character and regular church attendance. Foster said that he intended to speak in support of Harvey as well. Reverend Bonner agreed.

On the morning of the day of the hearing, Foster and Bonner met with Harvey's court-appointed defense solicitor, who said:

"The stolen items were found in the humpy next to his. Unfortunately, when the police questioned Hudson, he admitted to knowing his neighbor and that the items had been stolen. This makes him an accessory for not reporting it to the police. He's giving me the silent treatment, so I haven't been able to prepare much of a defense for him. It doesn't look good for him, Reverend."

"I'd like to talk to him, would that be possible?" Reverend Bonner asked.

The solicitor led the reverend to the jail. Bonner was taken to Harvey's cell.

"Harvey, how have they been treating you?" Bonner asked as they shook hands.

Harvey smiled wanly. "Orright, Reveren' Bonner."

"I want to help you, Harvey. But I need to know, before God, did you have anything to do with stealing those items from the dry goods store?—the truth now."

"I didn't steal nothin'. I seen those things, but it wasn't none of me business. I think Boss Foster had me arrested, 'cause we had a blue over me playin' fer the All Blacks."

"That's not fair, Harvey. Superintendent Foster was the one who told me you had been arrested and asked for my help, my word he did. He's going to vouch for you, as I will also.

"Your solicitor said you wouldn't tell him anything about your past. How can he defend you if you won't talk to him? If the court brings up any past arrests or other negative information, he'll have no defense for you, and I'll look stupid. If there are bad things in your past that are brought out, I can speak to such matters as your pastor. You have to tell me if there were any prior arrests that I need to know about."

"Nothin' serious, just stuff all us blacks git taken in fer."

"Like what?"

"Drinkin', eatin' fruit from farms where it grow natural like, vaggin', an' disturbin' the peace. They don't keep records of that stuff."

"They keep drinking and stealing violations, Harvey. Aborigines shouldn't drink, and they certainly shouldn't steal. How many times have you been arrested?"

"Only once before in Griffith. Nothin' wrong with blackfellas drinkin', Reveren'. Whitefellas git drunk too."

Frowning, Bonner said, "I don't drink—it adds nothing to the goodness of our society."

"Yer a pastor, Reveren', no one 'spects you ta drink. But when yer all alone like me, an' ya want ta be mates, drinkin' starts. I don't drink as much as others, 'cause I have ta take care of meself."

"Is that all, Harvey, nothing else I should know about, nothing else that might be recorded or come up? I don't want to be embarrassed by standing up for you."

"Well . . . when I was fifteen, they put me in Reeundah juvenile correction center."

"What was that for and for how long?"

"That family I told ya 'bout in Young that run a orchard? I didn't like no one there an' always felt kind of down. When I wasn't workin', all I did was sit in me room. I ate by meself. They always pushin' me, an' boss beatin' me with his belt. Got tired of it. They didn't pay me no money. I reckon, I can take care of meself. One night I go out on me ownsome.

"I had ta keep away from whitefellas, 'cause blackfellas in the fringe camps said p'lice was askin' 'bout me. They caught me pinchin' fruit. When I told them I wouldn't go back ta Young, they sent me to Reeundah juvenile correction center fer six months."

"What happened when you came out?" Bonner asked. "Where did they send you?"

"I was placed in another apprenticeship. But didn't like it no better than the first one. I left at sixteen. Since then, no problems, 'cept what I told ya about, Reveren'."

"Your hearing is in two hours, Harvey, I need to talk to your solicitor and Superintendent Foster." He excused himself. "I'll see you in a little while."

Reverend Bonner met Foster and Harvey's solicitor coming toward him in the hallway.

"Oh, Reverend," Foster said. "We've just had a conference with the magistrate. If you will vouch for Harvey's good character as a regular churchgoer, and if he will agree to live on the mission under my personal recognizance, the judge will let him go."

"I thought this was more a matter of his guilt or innocence?"

The solicitor spoke up. "Of course, Reverend. I'm pleading not guilty for Harvey. What we're talking about is what the magistrate can do if he's found to be an accessory or not. If he is found to be an accessory, which he has already admitted to, you can be sure he will be found guilty in the dock."

The hearing was just a formality. The magistrate listened to the arresting constable and ruled that Harvey was an accessory to grand larceny as charged. Then he said:

"Defense solicitor, before I set the trial date, I understand you have persons wishing to speak on behalf of Mr. Hudson."

Reverend Bonner spoke glowingly of Harvey's good character, hard upbringing as an orphan, and religious fervor. "I believe that he was not in any way involved in this robbery. I ask that he be released on the personal recognizance of Superintendent Foster and my care. Thank you, Your Honor."

"Superintendent Foster, please stand," the magistrate said. "Under the Aborigines Protection Act, Aborigines with fair complexions are supposed to join the white society to find work, not live on a mission at government expense. Can you tell me why I should remand Mr. Hudson to you?"

"Well, Your Honor, we're in a depression right now and it's a matter of circumstances and judgment, I reckon. First off, Your Honor, Mr. Hudson is only a half-caste, and as ya can see he's pretty dark. With over thirty percent of whites unemployed, it'd be right hard for him ta find work. Since he hasn't been sacked from a job, he can't qualify for susso, I mean, sustenance relief, Your Honor. Under these circumstances, living on the mission and attending church will keep him out of trouble."

The magistrate turned to Harvey. "Is this what you want, Mr. Hudson? If not, you're very likely to be found guilty as an accessory, perhaps even as an accomplice, and sent to jail for a year or longer."

"I go live on the mission, Your Honor, sir," Harvey answered.

"Let the court record show that Harvey Hudson is released on the personal recognizance of Superintendent Foster for a one-year probation period, during which time he is to remain a resident of the Murraroo Aborigines Mission under the supervision of Mr. Foster, who will report to this court if Mr. Hudson causes any further trouble."

*   *   *

With continued pilfering of his crops and little assistance from the police, Wing-yuen discontinued cultivating the outer acres of his property and planted only a few acres along Mill Creek. These few acres were hidden in the valley from the surrounding roads and were the least accessible. When even these crops were stolen before they were ripe, he decided to sack his remaining workers and to let his fields lie fallow.

Seven months later, Yue-kung, Wing-yuen's dependable headman, knocked on his door. After small talk while drinking tea, Yue-kung got around to what was on his mind. "It's been many months since we stopped gardening. I've been denied government sustenance and can't find any steady work. I have no money left, and my family is starving. I am *ashamed* to beg you for a loan."

Wing-yuen gave Yue-kung money and told him that he had been working on an idea for a new business. "Come back tomorrow at two o'clock to meet with my father and me to discuss my idea."

The next day, Sek-leih answered the door and led Yue-kung through the house and out into the garden where Wing-yuen and Min-chin were enjoying a warm, sunny September afternoon. Min-chin had suffered a bout of pneumonia during the winter and had spent three weeks in the hospital. The illness had compromised his health. He was lying on a cot covered by a blanket with a pillow under his head.

Yue-kung paid his respects to Min-chin. Wing-yuen told his father that he had an idea he wanted to discuss with him and Yue-kung.

"This Great Depression seems only to be getting worse," Wing-yuen said. "I think it will go on for many more years. I have given much thought to selling our land or finding some new use for it to provide us a living. I think I have the solution—a chicken hatchery.

"The police told me that a businessman can defend himself and his goods if his business place is broken into. I want to use our savings to build a large building to raise chickens for poultry and eggs. The building will be locked at all times. If robbers break in, then it is legal for the guards inside to fight them off."

Wing-yuen paused to let what he had just said sink in.

Min-chin motioned to Wing-yuen and spoke in a whisper into his ear, due to a persistent sore throat.

"A locked buildings is a good idea, Son. You will find many unemployed, large countrymen willing to fight the thieving *kwai-los* and Abos. But who will you sell to?" Then he started coughing and clearing his throat, which he spat on the ground on the far side of his cot.

While his father was dealing with his coughing fit, Wing-yuen asked, "What do you think, Yue-kung?"

"That's a white man's business," Yue-kung said. "They have many commercial chicken hatcheries and provide all the meat and eggs to Paddy's Market that is needed."

"I don't want to sell at Paddy's Market, and I don't want to compete with the white poultrymen. I have another approach. If I am the only Chinese poultryman, I think that I can capture all of the business of the Chinese restaurants in Chinatown, as well as the business of Chinese who shop in Chinatown."

Again Min-chin motioned Wing-yuen to draw near. "Chinese labor is cheap. You must sell at lower prices than the whites. The Chinese will not buy from you just because you are Chinese."

"I know I must sell at lower prices than the whites, Father," Wing-yuen said. "My plan is to undercut the whites' unionized high prices. First, we will sell door-to-door to the Chinese butchers and restaurants. Later, we can rent a building in Chinatown to process the chickens in the back and sell the meat and eggs in a retail store in the front. As our production increases and the word gets around that our meat and egg prices are less expensive than the whites, we can expand our business to include wholesale."

Yue-kung sat looking down, shaking his head slowly from side to side.

"What's wrong, Yue-kung?" Wing-yuen asked.

"I'm worried. The whites allow us to market garden because they don't want to dirty their hands and are poor farmers. The white poultrymen and their unions will not like us getting into their businesses."

"They won't know, because we will go door-to-door and won't sell at Paddy's. Later, when we are established, they will let us sell to the Chinese because it is only a small loss of business to them."

"It's dangerous."

"What choice do we have, Yue-kung? We must provide for our families. Will you help me?"

"Yes, Wing-yuen."

Min-chin had a wide smile on his face. He put his hands together and shook them toward the sky. Then he went into a severe coughing spasm that lasted several minutes. He drew Wing-yuen near.

"It's a smart business plan, Wing-yuen—cough, *cough!* I praise Kwun Yam, the Goddess of Mercy, Buddha, and all the gods that you've found a solution without selling our land!"

That night, filled with enthusiasm, Wing-yuen explained his plan to Sek-leih. Like Min-chin, she thought it was a good plan, though wondered if they could afford it. While they tried to discuss the particulars, they were interrupted time and again by Min-chin's loud hacking cough. After a while, his annoying cough stopped, and they were able to complete their conversation. In the morning, when Sek-leih entered Min-chin's bedroom with his morning tea, she discovered that he had passed away.

*　*　*

On April 25, 1938, Nigel marched with other war veterans in the Anzac Day parade down George Street. He took pride in walking with his slight limp rather than riding in a car with other men who had lost a leg. The worst of his war memories had receded, and the parade was now a celebration of life and mateship. With the Great Depression waning and the Armstrong Development Company experiencing renewed profitability, Nigel had fewer worries these days.

After the parade, he headed for the Anzac War Memorial in Hyde Park to meet his family. Archibald at age fifteen had expressed an interest in the Great War for the first time and asked to visit the memorial with him.

Walking toward the memorial, Nigel was impressed once again by its stately Art Deco appearance and its reflection in the Pool of Remembrance. Wilhelmina, Archibald, and two-year-old Lydia were picnicking on a blanket set on the lawn. Wilhelmina pointed out Nigel approaching, and Lydia ran toward him on unsure feet with outstretched arms.

"Daddee, Daddee."

Kneeling to embrace her, Nigel said, "Hi, sweetie," and hugged her. He picked her up and walked over to Wilhelmina and Archibald. Tired, he sat down next to Wilhelmina, who gave him a sandwich to eat. Looking around he thought what a verdant and peaceful haven the park was in the middle of the city, like Hyde Park in London, after which it was named. Having walked through London's Hyde Park, he concluded that Sydney's Hyde Park was much smaller.

"Look at the height of those pine trees around the memorial and reflecting pool," Nigel said to Wilhelmina and Archibald. "I planted one of them as a seeding, from the Lone Pine and Pine Ridge battlefields of Gallipoli, to commemorate Christopher's service at Gallipoli."

After lunch, Nigel and Archibald walked through the Anzac War Memorial. Archibald had many questions about the military exhibits. Nigel was struck how Archibald regarded the Great War as "history." Nigel laughed quietly to himself. I must be getting old, it seems like only yesterday to me.

Looking down into the awe-inspiring Tomb of the Unknown Soldier, Archibald asked, "What is the dead soldier lying on, Dad?"

"His shield. And his arms are draped across his sword."

"He kind of looks like Jesus on the cross, except lying down."

"Yes, I see what you mean. Maybe the sculptor meant it to look like that—representing all the dead soldiers who gave their lives for the good of others."

For the first time, Nigel saw his son as a young man who could go off to war . . . and be hurt or even killed. He's grown so handsome . . . a fine profile . . . has his mother's complexion and beauty.

They joined Wilhelmina and Lydia, packed the picnic basket, and walked north through the park. Approaching a large granite and bronze fountain with figures from Greek mythology, Nigel said, "We're coming up on your fountain, Archibald."

"I know . . . at least the same name," Archibald said. He walked up to the plaque and read out loud: "The Archibald Fountain is a gift from J. F. Archibald to his countrymen to commemorate the alliance between Australia and France in the Great War 1914-1918."

A change in the wind direction sent him reeling backward to avoid the fountain's spray. With Wilhelmina and Nigel laughing, a slightly wet Archibald joined them on seats set at the far edge of the wide, circular pavement around the fountain. They relaxed and enjoyed watching people promenade by.

Chapter 4

The Second World War

"What's the prime minister going to talk about, Dad?" Archibald asked. He sat down next to his father who was awaiting Robert Menzies's radio address to the nation scheduled for nine fifteen the evening of September 3, 1939.

"Hitler's invasion of Poland three days ago," Nigel said, massaging his right temple as if he had a headache.

"Turn down the radio a bit, won't you, dear?" Wilhelmina asked as she came into the parlor. "I just put Lydia to bed—you don't expect war, do you?"

"Britain hasn't declared war yet, although I'm afraid they'll have to soon, to honor their mutual defense pact with Poland. European war seems inevitable, but I hope Menzies will have a measured response tonight. Unfortunately, Parliament is united behind Menzies if he wants to join Britain in declaring war against Hitler. Though my immediate concern is Japan, not Germany."

"*Japan?*" Wilhelmina said, surprised. "They're fighting in China . . . why are you concerned about them?"

"After taking Nanking and then Canton, the Japanese have been making threats toward Hong Kong. I'm sure they'd like to get their hands on Australian iron ore, as well, and our other natural resources that we're withholding from them."

"Oh, they wouldn't *dare* attack the British in Hong Kong, would they?"

"Probably not. Their navy is no match for the British navy. But the pact Japan signed last year with Germany and Italy may require Japan to enter the war against Britain. If that were to happen, the Japanese would be an immediate threat to us."

Wilhelmina started to leave the room.

"Don't leave, Willa. Menzies is about to speak. You may want to hear this."

While the Armstrongs were talking, Britain had declared war on Germany promptly at eleven in the morning of September 3. Given that Canberra was ten hours ahead of London, Menzies's speech followed Britain's declaration of war by fifteen minutes. After some preliminaries, Menzies said:

"Fellow Australians, it is my melancholy duty to inform you officially that, in consequence of the persistence of Germany in her invasion of Poland, Great Britain has declared war upon her, and that, as a result, Australia is also at war."

"*Bloody hell!*—that was short and sweet!" Nigel said. "We are at—"

"*Dad!* I can't hear."

". . . there can be no doubt that where Great Britain stands there stand the people of the entire British world. Bitter as we all—"

"This is *terrible!*" Wilhelmina said. "If Japan declares wa—"

"*MUM!*"

". . . war will involve not only soldiers and sailors and airmen, but supplies, foodstuffs, and money. Our staying power, and particularly the staying power of the mother country, will be best assisted by keeping our production going; by continuing our avocations and our busine—"

"I'm going to enlist if they call for soldiers," Archibald announced seriously.

"You'll do no such thing!" Nigel said. "Listen!"

". . . in spite of the emotions we are all feeling, you will show that Australia is ready to see it through. May God in His mercy and compassion grant that the world may soon be delivered from this agony."

They sat looking at one another, astounded. Australia was at war with Germany again, only twenty-one years after the Great War to end all wars.

"Dad, I want to volunteer when they call for soldiers," Archibald said.

"You're too young. You'll have to be eighteen. There's no rus—"

"I'll be eighteen in eight months."

"Archie, we don't want to think about that right now," his mother said.

"Look, Wilhelmina, I'm going to join the citizens' air force—but just as an instructor and to serve on the home front if we're attacked. Archie, that's what I'd like you to do too. Join the Citizens' Military Forces to defend Australia, rather than go overseas. That way, you can serve, get your military training, and attend uni to get an education. That makes sense, doesn't it?"

"Ah . . . the militia's not real soldiers, Dad. The British are going to need all the help they can get. Just like you did in the Great War. It's my responsibility, just like it was yours. I wouldn't feel right if I squibbed it."

"Believe me, Archie, I know exactly how you feel. But, well . . . actually, I expect Japan will be declaring war on us soon—so whether you're in the AIF or CMF, you'll still be serving here to defend Australia."

Nigel was wrong. Japan did not declare war on the Allies before Archibald's eighteenth birthday and his enlistment in the Australian Imperial Force. It chose instead to consolidate its gains in China, while making plans to achieve an Asian colonial empire.

By the end of 1940, the Allies had pushed the Italian forces threatening British bases in Egypt back into Libya. In February 1941, Archibald's Ninth Division relieved the Australian Sixth Division in Libya at the same time that German General Erwin Rommel landed in Tripoli, Libya, with the Afrika Korps to reinforce the Italians. Rommel's surprise offensive threw the Allies back toward Egypt. Churchill and the Allied High Command decided on April 11, to abandon Libya, except for Tobruk, a fortified seaside town and strategic port, that if abandoned, would be used by Germany to resupply Rommel.

* * *

The forty-three men in Archibald's platoon strained to hear their
sergeant, Terence Cook, over the sound of artillery fire.

"General Morshead said we won't be evacuated by ship, so ya
can forget about that. Our job is to hold Tobruk to deny 'em the
port. There's two Australians 'ere fer every Brit, so this battle will be
remembered as an Aussie show. Just remember that, mates, when
the fightin' starts."

"Fighting *starts?*" someone yelled out in his platoon. "What
the bleedin' hell have we been doin' for three days, Sarge?"

"Yeah, righto, but it's goin' ta git a hell of a lot hairier. We've
done well against their probes; however, now Jerry knows where
our posts are and anti-tank ditches and minefields. The captain expects a major pointed assault by their panzer tanks tonight or tomorrow night intent on breakin' through."

"Hell of a way to spend Easter," someone grumbled.

Sergeant Cook acted as if he had not heard the remark.

"They'll come in with their tanks followed by infantry ta
mop us up. But the general has prepared a little surprise for Fritz.
We're goin' to use that inner perimeter we've been diggin' for the
past week.

"Our artillery will knock out as many of their tanks as possible
as they approach. If they come in force and we can't stop 'em, then
the posts at the main point of attack, upon receiving orders, are to
fall back to the inner perimeter. The plan is ta draw the panzers
into point-blank fire from our dug-in cruiser tanks, field artillery,
an' anti-tank units. The rest of us, along the outer perimeter flanks,
are ta keep our heads down until their tanks are engaged inside the
perimeter, then come out an' give their infantry hot hell. This will
be dodgy, so be sure of yer lines of fire."

In the twilight of April 13, Archibald focused his camera on
the slit trench where his sergeant and four mates posed behind
their rifles and a machine gun. "Don't look at me, smiling, look out
there." Archibald pointed into the desert in front of them. "Like
you're mean bastards shootin' Krauts."

"Get yer arse back in here, Armstrong, before ya get it shot off," Sergeant Cook said.

Archibald took two more photographs and jumped back into the twelve-foot-long slit trench. He picked up binoculars and focused them. Looking over the double row of sandbags stacked around the trench, he saw nothing unusual across the flat desert plateau that offered no cover for the Germans. Archibald's slit trench was one of hundreds of posts spaced out irregularly to form the outer defensive perimeter that ran for twenty-five miles in a semicircle around the town and port of Tobruk. Because the El Adem-Tobruk Road was less than two miles away, the posts in the central area of the perimeter were closely spaced, less than a hundred yards apart. Their trench was protected by barbed-wire, mines, and an anti-tank ditch. A Bren machine gun was their main weapon.

Sergeant Cook had chosen Archibald's trench because it was in the center of his platoon's seven trenches. He had replaced their sergeant, who had been killed a week earlier.

"Where are you from, Sarge?" Peters asked.

"Sydney."

"I'm from Sydney too, Sergeant, Bellevue Hill," Archibald said.

"Uh-huh, the hoity-toity end of town. I'm jus' hoi polloi from Stanmore," the sergeant said.

"Ya married?—and can we call ya, Terry?" Fishwick asked.

"Yeah, in this trench ya can. And I'm married twelve years with two kids . . . never looked at another woman."

"Bulldust," Pickering said.

"No, it's dinki-di. I'm a Baptist—Stanmore Baptist Church. I've got two great kids and a good wife; that's somethin'."

"I'm goin' to get married some day, but no way I'll be true," Pickering said. "Reckon I'll have a sheila or two on the side."

Smiling, Sergeant Cook shook his head. "Lots of problems with that, mate, when ya try ta butter yer bread on both sides."

As the evening light was failing, Cook reported to his captain, over the field telephone, that he could see a cloud of dust from enemy movement on the far side of the El Adem-Tobruk Road. Shortly after, their central area of the perimeter was hit with an intensive artillery bombardment and bombs from wailing Stuka dive-bombers.

"Shit, mates, looks like we're goin' ta cop it," Cook said. "Keep your heads down."

When Cook chanced a look out to report the location of the advancing German panzers, he was hit in the forehead by a piece of shrapnel that killed him instantly. Explosions and flares provided intermittent light showing that the attack was moving in their direction.

When the bombardment let up some, Fishwick yelled, "*That's it. They have to be close.*" He rose to look out. A shell exploded nearby sending him back to the floor of the trench. Archibald snuck a look and saw a frightening sight. Three hundred yards off to his right, a furious firefight was underway as panzers bore down on a reinforced concrete bunker in the outer perimeter. By the light of a burning tank, Archibald could make out a German breaching party clearing a path through the minefields and wire.

"Pete!—get the Bren up—*get it on the tripod!*" Archibald frantically pointed. "*They're right over there!*"

They set up the Bren and began shooting at the breaching party. To their left, a panzer saw their muzzle fire, swiveled its turret, took aim, and fired. The protective ring of sandbags around their trench exploded. Stunned, Archibald found himself on top of someone. He heard Pete's muffled voice:

"Get the hell off me!"

Coughing in the thick dust caused by the explosion, Archibald rolled forward onto his knees and landed with his hands on someone's chest. He ran his hands upwards to the face and felt a bloody stump where the head should be. Horrified, he recoiled and screamed—"*AHHHHH!*"—collapsing against the side of the trench.

In the dark, Pete found Archibald's arms and shook him hard.

"Get a hold on, Arch. They're all dead! The Bren's destroyed." He put a rifle into Archibald's hands. "We got to get out of here, mate! You with me?"

"Y-yeah . . . yeah, let's go," Archibald answered unsteadily.

Cautiously they looked out of the trench. The Germans had overrun the bunker and breached their outer perimeter. Panzers with infantry following were streaming toward town. A squad of

Germans was firing into the slit trench nearest to theirs. Going over the top, Archibald and Pete flattened themselves to the ground and began crawling toward their platoon's next slit trench. They were spotted. Bullets hit all around them. Shouting out their names so not to be shot by their own mates, Archibald and Pete ran to the trench and jumped into it. The Bren machine gun began to mow down the attacking Germans, some of whom jumped into the trench that Archibald and Pete had just left.

The Australian field artillery, tanks, and anti-tank units in the inner perimeter opened up on the exposed panzers and German troops. The battle raged through the night. The Germans retreated through the gap in the outer perimeter and back toward El Adem-Tobruk Road, receiving intense fire from Brens, shells, and mortars until out of range. With first morning light, the "Easter Battle" provided ample evidence of an Australian victory. The first Afrika Korps defeat cost the Germans seventeen tanks, a hundred and fifty dead, and two hundred and fifty captured.

Rommel tried again on April 16-17 and a third time from April 30 to May 2 to capture the Tobruk garrison. Frustrated with little ground gained, Rommel left the Australians and Britons in their holes, where they became known as the "Rats of Tobruk," an epithet proudly embraced by the Australian defenders. In October 1941, Archibald and the Ninth Division were relieved and evacuated by sea to Syria for occupation duties following the Allied capture of Syria in July.

* * *

"Heavy," as Harvey Hudson was called by his football mates, felt he was living a pretty good life compared to most Aborigines. After completing the magistrate's one-year probation period served on the Murraroo Aborigines Mission, he had no desire to give up football and return to the fringe camp. With little or no work available to Aborigines during the Great Depression, life was hard outside of the government's subsistence programs.

Coach Foster treated his star player well by making sure Harvey had enough to eat and assigned him the easy jobs of managing their rugby league team and running a crew that maintained the church. As the star player and captain of the unbeatable Murraroo All Blacks for the past five years, Heavy Hudson was a bit of a local hero. He had joined the choir after months of coaxing by Reverend Bonner and his wife.

In a secluded bush area near the mission, Harvey lounged on the ground with other Aborigines, five men and three women. They were enjoying the afternoon together and passed around a fifth of whiskey. While others were talking, Harvey thought about his life.

Me life is better now than when I was a scroungin' swagman. Or is it? I made me own way back then. Now I live on the white man's dole 'cause there ain't no place for me outside the mission. At least I'm a big man at Murraroo and a lot more sure of meself. I should be happy. But is this all there is to life? Am I goin' to make anythin' of meself? Hearing his name spoken drew him back in to the conversation.

"Yeah, Coach Foster said Heavy's good enough ta play fer the national team," said Steve, one of Harvey's teammates.

Seeing the group looking at him, Harvey said, "Coach is gittin' me a tryout with the Australian rugby league team. I'd like ta play in New Zealand, England, an' France."

Willie Langford, another teammate and Harvey's closest mate, said, "Don't git yer hopes up, Heavy, there's a war on."

"Only way ya git out of 'ere is in the army or state jail," said Tom. "Pass me the swill."

Willie passed the whiskey bottle to Tom, but Durey grabbed it too.

"Ain't swill, ya galah. T'is good stuff," Durey said, as Tom wrestled him for the bottle.

Tom said, "Too good fer you."

"*Stop it!* Ya goin' ta spill it," Katie said.

"Hey, hey, cut it out—Tom's turn!" Harvey said.

After the two men had settled down, Willie said, "Yer wrong there, Tom, the army ain't takin' us."

"What ya mean?" Tom said irritably. "Me dad go ta France in the first war!"

"I go with Jake ta army office in Gura," Willie said. "They say we gotta 'ave a dog license or look whitefella. They ain't takin' no half-castes without a dog license."

"What a 'dog license'?" Yulu asked.

"Piece a paper, give halfie the same rights as whites," Willie said.

"So now we need a license ta drink, vote, *and* join the army," Harvey said. "Bugger them—they can fight their bloody war in Europe without me, fer all I care."

"I bin ta see Jake in the infirmary," said Katie. " 'E look more crook than last week."

"What wrong with 'im?" Steve asked.

"Doctors don't know."

"*Payback!*" Yuyu said. "Killer badfella sing 'im Jake poorfella crook."

Harvey shook his head. "I don't believe in song magic."

"Me bin see poorfella die 'cause spirit Shade go."

" 'Ow'd it happen, Yuyu?" Willie asked.

"Men business, can't say 'cause gins 'ere."

Willie shooed the women away with the back of his hand. "I want ta 'ear this, ya three move away."

When the three women had moved outside of earshot, Yuyu spoke quietly. "Badfella steal part of poorfella spirit Shade an' rub it on sacred stone. Killerfella—"

Tom interrupted. "Steal *what* from poorfeller?"

"Part of 'im—blood, hair, piss . . . shit, anyt'ing from 'im body. Then killerfella dig 'im hole an' make 'im fire 'long bottom of hole an' put sacred stone in fire. Then killerfella sing payback chants an' poorfella spirit Shade come ta git back steal part 'im body. Fire burn bright, ma'be fightin' on stone an' sparks. Quicktime killerfella cover hole with heavy flat stone, keep 'im poorfella Shade spirit in hole. Can't go back ta poorfella. Without spirit Shade, poorfella go proper crook, ma'be die."

"Me auntie died from Black Magic say me sister," Tom said. "Ma'be song chant—"

"That's native magic; no one believes that no more," Harvey said.

Shaking his head in disagreement, Durey said, "Devilfella can steal other fella spirit. Me uncle strongfella bin die no reason 'cause bad business with Wuduminji people. Wuduminji killerfella song-man chants kill 'im me uncle dead."

"You two need ta go to church this Sunday," Harvey quipped.

"Whitefella god—why ya b'lieve in 'im?" Yuyu asked.

Now I've done it, Harvey thought. He really believes in song magic, jus' like I do Jesus. But . . . he's just a primitive fella . . . don't know no better. I don't want to get into this with him.

"My business," Harvey said.

"W'ere ya come from?" Durey asked. "W'at yer kinship to-tem?"

Harvey looked at him without answering.

Yuyu said, "Baiame send Sun Mother ta give life, not God-whitefella in sky. Rainbow Serpent make rivers an' billabongs, not Big Name. Spirit Shade go Sun-Down-Way fer good die an' easy huntin'. You no b'lieve in Dreamtime?"

"I was raised by whites an' don't have a totem," Harvey said. "I don't know yer stories."

"Yer *black* whitefella!" Yuyu said.

Katie heard what Yuyu said and thought he had insulted Har-vey. "You two full-bloods are *black*—and dumb and don't know nothin'.'"

"Shut-up, gin, yer dark too an' *guangi*, stupid." Durey said.

"Am not!"

"I got things ta do," Harvey said, abruptly getting up to leave, disgusted by the conversation.

"Me too," said Katie. "I don't 'ave ta listen ta poor, dumb, out-back swaggies."

While the two of them walked back toward the mission, Katie said, "Don't take no notice of 'em rubbish fellas, they don't know nothin'. They ain't got no schoolin' an' ain't modern, like fair-look-in' people."

"I don't know, Katie, at least they know who their people are an' have their stories. We ain't black an' we ain't white; we don't fit nowhere. Just wards of the state is all. I don't want ta live me whole life 'ere. Crikey, I'd like ta git out of 'ere an' go someplace."

"Me too. Where ya want ta go?"

"I don't know. Someplace where I feel good."

Several months later, Harvey married Katie after she had become pregnant with his child. Reverend Bonner had counseled him by telling him marriage was the right thing to do. He liked Katie, but was afraid that family responsibilities would seriously disrupt his life. His concerns were aggravated by Katie's insistent urging that he find a paying job.

"So many Gura whitefellas off ta war, ya can git a job doin' somethin' in town," she said. "Jobs at warehouse in Gura, they say."

"I 'ave work. I'm captain of the football team an' 'ave ta paint the church."

"That don't pay no money, Harvey. It's mission work ta git us our rations. Ya say ya want ta get off the mission, an' so do I. We need money. Ya don't want ta raise our child on the mission, ya say."

"I can make money playin' fer the national team. Coach Foster said so. He's tryin' ta git me a tryout."

"Ya say there bin no rugby league tests since the war started an' now Japfellas bomb America. This war goin' ta go fer long time. This yer chance to git work an' make money, while whitefellas are away."

Harvey didn't know what to say. He hadn't told Katie that Coach Foster had told him the national rugby league team had disbanded until after the war. It had been his ticket to get off the mission. Things had been going along just fine, but now this war and Katie were making it difficult for him.

"I don't know, Katie. I like playin' footy. If I git a payin' job, I'll have ta leave the team. I have ta think 'bout it."

A month later, while Harvey and Willie were walking to a hardware store in Gura, Willie asked, "The Japs bomb Darwin again, do ya think they come 'ere?"

"Don't know, seems they might." Harvey didn't feel much like talking. He had angrily walked away from Katie that morning after she nagged him once again about finding a paying job.

As they walked by the army recruitment office in Gura, Willie slowed and stopped. "I'm goin' inside ta see if they takin' halfcastes now."

Harvey followed Willie in. A recruitment officer, seated behind a desk, was talking to three young white men sitting in chairs lined up against the wall.

"What can I do for you two?" the officer asked.

Willie walked forward while taking off his hat and asked, "Ya takin' Aborigines, boss?"

"You want to volunteer for the Australian Imperial Force?"

"Yeah."

"You got a Certificate?"

"Certificate?" Willie said.

"A Certificate, a dog license, you know what I'm talking about, Jacko! . . . a Certificate of Exemption from the Aborigines Welfare Board because you're almost white."

"No, boss."

"You're not a full-blood are you?" the officer asked.

"No, boss—half-breed."

"Well, you're in luck, my *good* man," he said while snickering and looking at the three seated whites. "The rule's been changed for youse. The military board says if the doctor determines that you are a supreme example of the human race, you can join up. Sit over there. The doctor will be here right soon."

"I go talk ta me mate 'ere, boss," Willie said.

When Willie opened the door, the recruitment officer said, "You miss this time, and you'll have to wait until next week for the doctor."

Stepping out with Harvey, Willie left the door partially open.

"Heavy, I'm goin' ta see if doctor take me."

"Yer ready ta sign up, right now, if they take you?"

Before Willie could answer, they had to step aside for the doctor to enter the building. "I want ta git out of Murraroo, go someplace, an' fight 'em Japs. It our country the Japs want—it our fight now. They pay us the same as whitefellas, ya know. Sign up with me, Heavy, we can git away from 'ere."

"They pay us the same as whitefellas, dinky-di?" Harvey said incredulously.

"Yeah."

"I'll go if they pay us the same as whites. Katie wants me ta make some money, an' I want ta git out of Murraroo real bad. Let's see if they take us."

The recruitment officer confirmed that the pay was the same for Aborigines as for whites. They passed the physical examination and answered the recruitment officer's questions to his satisfaction. Sworn in as enlistees, Willie and Harvey were told that they were soldiers now and had to report back in four days to be sent to Greta Army Camp, New South Wales, for military training.

* * *

"Let's see yer papers, matey," the policeman said to Sam Kee. "What's in the box?"

Handing his identification papers to him, Sam Kee said, "Poultry delivery."

"Where ya goin' with it?" the policeman said as he looked at Sam Kee's papers.

"Whatta you care?"

"Now don't get cheeky with me, Johnny, or I'll take ya in. I want ta make sure ya didn't steal it. Ya got a receipt?"

"I told you, it's a *delivery* from my father's shop in Chinatown. I get stopped by you cops all the time."

"Well maybe ya oughtn't to be walkin' around at six o'clock in the evenin' outside of Chinatown. We're under an invasion alert, ya know, and people are scared. So where ya goin'?"

"Just around the corner—Huang butcher on Oxford Street."

"*Ah so*—Lee Kum's shop?"

"Yes."

"You speak pretty good English for a Chinaman."

"I should: we've been here since 1856."

"Ya don't look that old, heh-heh-heh—just kiddin' ya!"

Sam Kee looked impatiently at him. "Is this going to take much longer, this box is heavy."

"Put it down, I want ta see a bill or order or somethin'."

Sam Kee put the box down on the sidewalk and handed him

the invoice addressed to Huang Lee Kum. The officer looked it over and handed it back.

"Let me give ya some advice if ya don't like being stopped. Get rid of those black glasses yer wearin'. Ya look like that Jap in the poster behind ya. Lookee here," he said, pointing to a poster taped to the inside of a shop window that read in large capital letters:

THEY ARE COMING, BE PREPARED!

The poster showed a menacing Japanese soldier with exaggerated buck teeth and cruel eyes. He wore black eyeglasses with ridiculously large round lenses. Stepping from Papua New Guinea into the continent of Australia, he held a rifle with its long bayonet dripping blood. The red rays of the Rising Sun filled the background of the poster.

"Don't get me wrong. I know the Japs occupy yer country, and ya don't like them any more than we do. But you'd be doin' yersel—"

"*This* is my country!" Sam Kee said.

"What?"

"*This* is my country—*Australia!*—I'm Australian . . . *damn!*"

"Don't get touchy now, Johnno. Just take my advice and keep a low profile if ya want ta stay out of trouble. Now g'wan, nick off!"

Sam Kee was angry when he returned to the poultry processing building and walked into his father's office.

"That's the last time I make a delivery. I don't care if it is an emergency! It can wait until the morning!"

"What happened?" Wing-yuen asked.

"I was stopped *twice* and made to show my papers! This obnoxious cop told me to get rid of my black glasses, because I look like a *Jap!* I've had it! They can't tell the difference between a Chinese Australian and a Jap—or they just like to harass us. Which is probably the main reason."

"It's something we have to put up with until the war is over," Wing-yuen said. "They put all Asians in the same boat. They're afraid and want to strike out at someone."

"I don't *care!* I'm sick of being treated like a second-class citizen!"

"You're spoiled. You spend too much time being the great chef.

You live better than most Australians. Your mother and I have given you everything you ever wanted. Don't you think that I'm sick of it too? And I've had to deal with it much longer than you. You have to be tolerant during the war scare."

"What scare! The country's not going to be invaded."

"You *don't* read the newspapers. You *don't* know what you are talking about. You want to be treated like an Australian, though you *won't* even read the newspaper. You spend too much time cooking with your mother. Australia *is* in danger of being invaded! Singapore fell easily to the Japanese. The Dutch and British forces have surrendered in Java. Hollandia and Lae in New Guinea have fallen—do you know where those places *are?*"

"Yes . . . of course."

"Port Moresby and Darwin are being bombed. Do you know Darwin is in Australia? What does that tell you? Why do you think the American President Roosevelt sent his top general, Douglas MacArthur, to Australia? Japan intends to *invade us!*—*read* the newspapers, stupid boy. . . . It's late. I still have work to do. Tell your mother I will be home at nine."

Sam Kee stood looking at his father. This was the first time he had called him "stupid."

"Is it because you think I'm stupid that you haven't given me more responsibility and still send me out on deliveries?"

"That was an emergency. I don't send you out on deliveries very often. . . . I'm sorry, Sam Kee, I have a lot on my mind right now. You are only twenty-two. You have plenty of time to learn my business."

"I want to learn the business now. If you won't teach me, I'll have to find a way to start my own business. I want to make a lot of money, so I won't be treated like a second-class citizen my whole life."

"You're *Chinese!* You'll always be treated like a second-class citizen—all your life. You *better* get used to it. That's the hard lesson I had to learn. However, if it's revenge you want, then become *very, very* rich. That would be the sweetest revenge of all."

Wing-yuen saw the disappointment in Sam Kee's eyes.

"I'm sorry, Son. Sit down. I've been working on something important. I'll share it with you."

Sam Kee sat in the chair in front of his father's desk.

"I've hired a white front man to expand my poultry business. He starts in two weeks. After eight years, I've exhausted the growth of my business to the Chinese community. We are doing well, but I want to do much better. Through the white salesman, who will act like he owns the business, I can expand into the white wholesale market, selling poultry products to white butchers, restaurants, and hotels. With our cheaper Chinese labor, we will be able to undercut our competitor's prices. What do you think of that?"

"That's wonderful, Father. I can help you in the white community, because I dress well and speak upper-class English."

"No, Sam Kee, you don't understand. We will not show ourselves to the white community. We will be a *silent* owner, running the business behind the scene, providing and processing the chickens and collecting the profits behind a white front man—who will really be just a salesman. We will make a lot of money, and you and your sister Lin Yee will become very rich. So you see, we *will* work together, so you won't always have to be a second-class citizen."

*　*　*

"I'm sorry, Mother, I didn't mean to alarm you," Nigel said as his mother Anne dabbed her eyes with a hankie. The Armstrongs were seated in Nigel's living room after dinner on May 10, 1942. The drapes were drawn as required by the blackout, high-alert order. Nigel's 73-year-old father, Peter, sat with his elbows on the table and his chin resting in one hand.

Anne said, "I just never imagined it would come to this—our family being placed in such jeopardy."

"We aren't in any immediate danger, Mum," Nigel said. "If I thought we were, I'd pack us all up tomorrow and drive us to the mountains. I just want us to be prepared to leave quickly if the Japs get near enough to make an air attack on the naval facilities and ships in Sydney Harbour."

"We're far from the harbor," Peter said. "Won't we be safe in Bellevue Hill?"

"From bombs, probably, but not from antiaircraft fire or a downed plane."

"I can't walk along Bondi Beach anymore without thinking of the Japanese invading," Wilhelmina said.

"Yes, the double row of barbed wire along Bondi Beach does look pretty ominous," Nigel said, "though any invasion would start up north and proceed south, I reckon, so we should have plenty of warning."

"The Blue Mountains would be cold this time of year," Peter said.

"I love the brisk mornings in winter and the roaring fireplace," Wilhelmina said, trying to lift spirits. "Wouldn't it be wonderful, Lydia, to spend time with Grandma and Grandpa at the mountain house? We could hike to the Three Sisters and Wentworth Falls!"

"I don't want to," six-year-old Lydia said.

"Oh, sure you do," Wilhelmina said.

"Will you be going up with us, Nigel?" Peter asked.

"No. I'll be needed here. The mountain house is only an hour from Bankstown Airport, so I'll drive up as often as I can." Seeing the concerned look on Wilhelmina's face, he said, "Don't be worried, Willa, I told you I won't be shooting down any Japs. Our Wirraway fighter has proven to be obsolete against the Jap Zero, and the Yanks aren't about to let me fly their new Kittyhawk fighter. These young hotshot pilots think I'm an old man at forty-five. I'll continue training pilots in the Wirraway."

"You want us to leave Sydney and go to the mountains because of this naval battle in the Coral Sea?" Wilhelmina asked. "It was so far away."

"The naval battle was only four hundred miles northeast of Cairns," Nigel said. "That's close enough. I'd prefer that you all leave for the mountains tomorrow, just to remove you from harm's way, but since you want to keep the family together as long as possible, I'm asking you to be prepared to leave at a moment's notice. That means keep a full tank of gas in your car, Dad. According to Prime Minister Curtin the naval battle averted a possible invasion, yet he also said it could happen any day."

"Today's newspaper seemed to say the battle was a draw," Peter said.

"From our viewpoint, I'd say we won it, because the Jap troop transports had to turn back for fear of being sunk," Nigel said. "One report said the Japs were on their way to attack Port Moresby; however, another speculated that Cairns was their objective. Either place would have provided the Japs with an airfield to launch planes to bomb us in Australia.

"The Japs issued a communiqué claiming victory for sinking both American aircraft carriers, although the *Yorktown* is still afloat. The problem is, I'm pretty sure the Americans don't have any other aircraft carriers in our sector to protect us from another invasion."

"Where are the British? Their navy was supposed to be invincible and protect us." Anne said. "Why do we have to rely only on the Americans?"

"The British are spread too thin to help us," Peter said. "We all underestimated the Japs. No one thought their torpedo bombers could sink the British battleships *Repulse* and *Prince of Wales,* or Singapore would fall without much of a fight."

"Churchill has let us down because he's pursuing a 'fight Germany first' policy, Mum," Nigel said. "He's handed our defense over to the Americans. That's why Curtin said 'without any inhibitions of any kind . . . Australia looks to America, free of any pangs as to our traditional links with the United Kingdom.' We've realigned our military alliance toward the Yanks, because, effectively, the British have abandoned us."

Peter looked harshly at his son but decided not to disagree.

"Why then is Archie still fighting for the English in Syria?" Wilhelmina said. "Why isn't he back here with the Sixth and Seventh Divisions to defend Australia?"

"His Ninth Division was the last to go, so it will be the last to return to Australia," Nigel said. "Churchill and Roosevelt wanted to send our troops to Burma to stop the Japs from advancing toward India, but Curtin demanded they be returned to Australia."

"You shouldn't blame Britain," Peter said. "The bloody Japs have had their eye on our country for years!"

"*Peter!*" Anne scolded. "Don't use that kind of language in front of Lydia, my word."

"You know how I feel about that, Dad," Nigel said, "and our White Australia Policy."

"It's our country. We have a right to let in whom we want."

"I'm tired, and it's late," Anne said. She did not want Peter and Nigel to get into an argument. "Time to walk home, Peter."

Weeks passed without further concern of a Japanese air attack or invasion. On a Sunday at dusk, while Nigel and Wilhelmina drove north across the Sydney Harbour Bridge on their way to a dinner party, three Japanese "mother" submarines about six miles east of Sydney Harbour each released a two-man midget submarine.

The dinner was at a couple's house located high on Cremorne Point that juts out into Sydney Harbour. After dinner the three couples moved into a magnificent glass-enclosed room to enjoy the panoramic view of the harbor. All of the lights were turned off to meet the blackout requirements, except for the soft light of a single candle.

"Isn't this romantic," the hostess Elizabeth Fairbank said as they entered the room. She led the women to one end of the large room, where tea was being served, while her husband Bob offered the men after-dinner liqueurs at the other end.

There was a muffled *boom* in the distance. "Did you hear that?" Nigel asked the men. "It sounded like an explosion some way off."

"Yes, in the direction of Watsons Bay," Elizabeth said from her end of the room.

Everyone moved to the east side of the room facing Watsons Bay. Seeing no unusual activity on the harbor, they returned to their two ends of the room. The congenial evening continued until Wilhelmina walked over to Nigel.

"It's close to eleven, Nigel. I'd like to be home before midnight."

"We've had a delightful evening, Elizabeth, thank you so much." Wilhelmina said. "Betty and Mark live close by, but we have a bit of a drive."

Suddenly, several sirens sounded in the harbor one after another.

"There are searchlights all over the harbor!" Mark Holder said.

They all moved to the windows. Searchlights from several ships were sweeping the harbor. More warning sirens sounded. A heavy military cruiser attached to a buoy between Cremorne Point and

Garden Island focused its searchlights on something in the water near Garden Island that was moving toward the Sydney Harbour Bridge.

"There's something moving in that searchlight," Bob said.

As they tried to identify what was illuminated, the cruiser opened fire with tracer bullets that streaked like shooting stars, followed immediately by the *pom-pom-pom-pom-pom-pom-pom-pom* of rapid-fire cannons.

"They're firing antiaircraft pom-poms at something in the water," Nigel said. "I can't see anything in the searchlight."

Boom . . . boom. "What's that?" Betty asked.

Boom . . . boom. "Coming from Watsons Bay again," Elizabeth said.

Boom . . . boom. "Those are depth charges," said Bob, who had been a sailor in the Great War. "Near the anti-submarine net. There must be Jap submarines in the harbor!"

"Oh my God, the Japs have invaded!" Betty exclaimed. "Mark, the *kids!* They'll be scared to death. *Let's go!*"

BAM-BAM-BAM-BAM-BAM-BAM-BAM. The loud sound of rapid firing directed toward them caused the group to duck and drop to the floor. Nigel moved behind a column, but continued to look out the window, sensing that the firing was low and off to one side.

"*There's a sub!*" Nigel said. "I can see it. It's passing by Cremorne Ferry Wharf—a ship at Garden Island is shooting tracers at it."

"The Japs are here, they're here, oh dear God, what are we going to do!" Betty said from the floor.

The firing in their direction stopped.

"I don't know where the sub went," Nigel said. "I'm sure I saw it."

Everyone was standing, except Betty, who was sitting on the floor and crying.

"Don't get hysterical, Betty, for godsake," Mark said, helping her to her feet. "Sorry all." He looked at Nigel and Bob. "What do you reckon?"

Wilhelmina and Elizabeth comforted Betty on the couch.

"Dunno," Bob answered. "Subs could be the first stage of an invasion."

"No, it feels more like an isolated attack to me," Nigel said. "There's been no reports of a large fleet moving in our direction, no bombing of the harbor, no sounds of distant heavy guns softening up a landing site—I think they're raiders."

"The searchlights are going out," Mark said. "What's happening?"

They were all drawn to the windows, except Betty and Wilhelmina.

"*There* . . . a few are still on," Elizabeth said. "It's so quiet and eerie."

"Could be blackening out for fear of Jap bombers," Nigel said.

The central area of their view suddenly exploded into yellow, red, and white colors shooting to the sky followed by a terrific KAA*BROOOOM* that shook the whole house. They recoiled backwards from the violence of the blast, covering their faces for fear of exploding glass. Elizabeth fell to the floor again. The windows shuddered in their frames but held.

"My God, something big blew up, what was that?" Mark asked.

"A torpedo," Bob said.

"Yeah, it went up like a torpedo," Nigel agreed. "There must be more than one Jap sub in the harbor!"

From the couch, Betty yelled, "*Mark! The kids! I'm going home.*"

"All right! All right. We'll listen to the radio there." They quickly said good-bye. Bob let them out, locking the door after them.

"We have to go too, Nigel," Wilhelmina said.

"The bridge is sure to be closed," Nigel said.

"You stay here until it's safe," Bob said.

"I'm going to call Mum and Dad then," Wilhelmina said. "They'll be worried sick."

The Armstrongs stayed the night with their hosts, the Fairbanks. Gunfire and depth charges reverberated throughout the night. In the late morning, it was reported on the radio that two midget submarines had been sunk and a third was being sought. One of the submarines had fired two torpedoes at the heavy cruiser USS *Chicago* but missed. One of the two torpedos ran harmlessly aground on Garden Island. The other passed under the Dutch submarine *K9* and struck the sea wall of Garden Island against which the depot ship HMAS *Kuttabul* was moored. The explosion sank the *Kuttabul* killing twenty-one sailors and wounding ten others.

Nigel asked his family to go to the mountain house. Wilhelmina argued that since it was reported that there was no invasion fleet connected with the submarines attack, there was no good reason to leave. Nigel reluctantly agreed.

A week later, on June 8, Nigel felt better about his family staying in Sydney when the results of the battle of Midway became known. The American fleet had devastated a large Japanese armada attacking the island of Midway. Four Japanese aircraft carriers and a heavy cruiser had been sunk and 322 enemy aircraft shot down. The Americans had lost only a destroyer and 137 planes during the battle, although the *Yorktown* aircraft carrier was badly damaged. Nigel felt that the Midway battle success had turned the tide in the Pacific in favor of the Allies.

That night Nigel went to bed expecting a good night's sleep. At the same time that he was going to sleep, Japanese submarine *I-24* surfaced in the Tasman Sea and pointed its deck gun toward the lights of Sydney. Nigel was half asleep when he heard a thundering sound:

wizzzzzZZZZTHUD!

Wilhelmina rolled over. *"What was tha—"*

"A shell!" Nigel said throwing off the covers and rolling out of bed. "It hit not too far away—*near Mum's!* Where the *hell* is my prosthesis! Get up! Uh-oh, here comes another one!" It whistled over the house making the same sound:

wizzzzzZZZZ followed by a THUD! in the distance.

"Turn on the light!" Wilhelmina said frantically.

Frightened and crying, Lydia ran into their room. "Mummy, what's the matter? What's those sounds?" Half out of bed, Wilhelmina reached out for her.

Nigel turned on the light. "Another one, *get down!*" They dropped to the floor, and he threw himself over them.

wizzzzzZZZZzzzzthud!

"Jeez, we're under artillery fire!" Nigel said. He picked up Lydia and headed for the door. Wilhelmina stood and headed for the closet.

"Willa, forget your bathrobe! We've got to get down to the basement, *now!"*

He ran down the hall carrying Lydia, with Wilhelmina close behind. *"Hurry!"*

In the basement, Nigel placed them against the east wall knowing that the shells were coming from the direction of the sea.

"Stay against this wall, don't move. I'm going to Mum's."

In his pajamas, Nigel ran up the basement stairs two at a time and out onto Benelong Crescent. He tightened his prosthetic leg and ran up the steps to Victoria Road, crossed it, and ran through the park toward his parent's house on Bradley Avenue.

While he ran he thought how negligent he was.

I should have demanded that they all go to the mountain house where they would've been safe. Stupid, stupid, stupid. I was the only one who really knew what could happen. Damn it! Stupid! I should have demanded! If anything has happened to Mum or Dad . . . I'll never forgive myself. Oh, God, there's a crowd at the far end of Bradley Avenue in front of my parents' house!

He gasped, stumbled, and nearly fell, righting himself with an outstretched arm. In the distance, came the *wooo-wooo-wooo-wooo* of an emergency vehicle's siren. His stomach churned; he felt that he was about to be sick. Then he saw his parents in the crowd.

They're all right!

Exhausted, gasping for air, he slowed his running and then walked toward his parents, who were engaged in anxious conversations with neighbors. They did not see him approaching. He saw that a shell had passed through the roof of a house, blown through its side wall, and continued on to damage the wall of the next house. His parents' house was the next house on the corner.

"Mum . . . Dad, are you all right?"

"*Archie!* We're fine, nothing hit us," Peter said.

"Are Lydia and Wilhelmina all right?" Anne asked as she hugged her son.

"Yes. The shells flew over our house. It seems to be over now."

The submarine had fired ten shells within four minutes. Three shells landed in the Bellevue Hill neighborhood. Only one exploded because armor-piercing shells had been used. Two people were injured. Fortunately no one was killed. Later that day, Nigel drove the five of them to their house in the Blue Mountains.

* * *

France was what I was hopin' for when I signed up, Harvey thought to himself, or England. Ma'be I could've played some rugby league there an' showed 'em somethin' . . . even stayed on ta play fer a national team. Didn't git too bloody far!—Kokoda Track in Papua New Guinea is still in Australia almost.

Harvey was trying to sleep in a fighting pit without much success. Willie was on watch.

No bloody way anyone can sleep with Japs yellin' "*Aussie di-iie!*" an' "*We killll yuuu!*" and shriekin'"*Aaaaaaaaahhh!*" Harvey thought. Damn, fuckin' Japs . . . three weeks now . . . bin pushin' us step-by-step back to Port Moresby. Lost a lot of good blokes. . . . Had ta leave most of 'em unburied where they fell. Thank goodness for the native Fuzzy Wuzzy Angels who help the sick and wounded.

Men are startin' ta depend on me—'cause they afraid of the jungle . . . "jungle jitters." Another form of competition is all it is, us against Japs. Sarge wants me at point. I can *feel* things ain't right when the jungle gits too quiet, birds stop singin', an' animals stop movin'. Me eyes catch the odd movement, a slight break in a ray of sunlight, or a strange sound. I'd rather be point where I can see an' hear good. Don't like followin' another bloke whose senses and reflexes might not be as good as mine. They too noisy. If I walk us into an ambush, an' I'm killed, well, it'd be me own blinkin' fault.

Australian voices suddenly shouted: "*Fuck you Japs*" and "*We'll kill you*" and "*C'mon an' git it*" followed by a short burst from their submachine gun. "*Like that, do ya?*"

Aw dammit, 'em two stupid newies in the next fightin' pit are givin' away their position. They were told ta keep quiet an' to throw grenades if the Japs git too close. Their muzzle flashes an' voices tell the Japs they're only two. Silly buggers are shit-scared. I can't do a thing, or we'll give away our pit too. I'm goin' ta be right tired if I don't git some sleep soon.

Harvey heard Willie lowering himself to be next to him in their fighting pit. In the total darkness, Willie felt around and touched his leg and then his arm.

"Heavy, ya sleepin'?" he whispered close to his face.

"No."

"Ya hear those newies?"

"Yeah."

"What do we do?"

"Nothin', let me sleep."

Harvey tried to sleep.

I couldn't even see Willie right in front of me face. It's as black as inside a closet with the door closed at night. Them newies' fightin' pit is only twenty yards away, but in this fuckin' jungle, with a roof of leaves that shuts out the light of the moon and stars; it's a world away. Screamin' Japs in a pitch-black room would scare anybody.

Night b'longs ta 'em. Fearless night fighters. Smart, little, yellow bastards. They send out four or five ta keep us awake all night while the rest of 'em sleep. We should do the same, but no one is game.

Harvey tried to think of something else.

Why didn't I visit Katie when I had leave? She was mad at me fer joinin' up and hadn't had our boy yet, that's why. It's really me new born son I want ta see now. In the letter, she an' Mrs. Bonner wrote, she's happy I'm sendin' her money fer the boy. Usin' it ta buy things fer the baby, an' savin' some too, fer when I come home . . .

Harvey awoke with a start when Willie lightly touches his chest. *I bin sleepin'!* he thought, astounded.

Willie found his face, cupped his ear with both hands and spoke softly directly into his ear. "Japs bin crawlin' up on 'em newies fer past hour. Pretty close now. Ya listen, Heavy."

Harvey raised himself quietly and stood to listen. There were several of them. The one out front was about ten yards from the newies' pit. He found Willie's arm, pulled him down with him, and whispered directly into his ear.

"Them newies gotta be sleepin'. Let's throw grenades ta give 'em a chance."

Each pulled the pin of a grenade and threw them where the Japanese soldiers were. The explosions produced a loud shrill cry, followed by wild yelling as the Japanese rushed forward and jumped into the newies' pit. A screaming hand-to-hand struggle ensued for a minute or more. Harvey and Willie held their rifles with fixed bayonets toward the newies' pit, prepared for a Japanese charge, but heard nothing more.

About an hour later, sounds crept slowly toward them from inside the perimeter.

Harvey whispered into Willie's ear:

"Jap stunt."

Wily bastards moved into the interior of the perimeter ta make us think our own people are comin' ta help us. They gotta be guessin' where we are. Doesn't matter, Japs or our men—yer dead. Anyone movin' at night gits a grenade. That's the rule. No passwords. No *Don't shoot, it's me.* If ya have ta shit, you do it in yer pit and live with it fer the night. Two of them, about ten feet apart. Closer now. Anythin' movin' gets killed! That's the fuckin' rule. He found a grenade and readied it.

Willie, stepping back slowly and carefully to better position his bayonet, brought his heel down lightly on a stone sitting in water that produced a *squish* sound. He and Harvey froze.

Harvey heard something hit the front wall of their pit and fall to the bottom with a *thud. What the—! . . . Grenade!*

"*GRENADE!*" Harvey yelled as he quickly turned, lifted himself out of the pit and swung his legs away, involuntarily sliding down the slippery muddy slope in front of the pit. The grenade exploded, and Willie screamed:

"*AAHHHH-AHHH-AAHH-AHHH!*"

Willie lay screaming and writhing to the left of the pit where the force of the grenade explosion had flung him.

Without his rifle, Harvey pulled out his razor-sharp combat knife, took a knife-fighting posture, and steeled himself to fight. He couldn't hear anything, except Willie screaming.

The Japs can't see anythin' in the blackness. Yet they know there's at least two of us 'cause I yelled *grenade.* God . . . they know I'm here! Got ta do somethin' fast.

Willie's screams suddenly changed to a gurgle.

His throat's being cut, Harvey thought. He took three quick steps, and jabbed his knife forcefully above the sound of Willie's gurgle where the enemy had to be. Hitting a body hard, Harvey ripped the knife violently upwards and jumped back away from him. Slipping on the muddy slope, his feet went out from under him, and he slid down the slope on his knees with his knife arm extended. He stopped at the bottom of the slope and listened.

Jap I jus' stabbed is thrashin' around. The other sound is Willie's death rattle. Harvey stared ahead into darkness. *WHERE ARE YA, ya little bastard?*

The sounds of the wounded Japanese soldier worried Harvey that he would not hear the attack of the other soldier. Willie's death rattle stopped, and the wounded Japanese soldier quieted.

Where the HELL are ya? You gotta be right in front of me, within ten feet. He can't git me if I'm invisible—don't even breathe. Weak whimperin' sounds from stabbed Jap; he's done fer. I'm comfortable on both knees . . . good. *I know yer there, ya bastard*—I can wait as long as you can. A muffled sound. *He's in our pit!* Sure, they both jumped in ta kill anyone wounded by the grenade.

Harvey heard the sound of a grenade rolling down the slope toward him. Moving fast on his hands and knees, he reached the pit and swung his knife through the center of it hitting the unseen man, who screamed out. Harvey allowed his body's momentum to carry him headfirst into the pit. The grenade exploded. Again his knife connected with his invisible enemy while his left hand found the man's shoulder. He stabbed upwards into the man's neck and kicked backward away from him.

Only when Harvey leaned against the far wall of the pit did he realize that he was wounded. His side hurt like hell. He felt the warm, wet, gooey consistency of blood in his shirt, but did not care. The wound was not serious, and he needed to focus and listen. He listened and heard only the death throes of the Japanese soldier he had just stabbed, nothing else.

In the morning, Harvey looked over the engagement area.

Four Japs had snuck up on the newies' pit. Willie an' me killed one of 'em with our grenades. The newies killed another. The other two attacked us. Poor Willie . . . his legs are torn up. I'll bury ya, mate.

*   *   *

Archibald's Ninth Division left Syria on June 26, 1942, by train to join the Eighth Army fighting Rommel at El Alamein, Egypt. On the night of October 23, a massive artillery barrage heralded the long awaited Allied offensive led by Lieutenant-General Bernard Montgomery. After the battle, Archibald wrote a letter to his family:

November 22, 1942

Dear Mum, Dad, and Lydia,

By the time this letter arrives, it will be old news that we've won a hard crucial victory at El Alamein, Egypt. Rommel is the Desert Fox no more. He is in full retreat all along the line.

Don't be concerned by the hospital letterhead. I had several minor shrapnel wounds and was suffering from exhaustion, but now I'm almost back to 100% again. I'm afraid I can't write the same about most of my mates who copped it or are severely wounded. I'm simply amazed that I lived through the battle. We fought continuously for nine days without a good sleep. I can't write how insignificant I felt as a puny human being. There were several times when we were under such a storm of artillery, tank, plane, and mortar fire that I thought it was the end for me. I was actually happy when I saw only infantry attacking us, if you can believe that! My battalion came close to being wiped out and has been withdrawn for rest and reorganization. Our 9th Division was only a small part of the Eighth Army, but suffered four times the casualties of most British divisions.

The 9th was placed on the important north flank when the attack began. When the attack stalled after several days, Morshead ordered us to attack north on October 28 and again on October 30 to split the enemy line north of us. We crossed the El Alamein railway line and cut the coastal road trapping a large German force to the east. We were right up to the coastal dunes of the Mediterranean Sea. While we were fighting the trapped Germans on our east, Rommel sent a strong rescue force from the west that pushed us off the road and into defensive positions behind the railway embankment. For the next two days, our salient was continuously attacked from three sides.

We were told that Rommel thought we were leading the main attack west on the coastal road. Our diversion allowed General Montgomery to regroup and press his original attack southwest of us, where he finally broke through the German line on November 3.

There's talk that they are going to let us go home now. I hope so. I am sick of the Middle East and anxious to return to Sydney and see you all again.

Love,
Archie

Churchill in a speech celebrating El Alamein, the first British battlefield victory against the Germans, said: "Now this is not the end, it is not even the beginning of the end. But it is, perhaps, the end of the beginning."

* * *

Sydneysiders were elated with the faraway victory at El Alamein in November 1942, but were even more jubilant that the Japanese were in full retreat along the Kokoda Track, which allayed their fears of imminent invasion.

Harvey was with the Seventh Division when it reached the coastal plain of the Buna-Gona area on the north coast of Papua New Guinea. The jungle swamp area had been turned into a honeycomb of camouflaged trenches, fighting pits, machine-gun bunkers, and well-placed artillery.

He was now a corporal in charge of a section of fifteen men, yet still preferred to lead from the front. Before every patrol, he took his new men aside for special instructions.

"We goin' out ta probe an' find the enemy. I'm placing ya newies in the center as we advance. We walk in staggered "v-shape" with me at point. Give me plenty of room in front and don't bunch up. If ya see a cleared openin' stay away from it. It could be fire lane fer a Jap machine gun. There's snipers in tops of coconut trees. Look fer trees with a clear field of fire. Waste a bullet if ya think ya see one. We ain't sneakin' up on 'em. They hear us comin', but don't make any unnecessary noise, so I can hear what's happenin' in front of me."

It took over a month for the Australians to take Gona and the Americans to push the Japanese out of Buna to new positions in a coconut plantation to the east. On December 18, a final joint Australian-American effort began to drive the Japanese from the Buna-Gona coastal area. On December 25, the Australians and American troops shared a Christmas dinner and relaxed together in a rest area behind the front lines.

In the Australian and American armies, Harvey was an oddity; a black who gave orders to whites. The conversation gradually turned to race. As usual, Harvey sat quietly and didn't have much to say.

"Harvey somehow just *sees* the Japs, before anyone else. He's got this sixth sense. I don't know what it is," a member of Harvey's section said.

"It's an Abo thing, a bushman's sense," said another section member. "That's why they're good trackers. It's those magical powers they're supposed to have."

When a soldier in his section looked at him, Harvey just smiled. They *want* me to have magical powers, he thought. It gives them a special advantage in our daily life-and-death struggle.

An American took issue with the way the discussion was going. "Well, your colored people got to be a whole lot smarter than our niggers—we don't trust them to carry a weapon. Likely as not, they'd shoot one of us! Ha ha ha."

"One thing they are not is smart . . . at anything!" said another American.

"The Jap, now there's a stupid bastard!" said an Australian.

"No fuckin' respect for his own life. Comes runnin' at us screaming '*Banzai!*' right into our machine guns, knowing he's goin' to die. Now that's both insane and stupid!"

"Ugly, little vermin, no better than cockroaches," an American agreed.

"You blokes ain't 'eard from our professor, Sarge Baker, yet," said an Australian. "Tell 'em what ya think about the Japs, Professor."

"Bob's a stirrer, trying to get me into trouble," the Professor said.

"Jesus H. Christ—don't tell me you have something *good* to say about the Nips!" an American said.

"I respect the little bastards," the Professor said. "But then I lived in Tokyo for two years and know something about their values, eastern religion, and culture."

"What culture, Sarge?" an Australian said. "He ties himself to the top of a palm tree knowin' he's going ta die after he gets one or two of us—I call that pretty damn stupid."

"Righto, we hate him 'cause he fights dirty and to the death," the Professor said. "We expect him to fight face-to-face, man-to-man, like a European and give up when he's beat. But they don't think that way."

"Because they're cockroaches?" an American asked.

"No, because they live and die by *bushido*, the samurai code of honor, which places duty, obedience, loyalty, and fearlessness toward the enemy above life itself, with suicide as the only honorable alternative to defeat."

"Well then, I'm pleased ta send the buggers to samurai hell!" an Australian said.

"Yeah, the only dead Jap is a good Jap," Chuck, an American, said.

"Ha ha . . . Chuck . . . that's 'the only good Indian is a dead Indian,' " an American said.

"Yeah, well now it's the Japs."

The Professor stood up to leave. "I want to kill Japs as much as all of you—so I can go home. I just don't have to hate 'em ta kill 'em."

"Ah, get over yourself!" Darby, an Australian, said.

"Go to blazes, Darby," the Professor said. "And another thing, Harvey here has saved my life more than once, and I don't much like talkin' about how ignorant and stupid his people are, like he's not even sitting here."

"They don't mean nothin' by it, Sarge," Harvey said. "It's jus' talk. It don't bother me."

"Well it bothers me. I'm turnin' in, g'night."

Darby watched the Professor walk away, then he said, "What a wanker. I'm so sick of his mental masturbation."

Harvey chuckled along with everyone else.

Six weeks later, after the defeat of the Japanese army in Buna-Gona, Harvey's battalion was sent to Kairi Camp in Queensland for rest and relaxation. In a ceremony at the camp, Harvey was promoted to sergeant. Feeling a strong sense of acceptance and accomplishment, he decided to make the army his career.

A letter from Katie finally reached him there. She wrote that she had named their son James. Superintendent Foster had left the Murraroo Aborigines Mission, and the new superintendent made such disruptive changes that she and many others moved to the fringe camp in protest. Reverend Bonner also left as pastor of the Methodist church.

Harvey thought that he would visit Katie and his son, until his commanding officer asked him to teach a course in jungle fighting. He felt obliged to accept and gave up the opportunity to visit them.

* * *

Archibald's Ninth Division returned to Australia from North Africa in April 1943. After welcoming parades in Melbourne and Sydney, he was given three weeks of leave, which he spent with his family. In May, he was sent to Queensland for amphibious training at Trinity Beach followed by jungle training at Kairi Camp. Harvey was one of the instructors teaching jungle fighting to Archibald's battalion.

The Australian Seventh and Ninth Divisions took part in the Allied offensive campaign against Lae, Papua New Guinea, that began in August 1943. Archibald's Ninth Division made an amphibious landing east of Lae and moved along the coast toward the town. American paratroopers seized Nadzab airfield northwest of

Lae, which allowed a steady stream of planes to fly in Harvey's Seventh Division. His division advanced on Lae from the west. Caught in the vise of these converging advances, the Japanese garrison abandoned Lae. The Ninth and Seventh Divisions came together fighting a Japanese rearguard defense as their main body retreated north.

Archibald and two mates moved cautiously down a side street, involved in nerve-racking house-to-house combat. A Japanese soldier suddenly sprang from a burning building and shot at them as he ran. Archibald and his mates returned fire. Hit several times, the Japanese soldier dropped his rifle, staggered drunkenly a few steps and fell. Unsteadily, he slowly rose and wobblingly walked away from them, weaving as he went. Fascinated, Archibald and the others followed him while holding fire. He fell again in the street and began wildly squirming about kicking up dust. Archibald walked pass two dead Japanese soldiers and fired a bullet into the thrashing Japanese soldier's head to quiet him.

The three of them continued warily down the street. They were greatly startled by a short burst from a submachine gun immediately behind them. Whirling around, they saw a black Australian soldier bayoneting one of the two "dead" Japanese soldiers they had just passed. The other "dead" soldier had been shot several times and was shuddering in death throes. A submachine gun lay by his side. They were shocked to realize that at least one of the two "dead" Japanese soldiers was about to submachine them in the back.

"*God!* Thanks, Sarge!" Archibald said.

"*Jeez*, that was close," another said.

"Good on ya, Sarge—sweet!" the third soldier said.

"No worries," Harvey said. "But unless ya see maggots or brains spilled out, it's best ta bayonet every Jap corpse, jus' in case." Harvey turned and made a "forward" motion to his section coming up behind him. As he walked by Archibald and his friends, he said, "G'day, mates."

After Harvey had passed by, one of Archibald's mates said, "I'll be damned, that's the first Abo sergeant I've ever seen!"

"He was one of the jungle fighting instructors at Kairi Camp," Archibald said.

After the battle for Lae, Harvey's Seventh Division was ordered to follow the retreating Japanese garrison up the Markham-Ramu Valley, while Archibald's Ninth Division was given the task of taking the Huon Peninsula, both Allied advances to drive the Japanese from Papua New Guinea.

* * *

The Japanese base at Finschhafen was the objective of Archibald's Ninth Division's amphibious landing on the Huon Peninsula on September 22, 1943. The town's name Finschhafen was left over from before the Great War when the area was part of Germany's colonial Bismarck Archipelago.

From American landing crafts, the Ninth Division stormed Scarlet Beach, six miles north of Finschhafen. Encountering light Japanese resistance, the division advanced south toward the town. Two days later, the advance was halted by a Japanese complex of pillboxes and bunkers with coordinated fields of fire. The American navy shelled the complex, but a probing attack determined that it was little damaged. The Japanese were on high ground, with the sea on one side and bogs and swamp on the other. Two infantry sections were ordered to flank the enemy complex.

Archibald and thirty others waded single file through slimy, green, swamp water up to their chests.

I hope no snake or fuckin' croc gets me in this shit, Archibald thought. This fighting is more disgusting than fighting the Krauts at Tobruk and El Alamein. At least there, I didn't have to worry about being eaten alive by a damn croc! And we're supposed to move quietly, so not to give ourselves away. Bullshit! Any croc grabs me; I shoot!

Distant shots . . . start of the planned frontal attack intended to draw attention away from our flanking movement. Right on time. Sounds intense. Good—the front of this line is getting out of the water.

Crack . . . crack—crack-crack-crack.

Uh-oh. A scream—somebody's hit. They're on to us.

Rut-tut-tut-tuttututtuttututtut.

Shit! Now we're goin' to cop it, and I'm still in the damn water.

Archibald dropped lower in the water and swam with his left arm, using his right arm to keep his rifle just above the water. Bullets splashed and ricocheted off the water around him. A soldier in front of him was shot through the neck, nearly decapitating him. Archibald made it to the shore and crawled to a large fallen tree that had several men behind it. The roar of battle was now deafening.

Lowering himself to reload, his elbow banged against something hard. He turned and looked in terror at a flamethrower on the back of a combat engineer. Bloody hell! Archibald thought. I don't want to be next to this bloke!

The sergeant shouted for them to advance. Archibald charged with others. An explosion erupted in front of them taking out a bunker. The sergeant yelled to Archibald and a gunner to rush a pillbox with him. The pillbox machine-gun slit faced forward away from them. The gunner stuck his Bren light machine gun into the corner of the slit and fired a burst then backed away for the sergeant to throw in a grenade. Inside, the Japanese screamed and two enemy soldiers emerged from the opposite side of the pillbox. There was a muffled explosion inside.

Archibald was providing protective fire from the top of the earth mound over the pillbox and shot the first Japanese soldier to emerge from the pillbox. The second fired a submachine gun at him. Archibald slid a bit down the slope as a third soldier emerged from the pillbox also firing at him.

They threw two grenades at Archibald that bounced down the slope and exploded, killing the sergeant and badly wounding the Bren gunner. Archibald heard the combat engineer and his assistant yelling at him. They were positioning themselves to fire the flamethrower into the pillbox and motioned him away.

Archibald slid down the slope, while the Japanese soldier with the submachine gun charged up the opposite side. Reaching the top, he aimed his submachine gun at Archibald and the Bren gunner.

Archibald raised his rifle to shoot and heard a loud *whoooooooosh*. The flamethrower's burst engulfed the Japanese soldier in flames. Some of the napalm burning liquid hit Archibald causing an inconceivable burning pain.

I'm on fire—burning—got to get my clothes off!

He ran for the swamp, screaming and ripping off his clothes. A mate reached out to him.

Out of my way!

Looks of horror.

GOT TO MAKE IT TO THE WATER. STOP THE PAIN!

Then he passed out. Rushed to the field hospital, Archibald's life was saved by a surgeon experienced in treating napalm burns. His helmet had protected the top of his head, but his exposed right side, from his face to his right knee, had been burned in blotches. The surgeon quickly treated the third- and fourth-degree burns over twenty percent of his body by removing dead tissue and replacing it with biological dressings and a few skin grafts. He ordered intravenous narcotics for pain and antibiotics to control infection. A week later, Archibald was in a burn treatment center in Queensland.

*   *   *

"He's just a salesman. *I am* the manager, not him," Wing-yuen said to his son Sam Kee.

"Mr. Jeffreys is more than a salesman, Father. He has three white men working for him now."

"They don't work for him, they all work *for me!*" Wing-yuen said nearly shouting.

"Work *with* him, then," Sam Kee said. "He understands how to wholesale our products to white customers better than we do and deserves more money!"

"I understand the business better than Mr. Jeffreys does. It is you who doesn't understand our business. No, I will not pay them more money than they are worth. If they want higher union wages they can work for a union. I can hire another man to do Mr. Jeffreys's sales work."

"He's been with us for over two years and has done a good job. I don't understand why you won't pay him more."

"You have become too friendly with him. He is using you

against me. It is not your job to represent Mr. Jeffreys. Do you know what he is asking for?"

"More money. He said it was a fair request considering the business he's brought in."

"He's asking too much and is trying to strong-arm me. He said that if I don't pay him what he wants, he'll tell people that he doesn't own the business—that I do."

"Why should you care about that? It *is* your business. It's not illegal."

"You still don't understand, after all the times I've explained it to you. We would lose white customers. The unions could come down on us for paying lower wages. The government could come after us. He can cause us a lot of trouble. I will pay him some more, but I won't be taken advantage of!"

In June 1944, Wing-yuen fired Mr. Jeffreys after they had an argument. Neither man would confide in Sam Kee the real reasons for their dispute. A month later, Wing-yuen hired a new sales manager. By the end of September, Sam Kee felt that the white sales office situation was finally returning to normal. One evening, when Wing-yuen had not returned home by ten o'clock, Sek-leih called the office. When he didn't pick up the phone, she assumed he was on his way home. At eleven o'clock, when he he hadn't returned home and didn't answer the phone, Sam Kee drove to the chicken plant.

He found his father lying on his back in the chicken processing area of the plant. He was lying on a three-foot-square metal drainage grate. Sam Kee knew his father was dead as soon as he saw him. The color was drained from his face, and he was staring unblinkingly at the ceiling. His mouth was open and jaw slack. He wasn't breathing. Sam Kee ran to the office and called the police and then called home.

The police report said that there was no evidence of foul play. The plant had not been broken into and there were no signs of a fight. It appeared that Wing-yuen had gone to the chicken processing area and slipped on the greasy floor, cracking the back of his skull on the metal grate.

Later, when Sek-leih found bruises on the upper part of his right arm, the police said the bruises could have been caused in any number of ways having nothing to do with the accident.

Sam Kee thought his father's death was accidental until Mr. Jeffreys walked into his office unannounced three months later. He was with two large, mean-looking men whom he introduced as "business partners," but did not give their names.

"I was very sorry to hear about your father's accident, Sam Kee," Mr. Jeffreys said. "You know him and me had our differences, but I respected him. You received my sympathy card, I'm sure, but I came here today to express my condolences in person.

"You and me are friends. You've told me how your father never taught you the business. Word is that you are losing your white customers, and your business isn't doing too good. I want to help you out. You know I know the business and can get back your white customers. I'm going to make you a fair offer for the business that you can't afford to pass up. It's more than the business is worth right now, and I'm only offering more because you and me are friends. I advise you to take it."

Sam Kee thanked him and said that he would discuss it with his mother, who was the other owner of the business. Mr. Jeffreys said he needed an answer in one week, because "my business associates are real impatient."

Sam Kee discussed the offer with his mother Sek-leih and his sister Lin Yee, age eighteen and a first-year student at the University of Sydney. He did not tell them that the offer was made in a threatening way. Nevertheless, Sek-leih sensed that her son was frightened. She never believed that Wing-yuen's death was accidental and did not want to endanger the life of her only son.

"I never liked the business, Mother," Sam Kee admitted. "It's smelly and disgusting. I can never get the smell out of my clothes. The offer seems fair to me."

"We still own our land and the market gardening business," she said. "What do you want to do about that? You don't seem to like the gardening business either."

"Father was the business man. I've always been satisfied with a simpler life and spending time with my friends. I'd like to open a good restaurant in Chinatown where I can work with the chef and greet the customers. I've always liked cooking."

"I'd like that," Sek-leih said. "With the sales money we could buy a building in Chinatown and live above it. I've never liked Botany. We aren't accepted here. Most of my friends live in or near Chinatown."

"I could walk to Sydney University from Chinatown," Lin Yee said.

"We will let our market garden manager run the gardening business and always have fresh vegetables for our restaurant," Sam Kee said enthusiastically.

Sam Kee sold the chicken business to Mr. Jeffreys. By March 1945, the family had purchased a building on Dixon Street in Chinatown and moved into its second-floor, four-bedroom flat.

*   *   *

The Australian army carried out a series of campaigns in 1944 against isolated Japanese garrisons on the islands of New Britain and Bougainville and along the north coast of Papua New Guinea. In April 1945, Harvey was among the Australian and American forces being assembled on the island of Morotai for an Allied offensive to recapture Borneo.

Shortly after Harvey arrived on Morotai, he received a desperate-sounding letter from Katie dated January 22, 1945. She wrote that their son James had been stolen from her humpy in the fringe camp by the police when she was in town buying groceries. The Aborigines Welfare Board said he was "neglected." The real reason, she wrote, was that she and others wouldn't move back into Murraroo Mission. She begged Harvey to come home to get their son back. Referring to him as a "war hero," she knew they would listen to him.

Harvey's request for leave to return to Australia because of a family problem was denied. He talked to the Professor, who assured him that there had to be a mistake and helped him write a well-written, reasoned letter to the Aborigines Welfare Board in Sydney.

Seeing Harvey looking unusually despondent as their landing craft approached the beaches of Balikpapan, Borneo, the Professor got up and squeezed in beside him.

"You're worried about your son, aren't you, Sarge?"

"Yeah. I was hopin' ta get a telegram or a letter before leaving Morotai."

"It's too early. It'll take at least a month for our letter to get there and find the right department. Then it will take some time for them to correct their error and write or telegram you back. I bet you'll get it in a few days once we get settled in Balikpapan."

Harvey fretted. "But what if they can't change things?"

"You have to think about staying alive right now, Harvey. You can't do anything for your son over the next few days. Think about staying alive for him."

The American navy had pounded the port town before the Seventh Division landed. Smoke billowed from a burning oil refinery, blackening the sky. The enemy had moved most of its forces to defensible high ground in the jungle outside of town. The battle for the oil-producing area took the month of July. Sporadic fighting continued right up to August 15, 1945, when Japan surrendered.

On August 27, Harvey received a special delivery letter from the Aborigines Welfare Board. He carried it with him for a day, afraid to open it. When he returned to his barracks, he found a quiet spot, opened it, and read:

25 July 1945

Dear Sergeant Harvey Hudson:

With reference to your inquiry contained in your letter dated 21 April 1945, we have reviewed the case of James Hudson, of no fixed address, New South Wales. We find that the Aborigines Welfare Board acted, pursuant to the Aborigines Protection Act of 1940, subject to the Child Welfare Act of 1939, Section C.4.b. and the state policy of assimilation, in the best interest of James Hudson when, at the age two years and six months, the state accepted him as a ward.

The Aborigines Welfare Board established to the satisfaction of the Children's Court on 9 April 1945, in hearing number CCJ7854, that said child, James Hudson, was living in a deplorable condition and was neglected by his parents, necessitating the State to intervene on behalf of the child's welfare. The child has been adopted by approved parents.

In the interests of the child and adoptive parents, the public record has been sealed. Under The Aborigines Protection Act of 1940, it is a violation of State law for an Aboriginal parent or a relative to attempt to communicate, in any manner, with the adopted child.

As provided in the Child Welfare Act of 1939, it is the responsibility of the parents to provide for the welfare of their child, regardless of any extenuating circumstances or obligations. The absence of one parent for military service does not lessen that responsibility.

Sincerely,
Rufus William Sledmere
State Examiner

Harvey slumped. This was what he had expected. He lowered the letter to his lap and wept silently, blaming himself.

I've never even seen my son. The same thing is happenin' ta him that happened ta me. Why didn't I go home to visit him when I could've? Was I afraid of bein' a father? Or maybe afraid of bein' reminded that I'm an Aborigine . . . ?

I'm important here, but just a good-for-nothin' ward of the state on Murraroo Mission. I only feel good with my army mates. They need an' depend on me. Is it only because of the war? Am I tryin' to be white? Am I ashamed of bein' a black? I should be ashamed of how Aborigines are treated, not because I am one. What's happenin' to me is not fair—jus' because I'm an Aborigine.

Harvey showed his company commander the letter and asked

for emergency leave to go to Sydney to appeal in person to the Aborigines Welfare Board. His commander read the letter and sat Harvey down to counsel him.

"This seems like a terrible injustice, Sergeant, and I'm very sad
that this has happened to you. However, you have to remember
that it's not just Aborigines that have had their children placed in
institutions. White children are also sometimes neglected by their
mothers when their husbands are away. You have to find out more
about how your wife was minding the boy.

"You've proven that you're an exceptional soldier and a natural leader, Harvey. Your Aboriginality is less important in the army
than in civilian life. I think you have a great future with the army. I
tell people that you have a quiet commanding presence about you.
In fact, I've been thinking about recommending you as a candidate
for Officer Training School. Or, if you like, you could go to Japan
as part of the occupation force and attend Officer Training School
after that.

"Would you like either of those assignments?"

"What about my son, Major? I can't just forget about him."

"I know it's hard, Sergeant, but what can you do? The case is
closed. He's already been adopted. All you can do now is ruin your
future."

"I'll have to think about it, Major."

"Let me know soon, Sergeant. I have to submit a list of volunteers for the occupation force by the end of the week. I can't in good
conscience approve your leave to see you go to Sydney and get in
trouble, now can I?"

Harvey left feeling confused. He thought hard about it for
three days.

The major means well, but he don't understand Aborigines are
treated different . . . worse than poor whites. He don't know. We
don't have no rights. We can't say nothin'. They can do anythin' they
want ta us. We can't defend ourselves 'cause the system's against us.
Am I a man or not? Do I have a family or not? I'm tired of this kill-
in'. The war's over. All me mates will be goin' home. I want ta try an'
help my people somehow—startin' with my own son! I have ta do

what's right, or I can't live with meself. I owe it to Katie, 'cause I've treated her bad, sendin' money ain't enough.

Harvey applied for a discharge, which he received in Greta Army Camp, New South Wales, on December 17, 1945. The next morning he boarded a train to Sydney to reclaim his son.

Chapter 5

Populate or Perish

Harvey changed trains in Newcastle before proceeding on to Sydney. During the three-hour trip, the closer he got to Sydney the more pessimistic he became. He reread the letter from the Aborigines Welfare Board over and over again.

He went over the sequence of events in his mind. It's been eight months since the Children's Court allowed my son James to be taken from Katie. The boy was adopted by "approved parents" before the July 25 date of the letter to me. He's been livin' with these people fer at least five months, and probably longer. What chance do I have of gettin' him back? Next ta none! Why am I puttin' meself through this?

By the time Harvey arrived at Wynyard Station in Sydney he had lost his resolve. Nevertheless, he threw his duffel bag over his shoulder and headed for the Aborigines Welfare Board on Macquarie Street near Parliament House. Although officially discharged from the army, he was dressed in his sergeant's uniform in the hope that it would help him make his case.

It was a balmy summer afternoon in December. The sky was vivid blue with an eastern front of billowing white clouds out over the ocean. As he walked up Martin Place, he was drawn to an empty bench in front of the General Post Office building. He felt vulnerable and did not know how to act at the Aborigines Welfare Board. He looked at the World War One ANZAC Cenotaph.

Should I go in with my hat in my hand?—beggin'—or *demand* that they give my son back because it ain't right what they did while I was servin' me country? He began to think how he would approach it if he was leading a patrol.

I'm ordering meself to do this. Can't demand nothin' 'cause I don't 'ave the force. This is a search mission, without the destroy. Search out some information: Why'd they take the boy? Did Katie abandon him? Did another man, maybe livin' with Katie, mistreat 'im? Did he really git adopted, or is he sittin' in some orphanage? If he's in an orphanage, can I git 'im back, now that I'm out of the army an' will be able ta raise him? Who adopted him?—whites probably. If he's adopted, do the white people want ta keep him? 'cause maybe he's a problem. I won't get no answers if I don't stand tall an' make 'em listen up. Bear down just enough ta git their attention, but not too much. Let 'em know I can hurt 'em, but don't make 'em call the police.

Feeling that he had a plan, Harvey walked with renewed confidence toward the Aborigines Welfare Board.

As he entered the board's building, a rush of worries hit him. It was nearly three o'clock on a Friday afternoon. What would he do if Rufus Sledmere, the examiner who wrote him the letter, had left early for the weekend? Could he ask to see someone else? Where would he stay over the weekend if he had to return on Monday?

Harvey smiled at the receptionist and asked to see Mr. Sledmere. "Do you have an appointment?" she asked.

"I received this letter from 'im," Harvey showed her Sledmere's name on the bottom of the letter, "and wanta thank him for writin' me."

She called Mr. Sledmere on the intercom. "A Sergeant Hudson has a letter from you, Mr. Sledmere, and would like to thank you for writing him."

Mr. Rufus William Sledmere entered the reception area from a side door. He approached Harvey with his right hand extended, while saying in a booming voice:

"*Sergeant* Hudson, my pleasure, *what* can I do for you!"

His appearance and outgoing and jovial countenance reminded Harvey of a movie scene in a German beer hall where a large man
sang boisterously while swinging a huge beer stein from side to side.
He was three inches taller than Harvey, but out-of-shape and sport-
ing a large beer belly. The buttons of his suit coat appeared ready to
burst. He had thinning blond hair and pinkish full rounded cheeks.

Harvey shook Sledmere's large, soft, meaty hand and showed
him the letter he had received from him. Smiling, he started to read
the letter, then frowned, took a better look at Harvey, read a bit
further, and handed the letter back to him.

"What's the purpose of your visit, Sergeant Hudson?"

The thought passed through Harvey's mind to say: I want my
son back! But instead he said in military staccato, as if he were speaking to a superior "I-like-to-ask-some-questions, sir, if-ya-please."

"You know I don't have to talk to you about this, don't you? In
fact, it's kind of against the law for you even to inquire about it. Are
you aware of that?"

Remembering that the letter said something about this, Harvey looked at the letter in his hand and said, "What's done is done.
I can't find me boy, sir. I just 'ave a few questions, if ya please, sir."

Sledmere, who had not served in the war, felt he owed this re-
spectful Aboriginal sergeant some consideration.

"All right, Sergeant, I was about to leave for the day; however, I
can give you five minutes. Follow me."

Harvey followed him through a door and down a long aisle with
desks and offices on either side. It appeared that most of the employees had left for the weekend. They walked past a bank of vertical files,
past a woman behind a desk, and into an office. Sledmere indicated a
seat for Harvey and then stepped back out of the office to say something privately to his secretary. Harvey looked out the window at an
expansive view of The Domain and Sydney Harbour. Stepping back
into his office, Sledmere sat down behind his desk and said:

"Go ahead, Sergeant."

Harvey explained that he had served continuously in the army
since April 1942, and had been discharged only yesterday. He was
looking forward to being a civilian and had come to talk to Mr.

Sledmere as the first thing to do in his new life. He had no home leaves in 1942 and most of 1943, because of the desperate fighting he was in on the Kokoda Track and in Buna-Gona. When he could have visited home later, he instead taught jungle fighting because his commander had asked him to. He intended to tell him that he fought on after that and had never even seen his son before he was taken, but Sledmere interrupted his monologue.

"This is all very interesting, Sergeant, and I applaud your service, but it's not a *question*. You've already used up your five minutes. Do you have any questions? I have to be going."

Taken aback, Harvey said, "Is my son adopted?"

"That's what the letter says, doesn't it?"

"I just wanta make sure," Harvey said.

"Yes, for many months now."

"Is there much chance that the people who adopted 'im will give 'im up?—if they don't like him, I mean, or if there's a problem?"

"There's no chance of that, Sergeant. It doesn't work that way. Once the child is adopted, the adoptive parents have full responsibility for the child . . . as if the child were born to them."

Looking down at the letter, Harvey said, "How was the boy neglected enough ta take 'im away from his mother?"

Sledmere placed his hands on his desk and pushed his chair back. "Ahh, now you're getting into an area I can't discuss with you." Raising himself to his full height, he looked down at the seated Harvey. "I wasn't involved in the action, Sergeant, the Children's Court determined there was abandonment, the adoption has taken place, the case is *closed*. Now I've been very patient—"

Harvey rose from his seat so suddenly that Sledmere pulled back and fell backwards into his padded office chair with a loud *thump*. With both hands on Sledmere's desk, Harvey bent forward over the desk and said in a rock-hard frightening voice:

"I *have* a few more questions. It's *not fair* what happened. I *served* my country. My son *shouldn't been taken* away from my wife."

"*Mr. Sl-Sledmerre?*" his secretary asked in a quaking voice from the door.

Harvey turned his head toward her.

"*Now, Betty!*" Sledmere answered, and she rushed away.

Harvey stepped back. He had not touched the man, but he had gone too far. Still, before he was forced to leave, he had to get some answers. In one quick fluid motion, he rounded the desk and went for Sledmere, who cringed in response. Harvey slammed one hand on an arm of his chair and brought the other down hard on top of the chair and put his face next to Sledmere's.

"Did my wife, or anyone else, mistreat the boy or injure him in any way?"

"*I don't know!*" Sweat streamed down Sledmere's fat face.

"Why was he taken?"

"He was *neglected*, living in terrible conditions in a fringe camp next to the mission—inadequately cared for!"

"Who said?"

"The police. They took the child from a humpy. No one stopped them; he was *abandoned!*"

"Where was my wife?"

"*I don't know!*"

Harvey heard a loud commotion down the hall and knew he was in trouble. He sprang back into his seat and turned his head to see Sledmere's secretary leading a policeman and several men in suits.

As they entered the office, Sledmere rose from his chair, steadied himself on the desk with one arm, and pointing at Harvey.

"*Arrest him!* He attacked me!"

Harvey raised his arms with his palms up expressing mock surprise. "I didn't touch 'im, we were jus' talkin'."

"Did he hit you, Mr. Sledmere?" the policeman asked.

"Betty, tell him," Sledmere said.

"He was threatening Mr. Sledmere," she said.

"Stay calm, Sergeant," the policeman said to Harvey. "Stand up—don't be gettin' yerself into any more trouble."

Harvey knew not to fight when he couldn't possibly win. He rose to face them.

"I didn't do nothin'."

"We're arrestin' you for disturbing the peace, not assault," the policeman said. "We'll let the judge decide that. Turn around now and put yer hands behind yer back—don't be doin' nothing stupid."

At the jail, a jailer told Harvey that he would see a judge the next morning. On Saturday, he was taken to a holding pen in the courthouse where he waited all day. The same jailer took him back to the jail for dinner.

When the jailer placed Harvey in a cell for the night, he said, "You'll have to wait until Monday morning to be arraigned, Sarge, because the courts are closed on Sunday. It's your bad luck to be arrested on a Friday—not a good day to be arrested, Sarge."

Monday afternoon, Harvey was brought before a judge. The arresting policeman was there. However, the plaintiff, Rufus William Sledmere, was not.

The judge said, "I've reviewed your case, Sergeant Hudson, and assigned a clerk to look into it. The court has determined that while you physically threatened the plaintiff, Mr. Sledmere, a public servant of the Aborigines Welfare Board, you did not assault him. It appears to the court that there are extenuating circumstances. The Aborigines Welfare Board has decided to drop all charges against you, subject to three conditions."

"Thank you, yer—"

"Hold on," the judge interrupted Harvey. "Let me explain the conditions. You must agree not to go back to the Aborigines Welfare Board to seek further information or redress regarding the adoption of your son. Second, you must apologize to me for your conduct, and I will pass it on to the plaintiff. And finally, you must agree, as provided by the law, that you will not attempt to find or contact your child. Do you agree to these three conditions?"

Knowing that he had no choice, Harvey said, "Yes, I do, yer Honor. And I apologize to Mr. Sledmere fer pressin' him fer information. He's a nice man."

The judge was impressed by Harvey. He thought of his own young son and wondered what he would have done if his son had been taken while he was away fighting in the war. He had read the file and knew that James Hudson had been adopted by a childless white couple, the Bennetts, who lived less than three miles away in the upscale neighborhood of Bellevue Hill.

"If it's any comfort, Sergeant Hudson, I can tell you that your son has been adopted by a childless, well-to-do, white couple who are sure to give him an exceptional upbringing and education. You are free to go, Sergeant, and I wish you a happy Christmas with your wife."

* * *

"How's Archie today, love?" Nigel asked Wilhelmina as he entered the kitchen after a day at the office. He and Wilhelmina were seeing a gradual improvement in Archibald's demeanor over the past three months. They hoped he had finally progressed to the point that he could accept his disfigurement and go on with his life. Nigel had never admitted his fears to Wilhelmina, but several times over the past two years, he had been afraid that Archibald might commit suicide.

"He's had another good day. After lunch, he shared one of his poems with me. There's no doubt in my mind that his writing poetry is therapeutic and one of the reasons for his improvement, although I wish he wrote less morbidly."

Archibald's deep depression had returned briefly after an unsuccessful ninth operation when the doctors told him that the right side of his face could sustain no further cosmetic surgery. Family members tried to accentuate the positives of his operations. They assured him that the surgery had greatly improved his appearance and praised the eye surgeon who had partially restored sight in his right eye. They emphasized how fortunate it was that the left side of his face was untouched by the flamethrower's fiery napalm.

Hearing faint voices downstairs, Archibald presumed that his father had arrived home, marking the beginning of the high point of his day—the evening family meal. Undoubtedly, his ten-year-old sister Lydia would tell entertaining stories about her day, and his father would discuss current events, followed by listening to the evening news on the radio with his father. It was a welcome respite from his grinding daily routine of burn treatments, dressing changes, physical therapy, and naps when painkillers induced lethargy. Doctor and hospital visits were less frequent now, and there was no longer the need for a full-time private nurse, which meant that he had more time to read, listen to the radio, and write poetry. On the other hand, it also meant that medical science could do no more for him.

Archibald dressed for dinner and combed his hair in the mirror. As he did, he saw his two-sided Janus face looking back—handsome on the left side and disfigured on the other. The skin grafts on the right side of his forehead and cheek had healed with whitish scars along their edges. Second-degree burn spots and blotches on his forehead, nose, chin, and throat were an unnatural pale pink color and glassy smooth. The right side of his surgically restored lips produced a crooked smile. His hair had been saved by his helmet but the hairline had been burned back into an irregular line. He had no right sideburn and the ear was deformed. His heart sank every time he saw the shocked look of revulsion when he turned his face toward someone from his handsome left side.

"One good sign is that he hasn't blamed the doctors for months," Wilhelmina said.

"Although, I agree with him on that point," Nigel said. "They shouldn't have built up his hopes if they couldn't deliver. I think the scars are little improved, if at all."

"Not so loud," Wilhelmina whispered, "he might hear you. The doctors said the scarring and discoloration will become less evident with time. That's what we need to stress to Archie."

Nigel wished he had not raised the subject and reminded himself that Wilhelmina was with Archibald every day. He softly touched her on the shoulder. "I'm going to have myself a Foster's before dinner. Shall I make you a shandy?" She nodded yes.

Archibald's recuperation and self-consciousness about his appearance resulted in him spending most of the past two years in his room. An outpatient nurse had provided burn care by applying lanolin and other emollient creams to control drying, cracking, and itching of the skin grafts transplanted from healthy parts of his body. She helped him exercise to reduce scar formation and disabling contractures over his right elbow, knee, and hip and manage his pain with pills.

Wilhelmina had engendered Archibald's interest in poetry when she saw him reading Rudyard Kipling's *The Light That Failed* about an artist going blind, while being spurned by the woman he loves. She introduced him to a collection of Kipling's poems including the inspirational poem "If-" that lifted his spirits. Shortly thereafter, he asked to read from her library of poetry, searching for stimulating poems to his liking.

Wilhelmina's interest in poetry began shortly after marrying Nigel, when he showed her a trunk of family heirlooms, including jewelry, and told her that she could choose anything that suited her fancy. She found a leather case at the bottom of the trunk full of handwritten poems by Nathaniel Armstrong, the ancestor who had started the family line in Australia. Appreciating his poetry and realizing its historical significance to the family, she took it upon herself to have the poetry printed and bound with an aim toward having it published.

Wilhelmina dried her hands on a towel and looked seriously at Nigel.

"Archie mentioned again that he's thinking of taking English literature courses at a university. He's interested in becoming a writer."

"I hope you didn't encourage him this time," Nigel said. "I haven't had a chance to talk to him about it yet."

"I don't want to *discourage* him, if it gets him out among people."

Nigel thought to himself: He wants to write in solitude rather than work in an office where he'd have to face people.

"Remember . . . ever since he was this tall," he indicated a height of four feet, "he liked to go to construction sites with me and watch buildings going up. It was always his intention to join the company. I expected that he would earn a business degree before joining me."

Wilhelmina reassuringly placed her hand on his arm. "I know, Nigel, but let's get him into uni first and then go from there. This is the first thing that's interested him in two years. Please encourage him."

"What about his aversion to showing his face? He can't seriously expect to attend classes with half of his face bandaged."

"Initially, he sees that as the solution. He's become comfortable wearing the bandages to the hospital. We have to support him in this, Nigel."

"Of course I will . . . I know this is about him, not me."

"Ask to read his poetry and tell him it's good, and that he should take writing courses if that's what he wants to do. We have to build up his self-confidence in every way we can, to get him over feeling sorry for himself."

"You forget that I know all about feeling sorry for oneself: I went through that myself."

"Well, *don't* mention that to Archibald again," she scolded. "You know he feels your loss of the lower part of your leg *in no way* compares with his facial injuries."

"Darn it, Willa, I not saying it does! Don't be so protective of him. I'm not a boofhead. I'm just saying I know how it feels to suffer a serious war injury."

Wilhelmina would not moderate her point. "But no one *sees* that you're impaired in any way."

"Ah, let's drop it," Nigel said in disgust. "I'll talk to him about his poetry. I want him to get better as much as you do."

After dinner, Nigel and Archibald retired to the parlor to listen to the evening news on the radio. During an advertisement, Nigel said, "Your mother tells me you've been writing poetry."

"Yeah. I'm learning different ways to write it."

"Can I read any of it?"

"You never talked much about poetry, Dad. I didn't know you liked it."

"Actually, I don't know much about it. Your mother's the poetry buff. Of course, I can recite a few lines of 'Waltzing Matilda' and other Banjo Patterson's poems like 'Clancy of the Overflow' and 'The Man from Snowy River,' but that's not saying much—everyone can. I like some of Henry Lawson's poems too and a few of our ancestor's, Nathaniel Armstrong."

They stopped talking to listen to a news broadcast. The Minister for Immigration, Arthur Calwell, had proposed free and assisted-passage schemes to greatly increase the number of immigrants to Australia. The announcer summarized Calwell's speech:

"The minister said that Australia recently faced its gravest peril, and a third world war is not an impossibility. Without adequate numbers our country may not be held in another clash of arms. We are but seven million people and hold three million square miles of this earth's surface.

"Calwell announced that the days of our isolation are over. We must populate or perish. The government intends to bring to these shores the best possible immigrant types from the United Kingdom. Australia will also admit a limited number of displaced persons from the European continent as part of a humanitarian program. It is the minister's hope that for every foreign migrant there will be ten people from the United Kingdom. His ambition is to reach a target of twenty million as soon as possible."

Archibald said flippantly, "We should be offering free passage to Americans too."

"That was a curious statement," Nigel said. "Do you think Americans would come?"

"The ones I met during the war seemed to like it here. A lot of them married Australian girls—but I don't know how many stayed. It's just that we should be cozying up to America rather than returning to Britain, which didn't help us much during the war. America's running the new world order now."

"Although our historical ties are with Britain," Nigel said, "I have to agree with you. Britain let us down. We were saved from invasion by the Americans. It's as if we are unaware that our country is situated closer to America than England, or for that matter, that we live within the Asian sphere. Did you hear the crack that Calwell made about Asian immigration?"

"No."

"When someone said something like 'It's wrong to allow in only whites while we keep out all of our Asian neighbors,' he wisecracked, 'Two Wongs don't make a white.' I think that pretty much says it all. I seriously doubt that I'll see any change in our White Australia Policy during my lifetime."

Another interesting news report garnered their attention. When the news ended, Archibald rose while saying "Good night,

Dad, I'm tired." Nigel had intended to discuss Archibald's interest in attending a university, but decided the time wasn't right. He wished him a good night's sleep.

*   *   *

"Let's name 'im Paul like the apostle Paul," Harvey proposed to Katie. He was standing at the bedside of Katie who was nursing their newborn child.

Harvey and Katie had decided in early 1946 to try to have another child. He told her that he did not care whether she had a boy or a girl, but he secretly prayed every night for a boy to replace the son he had lost. His prayers were answered on March 13, 1947, with the birth of a healthy baby boy.

The first months back at the Murraroo Aborigines Mission had been very difficult for Harvey. Eight days after his reunion with Katie, on New Year's Eve, he learned from two mates that she had lived with another man for more than a year in the fringe camp. When he confronted her with this information, she did not deny it.

"Me bin think ya no come back," she said. "Ya in army, no visit 'ome fer three an' half years! Ya bin write *only* six times. Me bin think ya no come back. In yer letter ya say teachin' jungle fightin' better than visit yer own one-year-old child!"

"We was married!" Harvey said. "I was sendin' ya money!"

"The fringe camp bin scary, Harvey, an' me wit' yer baby. Me mate bin good bloke. 'Im bin make humpy an' git food an' git wood fer James an' me. One time, cops bin raid, 'im hide James!"

"Did ya lay wit' him?"

"What d'ya think!"

"Where was he when James was stolen?—where was you?"

" 'E bin go end of '44. Me ain't hear no more 'bout 'im. Me bin by meself when James stolen. Woman mate watch James when me go to Gura for food. Cops take James an' woman mate baby."

Angry, Harvey moved out of the married quarters and into single men's quarters. He turned again to the church for solace. He found comfort there, as he had many times before, since he was a boy in the Methodist Danedine Mission. Besides dealing with his resentment toward Katie and the loss of James, he had to contend with horrendous dreams of killing and mayhem. He studied the Bible every evening and sought the counsel of the pastor. Gradually, he came to forgive himself and Katie. They reconciled and moved back into married housing.

Harvey continued to suffer bouts of despair due to the terrible living conditions in the mission, which he saw more clearly than ever before, now that he had seen some of the world and had a different perspective.

He mulled over their situation: Our people 'ave little freedom an' are controlled in belittling an' petty ways. The superintendent acts like a prison warden. Everyone has ta sign in an' sign out. Visitors allowed only on weekends an' 'ave ta be scheduled ahead if they want ta stay overnight. Livin' quarters can be searched, day or night, usually fer alcohol. Break the rules an' out ya go, or rations cut, or already meager pay reduced. They don't respect us an' treat us like children. We can't demand respect an' fair treatment, because we don't speak good; because we ain't educated enough.

He wanted a better education for Paul and decided to discuss it with the elders.

"Our children are receivin' only five years of education compared ta twelve years fer white children. Their kids start school at age five, and our kids don't start until seven or eight. We grow up speakin' poor English an' don't learn how ta write good, read, or add and subtract as good as whites."

The elders decided to ask for additional years of education for the brightest Murraroo Mission children who wanted more schooling. Harvey was chosen as the best person to make the request. He discussed the matter with the schoolteacher and later with the superintendent. Both gave him essentially the same answer: The Aborigines Welfare Board was funded for only five years of education and that was that.

Harvey unintentionally got into the inadequate education issue with Katie one evening when he nonchalantly corrected her English. They were in their bedroom. Katie had just changed Paul's diaper and was playing with him on their bed, while Harvey repaired a broken window sash.

While tickling Paul to make him laugh, Katie playfully said, "Me love me little baby."

Harvey said without thinking, "You use 'me' too much . . . it sounds bad."

"What ya mean?" she said.

"You should say *my* baby, not *me* baby."

"Paul b'long ta me. Paul *me* baby."

"That's not right," Harvey said. "*My* goes right before something that's yers. I learnt that in the army when the drill sergeant kept tellin' me it's *my* weapon, not *me* weapon. We 'ave ta use better English if we want our son ta speak good."

"Ya say, ' 'Em blokes me mates,' " Katie said.

"That's 'cause I don't own 'em like *my* weapon. See the difference? And you should say *I* love my baby."

Katie thought for a moment. "You an' me love Paul—yeah?"

"Yeah," Harvey said as he continued to work on the repair.

"Then orright, Paul me baby; me love Paul."

"No, the rule I learnt is when it's just one person ya use 'I love Paul.' With two people, it's 'You an' me love Paul.' "

"Rules, rules," Katie concluded, "they don't make no sense."

"I had ta learn them rules meself," Harvey said. "I want my son ta learn 'em right in school."

*   *   *

She smiled at me again as we entered poetry class, Archibald thought to himself. I think she likes me. I should say something to her when we walk out of class today. Say something like . . . I enjoyed your poem yesterday—oh god, that's pathetic! . . . I could tell her I'm having trouble with the assignment and ask for some help—twenty minutes at the student union. Tell her I'm asking her because she's the best student in class. It'd be hard for her to say no to that. Then I could see how she feels about me. Maybe she's just being nice . . . though she doesn't seem like the type who'd feel sorry for me. Unless

I'm misreading her. The class only meets two more times .... There's a lot I like about her , , , sweet ... exotic ... petite ... delicate ... and intelligent. She has a friendly demure smile.

Archibald was in his second year of English literature at the University of Sydney, having entered in 1947 at the age of twenty-four. The woman he was attracted to was two years younger than he, but two years ahead of him in the university, because of the time he had spent in the war and convalescing. Archibald continued to wear bandages on his face, even though it was healed. He had convinced himself that he was not vain, but needed the bandages to retain moisturizers and to protect his scars from sunburn.

In the middle of his first year, Archibald had joined the university newspaper to practice his writing skills. By then, he was well known around campus as the "bandaged veteran." Within a couple of months, the paper dismayed him with a draft of an article explaining who he was and how he had been burnt by a flamethrower while attacking a pillbox. The article was entitled, "Hero with a Bandaged Face." Although he pleaded with them not to print it, the editors, thinking he was being modest, went ahead with the admiring character piece. After the article, he became something of a celebrity on campus. The bad part was the speculation of when his bandage would come off.

Friends at the newspaper began to sense his dilemma and cautiously encourage him to take off the bandage around the office, where sunlight could do no damage. Others said his scars were a badge of honor. Once he was comfortable without the bandage around the office, he began to venture to the occasional class without it. The responses he received to his scarred face were not as bad as he had expected. Some people were repulsed and avoided eye contact, as he had expected, but most people did not seem to care. A few acquaintance and teachers made a point of being engaging. Archibald became increasingly emboldened. Then he became attracted to Lin Yee Fong in his poetry class.

Lin Yee had wondered, like many other people in her class, what was under the bandage of the tall, handsome, sandy-haired veteran. She was intrigued because he was obviously interested in her. She was flattered and embarrassed when she would catch him looking at her from across the room. When she did a reading, he would ask a complimentary question. She had never had a boyfriend and had resigned herself to a life of professional service. In spite of her resignation to a single life, she began to have romantic thoughts about him.

He was one of only a few men in the poetry class. She liked his sensitivity and appreciated his intelligence; however, his poetry was harsh and disturbing. He was suffering from his war experiences and wounds, she concluded. She wouldn't have admitted it, but she wanted to soothe his troubled heart. The day he came to class without his bandages, she was distressed by the extent of his burns. The contrast between the handsome side and scarred side of his face was hard to take. Then she thought of the courage he was exhibiting and respected him. She wanted to know him better and decided to let him know that she liked him.

Archibald thought his ploy had worked. Lin Yee agreed to help him with the assignment. They walked together to the student union talking about the assignment. Once seated, Archibald turned the conversation around to her. He learned that she was twenty-two and was taking the poetry class as a break from medical school classes. She was in her fourth year of a five-year course. After two years of residency, she would become a doctor. He also found out that she had read the article about him and liked his poetry and the serious subjects they explored. But most importantly, before she rushed to her next class, he determined that she liked him. They agreed to meet in the library on Saturday at ten to work on the assignment together.

While Lin Yee walked to her next class, she glowed with the confirmation that he liked her, and she liked him. After only a few minutes of talking to him, his scars seemed less glaring. He was deep and sincere in his sentiments. He wasn't boastful when he let her know that his family had developed many of the office buildings downtown and owned hotels in Bondi and Manly.

As Archibald dressed for their meeting Saturday morning, he considered wearing his bandage but then rejected it. Today would be a further test.

They studied together for two hours and went to a restaurant for lunch. She was even more intelligent than he had thought, but more importantly, she radiated a centered, positive attitude that made him feel comfortable with her. She didn't seem concerned about his scarred face.

"Byron is one of my favorite poets," Archibald said.

"He's a bit too gloomy and melancholy for me," Lin Yee said.

"You probably wouldn't like Vernon Watkins and David Gascoyne then. They're apocalyptic poets in the difficult years between the wars," Archibald said. "They were the product of the World War One and the Great Depression and anticipated man's folly that led to World War Two. It's kind of heavy, still I like what they have to say."

"I'm not familiar with their poetry," Lin Yee said.

From her look, Archibald concluded that he was depressing her and should change the subject.

"I imagine being a doctor would be very demanding. There aren't many women doctors. Why do you want to become a doctor?"

"I'd like to open a practice to serve the Chinese community, which doesn't feel entirely comfortable with the healing methods of western doctors. Eastern doctors approach healing differently from western doctors."

"With different pills and remedies, or maybe with the use of herbs?" Archibald asked.

"Eastern doctors try to heal the mind as well as the body."

"Even if a fellow comes to you with a knife wound?" Archibald said with a playful smile.

"Well, while treating the person physically, I'd ask how he was wounded by the knife. Did someone wound him? Did he do it to himself? Was it an accident? . . . does he consider the wound disfiguring? These are the kinds of questions that would concern me beyond the wound itself. Most likely, a western doctor would treat the wound primarily, apply antibiotics, stitch him up, and send him on his way." She thought to herself, this is probably what happened to you. "I think Christian doctors have a more external way of treating illness and wounds."

"External?"

Embarrassed, Lin Yee said, "I'm not making sense. I'm sorry. It's very difficult to explain. Please, let's talk about something else."

"No . . . I'm sorry. Really, I'd like to hear more about your approach. I've talked to a lot of doctors over the past four years, but I've never talked to one about this."

"I'll try . . . I've never had anyone draw me out about the kind of practice I'd like to provide. You're the first. Our instructors don't teach what I want to do. And it's not psychiatry either. My approach is so entangled with my spirituality and eastern upbringing."

"From what little I know about psychiatry, I don't believe in it. But there I go again, interrupting. Please go on."

"I was raised in eastern philosophy and attitudes, which are different from Christian western ways of looking at things. I'm a Buddhist. I believe that 'self' is not the body you happen to occupy. Your body is just a vessel, it's not who you are. Christians don't look inward first; they seem to look outward, to community, for self-definition and healing. Buddha taught us to look inside ourselves first and heal within. He said that individual ego is a popular delusion; the objects with which people identify themselves, such as family, social position, wealth, possessions, education, and even appearance are not their true selves."

She saw an absorbed look on Archibald's face that she assumed was befuddlement.

"I'm sorry. I'm still not making sense, am I?"

"Yes you are," Archibald said keenly. "I'm just thinking. You're saying that westerners place too much emphasis on superficial appearances rather than focusing on the soul of a person."

"Yes . . . I mean . . . well, I think 'soul' is different than 'self.' Soul says something about afterlife, I think. And I don't mean to say that afterlife isn't important either, because it is, but each individual is responsible for development of his 'self' or *karma*—others can only help . . . or hurt. And . . . only the mind deserves to be called the 'true self.' So to improve the 'true self' and enjoy good health, one must first discipline and control one's own mind by realizing that misfortunes comes not from the east or from the west, but originates within one's own mind."

She paused and folded her hands on the tabletop and looked down at them. "I'm sorry. It's difficult to explain, but I think the mind is more important than the body."

Archibald was touched by what she had said. He had never thought about his personal responsibility to mend his own mind in quite this way. He thought how he had placed his great misfortune in the hands of the doctors to return his good looks to him and blamed them when they didn't.

"I think I understand what you're saying, Lin Yee. I've never thought of personal responsibility quite that way. I like the idea that misfortune doesn't come from the east or west, but is formed *within* one's own mind. It's all about perception, isn't it? It's how one *perceives* his misfortune. If a person convinces himself that misfortune is, for instance, not misfortune, but a character-building exercise and life goes on, then he can still believe in himself, and it doesn't matter so much what other people think."

"Yes, that's what I'm trying to say," Lin Yee said. "A doctor can help a patient heal himself and develop inner self-contentment, regardless of the condition of the vessel."

After they parted, Lin Yee knew she had a "boyfriend." She decided not to tell her mother or brother, because Sam Kee was sure to forbid it. As head of the family, he could not allow her to date a Caucasian.

Archibald did not want to tell his parents that he was dating a Chinese woman for fear of their disapproval. Wilhelmina, however, sensed that Archibald had a girlfriend by his improved mood and because he had stopped wearing his bandages to university. She did not say anything to him for fear of disrupting his recovery.

Near the end of the school year, Archibald asked his father if he could live in his grandparent's vacant house in exchange for renovating it. Nigel had inherited it from his mother Anne who had died in February 1946, a year after his father Peter passed away. A family had been renting the house until recently. Nigel was pleased that Archibald wanted to get back into construction. They walked over to the house on Sunday afternoon to look at its condition and to assess the work to be done.

As Archibald stood in the kitchen looking out into the un-fenced back yard, he saw a little boy climbing in their shade tree. He called to his father.

"Hey, Dad, look at this. There's a little kid climbing around Granddad's Moreton Bay fig tree."

"Well look at that. I wonder where he came from?"

From forty feet away, they could clearly see that he was a dark-skinned boy around six- or seven-years old. He had placed a three-foot-high box beneath the lowest drooping limb to climb up into the tree.

"Granddad wouldn't be too happy about this if he were here," Archibald said. "He gave that tree loving care when he planted it."

"Oh, it's well established now; that little boy won't hurt it. Where's he from? That's what I'd like to know. Let's go talk to him."

As they walked out the back door of the house, the boy froze in his climbing. He had nowhere to run. He looked at them like a robber caught in the act.

Nigel almost laughed out loud at the frightened look on the boy's face, but then realized he was staring at Archibald's scarred face and might panic and jump out of the tree, injuring himself.

"G'day little fellow, are you having fun?" he said with an overly jovial tone of voice.

"Yes, sir—is this your tree?" he asked while still looking at Archibald's face.

"Yes it is."

"Mr. Wakefield said I could climb it."

Standing beneath the tree and looking up at the boy, Nigel con-firmed his first impression: The boy was an Aborigine. "Oh, so you knew my renter. Where are you from?"

The boy started to lift his arm when they heard a call from the adjacent house.

"HELLO there, so sorry, that's my boy." A blond-haired man in his mid-thirties came hurrying toward them. "I'm sorry, are you the owner or renter of the house?"

"I'm the owner. I'm Nigel Armstrong and this is my son, Archibald."

The man shook hands with both of them. Looking at Nigel, he said, "You must be Anne's son."

"Yes, I am."

"I bought our house just a few months before your mother passed away. She was such a nice stately lady."

"Yes, she was. Sadly, I think she found it difficult to go on after Dad died."

"We were good friends with your renters William and Susan Wakefield. We were disappointed when he was transferred to Melbourne. Their son Freddie and my James were the best of mates. That's James up in your tree."

Looking up, Nigel said, "It's nice to meet you, Jamie."

Before the boy could answer, his father said in a conciliatory tone of voice: "We like to call him James rather than Jamie."

Without a moment's hesitation, Nigel said, "You can climb in our tree anytime you like, James."

"Thank you, sir," the obviously well-mannered boy said.

"Oh, I apologize. My name is David Bennett." Then he pointed toward his house. "And that's my wife Mary on the back veranda." He beckoned her. "Mary, dear, come here and meet our neighbors."

She walked over and they exchanged greetings. She was also a blond, very attractive, and appeared to be a bit older than her husband. Nigel and Archibald were thinking the same thing: The Aboriginal boy is obviously adopted.

In the course of getting acquainted, Mary said, "We moved here to have a large yard for James to play in. He and the Wakefield's son, Freddie, almost lived in your tree. It's the only one around that they could get up into. The Eucalyptus trees are all too tall. Are you going to be moving into the house?"

Nigel looked at Archibald, who said, "I'll be moving in shortly and making some improvements." Seeing the concern in David's eyes, Archibald added, "but I'll be sure not to be too noisy or messy."

"Oh, don't be concerned about that," David said. "It will be nice to have you as our neighbor."

"Do you have any children?" Mary asked.

"No, I'm not married yet."

Nigel caught the "yet" and the hopeful way Archie said it. Nigel made a mental note of it to discuss with Willa. Archie's attitude had been up for months; perhaps there was a romantic interest in his life that accounted for his desire to move into his own place.

*   *   *

Nigel wondered how best to tell Willa. He expected that she would take it poorly: the girlfriend being Chinese and all. He couldn't imagine why Archie hadn't told him that he had a Chinese girlfriend.

I've always been a supporter of diversity, Nigel thought, and have nothing against the Chinese. I don't care if she is Chinese as long as he's happy. And God knows he's been happy lately. I knew something was going on. And she's a doctor . . . well I'll be darned.

Nigel had found out that Archibald was dating a Chinese woman when he had stopped by his renovation to drop off some material samples. He wasn't in, so Nigel left the samples leaning up against the front door. While walking toward his car, he met David Bennett coming home from work.

Nigel asked him how his day went, and David asked him if it was his company constructing on office building on George Street. The construction sign said the developer was the "Armstrong Development Company." As they were about to part, David said:

"Oh, I enjoyed meeting Archibald's Chinese girlfriend and found her remarkably lovely and composed. She must be an exceptional woman to be a doctor."

Nigel didn't know what to say, so he said, "Yes . . . she must, thank you," and rushed off saying "dinner is waiting."

That evening, after dinner, Wilhelmina went into the library to read. Nigel went into the parlor to listen to the radio. After the news was over, he decided the time was right to tell her. He walked around the parlor rehearsing what he would say to her.

Wilhelmina could tell the moment Nigel walked into the library that he had something important to say. His ponderous look gave him away. He smiled, and she closed the book in her lap, giving him her complete attention.

"What is it," she said.

Realizing he had already botched his approach to the subject, Nigel affected an upbeat voice.

"Well, Willa, I think I know why Archie has been so happy—he has a girlfriend!"

"I was sure of it!" Wilhelmina said gleefully. "How did you find out?" She placed her book on the side table. "Did Archie tell you?"

"Actually, I wish he had. No, his next-door neighbor mentioned it to me in passing. I had gone over there to drop off—"

"How would his neighbor know, and we wouldn't? Where did this neighbor meet her?"

"Well, I don't really know. He didn't tell me, but she's a doctor. Isn't that grand?"

"A *doctor*." Wilhelmina made a grimace. "How old is she?"

"The neighbor, David Bennett, didn't say. I've only met him twic—"

"Nigel, please! I don't care about the neighbor. How do you know this doctor is Archie's girlfriend?"

"Well how many girlfriends do you think he has!"

"Don't get snippy like that."

"Then don't cut me off, Willa! I have to tell you how I found this out, but you won't let me."

"Go ahead—just get to the point."

"Ahh damn."

"Don't swear. Go on."

"The neighbor simply said that he had met Archie's *girlfriend* who was 'remarkably lovely and composed'—his words—who is a doctor. I didn't know what to say, so I thanked him for his compliment and got the hell out of there."

"You don't think Archie had this woman in his house, do you?"

"Where else would a neighbor likely meet her? Although that doesn't mean anything, because Archie may have been simply showing her his renovations."

"What kind of woman would go to a man's house unescorted?"

"Wilhelmina, aren't you the proper one," Nigel said, smiling, almost laughing. "This is 1949, not 1919, when we were courting.

He's not a boy; he's twenty-seven. I'm happy for him."

"You have to talk to him, or I will! It's not right. The neighbor saw what was going on. That's why he mentioned it to you."

"That's *not* why he mentioned it to me."

"If Archie had any respect for this woman, he wouldn't have taken her to his house. That's why he hasn't told us about her."

"That's *not* why he hasn't told us about her."

"Then why do *you* think he hasn't told us about her?"

"I imagine it's because he thinks we won't like her."

"Why wouldn't we like her?—because she a doctor? I'm not against women who want to work. I didn't work because I thought it was more importan—"

"She's Chinese."

"*What!*"

"The neighbor said she's Chinese."

"That's not possible!"

"Certainly is. We do have a few Chinese left in Sydney, you know."

"*Nigel*, this is *not* a joke! He's been seeing this woman for months—what if he wants to *marry* her."

"That's fine with me; I'd be happy for him. Remember, my parents were upset when I wanted to marry a woman of German descent right after World War One."

"German *and* Dutch descent, and *only* on my father's side. You married a *white* European, not another race from China."

"She's a doctor, for heaven's sake. Her family must be well off. She sounds sophisticated. You should be happy he's found an accomplished woman—or any woman! You were afraid that he wouldn't *ever* marry."

"But what about the children! They'd be half-breeds."

"Ahh, so that's what this is all about. You think you couldn't love your own grandchildren. You'll love them all right. I can tell you that."

"I'm not thinking of me. It would be so difficult *for them*. They wouldn't fit in. I hated my name Wilhelmina, because it wasn't an English name. I asked my teachers in each grade to call me Willa.

What do you do if you're half white and half Chinese? My goodness, I wouldn't wish that on anyone."

The next day, Saturday, Archibald began his day early to work on one of his many renovation projects: removing rotted areas from the bottom of the wood balusters in the balustrade around his back veranda.

At nine o'clock, James looked around the corner of the house and saw Archibald working. He smiled, gave a little wave, and walked toward him.

"Here comes My Little Assistant," Archibald said.

A pattern had developed over the past months of James wanting to help him. Archibald gave him little jobs that a seven-year-old boy could handle. This morning, Archibald showed him how to use a screwdriver to dig out the loose, disintegrated parts of the balusters down to good wood, then Archibald would follow him to do the final work. Over the months, James had been a real help with such jobs as pulling weeds, digging up the planting beds, mixing in topsoil, carrying in building materials, removing old carpet, sanding, and sweeping up. Archibald often left jobs that required four hands until James joined him. When he did not have a job for him, James would climb the fig tree, play nearby, or just sit quietly watching him work. It appeared that he didn't have any playmates in the neighborhood after Freddie had left. Archibald did not mind the boy's presence. He was courteous and quiet company.

When they were first working together, James persisted in calling him "Mr. Armstrong," even though Archibald asked him repeatedly to call him "Archie." When Archibald finally explained that they were mates working together and should use friendly first names, James said that his father made him call all grown-ups "Mr. and Mrs."

Archibald said that he didn't want to go against his father's rules, but they needed to find a solution. They discussed what to do and agreed that James would call him Archie when they were alone and Mr. Armstrong when his dad was near.

"That way, James, you will be doing what your father wants and doing what I want too." James was comfortable with the solution that became part of their special relationship.

A month after that, as they worked opposite each other, James paused in his work and asked, "What happened to your face, Archie?"

"I was a soldier, James, in the war. When I was fighting, I was badly burned. The doctors saved my life and did the best they could to fix my face, but they couldn't make it like it was before. Still, I'm glad to be alive."

James simply said "Me too" and never asked again.

While they sat on the veranda working on the rotted balusters, David Bennett rounded the corner, waved, and gave out a hearty "Good morning, Archibald."

David was a bit too stuffy to call him Archie. Archibald called him David, because he seemed uneasy with the more familiar "Dave."

Walking up to Archibald, he saw James.

"James—there you are. I wondered where you were. If he's bothering you, Archibald, just say so. I've told him not to make a pest of himself."

Seeing James's hurt look, Archibald said, "Oh no, I can't do without My Little Assistant." He turned back to James. "Can I, James?"

James smiled back at him and went back to work.

"James, go have some breakfast with your mother," David said in an authoritative voice. "I have something I want to discuss with Mr. Armstrong."

"I already ate, Dad."

"James, that's 'I have already *eaten,* not *ate*—you know that."

"Yeah, I forgot, Dad."

"Now go play somewhere else for a while, so Mr. Armstrong and I can have a private conversation. Go on now."

"Can I come back later, Mr. Armstrong?"

"Sure. There are a lot of posts left to do." As the boy moped past, Archibald said, "Seeya later, James."

After James was out of hearing range, David said, "Really, Archibald, please tell me if he's being a pest. I don't want him to be a problem for you."

"He's no problem, David. In fact, sometimes I can use two extra hands, and he's a good little worker once I show him what to do. I've been thinking of paying him in some way, if it's all right with you."

"Don't do that, *please*, it would only legitimize something I'm against. Mary's the one that allows him over here—against my better judgment. But if he's really no problem for you . . . ?" He took a long portentous pause and looked questioningly at Archibald, waiting for his response.

"He's no problem."

"Then I'll allow him over here until I hear otherwise from you. Actually though, that's not what I came over here to discuss. I think I may have let the cat out of the bag yesterday."

He described his chance meeting and how Nigel had acted surprised when he mentioned Archibald's girlfriend. "Since we've seen Lin Yee over here several times before you introduced us, I just assumed that your father knew her."

The look on Archibald's face told him otherwise.

"I blundered, didn't I?" David said.

"It's not your fault, David, it's mine. I've let this go too long. We've been talking about telling our parents for weeks; now we have to do it, that's all. Did you happen to mention she's Chinese?"

"I'm afraid I did. *Blast!* I didn't mean 'afraid,' there's nothing wrong with her being Chinese—I mean—I told your dad she's a doctor and a lovely woman. I'm sorry I spoke out of turn—my big mouth."

That evening, Lin Yee and Archibald agreed that they had to tell their families. Archibald wanted them to go together to tell his parents and her family, but Lin Yee said that would be too confrontational. She suggested that it would be best for each of them to tell their families separately. He disagreed but gave in to her wishes.

They had already professed love to each other; even so, they decided to tell their parents that they were good friends and only dating. In the course of the conversation, Archibald said he wanted to marry her. Crying with joy, she said she wanted to marry him too. They decided to marry after he completed his university studies in December 1950, but not announce an engagement for several months.

* * *

Lin Yee's brother, Sam Kee, was head of the family. She hoped he would approve her relationship with Archibald. For the past four years, he had talked of his responsibility to arrange the marriage of his single-minded, independent, six-years-younger sister and criticized her for a lack of interest in the husbands his match-making produced. He had recently told her that she was unmarriageable because of her age and higher education.

On the other hand, she thought, he embraced being Australian and a modern man. He called himself a Chinese Australian and took pride in his well-spoken English, western dress, and white Australian friends. He had recently decided to drop "Kee" from his given name, outside his family, to be know simply as "Sam." He had named his first child Edward rather than a Chinese name. The baby boy was nearly six months old.

Lin Yee knew there had never been a non-Chinese member of the Fong family. When Sam Kee had looked for a wife after the war, he considered only Chinese women. In 1947 he had married a Chinatown shop-owner's nineteen-year-old daughter Mei-lan.

If Sam Kee forbade her relationship with Archibald, Lin Yee did not know what she would do. Leaving the family was unthinkable. She decided to make a special offering to her ancestors to ask for their acceptance of Archibald and to request that they encourage Sam Kee to accept her chosen husband into the family.

Sunday morning, Archibald awoke with anticipation. He would tell his parents today, two days after his father had learned of his Chinese girlfriend, before they asked him about her. He called them and asked if he could join them for "Mum's Sunday dinner."

Nigel and Wilhelmina expected, and hoped for, his announcement. He did not disappoint them. They allowed him to tell the whole story of his evolving relationship with Lin Yee with very few interruptions. He stressed how she gave him confidence and a philosophy to go out without his bandages. They could tell that he loved her. When he finished, he was delighted by their wholehearted happiness for him. They hugged him and asked when they could meet this wonderful woman.

Thirteen-year-old Lydia had been asked by Nigel to leave the table when he realized that Archibald was launching into his romance with Lin Yee. She protested that she was old enough to listen, but Wilhelmina told her it was "adult talk" and to leave the dining room. The three of them knew she was sitting on the floor right outside the dining room door where she could hear every word. They did not mind if she heard, as long as she did not speak. At the end of the conversation, she rushed in and threw her arms around her big brother, smothering him with kisses.

Sam Kee was flabbergasted that his unmarriageable sister had found herself a mate. He was amazed that her intended was a member of the rich and well-known Armstrong family, office and hotel developers. His mind jumped immediately to how this could work to his advantage. Then, he thought of the Fong family line and his responsibilities to his ancestors, something that had not been foremost in his mind for years. He told Lin Yee that he had to think on it and would give her his answer in a day or two.

In fact, he had already decided. This was his home and where he would be buried. He was an Australian and had to live by their values. The ancestors would be asked for forgiveness and tolerance, because he could not stand in the way of his sister's happiness.

Over the next month, Lin Yee met Archibald's family, and Archibald met Lin Yee's family. These family meetings deepened their understanding of and commitment to each other.

Archibald had hired workmen to help him finish the renovation of his house more quickly and planned a summer barbecue and housewarming as the ideal way to bring the two families together. They sent out invitations to their families and Archibald's neighbors for the big event to be held on Saturday, February 2, 1950. Archibald sent a special invitation addressed to Mr. James Bennett, My Little Assistant.

The final coat of paint was applied on the walls of the living room on Tuesday the week of the housewarming. The carpet was laid the next day and pictures were placed on the walls that evening. Lin Yee and James helped Archibald dust, run the vacuum, and arrange the furniture on Thursday. On Friday, they added the finishing touches. Lin Yee brought fresh cut flowers to put in vases. Archibald finished an album that showed his snapshots of every major step of the renovation. He placed the album on his four-foot-square glass table that occupied the center of living room seating area opposite the fireplace. Next to the renovation photo album, he placed his prized photo album that displayed his most valued photographs from the time he was a boy, through his war years, and up to the present day.

After all of the guests had arrived and introductions made, Archibald gathered everyone together and took them on a tour through the house. It was a successful way to bring the disparate members of the party together. When the tour was over, he showed them the renovation photo album and encouraged them to go through it sometime during the day.

The party was catered, still Archibald felt the need to act as the barbecue chef. He made a bit of theater of it by putting on his apron, gloves, and white chef's hat while calling everyone together to view the steaks and vegetables displayed on a table in front of the barbecue pit.

"The barbie's been burning for hours and is *just* the right temperature to cook up a fine feast," Archibald announced. "Gather around and choose your steak, or steaks, if you like. We have succulent lamb, veal, and tuna for your dining pleasure. Where's My Little Assistant? Where's James?"

His mother Mary pushed James forward. He stood in front of his mother wearing a shy, excited grin.

"Ladies and gentleman, this is Mr. James Bennett, My Little Assistant throughout the entire renovation. I couldn't have done it without him. He should be first in line. Come on over here, James, with your mum, and start the queue."

As James pointed to a veal steak, Archibald bent down and said with quiet sincerity "Thanks for all your help, little matey."

The day was sunny and the temperature ideal for outdoor dining. Tables had been arranged in the back yard under the shade of the Moreton Bay fig tree. By midafternoon, everybody had eaten their fill, and the party had divided into small groupings. Archibald and Lin Yee were conversing with Sek-leih and Mei-lan, who had kept to themselves and appeared uncomfortable.

Mei-lan's husband, Sam Kee, had not sat with her. He was too busy talking to everyone else, including the caterer and his staff. Handing out his business card to each person to whom he spoke, he invited each to a free meal at his Golden Dragon Restaurant in Chinatown. He even sat down and seemed to have an animated conversation with James. Everyone called him "Sam," because he had instructed his sister Lin Yee to introduce him as Sam rather than Sam Kee. When Mei-lan finally obtained Sam Kee's attention, she and he went into the house to find the guest lavatory.

Suddenly, from the back veranda came a loud yell "*WAAAA!*" that made all heads turn in its direction. Sam Kee was bounding down the veranda steps yelling "*Look at this everybody!*" He was holding Archibald's prized photo album and hurried toward Archibald. "Come here, everyone, come here, look what I've found! *This is amazing!*"

He created such a scene that even the catering staff were drawn to him. Sam Kee had his finger in the album and flipped it open on the table in front of Archibald. He pointed to a photograph of an old, wizened Chinese man in a beautiful robe and two boys, one Chinese and the other Caucasian. He excitedly tapped his finger below the picture of the Chinese boy. "That's me." Then pointing at the Chinese man. "And that's my grandfather Min-chin. And that must be *you*, Archibald!" he said, pointing at the Caucasian boy.

"*You* were that little Chinese kid?" Archibald said. "Well I'll be *damned!—oh, sorry.*" He covered his mouth with both hands while looking at James.

Everyone guffawed at Archibald's faux pas.

"It was taken the day the Sydney Harbour Bridge opened," Archibald said.

People all started talking at once. Through the excited hubbub, Nigel said, "I took that picture with Archibald's first camera, a box camera. We had just bought it for him." Only those near heard him.

At the same time that Nigel spoke, Archibald was saying loudly, "This is unbelievable—just great, great." Then he exclaimed, "We must be about the same age, Sam, I'm twenty-seven."

"I'm twenty-nine," Sam Kee said. Then he started to laugh, "Ha-ha ha-ha ha-ha—this bodes well for the future."

Wilhelmina had worked her way to the table and was looking at the photograph over Lin Yee's shoulder. Lin Yee was bent over closely studying the robe.

"Oh my, Lin Yee, what an exquisite robe your grandfather is wearing."

"I was only six or seven when this picture was taken, but I can clearly remember this colorful embroidered silk robe displayed in our sitting parlor," Lin Yee said as she stepped aside, so Wilhelmina could take a closer look. "I think it was a gift from an old friend of his."

Wilhelmina lowered her face close to the photograph. "Your grandfather looks just like one of those imported Chinese figurines you can buy at David Jones department store."

* * *

At the relatively young age of forty-one in 1954, Harvey was permitted to sit with the elders in their determinations, a great honor in recognition of his community service and worldly experience.

The Murraroo Aborigines Mission was going through one of the worst periods of food shortages since the Great Depression. They were particularly short of meat. The superintendent, Kevin Thorne, blamed it on a variety of reasons that he said were beyond his control. For months the elders found ways to conserve and supplement the mission's food supply, wholeheartedly approved by the superintendent, but still their rations were inadequate.

The elders began to hear stories that Boss Thorne was unloading food from his truck at various commercial establishments in Gura. Harvey did not trust the superintendent and arranged for two young men to follow him when he left the mission. They confirmed that the superintendent was selling meat to Merrill Quality Meats and foodstuffs to Gura Grocery in town.

No one knew what to do about it. If anyone complained to the police, the superintendent would deny the allegation, as would the butcher and grocer, and the complainer and his family would pay a heavy price. Harvey was no more anxious to put himself in jeopardy than anyone else. Paul was seven and had just begun school. In a meeting of the elders, Harvey proposed a strategy to expose the superintendent's thievery.

"We 'ave ta let the Super know that we know what he's doin' without no one bein' pointed out as the leader. If he knows we all know his stunt, then ma'be he'll stop."

"How we do that?" asked one of the elders.

"We'll write 'im a note," Harvey said. "It'll say 'We know what you're doing' with the names of the butcher and grocer on it an' tack it to his door at night."

"Sounds like a dingo stealin' chooks at night," an elder said.

"No choice, we 'ave ta play the Super's stunt better than 'im." Harvey said. "He's lyin' an' cheatin' us. If we face 'im man-ta-man he'll make us pay. We don't have no choice but ta sneak around ta get what's fair."

The elders agreed to Harvey's proposal. Harvey wrote the note, and a young man tacked it to Superintendent Thorne's door at night. Over the next two weeks nothing changed. Harvey thought the note may have been poorly tacked and lost or possibly misconstrued by the superintendent, so a week later he wrote a second, more explicit note and tacked it securely to his door himself. Again nothing happened and the food shortages continued. The elders met to discuss whether anyone had seen any changes at all in Boss Thorne.

One of the elders said, "Me wife work fer Boss Thorne. She say he act different, not friendly like an' no trust her. I think boss know."

"I think he's kinda remote an' distrustin' too," Harvey said.

Others agreed, and the consensus was that Thorne had received the message.

"He doesn't care that we know," Harvey concluded. "'Cause he holds all the cards and thinks we can't do nothin'.'"

The elders grumbled on indignantly without direction or conclusion until an elder made a proposal.

"We ought ta go on strike to demand more food. No workin' 'til we git more food."

Several elders agreed, but others did not because it was illegal. An argument ensued with some name calling.

"Hold on!" Harvey said. "If we strike, police will be called an' strike leaders will be arrested, that means all of us. We should do 'secret' work slowdown that will show the Aborigines Welfare Board that Boss Thorne can't run the mission. Over next two weeks, more an' more of us git sick 'cause there's not enough food. When the work isn't done, the boss will lose his job. That's the way ta hurt 'im an' maybe get rid of 'im. He can't punish everyone 'cause we don't 'ave enough ta eat."

The elders agreed to Harvey's secret work slowdown. A schedule was drawn up of people willing to act sick. The slowdown started three days later. By the end of the second week, Thorne was angry about what was going on. He talked to the elders and others, but no one let on that it was more than illness from lack of food. Boss Thorne, though, was not a man to be underestimated.

A week later, at two o'clock at night, Harvey was awakened by loud banging on a door several units down and shouts of "PO-LICE, OPEN UP!" Harvey rolled out of bed and pulled on a pair of trousers. He could see torches passing by his window and heard many men's voices.

Katie asked him, "What's happening? Why are the police here?"

"I'll find out," Harvey said.

"What's wrong, Daddy? Harvey's son asked as he entered their bedroom. He reached out for his father.

Sweeping him up, Harvey said, "Let's look out the front window."

Before Harvey reached the window, banging on his own front door startled him.

"POLICE! Open up or we'll break it down!"

Harvey put his whimpering son down and answered, "AL-MOST THERE—COMIN'." He turned on the living room lights and opened the front door.

Harvey was blinded by three or four torches shining into his face. He shielded his eyes. "What do ya want?"

An unseen hand grabbed his arm and pulled him onto the front stoop.

"You're under arrest," a voice said from the darkness below him.

Harvey could not see the man who spoke.

"Fer what?"

"Step down here, *now!*"

Harvey felt a strong grip on his left arm. It took all of his self-control not to break the hold and strike out with his right fist, but he let himself be pulled down the two steps. His arms were drawn behind his back, and in the process, he was tripped up and fell face first to the ground. A knee landed on his back, and he was handcuffed. Several men grabbed and lifted him to his feet.

Harvey could hear Paul crying and screaming *"Let my Daddy go!"* and Katie shouting *"What he do?"*

"Ah shut up, gin, and go inside before we arrest you too!" someone shouted.

Harvey was crammed into the back seat of a police car with two other men—both elders. In the morning at their arraignment, the judge said:

"An informant has identified you three as the leaders of the work strike. Now you three elders know it's illegal to lead a strike on an Aboriginal station." He looked at them. "Well . . . don't you know that?"

"There's no strike, Your Honor," Harvey said, "people are gettin' sick 'cause we don't have enough to eat."

"That right, boss," one of the other elders said.

"I have a sworn statement from Superintendent Thorne indicating that you three organized a work strike. Even if you weren't the ringleaders, you are elders who will serve as examples that you cannot make trouble for the government without consequences. The Aborigines Welfare Board is doing the best it can for you people with limited resources."

The judge asked if they had anything to say for themselves before sentencing. Realizing that they were all going to go to jail, Harvey decided to expose the superintendent.

"We've been starving at the mission 'cause Superintendent Thorne been stealin' our food an' sellin' it ta Merrill Meats an' Gura Grocery."

Superintendent Thorne, who was seated in the courtroom, jumped up and shouted:

"*That's a bloody lie!* Your Honor. Libelous!"

"*Sit down*, Thorne. Another outburst like that and I'll have you ejected and charged with contempt of court. Now *sit down!*"

Looking at Harvey, he said, "Finish what you were saying."

"We elders decided ta carry out a work slowdown 'cause our children an' old folk are starvin' an' gettin' sick, Your Honor. We got it all written down with dates an' names an' how he's doin' it. The Aborigines Welfare Board should look into the crooked things Superintendent Thorne is doin'."

"If you have all this evidence of wrongdoing," the judge said, "why didn't you give it to the Welfare Board and ask them to investigate before going on strike?"

"Investigation takes time, Your Honor, or ma'be just hurt us with nothin' happenin'. Boss, I mean, Superintendent Thorne, would throw us off the mission straight away. None of us wanted to be hurt by the Super, Your Honor. We thought that if we let him know his stunt was up, ma'be he'd stop."

"Well, you've gone about this all wrong," the judge said. "Now, you'll have plenty of time to write your letter to the Welfare Board, because I'm sentencing each of you to three months in the county jail with hard labor."

"When you complete your letter, submit it to me. I'll forward it onto the Aborigines Welfare Board and ask them to investigate."

Harvey wrote his letter to the judge, who contacted the welfare board, as promised, and asked them to investigate the allegations. An investigation resulted in the dismissal of Superintendent Thorne. Harvey's time in jail was softened by frequent visits: Katie and Paul, the elders, and other people from the mission. Harvey felt it was the most purposeful and satisfying episode of his life. He and the other two elders served their three-month sentences and returned to the mission where they were greeted as heroes.

The only thing that worried Harvey about the entire affair was the effect it had on Paul. He seemed strangely detached, suffered frequent nightmares, and carried fear in his eyes.

* * *

"I'm very pleased that we are introducing you to the Sydney Symphony Orchestra, Lin Yee," Wilhelmina said, as she craned her neck to talk to her daughter-in-law in the back seat of the car. "Especially tonight. You are sure to enjoy Handel's *Water Music* and maestro Eugene Goossens's dramatic conducting." Wilhelmina was fond of Goossens, an Englishman of Belgian descent. "He's done wonders with the orchestra since he took over seven years ago."

She looked at Nigel, who was driving, to see if he had anything to add. They were on their way to attend the concert in Centennial Hall, the largest space in the Sydney Town Hall and in the entire city. She looked back into the rear seat again.

"We were lucky that your father was able to get tickets for you. Goossens has made the symphony so popular that all the tickets are sold to subscribers at the beginning of the season. Mr. Moses, the general manager of the Australian Broadcasting Commission, who manages the symphony, gave them to him."

Afraid that she was being long-winded, Wilhelmina stopped talking. When no one said anything after a few minutes, Wilhelmina said with a hint of impatience in her voice:

"Well, Nigel, aren't you going to tell Archie and Lin Yee about the premier's call?"

"Premier Cahill?" Archibald asked.

Nigel nodded yes. "He called me this morning to ask me to serve on a committee to oversee the building of a performing arts center in Sydney. As chairman of the Public Buildings Advisory Committee, I'd already received an invitation to the public meeting about the center, but I didn't expect to be named to the committee to get it done."

"That's quite an honor," Lin Yee said "Did you accept?"

"Yes. . . . And it *is* a bit of an honor, actually. I'll be the only private business person on the committee. The other five appointees are government and public-service types."

Wilhelmina turned in her seat and spoke to Archibald. "I expect your father was chosen, in part, because he raised £100,000 through a public subscription appeal as chair of the Elizabethan Opera Ballet Trust."

"Along with Charles Moses, who's much better at it than me," Nigel said. "He's also an appointee to the performing arts center committee, along with Goossens."

"Ah yeah, I remember reading about this in the newspapers," Archibald said. "Goossens has been calling for a new symphony hall at Bennelong Point for the past few years."

"Bennelong Point?" Wilhelmina said. "Isn't that where Governor Phillip built a small brick house for Bennelong, an Aborigine he befriended?"

"The very same," Nigel said. "Goossens has been promoting Bennelong Point as the best site for years. He finds it intolerable that Sydney doesn't have a proper concert hall, and his orchestra has to compete with other users of Sydney Town Hall. He's right. And his constant pestering of the council and state government has embarrassed them to the point they're finally doing something about it."

"Where is Bennelong Point?" Lin Yee asked.

"When you're standing at Circular Quay looking toward the harbor, it's the peninsula of land to the right," Archibald said. "There's a small park on the water and a large tram depot behind it. You know, Dad . . . lately, the newspaper seem to be calling for an 'opera house' more than a 'concert hall.' Is the Elizabethan Opera Ballet Trust attempting to add some class, to raise us out of the muck of our cultural backwater?"

"Well, I don't know about the muck," Nigel said, "but the 'opera house' name does seem to be catching on, although it shouldn't. It's really a performing arts center for the symphony, opera, ballet, and a drama theater. Opera enthusiasts are pushing for an opera house, because there's no place in Sydney to stage a grand opera. The stage in the town hall is too small for grand opera, there's no way to make stage set changes, and there's no orchestra pit."

Impressed, Lin Yee said, "I must say, Dad, you *should* be on the committee with all you know about this."

Chapter 6

The Cultural Cringe

Archibald and Lin Yee were invited to dinner at the Bennett's house one Friday evening. When they arrived, Mary apologized that David had been delayed at the office and was on his way home. He drove into the driveway ten minutes later.

"Hi, Archibald and Lin Yee. Sorry for not being here when you arrived. I had an emergency at the office regarding the upcoming SEATO meeting. Where's James, Mary?"

"He's in his room, dear," Mary answered.

"He *should* be down here, talking to our guests. I'll get him. I need to change my shirt anyway." Starting up the stairs, he paused and asked, "Mary, ask Alice to fix me a Scotch and water with ice, won't you? I'll be back down in a couple of minutes."

A few minutes later, David came down without James and thanked the maid Alice for his drink. He joined Mary, Lin Yee, and Archibald in the living room.

"What are you doing for the SEATO meeting?" Archibald asked.

"I have the food service contract for the three-day conference. That means providing food and drink for ministers and aides from eight different countries."

"Eight?" Archibald said.

"Yes. Australia, Great Britain, United States, France, New Zealand, Thailand . . . that's six, hmm." David thought. "Ah, Philippines and . . . Pakistan—that's eight."

"Is the purpose of SEATO to fight communism in Asia?" Lin Yee asked.

"Yes, to contain communism, as I understand it, and to promote economic cooperation," David said. "It's called the *Southeast Asia Treaty Organization* because Korea is stabilized now, and they want to support freedom in Indochina, Malaya, and other places in southeast Asia."

"That's why Menzies recently sent troops under SEATO to Malaya, to fight the communist insurgents there," Archibald said.

The maid came in and announced that dinner was ready to be served and then walked toward the stairs to let James know.

"That's all right, Alice, I'll tell James," David said as he hurried toward the stairs. Muffled angry voices were heard from upstairs, and David came down with James.

"Hello, Mr. and Mrs. Armstrong," James said with a warm friendly smile to Archibald.

Throughout the dinner, the twelve year old was distant and preoccupied. He asked to be excused after the main course, saying he did not want dessert, and went up to his room.

Strange, Archibald thought—*no dessert*—and he usually wants to talk to us for a while. This past summer he was happy and carefree, but since starting his seventh year of school he's been moping around. I haven't seen much of him lately. Probably having growing pains and difficulty adjusting to secondary school.

"It's a comfortable evening," Mary said. "Let's have our dessert on the terrace."

The maid placed the desserts, silverware, and serviettes on a tray and carried the tray out to a table at the far end of the terrace overlooking the garden.

Once seated and started on their desserts, David spoke in an unusually soft voice. "We're having a bit of a problem at James's new school and would like to discuss it with you, if you wouldn't mind. It seems that James has a thin skin and can't walk away from a nasty comment now and then. He's been getting into fights and is in danger of being expelled."

Now I see why we are on the edge of the terrace, Archibald thought, to be out of earshot of James.

"Not *expelled*, David," Mary whispered. "He's been placed on 'notice.' Although, if he has another fight, he could be placed on probation and then expelled if anything additional happens. We've met with the headmaster. It isn't James's fault, really, because some older students have been picking on him, and saying terrible racial slurs. I hate to repeat them, but horrid names like Abo, boong, and nigger."

"Racial taunts are so terribly hurtful," Lin Yee said, "when a young person is trying desperately to fit in."

"That's what I think, Lin Yee. Any young boy would be driven to fight if called such dreadful names," Mary said, looking at David.

"These fellows have been told to stop their harassment, but you know how it is, Archibald, older students will just keep it up when they see a student can't take it. I was called fatty, and other boys were called poofters and twits. It's all part of a boy growing up, Mary." David shook his head. "I told James he has to rise above such comments and show them it doesn't bother him. They'll stop if they see a stiff back. We all had to learn how to deal with schoolie bullies."

"He has a special burden of being an Aborigine," Mary said.

"Part Aborigine," David said. "Look, Mary, he's going through the difficult period of early adolescence. We'll have a bad year or two, then he'll come out of it. You are making too big a deal of this."

"He has his dark color to deal with that he cannot overcome," Mary said.

"So do a lot of other people . . . like reffos—Greeks, Jews, Italians—and other dark-complexioned people. Color is just a thing he has to deal with like other childhood concerns such as being short for your age, or having a carrot crop of hair, or for a girl not being pretty, or having a bad case of pimples for goodness sake. He's confused about life and a bit lost right now, that's all. Don't you agree, Archibald?"

"I felt displaced and lost at his age," Lin Yee said.

"Oh, Lin Yee, thank you," Mary said. "How did you deal with it?"

"It took a while. Th—"

"See Mary," David said.

Mary looked anxiously at David with her index finger in front of her closed lips. "Go on, Lin Yee."

"There was this group of girls who were so mean, they made sport of calling me terrible names, like Chink and Chow and worse, under their breath or right to my face outside of school. So for a while, I didn't want to go to school at all. My father and mother sat me down and told me how they had handled it when they were young, and that this is just the way it is. They said we are Chinese people in a foreign land and must learn to tolerate such bigoted name-calling, because there will always be petty, hurtful people. The important thing is to develop the inner strength based on knowing yourself and being proud of your heritage. The abusive language heaped upon us does not have to humiliate us if you have a clear sense of self-worth. This is part of our Buddhist teaching. They said that most whites are not mean, so seek out those who accept and like you and avoid the bad ones as much as possible."

"But James's problem is he *can't* look the other way, Lin Yee. He says he gets so mad that he can't hold in his emotions."

Looking at Lin Yee, David said, "We've been telling James *exactly* what your parents told you as an adolescent. There will always be bullies and mean-spirited students. Stay away from them. Don't let them get to you. When they call you names just laugh it off. Fighting them will only make it worse. Raise yourself above them is what I tell him. What do you think, Archibald?"

They all looked at Archibald. "Perhaps, we are overlooking something important that Lin Yee just said."

"What?" David said, not understanding.

"This is such a delicate emotional matter," Archibald said. "I don't wish to offend."

"Really, Archibald, we are at our wits' end," Mary said. "Well, at least, I am. I feel completely lost as to what to do. Frankly, we wanted to have this conversation with you and Lin Yee. You have a special relationship with James. He thinks the world of you. And we were hoping to get insights from Lin Yee, like she just gave us.

So please, if you have any thoughts to share, we would appreciate hearing them. Right, David?"

"Yes, please feel free to say anything that you think would be helpful, Archibald."

"Well, I was enlightened myself when Lin Yee said that her parents sat her down and explained the discrimination they faced and how they handled racism." Archibald paused.

"Uh-huh," David said.

"He's saying we haven't faced racial discrimination, David," Mary said.

"Ah . . . well, that's true, Archibald, but as I said earlier, there are all kinds of discrimination. I've discussed this openly with James, color is just one of many differences mean-spirited students can point to."

"It's cultural though, as well, David," Lin Yee said. "I'm proud of my Chinese 6,000 years of culture. Have you helped James to be proud of his culture, or is he humiliated by it?"

"He doesn't think about it, Lin Yee. We've raised him as our son with all the advantages of the white society," Mary said. "He's hasn't once said anything about Aborigines or asked any questions about them. I don't think that's the problem."

David nodded in agreement. "I know it may seem harsh to say it, but honestly and realistically, there's precious little to be proud of as an Aborigine. They're primitive people after all."

"But, still, that could be part of what James is feeling," Archibald said. "When he's called those horrid names, one needs something to grab hold of. If he thinks the names are justified, then he may feel just shame. That would be very debilitating, don't you think?"

"Well, if *shame* is part of his problem, I don't know what we can do about it," David said. "But, regardless, I think he'll get over it as he matures, and thank us for raising him white."

* * *

When Harvey returned to the Murraroo Aborigines Mission after serving his three-month jail sentence, he heard that the new superintendent had ejected two fair-skinned families from the mission. It wasn't long until Harvey was called into his office.

"As the new superintendent, I've been reviewing everyone's files. You appeared to me to be a half-caste who doesn't belong here under the Aborigines Welfare Board's long-standing policy of assimilation. Imagine my surprise when I read your file and found that you had been allowed to return to the mission for a "transition period" following your war service. That was nine years ago! I reckon we've taken care of you long enough, don't you, Mr. Hudson?"

"This is the only home I've known since I was twenty-one years old, Mr. Haswell. My church is 'ere, and my boy's school's 'ere."

"Bob Buckley, the DWO, District Welfare Officer, in Gura can help you. It's his job to assist assimilating families to find jobs and housing in the white communities in this district. Seems to me you should do quite well outside the mission, Mr. Hudson. You knew enough to make sergeant in the army and to get your way around here. If you contact Bob and work with him, I'll give you a couple of months to move off the mission. Good luck."

Harvey went directly from the superintendent's office to the parsonage to talk to Reverend Knapp.

"Is there an appeal process, or some other way my family can stay on the mission, Reverend?" Harvey asked. "It would be hard on my son ta leave school an' 'is friends."

"I don't know of any. This isn't against you personally, Harvey, you know. The federal government has found that the number of Aborigines has greatly increased. While this is a good thing, because it shows that the Aborigines protection policies have succeeded, the government must now get serious about forcing half-castes, like yourself, off government stations and missions and into white communities. They're doing it to reduce costs. I'll try to help you find a job in Gura, so you can continue to serve on the church board and stay in the choir."

While Harvey was in jail, Katie had withheld the bad news that families were being thrown off the mission, so she was not shocked when he told her that they were next. They were both upset by the uncertainty of their future.

"I'll go see Mr. Buckley in Gura tomorrow to see if he can help us," Harvey said.

Almost the first thing Bob Buckley said to Harvey was "Do you have a Certificate of Exemption under the Aborigines Protection Act?"

"Yes, sir. I got it when I served in the army."

"That's good. It will make everything easier and qualify you to participate in the state's Aborigines Dispersed Housing Program."

"Dispersed housin'?"

"Under the state assimilation program, the government is providing funds to help rent and buy houses for Aboriginal families in white neighborhoods, rather than build more projects. However, you have to have a job and keep it to qualify for the housing. So our first job is to find you a job."

"What about my son's schoolin'?"

"With your Exemption Certificate, a job, and a house in Gura, you can enroll him in school in town. He can get more than five years schooling; go all the way through high school if he's able."

Harvey was excited when he talked to Katie about his conversations with the welfare officer. "This could turn out ta be somethin' *good* fer us an' Paul. In town, he can get more than five years of schoolin' an' maybe even finish high school."

Over the next month, Harvey went to three job interviews: two arranged by Bob Buckley and another through Reverend Knapp, all without success. The third interview Buckley sent him to was with an employer who was a former rugby league player. He had played against the Murraroo All Blacks and remembered Harvey as its star player. Harvey's years of maintaining the church earned him the glorified job title of "assistant building maintenance engineer" of a plant that built and maintained mechanized harvesters, which were taking the place of crop hand pickers.

A month later, Harvey, Katie, and Paul left the mission with their few possessions and met Bob Buckley, who presented them with the keys to a partially furnished two-bedroom rental house in a poor white neighborhood in Gura. The Aborigines Welfare Board was supplementing their rent payment. Mr. Buckley walked them through the house.

"Since you're a maintenance engineer, Harvey, I reckon you'll take good care of the place. This dispersed housing is an experimental program, so I'll be looking in on you from time to time to see how you're doing. I have to send a monthly report to the board, ya see.

"Now this is a one-family house, so you can't have anyone one else livin' here with ya—no friends or relatives on a permanent basis. If you want to have anyone stay with you for more than a few days, you have to get my permission. Let me know if you run into any problems. I hope everything works out well for you here."

Harvey and Katie enrolled Paul in Dawson Primary School only six blocks from their house. With Paul going to a white school, Harvey's job working out well, and Katie happily cooking, cleaning, and painting the rooms of their first proper house, they were more optimistic about their future than ever before.

* * *

Wilhelmina was reading a magazine in bed when Nigel came in wearing his pajamas and carrying part of the evening newspaper.

"You know I don't like you to read the newspaper in bed, Nigel."

"I didn't have a chance to read about the Opera House yet. I'm not going to spread it out. I'll keep it folded as I read. I just want to see what it says about Jørn Utzon"—he had phonetically pronounced it as Yawn Ootson—"and his first meeting with us."

"What's he like?"

"Blond, blue-eyed, handsome—the archetypal Dane. He's young, under forty, and very tall; I'd say about six foot four, and slim. Speaks English well enough. I like him. He has an engaging smile and casualness about him that is personable."

"Were you impressed by what he had to say?"

"He's a bit dreamy. Here, I'll read you something he said: "I have made a sculpture; if you think of a Gothic church, you are close to what I have been aiming at. Looking at a Gothic church, you never get tired, you will never be finished with it—when you pass around it or see it against the sky. It is as if something new goes on all the time and it is so important—the interplay with the sun, the light, and the clouds, it makes it a living thing."

"He's a romantic," Wilhelmina said. "What else has he designed?"

"Not much—mostly housing, nothing monumental. He's a relative unknown. Evidently, he has never taken a major building through the construction process. All this would worry me if I thought his building was really going to be built."

"Why won't it be built?"

"Too many problems. Starting with the lack of funds to cover its estimated 5.3£ million cost, which seems too low, by the way, considering those unusual roof shells. I wouldn't know how to build those things."

"Isn't the state going to pay for most of it?"

"No. The Liberal opposition leader Morton won't support it, calling it repugnant to spend this kind of money on the wealthy opera-going set. The appeal fund can't hope to raise the money, especially with this controversial design. Premier Cahill has proposed a lottery, but the opposition is saying it's immoral to fund it through the lower-class's gambling vice. So I expect the project will just die from lack of funding."

"That would be a shame. I think it's an exciting modern design that seems just right for its site. The multiple white roofs will look like white billowing sails on the harbor."

"His whimsical design would be fine for a nautical museum or aquarium but, my goodness, not for an opera house. How can you like it when you thought the Paris Opera House was stupendous? Now that's an *opera house*. I'd like a building that people dress up for and look forward to entering—not this . . . *circus* tent. Actually, I can't take credit for that analogy. Frank Lloyd Wright called it a circus tent."

"How can you serve on the Sydney Opera House Executive Committee if you dislike the design so much?"

"I can't just resign because I don't like the design. Walter Bunning said it looked like 'An insect with a shell on its back, which had crawled out from under a log.' Although, the comment I like the best is 'A team of copulating turtles,' hah ha."

"Harry Seidler called it 'A magnificent piece of poetry,' " Wilhelmina said.

"The controversy swirling around this design is one of the many reasons I'm sure it will never be built."

"If the design is so bad, why did the distinguished panel of four architects select it unanimously over 232 other competition entries and say it was capable of becoming one of the great buildings of the world?"

"Mostly because of the American architect Eero Saarinen. He was the most famous architect on the jury and swayed the others. He arrived late and didn't like any of the shortlisted entries chosen by the other three architect judges. So he went through the rejected entries and liked Utzon's, declaring it the obvious winner. Seems the other three had rejected Utzon's entry because it didn't fulfill the competition requirements: his drawings were diagrammatic, lacked engineering details and dimensions, and didn't include the required perspective of the building. So Saarinen sketched up two perspectives himself, so the other judges could appreciate the brilliance of the design—as he saw it. Saarinen is an ultra modern architect; small wonder he liked Utzon's building."

Seeing a drawing of the Sydney Opera House in the magazine Wilhelmina was reading, Nigel asked, "What's that you're reading?"

"A very interesting article in the literary magazine *Meaning* about Sydney's cultural cringe, which, evidently, we are trying to compensate for by building the Sydney Opera House."

"I'd expect that from a Melbourne magazine," Nigel said. "Though they've got it wrong, the cultural cringe applies to all of Australia. The Brits and Europeans cannot even imagine that the words "opera" and "Australia" belong in the same sentence. They think Australians are rough, crude, and without culture, interested only in sports."

"Well, there's truth in that," Wilhelmina said. "The article goes on to say that we suffer an inferiority complex when it comes to Britain's and Europe's cultures. That we need to develop the confidence and maturity to create a distinctive Australian culture reflecting our peculiar society and environment. I agree with that."

"Yes . . . you would. We *have* to be worldly and sophisticated like our former maestro, Sir Eugene Goossens, who was your favorite person in the whole wide world."

"Why would he take a chance like that?" Wilhelmina said. "He must have a sex problem."

"He didn't expect customs to go through his baggage. The pornography was concealed in sealed folders marked with the names of composers, as if the folders contained musical scores."

"At his hearing, his counsel said he had been forced by threats to smuggle it in for others," Wilhelmina said.

"He could have been blackmailed, I guess. He was secretly involved in an occult sex group in Kings Cross."

"Occult sex group? Ha ha ha. What are you talking about, Nigel?"

"A group that believes in witchcraft, magic, and supernatural sex rites. Group sex."

"Goossens! I don't believe it!" Wilhelmina said.

"It's true! That's why customs went through his luggage. The vice squad was tipped off and waiting for him. They had photographs and letters from the lead witch's coven in Kings Cross that implicated him in their sex rituals. Once a celebrity gets involved in that sort of thing, he's open to being blackmailed."

"This is too much! *Who* told you all this?"

"One of my girlfriends in Kings Cross," Nigel said drolly.

Laughing, Wilhelmina jammed her elbow into his side.

Nigel grabbed his side and feigned injury. "Ohhhh, you broke a rib."

"I'll break a more important bone if you go to Kings Cross!"

"That would hurt you more than me. Well, maybe not. Ha ha."

"Have you ever seen pornographic photos?"

"I saw some during the war when I was in Egypt and Paris."

"What do they show?"

Nigel rolled over onto an elbow and started to untie the top of her nightie.

"What are you doing, you bad boy?" she asked, smiling.

He placed his hand on her breast. "They show things like these."

Running his hand down her front, he placed his hand between her legs. "And a thing like this."

Wilhelmina giggled. "I have problem, I feel a headache coming on."

Nigel growled and said, "I have a problem too—between my legs—that only you can help me with."

"Ooh . . . you're such a piggy."

* * *

It was customary for Lin Yee to have lunch with her brother at least once a week at his Golden Dragon Restaurant in Chinatown. Her busy private medical practice, serving primarily Chinese women, was located on Liverpool Street, on the northern fringe of Chinatown. Their weekly lunch had become their principal time to visit.

"Sam Kee, this *Foo Yung Har* is yummy," she said. "You consistently serve the best food in Chinatown."

"Thanks, but I'm not doing that well financially. I've advertised to whites and added a sign in English and serve quality food, yet cannot attract upscale white customers. They won't come to Chinatown. I can't raise my prices without white customers; therefore, I can't afford to serve the best gourmet dishes I'd like to prepare."

"Maybe you should open another Chinese restaurant outside of Chinatown to try out your ideas. Archie is building an office building on Alfred Street facing Circular Quay. You'd be right there to attract international passengers in ocean liners who may like Chinese food."

"There aren't any Chinese restaurants in the business district. There has to be a reason for that."

"Just because there aren't any, doesn't mean *one* wouldn't be successful. Maybe that's a plus—no competition."

Sam Kee put his chin in his hand, deep in thought. "Do you think Australian businessmen would eat Chinese food in a modern, sophisticated Chinese restaurant?"

"Not twenty years ago, but they would today, if it serves quality food, is classy and clean, and run by an English-speaking, entertaining, and attentive owner like you."

"Sydney *is* becoming an international city with a lot of overseas relationships. I'd bet many foreign businessmen want to eat Chinese food, but their Australian partners don't want to take them to Chinatown. I think you might have a good idea there, Lin Yee."

"I'll talk to Archie and see what he thinks. Maybe he'll give you a break on the rent to get started," she said enthusiastically.

That evening, over dinner, Lin Yee talked to Archibald who liked the idea. He discussed it with Nigel, who thought it was worth pursuing. A few days later, Sam Kee sat in Archibald's office at Armstrong Development Company.

After pleasantries, Archibald showed Sam Kee the second floor space that had been set aside for a quality restaurant to enjoy harbor views. He discussed the rent and conditions, including giving him a "family-member low rent" for the first two years. Then he sat back in his chair to hear Sam's response.

"Your 'family-member rent' for the first two years to see how the restaurant does is a real incentive, Archie, and I appreciate it. I'm really pleased that you think a quality Chinese restaurant makes sense and could be successful. I've always wanted to prepare gourmet food for an upscale clientele. I envision myself as an outgoing Chinese restaurateur welcoming sophisticated business and international diners to his first-class, modern Chinese restaurant serving quality dishes. I think I have the personality for it."

"I do too, Sam," Archibald said encouragingly.

"My idea is to play down the Chinese characters on the building facade. I think this scares away white customers. The name of the restaurant has to say clean, sanitary, and quality food. What do you think of the name Modern Chinese Palace?"

"That's good. 'Modern' is up-to-date, like our building. 'Palace' evokes images of Chinese emperors living in lavish surroundings—first class. It tells you it's a Chinese restaurant without being too exotic. I like the name."

"Here are a few of my ideas. Plenty of glass and lots of light inside so people can see that the restaurant is bright, clean, and cheery. Too many Chinese restaurants are dark, dingy, and foreboding, run by old world people. Do you have a place on the ground floor where I can display enticing photographs of my best dishes in the front window with the names of the dishes below in English to entice people in?"

"Yes, we can do that—it's a good idea."

The menus will also show appetizing photos of my food with large English names beneath and smallish Chinese characters beneath that. I expect some Australian businessmen will bring their foreign customers for Chinese food, but may themselves prefer western dishes. So I'll offer a mixed grill, Chicken Maryland, king prawns, and lamb chops."

"Any fish and chips?" Archibald said with a chuckle.

"Definitely not," Sam Kee said with a smile. "Also, I'll have fresh seasonal flower arrangements delivered daily."

"That sounds like the first-rate, quality restaurant we had in mind for the space, Sam."

"I'll continue to advertise in the newspapers, international travel magazines, on the bulletin boards of the overseas terminals, and probably on the radio."

Over the next seven months, Archibald and Sam Kee worked closely together with Sam Kee's architect to prepare the plans for the restaurant.

*   *   *

Nigel asked Archibald to join him for lunch to try out Sam Fong's Modern Chinese Palace. The hostess was appalled by Archibald's scarred face and was leading them to a table near the kitchen when Sam Kee saw them.

"No, no, Tam-ho, these are *very* important men. This is my brother-in-law Mr. Archibald Armstrong and his father Mr. Nigel Armstrong. They own this building and built our restaurant—very important men."

The young woman blushed and bowed deeply. "So very sorry, Mr. Armstrongs."

"She is new, only started this week," Sam Kee said. "She is learning who my most important customers are. Let me show you to the best booth in the restaurant by a window." He led them to a booth and removed a "reserved" sign from the table. "It has a view of the bridge and harbor. Is this to your liking?"

"Very nice, Sam," Nigel said.

"Please be seated. I know you like soup, Archie. Today I have special *Gai Arp Wun Tun*, very tasty, young duck soup. We also have oysters, fresh from the fishermen's market this morning. I can serve them to you on the half shell or in *Cheow Foo Yung Hoow*, fried oysters and eggs." Sam Kee stepped back. The hostess, who had been standing quietly behind him, said, "Here are your menus, Mr. Armstrongs. I hope you enjoy your meals. The waiter will be with you shortly."

"Thank you, Tam-ho," Sam Kee said.

Noticing that only half of the tables were filled, Archibald asked, "How's business, Sam?"

"Not bad for three months. Did you hear my advertisement on the radio?"

Archibald and Nigel looked at each other and each said, "No."

"Station 930 at eleven in the morning, Monday through Friday, five times a week. And I'm writing a spot ad for television. The Modern Chinese Restaurant will show it's modern by using this new way to advertise."

Sam Kee's attention was diverted to a group of four men who had just entered the restaurant. One of the men waved at him, and he waved back.

"Excuse me, please, I'd like to welcome Mr. Thompson. Look over your menus, your lunches are on me. I'll be back. I have something I want to ask you." Sam Kee hurried over to greet the party.

Archibald raised his menu and began to read. Nigel looked around the restaurant and then interrupted Archibald's reading.

"I've told you, haven't I, what a professional job you did as project manager of this office building and this restaurant?"

"Yes . . . thanks, Dad."

"The use of mirrors and stainless steel in here is just what this restaurant needs to look clean and modern."

"I like real estate development and construction. It's interesting, challenging, and varied. It'll never get boring."

"You heard that Edgar is resigning to join Quadrangle as its president?"

"Yes, it's a good move up for him. I wish him well."

Nigel paused and then said tentatively, "What do you think of Bill Horne taking his vice-president's position?"

"He deserves it," Archibald said. "He's been with you a long time. I've learned a lot from him."

"He's fifty-eight and will retire in five or six years, and you'll be able to take his place by then. It wouldn't be right to advance you to vice-president now, after only six years."

"I'm not ready yet. Bill's a capable nice fellow. Here comes Sam back."

"Did you order yet?" Sam Kee asked.

"No, we've just been talking," Archibald said.

"Do you want to order?"

"We have time, Sam, go ahead with what you want to ask us," Archibald said.

Sam Kee grabbed the arm of a waiter passing by. In a commanding voice, he said, "Chung, your customers haven't been waited on yet. Bring them green tea and a *dim sum* delicacy basket."

The waiter rushed off, and Sam Kee returned his attention to Archibald and Nigel.

"My biggest problem is getting good people," Sam Kee said. "Relatives make the best workers in a family business. I'm planning my first trip to Canton to visit distant relatives. I want to sponsor those who wish to immigrate here to work in my restaurants. Since the Immigration Restriction Act was repealed last year, I think it should be easier to bring in relatives now, don't you?

"I think it should. What do you think, Dad?"

"Well, everything's been moving in the direction of a more liberal immigration policy. The Colombo Plan that allowed Asian students to study here has been a moneymaker for the universities. The government is loosening its immigration policy because of our growing trade with Asia. Businesses want it for economic reasons.

Churches want it on moral grounds. Who would have thought that we would sign a trade agreement with Japan only twelve years after the war?"

Sam Kee had made eye contact with a couple waiting to be seated. "I've interrupted your lunch too long. Please excuse me." He walked over to greet the couple.

"I recall you said once that you didn't expect to see any changes in the White Australia Policy during your lifetime."

"I didn't want to be negative in front of Sam, but the Menzies government still supports the White Australia Policy."

"They've repealed the infamous dictation test," Archibald said.

"True, but the government's new standard is nearly as restrictive—a 'distinguished and qualified' requirement to allow in only skilled workers. The dictation test had been exposed as outdated and reprehensible; it was an embarrassment that had to be replaced."

"Well, I still think it's a step in the right direction," Archibald said, undeterred.

"And so do I," Nigel agreed.

The waiter arrived with the tea and dim sum, and they began to eat.

"Premier Cahill's sudden death was a shocker, wasn't it?" Nigel said.

"Yes. . . . went into Sydney Hospital with stomach pains and dies from a heart attack."

"He was just a few years older than me," Nigel said.

"You're in a lot better shape than he was, Dad. You don't look sixty-two."

"I still swim, but haven't surfed for more than ten years. I've been thinking about givin' it a go again. Just to see if I can still do it."

"That would be impressive. You better not tell Mum."

They sat eating without conversation for several minutes, then Nigel said, "With Edgar leaving, I'll need an alternate on the Sydney Opera House Executive Committee. Are you interested?"

"Wow, do you think they'd accept me?"

"I can choose anyone I want as my alternate. You like the design don't you?—like your mother."

"I think it's going to be a masterpiece."

"Good. You and Jørn Utzon will get on famously. In a year or so, you can take my place on the committee."

"In a few years it will be built."

"Who have you been listening to? This thing will take five or six more years, at least. That is, if it's *ever* completed. Utzon keeps comparing it to a cathedral and acts like fifty years wouldn't be too long. I got involved in 1954, five years ago, and we've only begun construction of the first stage of three."

"Would I be your alternate on the fundraising committee as well? I don't know anything about raising funds."

"Other committee members can take the lead; in any case, the appeal fund has been eclipsed by the lottery that has already raised six times what the appeal fund has. If Cahill hadn't pushed through the lottery, we couldn't possibly afford this increasingly expensive building."

"Why are you so down on it?"

"I'm one of the few people on the Executive Committee who understands the design and construction process, so it's too frustrating for me to stay involved. You might not want to become involved either, once you understand the quagmire we've got ourselves into. I saw it coming, though I'm just one voice on the committee. Still, I feel responsible."

"It can't be that bad; it's under construction."

"Unfortunately, that's part of the problem—it *shouldn't* be under construction! Premier Cahill made them start Stage One, the 'podium,' which includes the concrete foundations and its four-story building, because he was afraid the Opera House would be scuttled if he wasn't reelected. They started the damn thing with only Utzon's floor plans. They didn't have construction plans! The structural engineer, Ove Arup and Partners, is doing the construction plans as they proceed. Have you ever heard of starting a massive building of some 900 rooms without finished construction drawings?"

"The podium is a four-story building?—with 900 rooms!" Archibald said.

"Yes, it's all concrete and will support the weight of the three roof shells. The shells are Stage Two, and the interiors are Stage Three. Another problem is that they don't know how to build the damn roof shells, so they can't estimate the building cost or when the project will be completed. The last time Utzon visited us, he said, 'The roof shells will be made of netted wire and sprayed with reinforced concrete, which will later be tiled.' The only problem is, he and Ove Arup can't agree on a structural design to support the heavy reinforced concrete roofs without deflection and cracking like an egg."

"They'll figure it out," Archibald said.

"I don't know. It would help if Utzon was here while his building is being construction, or at least had a representative involved. The government is saying, in effect, that since Utzon has never built a major building and Ove Arup and Partners has an outstanding, worldwide reputation for structural engineering and managing construction, it should build the concrete foundations and four-story building without any significant involvement of the architect. I've never heard of such a thing, and it is sure to lead to problems."

"Yeah, I agree," Archibald said. "I'm surprised that Utzon agreed to this arrangement."

"The government didn't give him a choice. Arup isn't working under Utzon. They have separate and distinct contracts—they're equals in effect. Happily, they seem to be working well enough together, in spite of everything."

Archibald was content to eat his lunch and say little while his father continued to vent his frustrations. Regardless of his father's complaints, Archibald was looking forward to working on the Sydney Opera House, a project he felt sure would produce *the* iconic building of Sydney.

* * *

Five years after Harvey's family moved into the town of Gura, Harvey received a curious telephone call at home. A serious sounding man, who Harvey assumed was white by the sound of his voice, gave his name as Jacob Elliman.

"I'm assisting the AAA, the Aboriginal Advancement Associa-

tion, located here in Redfern, Sydney. Have you heard of the organization, Mr. Hudson?"

"No."

"It's a four-year-old association of mostly Aborigines and some
whites interested in a fair go for Aborigines. I'm a trade unionist
organizer assisting the AAA in its study of rural segregation in New
South Wales. Gura will be one of the study towns if an Aborigine,
like yourself, Mr. Hudson, would agree to participate in the study."

Suspicious, Harvey asked, "Where'd ya get my name?"

"From two elders at the Murraroo Mission, Alfred Parbury and
Dowie Cadigee. They told me you had been an activist at the mission and would likely help the AAA in its study."

When Harvey remained silent, Elliman went on.

"You're exactly the kind of Aborigine the association is seeking,
Mr. Hudson. You're a veteran, employed family man, and a resident
of Gura with a son in public school. Also, you're a renter in the government's pepperpot dispersed housing program to promote assimilation. You are perfect for our study, Mr. Hudson."

"I'd like ta help, Mr. Elliman, but I don't 'ave time ta do no
study," Harvey said, "an' I'm not much of a writer."

"Oh, you won't have to write anything, Mr. Hudson, it's our
study; you'd just be a participant. I can even withhold your name if
you like. This is simply a study of acceptance of Aborigines partici-
pating in the AWB's, sorry, Aborigines Welfare Board's assimilation
program.

"What?"

"Let me put it this way, as a straightforward question, Mr.
Hudson. I hope you'll answer it truthfully. Are you accepted by
your white neighbors and is your son accepted in his white school?"

"I don't know how ta answer that, Mr. Elliman."

"I know the answer is usually 'No,' Mr. Hudson. Aborigines in
the pepperpot housing program in Coonamble, Walgett, and Lis-
more are part of our study. Have you heard anything about that?"

"No."

"Well, those are towns where Aborigines are experiencing the
same problems of no acceptance that you are. Once we complete

our study, we intend to change the Aborigines Welfare Board's assimilation program to benefit Aboriginal participants. That's why
we want you to simply inform us of businesses and institutions that
discriminate against you in Gura. It will only take a day or two.
Would you be willing to participate, Mr. Hudson, for the good of
your family and the Aboriginal community?"

"I don't know, Mr. Elliman. This is kinda sudden. Let me think
about it an' talk ta my wife."

"Fair deal, Mr. Hudson. How 'bout I call you back in a few days
after you've had a chance to talk to your wife and think about it?"

"Orright," Harvey agreed.

Elliman had called at the right time. Harvey and Katie were
sick of the discrimination they had experienced since moving into
their house. Their neighbors were unfriendly and critical, constantly looked for reasons to complain about Paul, their dog, the yard,
and upkeep of the house. Bob Buckley added to their problems
by not making repairs in a timely fashion. He used his key to visit
whenever he cared to, once walking in on Katie while she was taking a bath. Unhappy as renters, Harvey and Katie had started saving
to buy a small house near the mission.

They were particularly concerned with the discrimination
at Paul's school and how it had demoralized him. He had started
school in a small class of eight Aboriginal children, ostensibly to
receive remedial education, until he could join his white classmates.
After two years, Harvey and Katie gradually came to realize that the
real reason was to segregate the black children, as finally confirmed
by Paul when he admitted that the school had white and black
restrooms and the playground had a fenced off area for blacks to play.

Harvey and Katie joined with three other Aboriginal parents
to meet with the headmaster to complain about the segregation.
When they arrived for the meeting, they encountered an intractable group of four teachers and the headmaster. The educators indicated that they had no choice but to segregate the classrooms
because the Aboriginal children were years behind and too old to
mix with the younger white students at their grade level. Also, the
Aboriginal children suffered from lice and hook and threadworm

infestation that would infect the white children. The headmaster said they had created the separate Aboriginal play area in response to complaints by white parents that their children were coming home with bruises because the Aboriginal children played too roughly. Nevertheless, the teachers contended that the Aboriginal students were receiving an education far superior to that provided in the Murraroo Aborigines Mission.

By his fifth year, Paul was skipping more school days than attending. For years, he had taken the occasional day off to spend with his friends at the mission, but in his fifth year his truancy led to his dismissal from Dawson Primary School. Harvey and Katie were able to convince the headmaster to take him back at the start of the school year to redo his fifth year, but Paul returned to his old habit of skipping days and was quickly in danger of being expelled again. Harvey had recently smelled alcohol on his breath and had decided that he had to have a serious talk with him, soon.

Harvey was inclined to assist the AAA; however, first he had to make sure that it would not endanger his job. He had been promoted to the position of chief building maintenance engineer and supervised two assistants, one Aborigine and one white. His white employer was fair and sympathetic to the plight of Aborigines. He agreed with Harvey that the discriminatory practices of some businesses and retailers in town was wrong and should be exposed. He encouraged Harvey to participate in the study as long as he did so on his own time and the name of the company was not mentioned in the study, except positively as an employer of Aborigines.

When Elliman called back, Harvey agreed to participate in the study. Elliman arrived two weeks later and unexpectedly asked if he could sleep on their living room couch for two nights. Too late to find other accommodations, Harvey reluctantly agreed. That Friday night, Elliman and Harvey had a long talk about the study and its finding so far.

Saturday morning, Harvey walked Elliman around town, pointing out places that discriminated in one way or another against Aborigines: providing seating in only the front rows of the picture show; excluding them from the public swimming pool; forcing the purchase of women's clothes and shoes if tried on; barber shops, beauty parlors, eateries, and milk bars that would not serve them; and the Returned Soldiers League club that did not accept Aboriginal veterans. He took Elliman to Dawson Primary School to show him the segregated play area and spoke of the discrimination his son had endured.

They returned back at Harvey's house at 4:30 in the afternoon. Katie offered them cold beers and gave a cold soft drink to Paul. The four of them sat down around the kitchen table to discuss Elliman's opinion of the situation in Gura as compared with other towns in the study.

Unexpectedly, there was a knock on the door, which Harvey answered. It was Bob Buckley.

"Hello Harvey, I was wondering if you're goin' to the assimilation meeting at eight o'clock tonight in the town council building?"

"I'm thinkin' 'bout it, Mr. Buckley," Harvey answered.

"You're benefitin' from the dispersed housing program, Harvey. You really should be there to hear what people are sayin' about it. The Gura Aborigine Welfare Committee and the Country Women's Association will speak in favor of the program. They're good, kindhearted, Christian organizations that care about the needs of Aborigines. You know there will also be racist groups there opposin' the program, so we need your support."

"I'll try ta make it, Mr. Buckley."

"All right, don't let me down now, Harvey."

When Harvey returned to the kitchen table, Elliman, who had overheard the conversation at the door, asked, "Are you going to the meeting?"

"I was at an Aborigines Welfare Board meeting once, and all they did was complain 'bout us," Harvey said. "Buckley jus' wants some black faces in the audience."

"Why don't you speak at the meeting when they open it up for public comment. Tell them about the places that discriminate against Aborigines in town. The list we drew up today. Tell them it isn't right. That's the purpose of the meeting according to what I just overhead."

"I can't do that, Jake," Harvey said. "I can't talk at a public meetin'."

"As an army sergeant you must've talked in front of your men?"

"Yeah, but that was different."

"We'll keep it short, Harvey. One page and then read the list of places that discriminate to expose them. I'll write it with you, and you can practice saying it. You can expose the hypocrisy of their assimilation program. You fought on the Kokoda Track, so I know you have the balls for it. All you have to do is read it."

"Do it, Dad," Paul said. "I'll go with ya. I'd like ta see what they do when ya say it to their faces."

"I go too, Harvey," Katie said. "Someone gotta speak up."

"It's best if you go as a family," Elliman added.

"Now let's not get carried away 'ere," Harvey said. "Katie, ya never know what's goin' ta happen when ya do somethin' like this. And Paul's too young ta get involved in this."

"I'm thirteen. I know what's happenin'—they treat us like dirt—I'm not afraid of 'em."

Elliman looked from Paul to Harvey to Katie. "No better school than the school of hard knocks, Harvey. If I had a son, I'd want him to learn from an experience like this. This is reality. They won't like what you're saying, though as long as you don't lose your temper, nothing will happen bad in a public town council setting. The police will be there, I'm sure."

"I'm forty-seven an' past lettin' anyone bother me, Jake. . . . Katie and Paul, if ya want me ta do it, I will. But we takin' a big chance ta try ta do somethin' good."

After an early dinner, Elliman and Harvey set about writing a one-page speech and a list of discriminating establishments. Harvey read and reread it and then gave his speech to them until he delivered it well.

"This is a short, to the point speech, Harvey," Elliman said. "The council won't like it but will let you go on until you start naming discriminating business. Then they'll start beating the gavel hard to try to make you stop naming names. You just keep reading louder. Some hecklers may try to yell over you, but you have a strong, deep baritone voice that will carry over them. Now here's the thing—don't take *anything* they say personal. If you get mad or injure anyone, then everything will be lost, and they'll throw you out on your ear, or worse."

The four of them sat together in the meeting room attended by well over 100 people. There were only a few other blacks in the crowd. A panel of city council members, town employees, and representatives of the Aborigines Welfare Board sat at four tables lined up on a dais. Chairs were arranged in rows with an aisle down the center leading to a speaker's lectern in front of the panel. The mayor of Gura chaired the panel and opened the meeting. The panel discussed the successes and difficulties of the dispersed housing program and the challenges of assimilation and then opened the meeting to the public.

When Harvey started to raise his hand to speak, Elliman stopped him.

"Don't raise your hand to speak yet, Harvey," Elliman said. "Let's wait until several others speak, and you have a good person to follow. I tell you when."

There was a noticeable murmur of surprise when Harvey raised his hand to speak. To Harvey's dismay, the mayor immediately recognized him as the next speaker.

When Harvey was close to finishing the first page, a loud, dissenting male voice was heard shouting from the back of the room.

"You Pepperpotters git free housin' an' the dole—isn't that enough fer you! *We work for a livin'!*" Harvey turned his head to see that the shouter was a tall, wiry man in his mid-thirties.

The mayor said, "Shut up back there, you'll get your chance to speak."

The man did not sit down, instead he pointed at Harvey. "He's a communist"—and then pointing at Elliman—"and his white mate is a Red too!"

Harvey did not know what a "communist" was and his incomprehension showed on his face.

The man read Harvey's perplexed look. "You don't even know what a commie is! You're a bloody pawn, *ya stupid Abo!*"

The insult jolted and quieted the room. There was no rebuke

from the mayor. Everyone was waiting to see what was going to happen next. Harvey looked at the heckler with unafraid threatening eyes. The heckler beckoned with his hands for Harvey to come to him. The entire room was dead silent.

The mayor suddenly broke the tension. "You back there—*sit down!*—or I'll order the constable to remove you."

The heckler smiled insolently. As he sat down and Harvey turned back to face the panel, the heckler said under his voice loud enough for all to hear "Coon coward."

Harvey lost his composure. He could not ignore the second insult in front of his wife and son. He laid his speech down on the lectern, turned and, in measured steps, walked toward the heckler who jumped to his feet. Two men on opposite sides of the aisle rose from their seats as Harvey approached. The nearest man said "Don't" and reached for Harvey's arm. Harvey walked by him with a straight arm to his chest that drove him back. The man standing on the other side of the aisle, lowered his head and attempted to grab Harvey around the waist. Harvey rammed his hip into the shoulder of the man sending him backwards onto his seat. Two policemen rushed from the front of the room toward the melee.

A third man grabbed Harvey from behind around the chest, as the first man, recovered from the straight-arm push, piled onto his back. Straining to reach the heckler, Harvey carried the two men with him until a third man threw his shoulder into Harvey's midsection. Another man with outstretched arms jumped between the heckler and Harvey. While Harvey was being forced back, the heckler pushed past the referee and threw a punch, hitting him on the shoulder. The unfairness of the punch raised voices of outrage. The two policemen pulled the group apart and ejected the heckler. Unhurt, Harvey walked back to the lectern with a look of calmness. As the crowd settled down, Harvey stood at the lectern trying to find where he had stopped reading.

"I think we've heard enough from you, sir," the mayor said and beckoned to the policemen reentering the hall. "Constable, would you please escort this man from the room. We've heard enough from him."

No dissenting voice was raised.

Not knowing what to say, Harvey left with Katie, Paul, and Elliman.

At Harvey's house, the adults had a long discussion into the night and drank many bottles of beer. By two o'clock, the three of them were a bit drunk, blurry eyed, and Harvey and Katie understood less and less of what Elliman was saying.

"This bloody assimilation is a form of sociological and psychological cruelty that forces Aboriginal people to give up their heritage and accept all that is foreign to them," Elliman said. "Do you understand what I'm sayin'? It's especially damaging when it leads to lookin' down on your own people, when at the same time you're being rejected by the so-called civilized and respectable people you're tryin' to join. You're not even counted as citizens of your own country; the one they stole from you. It's all such egregious bullshit."

"So what can we do, Jake?" Harvey asked.

"Don't lose respect for your own people and don't try to fit in with whites who don't want ya. Live your own life and teach your own children. Don't take nothin' from the bastards because the price is too bloody high."

Then Elliman stood, walked into the living room, fell onto the couch and immediately went to sleep.

*   *   *

For the second time in a week, James stormed out of the house after he and his father David exchanged angry words. David came into the kitchen and poured himself a coffee.

"I don't know what's wrong with him, Mary," David said as he sat down at the kitchen table. "I can't say anything without setting him off. I'll be happy when summer's over, and he's off to Sydney University."

"But he says he's not going," Mary said.

"What else is he going to do? He's going all right! He's not staying in this house with his smart mouth and miserable attitude.

That's not going to continue. He's going to board at the university."

"He said he wants to take a year off and go on a 'walkabout' around the country to see how Aborigines live."

"See—that's what I mean! He uses terms like that to bait me, make me angry, like he's some kind of native outbacker or something. Ridiculous!"

By the end of 1961, David and Mary Bennett had suffered James's resentment through his junior and senior years. He had developed an attitude of rudeness toward his adoptive parents and treated them dismissively. Working evenings and weekends in Bondi as a short-order cook, he ate meals at the restaurant to avoid his parents, bought himself a car, and covered most of his own expenses.

James had done well in secondary school, but showed no interest in going on to tertiary education. He had refused to attend his high school graduation to spite David, who had been looking forward to the ceremony. None of David's threats could force him to attend. When James refused to apply to university, David obtained an application from the University of Sydney and filled it out himself. When he told James that he had been accepted, James said he was not going.

"We should have tried to find his parents," Mary said. "That's what's behind all this."

"Don't say that, Mary. Don't blame yourself. There's nothing we can do. Those records are sealed. They wouldn't tell us even if we asked."

Mary stood and walked to the kitchen sink and washed her coffee cup recalling the questions James had asked them, and they couldn't answer: The area where he was born, the ages of his parents, his tribe or clan or whatever group he belonged to, and whether he had brothers and sisters. He's having an identity crisis, she thought. He resents us for adopting him and withholding information he thinks we have. We have to find a way to reach him.

"Let's go on a two-week cruise with him before he leaves for university," Mary said. "If we are on a ship together, visiting places and eating meals together, perhaps we can mend our relationship a little."

"He won't go."

"Then pick somewhere he wants to go."

"Ships don't sail into the outback," David said.

"Be serious. Tell him we want to go someplace to be together, and ask him where *he* would like to go. Better yet, I'll ask him. He's more likely to go if I ask him."

"Fine with me. He's not going to go anyway, but you can ask him."

Two days later, David overheard James and Mary talking.

"I can't take time off work, Mum. I have to save enough money to travel around Australia. I'm going to start with New South Wales Aboriginal stations."

David entered the kitchen as James was talking.

"Look, James, if you want to visit some Aboriginal communities, we can take a week off and visit them together."

"With *you* and Mum?" James said derisively.

David looked at Mary who appeared annoyed by his proposal, which he had not discussed with her beforehand. "With your mother, if she wants to go, or just you and me. You'll quickly see that you have little in common with them. I think it will answer many of the questions you're wrestling with."

"I'm not *wrestling* with anything. I just want to see how Aborigines live and understand who they are. I can't do that in a *week*. And I can't do it with *you*."

"Why?" David said.

"Because they'd see I'm an adopted kid of whites."

David was angered by James's disdainful look and contemptuous words. He acts like I'm a white oppressor, David thought. Like his enemy! *This is bullshit!*

"So you think you're going to drive up in your Ford Zephyr and say 'Hi, I'd like to get to know you,' and they're going to say 'Happy to meet you, mate.' Don't be so naive. These are people who have had tough lives. They're uneducated and ignorant. They're going to take advantage of you one way or another; you can be sure of that."

"So you think all Aborigines are dumb and ignorant, *right?*" James said.

"You know what I mean. They aren't educated. Don't try to twist my words. Indigenous natives can be improved, if they are given the same advantages as white people and a better environment."

"Like me?—your *grand experiment!*"

"I've had about enough of your smart mouth. *Go* on your little *walkabout.* You'll be back here in two weeks after you realize how good you've had it. In fact, I'd *like* to see you try to get by on your own, that would be a laugh!"

"You're the *laugh!*" James said as he headed out the door.

Mary frantically called David at work the next day to tell him that James was packing to go on his trip around Australia. He intended to leave before David returned home.

David was furious that he had to cancel an important meeting for this foolishness. He walked through the front door to see Mary crying in the foyer as James came down the stairs with a cardboard box to load into his car.

"You're not going anywhere, James! What do you mean leaving like this? Look at your mother!"

As James tried to walk by him, David grabbed at his box, upsetting it. Some of its contents fell to the floor.

"That's it—*go to your room!*—you're not going anywhere. We'll discuss this later, like adults."

James ignored his father's order, got down on his knees and shoveled the fallen items back into his box. David dropped to one knee to stop him. James pushed him away, causing David to fall on his backside.

David reached for James's savings account book lying on the floor, but James grabbed it first.

"You're leaving that here!" David ordered.

"No I'm not. It's *my* money!"

"You saved it because you lived here for *free!*"

James stuffed the savings account book into his pocket and stood up to leave, but both his mother and father blocked his way.

"*Pleeaase, James,* don't leave like this!" Mary said tearfully. "Where are you going? You could be hurt—don't be foolish."

James lowered his head and pushed by his father. As they jostled, David said, "If you walk out that door, you'll never be welcomed back here again."

David grabbed the box as James tried to back out the door.

James punched him in the face, knocking him to the floor. Carrying the box, James ran toward his car. Mary bent down to help David, giving him her hankie to cover his bleeding nose. They rushed out the door as James started his car.

David ran toward the car, his nose bleeding profusely. "Don't expect us to take you back, because we *won't! Leave!* I never want to see you again! You've been nothing but trouble!"

He reached the driver's side window as James, looking straight ahead and crying, drove down the driveway.

David beat on the window and yelled, "So this is the thanks we get! *I wish we'd never adopted you!*"

* * *

Several people milled around the discount book table in a Double Bay bookstore. One of them was Lydia Armstrong who considered herself lucky to have found a beautifully illustrated book of impressionist painters. While she slowly leafed through the large book, she noticed a handsome man looking at her.

Without drawing his attention, she took furtive glances as he nonchalantly walked around the table randomly picking up books. Luminous grayish-blue eyes . . . full lips turned up at the corners, strong jaw . . . thick brown hair sophisticatedly combed back. About five feet eight inches, she reckoned. Broad chest and thin waist. Late twenties. Exotic and sexy but what nationality? He smiled (at me?) showing unusually white teeth contrasting with his olive complexion. Pleasing smile.

The handsome man was trying to make up his mind. He did not usually pick up women at bookstores, but she looked fast. He looked over her provocative appearance: tight red wool sweater with a low, rounded neckline; long, heavy, beaded necklace with the pendant depressing the sweater between her breasts; short form-fitting black skirt; svelte; sexy dark nylons; nice legs; long hair; large, round, pierced gold earrings; ostentatiously artsy bracelets on her right wrist; expensive gold watch on her left; heavy eye shadow—too much makeup; red fingernails to match her red lipstick and sweater; around twenty-four; no wedding ring; and alone at four-thirty on a Saturday afternoon, looking at a book of impressionist painters—a perfect ice-breaker. But she's not really my type.

His preference is shorter women, younger, more buxom and shapely, blue-eyed, long-haired blonds, which he cannot believe Sydney has so many of. This sexy woman was only pretty, a bit too tall at five six or seven, too thin, and a brunette with brown eyes. Regardless, he cannot resist trying his luck with her.

He moved next to her and looked at the book. "Excuse me, miss; unfortunately, you seem to be looking at the only copy of *Impressionist Painters*. I'll wait until you're finished with it, but I was wondering if you intend to buy it?"

"I was thinking I would," Lydia answered with no sound of offense in her voice.

Feeling confident, he asked, "Could you tell me if the paintings and posters of Toulouse-Lautrec are included? He's one of my favorite impressionists."

"Oddly, he is. He's usually classified as a *post*impressionist, but this book lumps impressionist and postimpressionist together."

Surprised by her knowledge of art, he asked, "Are you an art historian?"

"No, an artist . . . a painter." Lydia smiled demurely.

"A painter! I've studied art too. I'm an architect."

"Really."

"What kind of painter are you? if you don't mind me asking."

"I haven't found my personal style yet," Lydia said. "I'm preparing a series of impressionistic landscapes for an exhibit right now, using oils, watercolor, and gouache."

"Toulouse-Lautrec worked in gouache, didn't he? I believe he learned it from Edgar Degas."

"Yes, they both worked in gouache; the technique goes back to the Egyptians."

"I'm impressed," the man said. "I'd love to look at the book and discuss it with you. Would you allow me to buy the book for you and treat us to a coffee next door to discuss it? Then when we're done, you can have it as a present from me, with my thanks."

She hadn't been taken in, but didn't mind spending some time with this handsome man who cared enough to give her a creative line. She had nothing planned for the rest of the day; however, found herself lying to him:

"I'd like that, but I have to leave before six, because I'm going out tonight."

"Oh . . ." (he wondered if he cared enough) "we'll be done before then, thanks. My name is Ferenc Károlyi by the way." He offered his hand.

"I'm Lydia," she said, shaking his hand.

While waiting in a queue to buy the book, Ferenc congratulated himself on his smooth move on her and thought about his obsession with women. *The Australian women I attract tend to be fast. After I get to know them, they always say, in one way or another, that it was my "animal magnetism" that attracted them. My dark, masculine appearance repels some women and attracts others. There doesn't seem to be much middle ground. I can tell within seconds if a woman finds me attractive or not. This one likes me.*

I didn't have such unreal success with Hungarian women. Are Australians more promiscuous? My appearance seems to be a plus here, and my accent helps. The most important reason, though, is that I treat women better than Australian men do. They seem to be so uncomfortable around women; always grouping together with their "mates." Aussie men don't know how to romance their women; in fact, they ignore them. The women here are starved for attention. Makes it easy for me. All I have to do is charm them with my worldly, cosmopolitan, European savoir-faire and use my artistic cachet of being an architect—and I'm in.

In four and a half years, I've had sex with more women than I can remember. Although it's getting a bit old—I'm getting a bit old—twenty-nine in four months. I ought to find the right woman—a rich woman. I've completed the architectural practice requirement and can sit for the registration exam. Marrying a rich woman would eliminate my money worries and allow me to start my own architectural firm immediately after becoming registered.

After buying the book, Ferenc and Lydia walked next door to a coffee shop. When they sat down, Ferenc offered Lydia a cigarette. She accepted. He took out his gold-plated lighter and lit it for her, and they ordered coffee.

Ferenc had several rules that he had learned from experience. Number one was to start the conversation talking about *her* and what she was interested in. And then *listen*. He knew he had an exciting, romantic story to tell her about himself, which just happened to be true, but it worked best later in the conversation. He opened the art book, and they began to discuss her art relative to the art works in the book. While they talked, Ferenc drew out information about her. She had graduated from university in art in 1959 and then followed her boyfriend to England. They traveled around England and Scotland, where her ancestors were from, and later to Paris. The relationship ended, and she returned home in 1960 to live with her parents.

"I decided to get serious about my art and change my conservative attitudes. I may never marry," she said. "I found this lovely studio with a lot of natural light in Double Bay and moved in three months ago. Peter Rothwell, the art gallery on Bay Street, likes my work and has agreed to sponsor a show when I have twenty suitable pieces."

She was captivated by his translucent grayish-blue eyes that bored right through her, causing her to feel self-conscious and look away. His mannerisms were graceful: the way he held his cigarette and habitually brushed back errant strands of hair.

"Tell me about yourself," Lydia said.

"I was a student Hungarian freedom fighter and sought asylum here in early '57," Ferenc said with an air of studied nonchalance.

"I remember that," she said.

"Your wonderful, democratic country has accepted fifteen thousand of us escaping Soviet tyranny. I was one of the student leaders at Budapest University and helped to organize the Hungarian Revolt."

"Were you involved in the fighting?" Lydia asked.

"Yes, I threw a few Molotov cocktails at the Soviet tanks and shot a rifle at them. My best friend was shot and died in my arms.

We were no match for the Soviets and so idealistic to think we could win. They knew who I was, so I had to escape. We made a dash to get out of Budapest and hid in a friend's barn for a few days. The borders were being watched, so we went through the forest at night to cross into Austria."

Pulling at her heartstrings, Ferenc said, "I haven't seen my mother, father, or my two little sisters since I escaped over four years ago. The Soviets would have killed me if I had stayed. It's been difficult and lonely here not knowing anyone."

"Oh, my goodness, it's nearly six o'clock. I should leave," Lydia said, gathering up her things.

"Couldn't you call," Ferenc said with a hopeful look. "We're having such a nice conversation. I'd like to take you to Szabados Hungarian Restaurant on Knox Street."

"I was there once, but didn't know what to order," Lydia said.

"I can take care of that," Ferenc said with an engaging smile. "I'll choose two classic, traditional meals. Could you call to get out of whatever you have to leave for?"

"I'll see. I'll use their phone."

Lydia returned and said, "That takes care of that," without saying what "that" was.

Seated in Szabados restaurant, Ferenc talked about how Double Bay was the most European community in Sydney. "It reminds me of a community in Budapest. Have you ever been there?"

"No, I haven't"

It's a beautiful city divided into two parts: Buda is on the hilly side west of the Danube River, and Pest is on a flat plain east of the river. The hills around Sydney Harbour remind me of Buda where the university is located next to the river. I couldn't live away from water."

"I love the water too."

"And where else can you find a coffee house like the one we were in today?" Ferenc said. "Hungarians are a cafe society, and Double Bay has a little of that feeling with its ethnic restaurants, shops, cinemas, bookstores, and after-hours spots. This is the only place I've found a Jewish delicatessen with the kinds of meats, cheeses, fish, salads, and pickles we have in Hungary. That's why I moved here two years ago into a one-bedroom flat on South Head Road."

"Double Bay was a sleepy little village until the postwar boom," Lydia said. "It became *the* address for immigrants from central and eastern Europe after the war. In just a few years, they've transformed the village with great restaurants, cafes, and shops—it became cosmopolitan almost overnight. That's why I'm here too." She decided to change the subject. "Where do you work?"

"I'm working on the Sydney Opera House that's being built at Circular Quay," he said, a little too proudly.

"Really," Lydia said, somewhat incredulously. "For Jørn Utzon or Ove Arup?"

Ferenc was dumbfounded. He had never met a person outside of work who knew the structural engineer was Ove Arup. "How do you know Ove Arup?"

"My father and brother serve on SOHEC, the Sydney Opera House Executive Committee."

Lydia had not offered her surname, and Ferenc had not asked. "What! I know every person on the committee. The only father-son team is Nigel Armstrong and his son Archibald."

"That's my father and brother."

"This is unbelievable! I've never met them, but I know them."

"Who do you work for?" Lydia asked again.

"The Department of State Planning in its special projects branch. I was placed there by the federal government to fulfill a two-year service commitment for my free immigration passage here. I already had a civil engineering degree and was within two years of finishing my architectural degree when the revolt started. I finished my architectural degree going part-time at the University of New South Wales while I was working full-time for the government. I'm going to take the architect's registration exam soon and then open my own private practice."

"What do you do on the Opera House?"

"Well . . . I advise my architect boss on mostly structural engineering matters, and he advises Stan Haviland, the head of the department, who serves as chairman of the SOHEC. It's been my main job for over three years."

"How do you like it?"

"I have to be careful what I say now, knowing you're an Armstrong," Ferenc said with a smile.

"Why?"

"A lot of politics, you know. Very dicey. I really can't say too much, Lydia. Your father could take it wrong. I don't want to get in trouble."

"You make it sound like an intrigue," Lydia said. "I'm not going to tell him. I hardly even see him since I moved out."

"God, I sound like a scared-for-his-job government employee, don't I? Oh, what the hell. I'm leaving soon anyway, and they can't fire me in government. Actually, I can't wait to get out of there . . . away from all the politics and pettiness. Well . . . your father . . . um . . . he's one of our enemies. He thinks the Department of Public Works should be running the project."

"Why?—is he right?"

"Uh . . . he's right, to be truthful. The Public Works Department is the normal building authority and has broad experience in project management. My department has only a small architectural services branch and primarily advises local governments. Premier Cahill gave it to the NSW Department of State Planning because he had been its minister and liked Stan Haviland. An act was recently passed making Paul Ryan, Minister for Public Works, the 'constructing authority,' while retained us as the implementing department and bill payer. So Ryan has no real power. Stan Haviland is just ignoring him, and we continue to work with your father's SOHEC. . . . though there are more serious problems than departmental politics and mismanagement of the project."

"Like what?" Lydia asked, genuinely interested in Ferenc's insider information.

"Problems between Jørn Utzon and Ove Arup. Let me restate that. I don't know if they have personal problems with each other, but their firms sure do. It's all about structural engineering—pretty boring stuff."

"Keep going, I'm interested," Lydia said.

"They cannot resolve the structural design of the roof shells.

Meanwhile, the four-story base building is under construction, and Arup doesn't know how massive to make the concrete columns to support the roof shells. See the problem?

"It all goes back to the beginning with Utzon's freehand sketches of the roof shells. At their first meeting, Ove Arup told Utzon his thin-shelled reinforced concrete roof shells had no geometric order and were too low-slung, wide, and extended to be structurally sound. He felt they had to be more upright and less squat to avoid deflection and cracking. Utzon disagreed and said that changing his sketched shapes would completely destroy the architectural character of the building. So for nearly four years, Arup has been trying unsuccessfully to come up with a structural design scheme that would satisfy him. Utzon is a purist when it comes to the truthful use of materials and organic solutions that respect the laws of nature. He has a disdain for forced engineering solutions and is a perfectionist unwilling to compromise his high architectural ideals.

"Last month, Hugo Mollman at Arup, who was directly responsible for the roof design, resigned in protest because Utzon rejected his latest engineering design for the roof shells. Then last week, Arup partner Ronald Jenkins, Mollman's boss, also resigned in frustration and anger saying he had run out of engineering solutions for the unworkable shapes of the roof shells. That's how serious everything is now. Utzon's going to have to be more flexible, or the project isn't going to be built."

"I haven't heard about any of this."

"They're keeping it quiet. They don't want the press to know that the roof shells are in trouble and the architect and engineer are at odds. Now you see how you can get me in trouble if you tell your father about this."

They left the restaurant at ten and walked on Bay Street to Steyne Park and then along the beach. Arriving at the door of Lydia's house, a block from Double Bay beach, after eleven, Ferenc asked to see her paintings. She said it was late, and her place was a mess, but gave him her telephone number saying she had a wonderful day. Ferenc shook her hand good night, and said he also enjoyed the day. He decided not to kiss her to indicate he wasn't the mover she probably assumed he was.

*   *   *

In November 1961, Harvey and Katie bought a two-bedroom, dilapidated house on a small plot of land on the road leading to the entrance of the Murraroo Aborigines Mission. After dinner and on weekends, Harvey and Katie worked on the house to improve it for occupancy. Paul helped initially but soon lost interest. Nearing fifteen years old and out of school for a year and a half, he rarely stayed with them anymore, being gone for days at a time. In an effort to see him more and instill a work ethic, Harvey paid him by the hour to work on the house. His work was so shoddy and slow, though, that after three months Harvey stopped giving him jobs.

Harvey and Katie moved into their house on February 26, 1962. For the first time in their lives, they felt completely independent, free from government control, rules, and harassment.

Two weeks after moving in, three elders from the Murraroo Mission came to visit. In the course of conversation, Harvey learned that the superintendent had told them that the Aborigines Welfare Board intended to demolish some of the old cottages on the mission.

"How many houses are going to be demolished?" Harvey asked.

"Don't know," they said.

"Are new cottages going to be built to replace them?"

"Yeah, sure," one elder said while the other two shrugged their shoulders.

"There's plenty of land," Harvey said. "Ya ought ta ask the Super ta build the new cottages first before tearin' down the old ones, so families don't 'ave ta double up. Do ya know what families gotta move?"

The elders looked at each other and shook their heads no.

"What about a plan? Is there a plan of how it's all going ta look when it's done?"

The elders said, "No."

"Ya can't trust 'em," Harvey said. "This could be the first step in closin' the mission. Lots of missions an' stations bin closed. Ya ought ta demand the new housin' be built first, so people 'ave a place ta move into without doublin' up or bein' forced off the mission."

The elders returned four days later to tell Harvey that a large bulldozer had been unloaded from a flatbed trailer and placed in a field.

"Boss say they bin sign demo fer seven or eight buildin's. He think board goin' ta build new housin', but don't know fer sure."

"Did ya ask if there's a plan?" Harvey asked.

"No plan, Super say."

"What are ya going ta do?"

The elders felt that they could not do anything. Then one of them said, "What do ya think we should do, Harvey?"

"Well it jus' ain't fair or right," Harvey said. "If ya want, I know a person in the Aboriginal Advancement Association in Sydney. I can ask his advice."

The elders talked among themselves, and then said, "Yeah, Harvey, do that."

Harvey called the telephone number Jacob Elliman had given him and asked for him. Told he no longer worked as a consultant to the association, Harvey talked to an administrator who listened patiently.

"So the elders have asked the mission superintendent for specifics, and he's unresponsive," the administrator said. "Is that right?"

"That's right. They aren't being told what this is all about," Harvey said.

"That's standard operation. The only way the elders and other residents of the mission can get their attention and not be walked over is to protest the planned demolition. If they are willing to do that, we can provide assistance."

"I think they are, but I 'ave ta talk to 'em," Harvey answered.

"Well find out and call me back. You'll have to get most of the residents to protest, because if it's just a few, they'll be thrown off the mission."

Two days later, Harvey called the AAA back. "I've talked to the elders an' they talked to the residents, an' most agree ta protest the bulldozin'."

"This comes at just the right time, Mr. Hudson," the administrator said enthusiastically. "You know that we have been campaigning for the abolition of the state Aborigines Welfare Board and dismantling the national assimilation policy. We want to change the federal constitution to make the commonwealth government responsible for Aboriginal affairs. If we can make the board look insensitive and harsh at Murraroo, it will be a big help right now.

"Also, the United Nations has been criticizing Australia's human rights and the Commonwealth Parliament is about ready to enact an amendment to the Commonwealth Electoral Act to give *all* Aboriginal people the right to vote. So we have a lot working right now, and your protest can help." The administrator made arrangements with Harvey for an employee to visit him.

An Aboriginal AAA man came and stayed with Harvey and Katie. Harvey had the elders come over to his house to meet him.

" 'Ere are five petitions ta collect signatures demandin' that the cottages should not be demolished without an overall plan, an' families put out should be given at least a two-month notice," the AAA man said. "I also 'ave this 'ere press release ta give ta the local newspapers, but they won't print it without action photos, like women lyin' down in front of the bulldozer. Ya need ta pay a photographer ta take some good pictures. With good pictures, we'll get ya national exposure. I also 'ave a list of grievances that the elders can read to the press. Biggest point is the Aborigines Welfare Board can't give away Aboriginal people's land. This is important because the AAA is calling fer the return of our traditional indigenous lands, stop closin' Aboriginal stations an' reserves, an' assistance to develop our lands along cooperative lines."

At the end of the AAA man's visit, he gave Harvey two hundred dollars to pay for a photographer and to help cover other expenses.

Within days the petition was signed by most of the residents. When the superintendent realized this was about the planned demolition of the cottages, he identified the cottages to be demolished by telling the occupant families they had a week to double up with relatives and friends. The protest day was quickly organized, and *Gura Daily News* was advised. Harvey hired a photographer. Protest signs were prepared.

The bulldozer was driven and parked close to the cottages to be demolished. That evening, Harvey met with the elders and planned the protest for the next day in front of the bulldozer.

Before Harvey and Katie went to bed, Paul arrived home to sleep. He was obviously intoxicated as he staggered to his room. Harvey went to his room where he was bent over on the edge of his bed awkwardly trying to unlace his shoes.

"We're protestin' the demolition of the cottages tomorrow, Paul. We need everyone ta protest. Can ya get yer mates ta meet us in front of the bulldozer at noon?"

"What's the point, Dad?" he said as he fumbled with his shoes. "Nothin' goin' ta change . . . waste of time." His words were slurred. He finally took off his shoes and then worked at unbuttoning his shirt.

"What ya doin' that's so important ya can't help out fer an hour?" Harvey said, more disappointed than angry.

"Ya always git involved in these things, but ya don't see it don't make no difference. I just don't care," he said, as he fell back on the bed and immediately fell to sleep.

Harvey undid the remaining buttons on his shirt, sat him up, and removed his shirt. He unbuckled his pants and pulled them off. As he did, he noticed a plastic bottle under the bed. He picked it up and smelled it. The bottle had a residue of petrol in it. He pulled a cover over Paul and carried the bottle into his bedroom to show Katie.

"Oh God, Harvey, he's a petrol-sniffer," Katie exclaimed when she smelled the bottle.

"I thought it was just the grog," Harvey said in a voice of despair. "This stuff can burn yer brains out—make ya a droolin' idiot."

Paul was still asleep when Harvey left an hour early for work the next morning, so he could take a long lunch hour to attend the protest.

The first act of the protest was for women to lie down in front of the unoccupied bulldozer. Harvey wanted to make sure the photographer he had hired took photographs of this before the bulldozer was moved. About the same time, a *Gura Daily News* reporter and photographer arrived. The superintendent stupidly improved their photographs by having the bulldozer operator climb up into the bulldozer and sit down before backing it away and parking it in a distant field. The photographers took pictures of the protesting Aborigines and their signs. When the police arrived and a scuffle ensued, dramatic photographs were taken of that too.

The reporter listened to an elder reading the list of their grievances and the claim that this was Wiradjuri land for 50,000 years and could not be taken from them. The superintendent could not be found for comment. The press was given copies of the petition and the press release. As the police broke up the unlawful protest without arresting anyone, Harvey left and drove back to work arriving at two o'clock.

Harvey had a man-to-man talk with Paul about the dangers of getting high by petrol sniffing. Paul said it was the first time he had tried it and didn't like it. He agreed it was stupid and self-destructive and promised not to do it again.

To Harvey's and the elders' surprise and satisfaction, the bulldozer was removed from the mission the next day and the planned demolition faded away as an issue. The photographs taken by Harvey's photographer were given to the Aboriginal Advancement Association. They generated newspaper articles throughout Australia and continued to find their way into published articles for years afterwards.

*　* 　*

On Ferenc and Lydia's first real date, the Saturday following their first meeting, Ferenc realized that he had misjudged her as "fast." She had been playing a role, that of the avant-garde, liberated woman, and had overdone it. She was, in fact, the opposite of "fast." He guessed that the boyfriend she had followed to England was her first and only lover.

On their date, she was extremely wary of him and maintained a certain distance. He wondered if she was reserved, distant, and untrusting by nature. Ordinarily, he would have lost interest after such a date, but he appreciated her intelligence, class, and family. He had great respect for Nigel Armstrong and his well-known integrity. Ferenc had listened to him once impressively debate an issue at a committee meeting. He did not know much about Archibald, other than his face had been badly burned in the Pacific war. Ferenc could easily imagine designing buildings for the Armstrong Development Company, one of the most successful developers in Sydney.

Lydia did not feel comfortable with Ferenc. He was too smooth and sure of himself for her. His piercing eyes, masculinity, and aggressiveness were intimidating. She felt he was too good-looking for her and questioned his sincerity. After their date, she decided to stop seeing him.

Ferenc felt the brush off immediately. He knew the tone of a woman's voice when she was fabricating reasons for not seeing him. He did not care that much; he had found another woman. If he wanted to put out the effort, he felt he could date Lydia again. Also, he was sure to see her in the bookstores, cafes, restaurants, and shops they frequented. He sent her a bouquet of spring flowers with a note saying how much he had enjoyed their two meetings and went on with his life.

Three months later, Ferenc received an engraved invitation from the Peter Rothwell Gallery in Double Bay to attend the exclusive exhibition launch of impressionistic landscapes by Lydia Armstrong. He went and encountered a changed, warmly encouraging Lydia. She had hoped that he would attend. When he did and enthusiastically praised her work, she knew that she cared for him.

Ferenc's lovemaking was so much better than the boyfriend she had followed to England, who had been no more experienced than herself and left her feeling unfulfilled. Ferenc enjoyed the sensual pleasures of sex. He was proud of his muscular body and playfully made love on top of the sheets instead of under them. He took his time and spoke in an easy, teasing voice during sex, asking if it was all right to try each new position or sexual pleasure. He made sure that she was satisfied before him. And he was as attentive after sex as before. She concluded that she had never really enjoyed sex before and found she wanted to do it as often as possible. After a two-month torrid romance, Lydia invited Ferenc home to meet her parents.

"How long have you been in Australia, Ferenc?" Wilhelmina asked.

"Since February 1957, Mrs. Armstrong, five years."

"How do you like it?" she asked.

"I haven't seen much of it, but I *love* Sydney. It's paradise here for me—the political freedom, weather, beaches, friendly people, and the city is beautifully sited on Sydney Harbour."

"How did the government transport you here?" Nigel asked.

"They flew me here, sir. My name was on a list of freedom fighters the Russians wanted returned to Hungary. That made it easy for me to request political asylum in Australia, my first choice. Austria wanted us out of their country as quickly as possible. I feel I was given a wonderful *gift* by being sent here."

"A *gift* . . . a gift of Sydney, so to speak," Nigel said. "Lydia told us you're both a civil engineer and an architect in the State Planning Department and advise Stan Haviland."

"Not quite, sir." Struggling not to look concerned, Ferenc smiled at Lydia, deferring the response to her.

"That's not quite what I said, Dad. Ferenc advises his boss who advises Mr. Haviland."

"Oh, do you work for John Raleigh then?" Nigel asked.

"Yes, sir. I've actually met with Mr. Haviland only about ten times since I've worked there. I've been reviewing the Opera House plans for nearly four years and giving my recommendations to Mr. Raleigh, who meets regularly with Mr. Haviland. I did attend a meeting of your Executive Committee once though . . . when you eloquently argued against starting construction before the plans were done."

"Evidently not eloquently enough," Nigel said with a chuckle, "but thanks for the compliment."

"As an architect, Ferenc, what do you think of the design?" Wilhelmina asked, looking impishly at Nigel. "Isn't it *just* marvelous?"

"Hold on now, Willa, don't lead the witness," Nigel said with both hands raised in feigned distress. "Now you've ruined any chance of an unbiased opinion."

"Actually, I already know your opinion, sir, that you would have preferred a more conventional design."

"I've been that transparent, have I? Well, I guess I've said on more than one occasion that we should have chosen a design that we knew how to build and looks like an opera house. But go ahead and give us your honest opinion."

"Do I have to?" Ferenc said as he laughed quietly. "I'd rather not, actually, if I may be so rude."

"See he agrees with me, dear," Wilhelmina said with a broad smile. "He doesn't want to *offend* you."

"Please go ahead, Ferenc," Nigel said reassuringly. "I'm a big boy and can take it. *Really* . . . I'd enjoy hearing the candid opinion of a trained architect. I promise you that I won't hold it against you or tell your boss. Please, go ahead—and don't feel that you have to agree with my wife, either!"

"Well, I'm a guest in your house, so you're forcing me to do it. To be completely honest and candid, Mr. Armstrong, I think it's a brilliant design and perfect for its peninsula site. The building sits as if in an arena, viewed from all directions *and from above*: from the tall office buildings, from the Sydney Harbour Bridge, from the apartment towers on the hills in Kirribilli and beyond, and from tall ships coming and going. The glazed white tiles of the gleaming roof shells, like sails in the harbor, will be appreciated from all angles. And they will hide all the building systems equipment that ordinarily would be exposed to view on a conventional rooftop. Utzon's new spherical solution for the roofs that makes them more upright will complement the arc of the Sydney Harbour Bridge beautifully, especially from the east. Photographs from that direction of both the Opera House and the bridge will be sent around the world, making Sydney a tourist attraction."

"Almost exactly my opinion, Ferenc," Wilhelmina said, self-satisfied.

"Nicely said, Ferenc, and I'd agree with everything you just said if the building was an aquarium or maritime museum—not an opera house. And I've suffered over the years because we didn't know how to build those roof shells until four days ago."

"What's changed?" Wilhelmina asked.

Nigel answered. "Jørn Utzon and Jack Zunz, Arup's partner in charge, flew here to deliver the news, in person. Seems Arup's latest ellipsoid structural scheme is out and a new spherical scheme originated by Utzon is in. Evidently, the engineers at Arup have wasted four years of structural design, and Utzon had to come up with the solution using concrete ribs to support the roofs. You can probably explain it better than I, Ferenc."

"I don't know if I can, sir, but I'll try," Ferenc said. "Certainly, Utzon deserves credit for coming up with the innovative spherical solution for the roofs, sir, but it's been a continuous evolving process with Arup to be fair about it. With all due respect, Mr. Armstrong, I wouldn't say Ove Arup and Partners wasted years of structural design. I'd say it was a continuous collaborative effort that resulted in the solution. Arup came up with the idea of using reinforced concrete ribs, not Utzon, by the way, in its ribbed ellipsoidal Scheme J, if you recall."

"I can't keep all the different schemes straight, to tell you the truth," Nigel said. "Can you explain for a layman how Utzon's spherical solution solved the problem of how to build the roof shells?"

"Utzon convinced Ove Arup, at the start, that his sketched low-slung shells were what won him the competition and were what the client wanted, in other words, his sketches were sacrosanct. Arup's engineers spent years developing different structural schemes for the shells that were all rejected by Utzon. The surprising thing is that these numerous schemes very slowly evolved into more structurally upright profiles. Finally, Utzon realized that there wasn't much difference between the various shapes of the roof shells anymore, and they could all be cut from a sphere. The sphere's radius is now the repetitive geometry that allows every part of the roof shells to be calculated in shape and size, so they are all the same in profile; only the sizes of the three roof shells differ. That's as clear as I can explain it."

"And this took four years to come up with!" Nigel said.

"No one has ever built anything like this, Mr. Armstrong; it's a revolutionary concept of design and construction."

"Do you think Utzon's innovation is going to reduce the latest cost estimate of £13,750,000?" Nigel asked. "It's four times the original estimate."

"I don't know, Mr. Armstrong. The concrete roof shells aren't going to be cheap. There's no way to estimate the entire cost of the Opera House accurately until we see Utzon's Stage Three plans for the interior of the building."

"I can't believe Utzon hasn't produced all of his plans by now. Four and a half years ago when he signed his contract, he told us it would take him eighteen months. Then later he said he'd complete all of his drawings by no later than mid-1959. On Tuesday, he told us he won't be done until March 1963. Do you know why he's so slow, Ferenc?"

"No, sir."

The evening proceeded convivially. Lydia felt that Ferenc had charmed both her mother and father. She was particularly pleased when, near the end of the evening, her father thanked Ferenc for respectfully using "sir" and "Mr. Armstrong" all evening, and then asked him to call him "Nigel" from now on.

*   *   *

"Here's something interesting to do tomorrow, Archie," Lin Yee said. It was Friday, and she was reading the Weekend Events section of *The Sydney Morning Herald*. "Listen to this. 'After operating for over one hundred years, electric tram service ends in Sydney tomorrow with the last tram trip to La Perouse, the end of the line. After it drops off its last passengers, it will proceed to a Botany junkyard. People are expected to line the route to wave their farewell.' "

"I'm not much interested in waving at the last Sydney tram," Archibald said.

"I'm talking about going to La Perouse. It looks like a nice little community down there, and it has a beach. Look at these pictures." She handed the newspaper to him. "Have you ever been there?"

"When I was around ten, our family took a drive looking for where Captain Cook, or was it Captain Phillip? was supposed to have first landed in Australia. I remember being mesmerized by an Aboriginal snake charmer and seeing native boys diving for coins that people were throwing off a pier. Dad bought me a boomerang, and Mum bought a beautiful display of shells from a native woman that still sits on their mantelshelf. It was the first and only time I've seen an Aboriginal mission. There wasn't much of a community back then."

"Well, it is now. There's a hotel, restaurants, a small museum about the French explorer La Perouse, and Pere Receveur's grave, one of the two chaplains in the La Perouse expedition. He died on February 17, 1788, and is buried there. His grave is the earliest known marked grave of a European on the east coast. The first Frenchman buried in Australia. Visiting French ships leave wreaths on his grave. There's also a World War Two fort. I'd like to go for the sights and then be there for the ceremony when the last tram passengers are dropped off."

"I think the beach is called Frenchmans Beach for obvious reasons," Archibald said. "Let's go; it sounds like fun."

They arrived in La Perouse at eleven in the morning, walked around for an hour enjoying the sights, and decided to have lunch at a small beach restaurant with a view of Frenchmans Beach and Botany Bay.

A smiling waiter greeted them. Archibald and Lin Yee were astonished to see that the waiter was James Bennett.

"Surprise, surprise, Mr. and Mrs. Armstrong," James said. "I saw you standing outside before you decided to come in."

"*Archie* to you, James. You're working here . . . that's dumb; *of course* you are, since you're wearing a waiter's apron. *How are you?*"

"I'm good! How are you two?"

"We're as happy as can be," Archibald said gaily. "How long have you been working here?"

"About two months now. And if I want to work here much longer, I'd better show you to your table." There were ten tables. James took them to the only available one set in a corner with no view of the beach.

"I'm sorry this is a lousy table, but we're really busy with the cere-mony today and all. Here's your menus. I'll be back in a few minutes."

There was an Aboriginal man running the restaurant and also taking orders, two female cooks, one who appeared to be his wife, and James. The restaurant was full and the service slow. Archibald and Lin Yee had no time to talk to James, except to arrange to meet him after work at the hotel restaurant for dinner at six.

After saying goodbye until later, Archibald and Lin Yee won-dered whether James would show at the hotel restaurant; never-theless, they walked over to the restaurant and made a reservation. Then they took a walk along the beach. Halfway up the beach they came to a sea-bitten, white-painted, wood fence that ran parallel to the beach marking the western boundary of the seven-acre La Perouse Aborigines Mission. Poorly constructed weathered wood shacks were scattered among the dunes and up the hillside. On the top of the hill, the steeple of a wood church projected over cottages and a barrack-like building.

After seating themselves on their beach blanket, Archibald said, "James has matured from his experience. He must be twenty years old now."

"He left in early '61, was it as early as January?" Lin Yee asked.

"That would be about right, around a year and nine or ten months ago."

"And no word," Lin Yee said, shaking her head in disbelief. "How are we going to handle this with Mary and David?—we have to tell them."

"Let's see what he says before we decide that. Hopefully, he won't place us in an impossible position. He doesn't appear any worse for the experience, I must say. I was dumbfounded how he just walked up to us smiling away, like nothing had happened. I was completely taken aback."

The last tram arrived at four. The speeches were boring, so they walked away from the crowd and crossed the footbridge to enter the impressive World War Two fort on Bare Island. After that, they leisurely walked across Botany Bay Park and arrived at the hotel at 5:40 p.m. After refreshing themselves in the lavatories, they waited for James in the lounge. He arrived promptly at six o'clock.

Archibald waited until their drinks were delivered and meals ordered before asking "Where have you been since you left, James."

"Did my parents tell you how I left?" He looked at them with questioning eyes.

"We know that you left in a huff," Archibald said, "without telling them where you were going, but nothing much more than that."

"Except that they were terribly distraught the way you left," Lin Yee said, "and that you haven't written or contacted them. Mary, in particular, is still sick about it and worries what has become of you."

James thought to himself, they were too embarrassed to tell Archie and Lin Yee that I struck Dad—typical, keep up the appearances.

"I just had to get out of there. My father was driving me crazy. I just drove west, sleeping in my car along the way. I didn't know where I was going. I was so mad and fed up with him and everything. I was just looking at things—the landscape and the towns: Katoomba, Bathurst, Dubbo, Broken Hill. I just kept driving west, thinking maybe I'd drive to Alice Springs.

"I was afraid to talk to anyone for some strange reason. I started driving to Adelaide, then decided I'd better stay away from the big cities. I guess I thought the police could be looking for me. Maybe they were. So I drove all the way to Alice Springs before I started talking to people. Do you know if my parents called the police to search for me or anything?"

"They thought you would be back in a few days or a week or two, James," Lin Yee said. "It didn't occur to them to call the police. Mary thought you would write her within a month. When you—"

"Actually, your father filed a Missing Person's report a week after you left, James," Archibald said.

"What?" Lin Yee said. "You never told me that."

"He asked me not to tell anyone," Archibald said. "That's how worried your Dad was, James."

"What you've done to your parents is not fair or right, James," Lin Yee said.

Archibald seldom raised his voice to Lin Yee or anyone else, but he did now, ever so slightly:

"*Lin Yee*, please, let's *not* pass judgment on James. We don't know his side of the story. We don't know what went on, or why he felt the need to leave in this unhappy way."

James looked fondly at Archibald. "I really don't like my dad. You don't know how mean he can be. Everything has to be *his* way." He looked at them to see how they were taking this. "My mom won't stick up for herself. She's afraid of him. *Every single day* he told me exactly what he wanted me to do. If I didn't live up to what he wanted, in any way, he'd fly into a rage and yell at me. I had to thank him a thousand times for *every little thing* he did for me. I just couldn't take it anymore.

"I started thinking, *you're not even my real parent!* You don't have any right to treat me like this. You're just trying to make me into this perfect Aboriginal kid, like I was some kind of science project. Then, when I started to ask about my real parents, I had hell to pay. They wouldn't tell me *anything* about them. I know they must know *something*. When I drove away, he ran right up to my window and yelled through the glass that he wished he'd *never adopted me!* That goes both ways is what I thought. I can get by on my own. I don't want his help or anything from him. I'll do it all on my own."

Archibald could not think of anything to say. It was too ugly. He was greatly saddened by James's youthful resentment of his father. It bordered on hate.

"What did you do in Alice Springs when you started to talk to people?" Lin Yee asked.

"I started to learn about my people. I visited some Aboriginal communities. I learned some of our history, our beliefs, laws, and customs. Dad told me I wouldn't have anything in common with them, but he was wrong. They aren't *stupid,* just because they aren't well educated. They accepted me for the most part. I liked a lot of them and made some good friends. Some of them will give you their last scrap of bread. Some others . . . I didn't like too much, to be honest—like the ones who stole my car. After that, I traveled like a swagman working odd jobs as I found them. I was nearly arrested a couple of times, except for my trusty savings account book. I made my way back to Sydney about five months ago and reapplied for

Sydney University. They accepted me. I start in February."

"That's wonderful, James!" Archibald exclaimed.

"Mary will be so pleased!" Lin Yee said.

"I don't want my parents to know! Not until I'm through with my first year. I'll tell them then. After I'm twenty-one. I want to do this on my own terms."

"James, you can't treat your parents that way," Lin Yee said. "It's not right, and it's so unfair. Mary loves you and is worried sick about you. She doesn't even know if you're alive."

"I reckon my parents know I'm okay. They just don't know how to contact me."

"How would they know you're okay, if you haven't contacted them?" Archibald asked.

"I was picked up in Wagga Wagga. The police called them to confirm who I was, but I wouldn't talk to them. They can check my bank to see I'm withdrawing from my savings account. I think they know I'm okay."

Lin Yee shook her head. "Well I can't say I haven't seen you."

"Just don't tell them you saw me. They won't ask. Don't tell them I'm working here, that's all."

Wanting to change the subject, Archibald asked, "Where are you living, James?"

"Near here, Archie. Not in the mission, but just outside it. Six of us share a house. It's not much rent."

"Are you going to live on campus when you start at uni?" Archibald asked.

"I can't afford it. I'll take the bus from here."

"That will take you an hour or more one way!" Archibald said. "Get a cheap room off campus or share a flat with someone near the campus."

"It would still be three or four times what I pay here, Archie. I can live here for almost nothing."

"Even when you add in bus fare? Have you figured that in?"

"I need to live in La Perouse to work at the restaurant, while I attend Sydney Uni."

While they talked about the costs to attend the university, it became obvious to Archibald that James needed financial assistance.

"James, your lack of money is going to make your chances of success in your first year very dubious. I know you want to do it yourself; I respect that desire and why you feel that way, but I don't want to see you fail your first year. When I build an office building, what do you think I do?"

"I don't know what you mean, Archie."

"I borrow money . . . from a bank to pay for the construction of the building, and then I pay back the loan over time from my profits. That's what I want to do for you. I want to lend you money to go to uni and graduate, and then you pay me back from your salary when you have a job. What do you say, James?"

"I can't take money from you, Archie. I wouldn't be doing it on my own."

"James, you *would* be doing it on your own. We'd sign a legal agreement with interest and a payment schedule for after you graduate. I'll sue your sweet arse if you don't pay me back with interest. Look, traveling from La Perouse to Sydney University and back everyday is a prescription for failure. And I'd hate to see you fail when I can help you to succeed."

"James, this makes a lot of sense," Lin Yee said. "It's like borrowing from a bank, which rich people do every day, but you can't, because you have no collateral. Archie is offering you a golden business opportunity. Take it."

"All right, Archie. But I'm going to pay you back, no worries. You'll see. I don't want ya suing my arse! Ha ha ha ha."

"Great, James. Now let's talk about Lin Yee's problem. You don't want to tell your parents until you've finished your first year and are twenty-one. I understand that. But Lin Yee can't wait until then. I understand that too. Your father is *not* going to remove you from Sydney Uni, we know that as well. How about you, James, telling your parents where you are after your first semester, and you, Lin Yee, avoid any conversation with Mary until then. Is that a possible solution?

Lin Yee and James agreed to Archibald's proposal, and they all shook on it. With smiles all around they ordered dessert.

Chapter 7

Dissent and a Fair Go

Lydia and Ferenc married after dating for seven months and moved into her rented two-bedroom house in Double Bay. Eleven months after that, Lydia confirmed that she was four-months pregnant. This Saturday morning in August 1963, they were driving to Paddington to inspect two adjacent boarded-up terrace houses on Duxford Street that they were interested in buying and renovating. Nigel had agreed to meet them there.

"Do you *really* need my father's advice?" Lydia asked.

"Yes, he's a builder and will be knowledgeable on the condition of the terraces and how much it will cost to renovate them."

Lydia did not believe Ferenc. She had come to know his devious and manipulative side. "We don't have the money to buy two terraces and pay the cost of renovating them."

"It all depends on their condition and the renovation cost."

"Okay . . . but don't try to mooch money from my father."

Ferenc looked askance at her. "Your father *gave* Archie your grandparents' house."

"My brother renovated the house, and paid for it after he was married!" She wasn't entirely sure of this, but said it nevertheless. "It's none of our business anyway."

"Yes it is. It would have been part of your inheritance."

"Dad was paid for the house, so it's still part of my inheritance!"

"They'll spend it."

Ignoring his speculation, Lydia said, "If it's going to cost too much to buy both terraces and renovate them, we'll buy only one or continue to look around."

"You said you loved the look of these houses and the neighborhood."

"That was before we figured out how much it's going to cost, and you asked my father to walk through with us."

"They each have only two bedrooms upstairs," Ferenc said. "We need at least three bedrooms and an artist studio for you. You want to keep painting after the baby arrives, don't you?"

"We don't have to move right away," Lydia said. "We can extend our lease and turn my studio into the baby's room. I won't be painting for a while anyway."

"Lydia, these two terraces are perfect for us. I thought you wanted to live in Five Ways as much as me."

Ferenc had become enamored with the Victorian architectural charm of Paddington, the first community to be gentrified in Sydney, which began in the late 1950s and would continue into the 1980s. He particularly liked the picturesque Five Ways neighborhood, with its shopping hub centered on a roundabout where five streets came together.

They drove in silence on Duxford Street and arrived at the terraces to see Nigel standing in the front yard talking to the owner. After greetings, Nigel excitedly said, "This entire row of ten terraces was built by your great, great, great aunt Eleanor Armstrong, whose married name was Norman."

"How do you know, Dad?" Lydia said, thrilled.

"Look at this." He pointed above the brass doorbell pull. "Norman Builders placed a glazed plaster brick plaque like this on every house it built with the date of construction in large numerals, 1876 in this case, and "by NB" in smaller lettering below. It's still a handsome plaque today."

Ferenc said to the beaming owner "This doesn't mean we have to buy it—just so you know."

They all laughed.

After inspecting both terrace houses and telling the owner that they had to talk among themselves before considering an offer, the three of them walked to one of Ferenc's favorite restaurants in Five Ways.

"Why do you want to buy in such a seedy, run-down neighborhood?" Nigel asked.

"Many of our friends have moved here, Dad," Lydia said. "It's an up and coming neighborhood for people like us: artists, architects, writers, academics . . ."

"European immigrants, like me, are moving here because we're used to living close together," Ferenc said. "We like to be able to walk to neighborhood pubs, shops and restaurants. The house prices here are reasonable, and we can renovate over time. Also, there are better views of the harbor from up here than in Double Bay."

"It *would* be something special, you living in Eleanor Armstrong's terraces," Nigel said. "The houses are old, but well constructed and nicely detailed."

"These two joined terraces will be beautiful when I'm done with them," Ferenc said. "As this community is renovated, I think our house will be a great investment. We have enough for a down payment, but we'll have to renovate it over several years as we have the cash."

"That's not a good idea, Ferenc, with a baby in the house," Nigel said. "There'll be a lot of dust. I'll help you with the cost, so you can renovate it before you move in."

"*No*, Daddy, we don't want to ask you for money," Lydia said.

"No worries, I helped Archie to renovate his house. You can pay me back when you're able."

"*Thanks,* Dad, that'll be a big help," Ferenc said. "I was recently promoted another grade, yet still don't make that much; living costs being what they are here."

"Archie told me you were promoted. You're attending the construction meetings at the Opera House site office now, I understand."

"Yeah, I was appointed the department's site liaison nearly two months ago."

"Archie's been attending most of the Executive Committee meetings for me, so I'm not quite up-to-date. When will the dynamiting of the twenty columns be completed?—it's been nearly four months."

"They have two columns to go," Ferenc said.

"I'm so sorry to see Ove Arup copping it unfairly," Nigel said. "A 'shocking engineering blunder' is the way the newspapers see it. The press can't understand and won't accept that the structural engineer couldn't correctly calculate the size of columns because the roof shells hadn't been designed yet."

"Friends keep asking Ferenc if the dynamiting and lack of progress mean the project isn't going to be completed," Lydia said.

"It's a fair question," Nigel said. "Have you worked much with Jørn Utzon since he came to live here?"

"Not much," Ferenc said. "He's been working mainly on preparing Stage Three plans for the interior. I've been working mostly with Michael Lewis, Arup's partner here, and Hornibrook's director of construction on Stage Two plans for the construction of the roof shells. Utzon isn't interested in our construction meetings and attends only if Lewis asks him too. But I've developed fairly good relations with both sides."

"What do you mean, *both sides*?" Nigel asked.

"Well . . . you know, Utzon and Arup have had this big falling out."

"Ah *great*, that's just what this project needs," Nigel said shaking his head. "How bad is it?"

"You don't know about it?" Ferenc said, amazed.

"No. I only attend meetings now and then."

"Utzon bricked up the door between his site office and Arup's and told Michael Lewis to make an appointment to see him from now on."

"*Why*, in God's name?"

"Things have been going badly for months. I'm not sure why."

"That's not true, Ferenc, we've come up with the reasons," Lydia said. "He's been bothered about this for months, Dad."

"We have a theory, that's all, Lydia."

"What is it, Ferenc? You're in a position to know."

"It's just a theory, Dad, that I think comes down to three or four main points. Ove Arup is literally sick about his company doing most of the work and being blamed for all of the project's problems. Arup has prepared all the construction working drawings, manages the construction and is responsible for approving payment to all the contractors, subcontractors, and consultants. He's basically acting in the role of an architect, not like a consulting structural engineer at all."

"Tell Dad what Michael Lewis said about Arup's financial problems," Lydia said.

"Lewis told me they are working at a loss, and the project has put the company in financial hot water. Utzon is being paid better than them for half the work. On top of everything else, Arup is being called incompetent while no one is blaming Utzon for anything.

"So Ove Arup wrote Utzon proposing that they share equally the fees and recognition to complete the project, *or* Utzon could take over the architect's traditional role and run the entire project, treating Arup as just another consultant. This angered Utzon who resented Ove Arup pretentious co-principals proposal. He said that Ove Arup's problem is that he has ambitions as an architect."

Nigel said, "Utzon doesn't have the experienced staff to run a complex project like the Opera House."

"That's not what Utzon thinks, evidently," Ferenc said. "He wrote Ove Arup a curt letter saying he will take over management of Stage Two and Three because 'Management is in a way the easiest part of the job, something which most people can learn.' Well, he's never done construction drawings for any major building or managed its construction, is not doing it now, and as far as I can see, except for paying his own Stage Three consultants, nothing has changed. Now since they are hardly speaking, it looks like Arup will have no choice but to prepare all the construction drawings for Stage Two roof shells and run construction just like it did for the Stage One's concrete foundations and four-story building. That's about where it is."

"You forgot Ove Arup's 'total design' concept that Utzon dislikes," Lydia said.

"Oh, yeah. Ove Arup has been writing articles and speaking at international conferences about his concept of 'total design of the built environment.' He thinks multidisciplinary collaboration of planners, architects, engineers, landscape architects, and others, working together, as equals, under one roof would provide the best solutions. Needless to say, architects see this as a direct attack on their creativity and dominance. Famous architects . . . Mies van der Rohe, for one, have ridiculed Ove Arup openly. Nevertheless, he's formed Arup Partnership with architect Philip Dawson to try out his concept. When Utzon heard ab—"

"Uh-*huh*—you can stop there," Nigel said, nodding knowingly. "Utzon thinks Ove Arup is out to steal the Sydney Opera House from him."

"Yes, that's the way I see it. Utzon then wrote Ove Arup that he would administer any structural design issues in Stage Three 'to the maximum extent,' which sounds like he intends to sack Arup if they disagree on any structural issues."

"How very sad," Nigel said, "that disorganization and the problems created by this unconventional building have led to this fallout between Jørn Utzon and Ove Arup."

*   *   *

"*Wow*, did I get an earful today, Lydia," Ferenc said, arriving home late from work.

"Utzon was mauled today by Premier Renshaw and his group. I knew it was going to be a tough meeting for him but not this bad. The premier demanded that both Utzon and Michael Lewis be there, but it was Utzon they were after and beat up."

"Were you in a meeting with the *premier*?" Lydia asked, impressed.

"I met him. We used my car and Eggert's car to drive a big stack of Stage Three drawings over to the meeting with the premier."

"Who's Eggert?"

"One of Utzon's Danish architects—a nice fellow. We carried the drawings into the meeting room and met the premier and the deputy premier. Then we waited in an adjacent room and heard everything they said.

"They wanted to grill Utzon about not doing construction drawings and not being adequately staffed to get the job done. You know what that's all about."

"What do you mean?" Lydia said, looking confused.

"William Wood—Public Works's spy I told you about—he's behind this. He's my counterpart sent over a couple of months ago by the Minister for Public Works Norm Ryan to find out what Utzon's been doing. Public Works wants to take over the project from my State Planning Department. They want to expose that Utzon isn't doing construction working drawings yet and hasn't solved many of the design issues yet."

"Such as?"

"The problems of seating in the multipurpose halls, acoustics, ceiling design, how to construct the glass walls—you name it."

"Ah, Wood," Lydia said. "He's the fellow Utzon tried to throw out of his office."

"Yeah. Wood is in his late fifties and pretty experienced. He's both an architect and structural engineer. Utzon saw immediately why Ryan sent him over and didn't like it. That's why he wrote Ryan saying Wood was interfering with his staff and slowing work production. He then denied him access to the drawings and documents, and all but pushed him out of his office. Wood is a lot less sympathetic to Utzon than I am. Ryan demanded that Utzon allow him back in to do his job—and this is the result. Ryan was in the meeting.

"They went through all of Utzon's drawings and concluded that only five were working drawings capable of being built; all the rest were preliminary sketches lacking dimensions and details. The Deputy Premier Pat Hills said, 'Stage Three is nowhere near being ready to tender construction. What have you been doing with your time, Mr. Utzon?'

"Utzon said, 'Are you losing confidence in my ability to perform by asking such a question?'

"The premier said, 'How do you have time to win the competition for the Zurich Playhouse when you don't have time to produce working drawings for the Opera House?'

" 'I and my colleagues worked on those Zurich Playhouse plans just for fun as a hobby for six months in our spare time.' Utzon said.

"Premier Renshaw said, 'Well, you've won first prize—good for you. We'll have to talk further if you accept a contract to build it.'

"Hills said, 'We wonder where you get all this spare time, Mr. Utzon. You've submitted competition plans for the National Opera House in Madrid. You've also submitted unwanted sketch plans for underground car parking for the Sydney Opera House and for the redevelopment of Circular Quay East. You have not been engaged to design these, Mr. Utzon. Keep your nose out of other people's business. We want you to work on what you are being paid to do—preparing buildable plans for Stage Three.' "

Lydia said, "My gosh, they went for the jugular!"

"Utzon was calm and cool, though. He said, 'The Sydney Opera House Executive Committee asked me to look into the need for parking and to consider the environs of the Opera House. All objects in this district are seen together with the Opera House, and if they are wrongly formed, they will destroy this building.'

"Premier Renshaw said, 'You are, of course, aware that the Opera House project is being called one of the biggest bungles in our state's history. Parliament is considering a Royal Commission of Inquiry into its mismanagement and increasing cost. The original cost estimate in 1957 was £3.5 million. Unfortunately, two weeks ago, quantity surveyor Rider Hunt came out with a cost of £17.4 million. So, you can imagine our chagrin when you publicly contradicted us by saying there are no economies to be found to reduce this amount.'

"Utzon said nothing.

"The premier said, 'I'm directing you today to consider Minister Ryan, here, as your client rather than the Sydney Opera House Executive Committee. We have to place this project in professional hands.'

"Utzon was really on his toes. He said, 'Under the Opera House Act, I am legally required to consider the Executive Committee as my client. As premier, Mr. Renshaw, you are its president and my ultimate client. Norm Ryan is your chosen minister, whom

I already work closely with as the construction authority.' The premier didn't have a response.

"So Ryan jumped in and asked, 'How will you ever complete the great volume of drawings required to build Stage Three with only ten architects on your staff?'

"Utzon said, 'I have more than ten here. There are nearly twenty architects working on the project, in total, when those in my Denmark office are included. I'll increase my staff as needed. It's not a problem.'

"Near the end of the meeting, Eggert and I were asked to collect the drawings and drive them back to the office. I was working on the second floor of the site trailer when Utzon and Lewis returned from the meeting about five-thirty. They came in saying they needed a drink after that 'ghastly meeting.' I guess they opened a bottle of champagne, because I heard a *pop*.

"Lewis said, 'I was shocked by their rudeness and aggressiveness. With the state election coming up, they're running scared. They don't want your parking proposals to throw light on their failure to provide parking and include its cost in the escalating total.'

" 'They have no right to tell me how to run my office,' Utzon said, 'or how many people to employ. This is all William Wood's doing.'

"Lewis said, 'Jørn, you've got to do something about this lack of working drawings. I kept my mouth shut, when you told them you have more architects than you do, because I didn't want to embarrass you. You've got to get someone to prepare the working drawings and other documents to build Stage Three. You haven't got in your staff the sort of experienced people you need, and you are never going to get there. You should utilize the services of a large established Sydney architectural firm, like Peddle Thorp & Walker, who are a short walk from our site office to help out.'

" 'I don't believe an architect should employ another architect for that,' Utzon said. 'All the great architects like Le Corbusier, Alvar Aalto, Mies van der Rohe, and Frank Lloyd Wright have tried that and it doesn't work. I must do everything myself; that's the only way this Opera House can be built.'

"Lewis said, 'Well, if they are prepared to give you fifty years to build it, there's just the possibility you might finish it; otherwise, you haven't got a chance . . . Look, I might as well tell you something. You're going to hear it from someone anyway. I was really frustrated last week and wrote Ove Arup and Zunz that you've been promising me for over a year now that "within the next three weeks" you'd send me the architectural drawings for the major and minor hall acoustical ceilings and the glass walls. My structural engineering staff can't do their work, if you aren't doing yours, Jørn.'

"It became real quiet then. I looked out the window and saw Utzon walking away in a huff."

The fateful meeting with Premier Renshaw put Utzon into a state of depression. He had only recently returned from six weeks in Europe to attend the funeral of his eldest brother Leif, who had died suddenly at the age of forty-eight of a heart attack.

On the plane flight back to Sydney from Denmark, Utzon had time to dwell on the fact that both his brothers and his mother were now dead, leaving only his father, nearly eighty, alone in Denmark, too far from Australia for Utzon to assist him in his declining years. At forty-six, Utzon was concerned about his own health for the sake of his family. Thoughts of his mentor and architect friend Eero Sarineen entered his mind. Sarineen had died at the young age of fifty-one of a brain tumor.

Two months later, in September 1964, to reduce everyday stress and to get away from Michael Lewis, William Wood, and the press, Utzon split his office into two. He moved his senior design section into a former boat shed on the west side of the Palm Beach peninsula, a two-hour drive from his Opera House site office. He did not install a phone, preferring to be reachable only by mail. He moved his family from Bayview to be near his Palm Beach office.

Within weeks, the Opera House site office was left with little design work. Feeling less valued and subjected to the daily demands of construction issues, without adequate direction, three staff members at the site office resigned, including a key administrative architect.

*   *   *

The Aboriginal Advancement Association (**AAA**) listed Harvey Hudson as one of its community activists. On January 23, 1965, the AAA president called Harvey.

"I'm calling to request your assistance, Mr. Hudson. The elders of Nanima Aboriginal Reserve want to improve their community and have asked for our advice. The reserve is near Wellington, about two hours north of you. Have you heard of it?"

"No."

"Well, we are sending a white community organizer Peter Gibbs to the reserve to conduct a one-day training session. They'd like to learn how to become community activists to get what they need. Something you already know, Mr. Hudson. It's going to be on Saturday, February 14. If you could accompany Mr. Gibbs, it would be very helpful to us and the elders. Gibbs would pick you up at 9 a.m. and have you back home that night by 9 p.m. Would you be willing to give us a day to help the cause, Mr. Hudson?"

"I'll help out if I don't have ta give a talk."

"Uh, it's goin' to be very informal, Mr. Hudson. It's a small community, but we think their leaders are pretty good there. You'll be there mostly to serve as an example and answer their questions. Does that sound all right, Mr. Hudson?"

"Orright."

"Thanks, Mr. Hudson. I thought we could count on you. Peter Gibbs will call you a few days before February 14 to confirm the particulars. Thanks again, Mr. Hudson. G'bye."

Entirely by coincidence, James Bennett, would also be in Nanima Aboriginal Reserve on Saturday, February 14. James had completed two years of education at the University of Sydney and would start his third year on March 1. Before then, from February 13 to 25, he would be one of twenty-nine students traveling in a rented bus to conduct a fact-finding survey of Aboriginal living conditions in New South Wales. If they came upon segregation in such places as milk bars, restaurants, picture theaters, hotels, and swimming pools, they would demonstrate against it. The bus tour would become known as the "Freedom Ride."

The fact-finding tour was organized by Student Action for

Aborigines, a University of Sydney student organization. Its pres-ident, Charles Perkins, an Aboriginal student, was a year ahead of James. All other members of the group were white. Expecting that their tour might encounter violent opposition, the group adopted a nonviolent resistance policy, read the writings of Mahatma Gandhi and Martin Luther King, and ran compulsory nightly seminars to prepare for possible confrontations.

On Friday, February 13, the students met at the university to board the bus. A large group of well-wishers were there to see them off, including James's adoptive parents, with whom he had recon-ciled, and a group of American black entertainers who sang "We Shall Overcome." A few journalists took statements from the stu-dents for their newspapers.

The bus traveled west over the Blue Mountains and stopped for the night in Orange, a town with few Aborigines. The next morning, they boarded the bus to go to Nanima Aboriginal Reserve. As the bus drove out of Orange into the countryside, James hunkered down in his seat, rested his head on the window glass, and thought about his reconcilement with his adoptive father, a six-month ordeal.

Fulfilling his promise to Archie and Lin Yee, he had contact-ed his parents after completing his first semester at the University of Sydney. He called during a workday, hoping his father would be away at work.

"Hello, Mum, it's me, James" was all he got out before his adop-tive mother gasped and started to cry. Sobbing, Mary tried several times to speak, but was too overcome with emotion.

When she could finally speak, she asked question after ques-tion about his health, his travels, where he had lived, and his experi-ences over the past two and a half years. He realized that she knew generally where he had been but little of the specifics of what he had done. When she asked how he was doing at the University of Sydney, before he had a chance to tell her he was a student there, he became angry.

"*Did* Lin Yee tell you I'm attending Sydney Uni?"

Surprised by his sudden anger, Mary answered, "She didn't tell me; I *told* her."

Hearing his mother's guileless answer, he realized he had blundered.

"How would *she* know?" Mary asked.

Exposed, James felt he had no alternative but to tell her the truth of his chance meeting with Archie and Lin Yee and how they had reluctantly agreed to keep his whereabouts to themselves until he had finished his first semester.

"I wanted to make sure that I could do well at uni before contacting you and Dad."

His mother started to cry again and through sobs said, "I c-can't . . . can't believe that Lin Yee . . . *lied* to me!"

James decided to get everything out into the open. He told her that Archibald was helping him cover the costs of university.

"I'm sorry, James . . . I have to hang up. Your father will be home any minute. If he finds me in this state, he'll be very angry. Give me your phone number, dear, and I'll call you tomorrow or the next day. I have to find the right time to talk to your father. He's not going to take this very well, I'm afraid."

James learned two months later that David had stormed over to Archibald's house that evening and angrily accused him of meddling in his family's private affairs. The two couples did not speak for weeks after that.

Mary called James back, and they met several times without David knowing. After finishing his first year of university, James and his adoptive father finally reconciled. James reluctantly allowed David to take over his financial assistance only if he agreed to make no attempt to pay off Archibald's loan amount, which James considered his personal obligation.

James thoughts were interrupted by loud voices coming from the front of the bus. The bus driver was lost and there was an argument about the location of Nanima Aboriginal Reserve. They stopped at a petrol station to ask directions.

The reserve was out of sight of Wellington, over a hill, past a rubbish dump, and at the end of an unpaved road. Because it was an "unmanaged" reserve, there was no superintendent to contend with when the bus pulled into the Aboriginal community, unexpected and unannounced. The residents were perplexed to see young, clean-cut, white men and women empty out of the bus, most carrying clipboards.

The students were shocked by the extreme poverty of the place. There were about twenty tin shacks and a few humpies providing shelter, all with mud floors. Water had to be carried from the river. The community felt overcrowded for its few dwellings.

Charles Perkins asked to speak to the elders and tried to organize a meeting, but his efforts were lost in the general confusion of greetings and questions. The students did not have a plan, except to fill out questionnaires and survey living conditions. They set about their tasks, asking questions, evaluating facilities, and requesting permission to look into dwellings.

Harvey and the AAA community organizer, Peter Gibbs, arrived amid this hubbub. The elders were expecting them and greeted them as they stepped out of their car. The head of the community explained the unexpected visit of students from the University of Sydney who were surveying Aboriginal living conditions in New South Wales.

Gibbs stopped a student passing by, who happened to be James Bennett, and asked to meet their leader. James saw Perkins in the distance and brought him to Gibbs. Several of the other student leaders followed. Awkwardly, people began to introduce themselves. Gibbs asked an elder if there was a room in the community building where the group could sit and talk.

Most of the community building was divided into makeshift rooms for families and single adults, but one end was retained for group activities. The students unfolded three tables and formed them into a U shape and arranged folding chairs around them. Gibbs seated himself in the center of the central table, Harvey sat to his left, Charles Perkins to his right, and James sat next to Perkins. Residents and students took the remaining seats and others leaned against the walls.

Peter Gibbs directed the conversation.

"I've heard of your group, Student Action for Aborigines, and your planned bus tour. I commend you for your activism. Your visit to Nanima Reserve is a surprise though. So this is a real treat for me to meet you all." With a hand gesture, he said, "This is Harvey Hudson, a community activist from Murraroo Aborigines Mission who will help me present a training session here today."

Harvey did not correct him that he lived outside the Murraroo Mission.

Perkins said a few things about himself and the reasons for their visit. He then asked James and several other students to tell why they were fighting for Aboriginal rights. Harvey was impressed by the eloquence and intelligence of the two Aboriginal students, Charles Perkins and James Bennett. He thought to himself, this is what we can become with proper education. The meeting concluded somewhat abruptly, because the students had to leave to find the Anglican church in Wellington where lunch was being prepared for them.

After Harvey returned to Gura, he followed the news about the students' bus ride and was delighted that they picketed the Walgett Returned Soldiers League club for not admitting Aboriginal veterans. He was upset, though, to read that outside Walgett a truck rammed their bus three times forcing it off the road. Fortunately, no one was injured. The police were searching for the truck driver. Several days later, in Moree, the students confronted the mayor, police, and five-hundred booing and shoving locals when they brought Aboriginal boys from a nearby reserve to swim in the segregated municipal swimming pool. The students used passive resistance by falling to the ground and covering their heads with their hands when punched by the mob and threatened with arrest by the police. The arrival of the press and photographers changed the ambience. The mayor relented and allowed the boys and Aboriginal adults Charles Perkins and James Bennett into the pool. Photos of their joyful swimming with the boys were printed in newspapers throughout Australia under the banner headline "Aboriginals Swim in Moree Segregated Pool!"

The press coverage was better than anyone expected. The thirteen-day "Freedom Ride" became national and international news and stirred the conscience of the nation.

*　*　*

The Labor Party was defeated in the New South Wales polls on May 1, 1965, and a coalition of the Liberal and Country Parties took over under Premier Robert Askin. They were elected, in part, on a campaign promise to control the escalating cost of the Sydney Opera House and complete it in a timely fashion. Davis Hughes, leader of the Country Party, was so enamored with the Opera House project that he chose to become Minister for Public Works rather than deputy premier.

In spite of the fact that Hughes had vowed to clean up the Opera House mess, Utzon was optimistic that the change would work to his advantage. The previous premier and his ministers had clearly turned against him. He had not seen the Public Works liaison, William Wood, for months and hoped that Hughes would discontinue Wood's liaison responsibilities.

Ferenc had become friendly with Bill Wood. They were both architect-engineers and liaisons from the two NSW departments most involved in the project: Ferenc from the State Planning Department and Wood from the Public Works Department. And, they were both frustrated by Utzon's move to Palm Beach. Their jobs were to liaise with both Arup's partner-in-charge Michael Lewis and Jørn Utzon, but every attempt to visit Utzon's Palm Beach office was thwarted. Their letters proposing a date to visit went unanswered, and requests through Utzon's construction staff at the Opera House site office were unfruitful. They could not call Utzon, because he had not installed a phone. He refused to attend weekly construction meetings at the site office and would attend Stage Three design meetings with Arup personnel only under duress. This left Ferenc and Wood with little knowledge about Utzon's Stage Three interior design progress.

Jørn Utzon did meet with Davis Hughes, the new Minister for Public Works, three times in June. Each meeting was more contentious than the last.

In late June, Wood showed Ferenc a draft of a letter he was writing for Hughes. The most critical part of the letter said:

You assured the previous premier, Mr. Renshaw, in a meeting on July 23, 1964, that you would have your Stage Three drawings for the interiors well along by now. It is a matter of great concern that you have few working drawings and supporting details in a form suitable to hand to a contractor for pricing and carrying out the work of Stage Three.

Whilst I can see that some drawings could not be completed in the major and minor halls of Stage Two, before the problems of acoustics are resolved, I see no reason why working drawings have not been completed for practically the whole of the Stage One interiors. I have walked through the basement and the three levels above, where there are some 900 rooms constructed in concrete. Mostly, you have shown me only sketch floor plans for the podium's theaters, music rooms, rehearsal and recital halls, administrative offices, box offices, conductor's suites, dressing rooms, kitchens and dining rooms, lavatories and lounges, workshops, storage rooms, and mechanical and electric rooms.

Regarding your request for funds to build plywood prototypes, I cannot proceed until they are in the form of working drawings, specifications, and approximate quantities that can be put out to tender.

In view of the number of years which you have had to work on Stage Three design of the interiors of the Sydney Opera House, it is no longer possible to recommend to Parliament further financial appropriations until you produce the working drawings and supporting details to allow reliable estimates of time and cost to be made.

On July 12, Utzon replied to Hughes's letter. "If it is now necessary for you to be presented with a full set of working drawings, etc., before you can receive an appropriation of funds, there will certainly be a delay in the project, for this has not been the program set for me up till now."

On Aug 11, 1965, Hughes met with Wood to decide how to force Utzon to produce working drawings, specifications, and quantity estimates. They came up with three initiatives: (1) Begin "checkbook control" of monthly fee payments to Utzon commensurate with the number of working drawings and the production of specifications and quantity estimates, (2) require that he immediately hire additional staff or subcontract with a local architectural firm to achieve item one above, and (3) require him to prepare and commit to a critical path method schedule for managing Stage Three production and construction.

Hughes meet with Utzon to discuss the three initiatives and to illustrate his hands-on approach to manage the process much better than had been done under Labor's administration. Utzon was shocked and repulsed by Hughes's haughty attitude and aggressiveness.

On August 25, Hughes submitted a memorandum to Premier Askin and his cabinet ministers, summarizing his progress in resolving the Opera House fiasco. It was leaked to the press. Utzon read the memorandum's main points in the newspapers the following day. One paragraph, in particular, threw him into a rage:

> The government will insist that Utzon prepare proper working drawings and specifications for tendering work. I foresee that this will involve a considerable increase in the number of staff employed by Utzon, or he will have to let out some of the work to a capable Sydney architectural firm to assist in the preparation of working drawings, specifications, and other documents. It is necessary that Stage Three proceed in a professional manner similar to Stages One and Two, which were largely engineering achievements carried out by Ove Arup and Partners.

Utzon immediately wrote a letter to Hughes and had it hand-delivered that same day:

> You obviously do not realize that everything that exists at the Opera House today I have been doing personally in my office. Every single piece of concrete has been

completely designed and controlled by me. If you do not accept my way of working, I am sorry, but you will have to find another architect to carry out the rest of the job.

Hughes had not intended to make his memorandum public and accepted Utzon's understandable temper tantrum. It did not have any influence on how he intended to proceed.

A month later, Archibald called his father. "Dad, I've just come out of a Sydney Opera House Executive Committee meeting with Davis Hughes. With the backing of Premier Askin, he's taken over our role as 'client' and reduced the Executive Committee to an advisory body. Hughes's Public Works Department has finally taken control of the project from the State Planning Department. Ferenc isn't going to be happy when he hears about this."

* * *

Nigel greatly enjoyed a family barbecue on a summer day. There was ample shade on his property and a cooling sea breeze to moderate the temperature. He held his two-year-old grandson on his lap as the boy pushed a toy truck up and down his arm.

Sam Kee, Mei-lan, and their son Edward were there. Archibald and Sam Kee shared a friendship based on compatible temperaments and business. Nigel was proud that his children, although born into wealth, were egalitarians and embraced cultural diversity. He noticed that Archibald was talking with Edward in what appeared to be a serious conversation.

Edward's main reason for attending the barbecue was to talk to Archibald about the army. He had grown up knowing that "Uncle Archie" had been badly burned as a soldier fighting the Japanese in World War Two. Seeing Archibald sitting alone, he had walked over to him and asked, "Can I talk to you about something private, Uncle Archie?"

Archibald was a bit taken aback by his direct approach, but said, "Of course, Edward—anything. Take a seat. What's on your mind?"

"I'm thinkin' about joining the regular army when I graduate in a year and wanted to see what you think about it. I'm a first lieutenant in my senior cadet unit in high school and really like the military. You were a soldier in World War Two, and your father was a fighter pilot in the First World War, but no one in my family has ever been a soldier. I feel like I should be the first to serve my country."

"Do you want to make a career of the military?" Archibald asked.

"I don't know... maybe. Dad doesn't want me to. He wants me to go to university first, and then if I still want to go in, enlist as an officer."

"That sounds like good advice to me, Edward."

"Call me Eddie, okay, Uncle Archie?"

"Ah, yeah, I forgot," Archibald sputtered, remembering Edwards's preference to be called "Eddie."

"There's a real war on now, fighting the communists in Vietnam," Edward said. "If I go to uni first and become an officer six years from now, it'll be all over, and I'll be sitting in some office in Canberra or someplace. If I'm going into the army, I want to be a dinkum Aussie defending my country. Communism is spreading through Vietnam, Thailand, and the Malay Peninsula and movin' toward Australia. The Communist Chinese are behind it, and Chinese Australians, like me, should be fighting against it."

Archibald said, "I went into the army as a lowly enlistee and wouldn't recommend it, Eddie. The life of an officer is much better, more responsible, and better paid. You're a cadet officer, so you obviously have leadership abilities. I'd recommend university and then you can go into officer training school."

Having said his piece, Archibald was happy to hear the cook announce that the food was on the table and ready to eat. He and Edward rose and headed for the large round picnic table that would seat all ten of them.

When they were seated around the table enjoying their lunch, Lydia asked how everyone felt about Australia giving up pounds and the pence for dollars and cents, which had begun a week earlier.

Edward had been waiting for a topic like this. Secure in his quick wit and ready repartee, he had found acceptance by entertaining people. They found it unusual and comical to listen to a Chinese bloke using Australianisms to tell good-humored stories and jokes, replete with Australian idiom and youthful slang.

When telling a story or a joke, Edward displayed the natural timing of a stand-up comedian. He knew how to pace himself and deliver a punch line. He seemed to enjoy the telling as much as people enjoyed listening.

"I don't like it!" Edward purposely said too forcefully. "I don't want to give up the word *quid!*" Now he had everyone's attention. "I *like* saying: I'll give you a *quid* for that, mate! It's terrible with the changeover. I'll give you a *dollar* for that, mate! It doesn't sound right."

This leadoff was his warm up. He had gotten a few smiles and a snicker or two and launched right into his second offering. "Now what's goin' to happen to *quid* pro quo? What's your *dollar* pro quo?"

He paused briefly as more of his audience laughed, then continued before they stopped. "And how can I use my favorite putdown? He's not the *full quid!* I can't putdown anyone with *He's not the full dollar!*—nobody will even know what that *means!*"

Sam Kee had a sense of humor, but felt that Edward often played the fool for attention and acceptance. He was often embarrassed by him. In spite of the laughter, he said, "That's enough, *Edward*, the great entertainer. You talk too much."

"Dad thinks I'm an *earbasher*," Edward said with a smile and shrug, to have the last word.

Sam Kee called his son "Edward" when he was annoyed with him or in formal occasions, and "Ed" in casual situations. He did not like to hear the childish "Eddie." Edward told everyone to call him Eddie, because his father did not like it.

After eating, as people were getting up from the table, Eddie came over to Archibald and asked, "Where's the head, Uncle Archie? I have to point Percy at the porcelain." Archibald laughed and told him where to find the lavatory.

Archibald saw Ferenc standing alone. Sam Kee walked toward Archibald at the same time. "How did your first three weeks of self-employment go, Ferenc?" Archibald asked.

After three years of saying he was going to leave State Planning to start his own architectural engineering practice, Ferenc had finally done it as a new year's resolution.

"It went pretty well, but working out of home is driving me crazy. Being around your sister all day, every day, is no bloody picnic, mate."

"She was there first, Ferenc," Archibald said, smiling.

Sam Kee laughed quietly.

"Too right . . . I've been looking for office space."

"Do you have any clients yet?" Sam Kee asked.

"Yes, before I left the government I'd been working nights on a private residence in Seaforth, and two weeks ago, I signed a contract for a warehouse in Woolloomooloo. Those two jobs ought to keep me busy while I do a million other things necessary to open an office."

"The sails of the Sydney Opera House are really taking shape," Sam Kee said. "You should be very proud of how beautiful it looks. Will you miss working on the Opera House?"

"I'm glad to be out of that whole screwed-up mess, Sam. I couldn't stand another minute of it, to tell you the god-awful truth."

Archibald said, "Seems like Hughes is really going after Utzon."

"And he should!" Ferenc said forcefully.

"Uh-oh, I sense some pretty strong feelings there," Archibald said. "I thought you were out of it."

"I can't help myself. It's such a drama coming to a head. I still have lunch with the people I worked with—Bill Wood, Eggert, and Michael Lewis."

"I don't attend many Executive Committee meetings anymore, since we've become an advisory body," Archibald said. "What's coming to a head?"

"Utzon arrived back from a six-week Christmas holiday to Japan and Hawaii to find that Arup had submitted a structural engineering report to Hughes concluding that the plywood ceilings for Utzon's major and minor halls were too heavy to be suspended from the roof shells. Which is fine with Hughes, because he doesn't want to use the plywood subcontractor Ralph Symonds Limited because it's in receivership."

Overhearing their conversation, Nigel sidled into their group and said, "So Utzon and Arup are still at it?"

"It's more like Arup *and* Hughes against Utzon," Ferenc said. "Hughes had asked for the structural report and didn't want to wait for Utzon's return, so Lewis gave it to him. Lewis told me that Utzon then wrote a personal letter to Ove Arup complaining about him. Utzon wrote that Lewis was 'an absolutely hopeless amateur by submitting the report to Hughes behind his back.' He asked Ove Aup to withdraw the damaging assessment of the plywood ceilings. Ove wrote back saying that Utzon had avoided contact with Lewis over the past year since he retreated to his Palm Beach office, and that the entire trauma could have been avoided if he had worked out the design of the plywood ceilings with Lewis. Then he said that Utzon had killed the joy of collaboration for him, or something to that effect."

"I think both Lewis and Utzon are at fault," Archibald said. "They have no regard for each other."

"Well, then—get this," Ferenc said. "A few days ago, unexpectedly, Utzon invited Lewis to lunch and told him 'I think that I'm going to resign,' probably hoping Lewis would be horrified and withdraw the negative plywood ceiling assessment. Instead, Lewis simply said, 'Resigning does not solve anything.' To which Utzon said, 'Oh no, if I resign, they'll come back to me and that's when I'll get exactly what I want.' To that Lewis said, 'Well, I think that is a pious hope.' "

"Sounds like Utzon's wants to resign before he's sacked," Nigel said.

"I can't imagine that the architect of the Opera House would be *sacked!*" Sam Kee said.

"I doubt that anyone is going to be sacked, Sam," Archibald said. "Minister Hughes just has to make a good show of doing something about the escalating cost of the Opera House, after all the political rhetoric of the state election."

"Hughes can sack Utzon for nonperformance," Nigel said. "Utzon admitted in a letter to Hughes that he needs another year to prepare construction drawings, and this after eight years on the job!"

"I have a Swedish architect friend who has me convinced that

Utzon will never produce construction drawings and specs because it's not the 'Scandinavian' way of working," Ferenc said.

Archibald grimaced and looked inquisitively at Ferenc. "Do you want to explain that—'Scandinavian way of architecture'?"

"The Scandinavian 'craft' method of architectural design and construction is different from your Australian way. Their architects produce design drawings and identify the materials to be used and then hand this to their chosen 'craftsman' subcontractor, who does the detailed 'shop drawings' for the approval of the architect. These shop drawings provide sufficient detail for the item to be made by the subcontractor and then the general contractor adds the item to the building's construction. Scandinavian architects spend a lot of time finding the right 'craftsman' to work with as subcontractor, rather than tendering the work to find the lowest price bidder. Utzon made the roof tiles this way. He provided the design and found Höganäs Ceramics. It did the shop drawings and manufactured the roof tile lids that the general contractor Hornibrook added to the roof shells. It wasn't quite that simple, but you get the idea."

Sam Kee was lost in this conversation. He walked away.

Acknowledging that Sam Kee was leaving because of their esoteric conversation, Ferenc smiled knowingly at Nigel and Archibald, and then continued: "Utzon probably doesn't have the stockpile of typical working drawings details that Australian architects have or previous specifications to use for tendering. He doesn't even think that way. I expect that he has never produced a set of working drawings and specifications to the level of detail that the Public Works Department wants to tender to subcontractors."

"That craft approach is not practical for a large, complex project like the Sydney Opera House," Nigel said.

"I agree with you, Dad, *if* the project has to be done quickly. Utzon never intended to do it quickly."

"Look," Nigel said. "I think it comes down to Utzon being a *design* architect, pure and simple. He's good at it and enjoys it. That's why he constantly enters design competitions. He doesn't like the drudgery of working drawings and specifications. Plus, he's a bit over his head."

"Michael Lewis gave him a way out when he suggested he use Peddle Thorp & Walker to prepare working drawings, but Utzon is too proud to share the glory," Ferenc said. "He's dug his own hole."

Sam Kee had walked over and joined Mei-lan, Lin Yee, Lydia, and Wilhelmina, who were examining plants in Wilhelmina's herb garden. Sam Kee knew quite a lot about herbs and enjoyed talking about their cultivation and uses in cooking.

While they were examining various plants, Edward walked over to them. He waited for an opening. When Wilhelmina mentioned how perishable coriander leaves were, Edward said, "Talk about perishable. I was in a green-grocers yesterday testing some fruits for freshness, and the Italian grocer walked up behind me and tapped me hard on the shoulder. When I turned around with one of his peaches in my hand, he pointed at a sign on the wall. It said in large black letters: *'DON'T SQUEEZE ME TILL I'M YOURS!'*"

They all laughed, including Sam Kee.

* * *

"*Utzon has resigned!*" Archibald said over the phone to his father. It was Monday afternoon, February 28, 1966. "I called Hornibrook's construction director about another matter, and he told me. Then I called Michael Lewis, who confirmed it. They were both called this afternoon by Davis Hughes who asked for their assurances that they wouldn't resign along with Utzon."

"Did they give it?"

"Yes."

"Oh, thank goodness." Nigel said. "How'd it happen?"

"Utzon had a meeting with Hughes at his office about his fees, and they got into Arup's adverse report about the heavy plywood ceilings. Utzon wanted the report withdrawn because he and Michael Lewis were close to working out a solution, but Hughes said Arup's report stands until he's satisfied that the heavy plywood is not a problem. Then he said they didn't want to use Utzon's chosen plywood supplier Ralph Symonds because it's in receivership and may go bankrupt during the job."

"Uh-oh, that would have set Utzon off," Nigel said.

"It did, evidently, but that wasn't the last straw that broke the camel's back. Utzon was there to collect over $100,000 for past work; however, Hughes offered him only an advance of $20,000 per month to carry his staff. And even the advance would not be made until Liaison Officer William Wood confirmed that progress had been made on working drawings or contracting with another architectural firm to do them. Utzon said something like I will not work under the purview of William Wood as my overseer. I must have the freedom to run this project as I see fit, or I will resign.

"Hughes said that he was sick of hearing him threatening to resign and that if he did it again, he'd accept his resignation straightaway. That was too much for Utzon, who jumped up and said, well, then, goodbye Mr. Minister, and walked out of his office."

"So they had a blue," Nigel said, "that doesn't mean he has resigned."

"Hold on," Archibald said. "Utzon went right back to his office and wrote out a resignation letter and had his secretary deliver it to Hughes."

> Minister Davis Hughes: February 28, 1966
>
> You have forced me to leave the job. There has been no collaboration on the most vital items of the job in the last months, you have not paid fees owed to me, and I see clearly that you do not respect me as an architect. I have; therefore, today given my staff notice of dismissal. I will notify the Consultants and Contractors, and I will have cleared the office of my belongings, and you will receive my final account before March 14, 1966.
>
> **Jørn Utzon**

February had been a terribly difficult month for Utzon. He faced an insurmountable number of converging and profound problems. Feeling beleaguered, he was in no mood to endure Hughes's intractable attitude and his "checkbook control," because he desperately needed funds to pay his staff.

Four days earlier, the Australian Broadcasting Commission, managers of the Sydney Symphony Orchestra, had met with the Sydney Opera House Executive Committee and threatened to stay in the Sydney Town Hall until changes could be made to the Opera House or a proper symphony hall could be designed and constructed elsewhere. Its analysis of Utzon's latest plans for the dual-purpose major hall indicated inadequate seating, unsatisfactory acoustics, too small rehearsal rooms, and poor provisions for televising and recording concerts.

Then the next day, he received an unexpected income tax bill of $91,300 from the Australian Tax Office for income taxes owed since he moved to Australia. Although he was paying taxes on his Australian earnings in Denmark, he was unaware that no agreement existed between Australia and Denmark to avoid double taxation. He would have to apply to the Australian Tax Office in the hope of receiving some relief in the form of credits for Danish taxes paid.

And, he was concerned about what all this stress was doing to his health.

Unbeknown to Utzon, Hughes sent a memorandum to Premier Askin and his cabinet ministers on Tuesday morning.

> Jørn Utzon has resigned. Anticipating that this may arise, I have discussed the method whereby the Sydney Opera House could be completed with the Government Architect and Senior Officers of the NSW Chapter of the Royal Australian Institute of Architects (RAIA). I am satisfied that a means can be found to complete the planning and supervision of the work. I have already taken steps to ensure that progress on Stage Two will not be interrupted.

At the same time, presuming that Hughes would want him back, Utzon prepared a list of nine demands to which Hughes would have to agree before he would return to the job. The list reinstated him as the "Architect-in-Charge" with final approval over all details of the Sydney Opera House, required Hughes to go through him in dealings with Arup and other consultants, and removed William Wood as Liaison Officer.

Hughes was contacted and agreed to meet with Utzon and two key staff members at 6:00 p.m. at his minister's office at Parliament House. Utzon presented his nine demands. Hughes rejected them all with the comment: "The spirit of your nine demands indicates an attitude that does not promise prospects for reconciliation."

Ferenc received a telephone call from his friend Eggert in Utzon's office. "I want to let you know that Harry Seidler and other architects are coming tomorrow at noon to the Opera House construction site for a 'Bring Back Utzon' demonstration. There will be speakers and then we will all march to Parliament House and demand to deliver a petition to Premier Askin."

"Damn, I have an important meeting with a client tomorrow," Ferenc said. "But I'll try to cancel it and see you there."

Eggert said, "A petition is also being circulated among the eighty-five architects who work for Public Works. It looks like most will sign it with a little encouragement. Give a call to anyone you know over there to sign it, will you? It will embarrass Hughes hugely."

"Sure, Eggert. Hopefully, I'll see you tomorrow."

On Thursday, March 3, several hundred supporters of Utzon's reinstatement took part in the protest and listened to speakers. From his Opera House site office, Utzon described the protest as "marvelous." Shortly thereafter, he received a long-distance telephone call from Ove Arup in London. He refused to talk to him, treating his call with disdain.

The protesters marched to Parliament House. A deputation delivered a petition of 3000 names. Askin agreed to meet with Utzon the following day.

On Friday, Utzon met with Premier Askin and gave him a copy of his nine conditions to return. The Royal Australian Institute of Architects pressed Askin to support Utzon for fear that no other architect of any status and ability would take his place. Askin said, "I'm concerned about the Minister for Public Works losing face."

Ferenc called Eggert on Monday morning, March 7. "I'm sorry that I missed the protest Thursday. I couldn't cancel my meeting with my client. Though I did call over to Public Works to encourage a few friends to sign the petition. It's going well, evidently, seventy-five out of the eighty-five government architects have signed so far."

"That's fantastic news, Ferenc. Everything is going really well here too. Hughes has given into the pressure. He called us this morning to request a meeting with Jørn at 3:00 p.m. today. I think he's going to have to give Jørn what he wants because he's afraid of being removed himself."

Hughes presented Utzon with a "Basis of Proposal to Re-engage Architect Jørn Utzon" and explained its purpose. After his presentation, Utzon, Eggert, and Wheatland withdrew to another room for forty-five minutes to consider it.

When they returned to Hughes in his office, Utzon said, "Your proposal makes me a design architect with limited oversight. It would seem I am merely to prepare designs in accordance with instructions and leave it to others to prepare the detailed drawings and supervise construction. Such a proposal is not only unpractical but quite unacceptable to me. I am at all times prepared to work with them as your representatives, but not under them. Assuming you can find an architect to take my place, he would be starting from zero and would be coming straight back to you as soon as he realizes the difficulties and ask you to bring me back."

The next morning, Hughes met with Askin and his cabinet and explained that Utzon had rejected his latest proposal and asked for their support, which they gave. With the support of Premier Askin, Hughes made a press statement: "An attempt at reconciliation with Mr. Utzon to re-engage him as a design consultant with limited oversight has failed. Therefore, the government confirms Jørn Utzon's removal from the Sydney Opera House project."

After the press statement, a reporter overheard Hughes say, "Utzon got to a stage that he didn't know how to go ahead. I'm glad that he didn't take the subordinate role of 'design architect,' his ego couldn't have stood it. I did him a favor by giving him a way out of his own mess."

The Sydney Morning Herald printed Utzon's response the next morning: "The Basis of Proposal was insulting and no self-respecting architect could compromise his values to agree to it." The article went on to say, "It was not Utzon's fault that a succession of

Governments and the Sydney Opera House Executive Committee should so completely have failed to impose adequate control or order on the project. . . . Utzon's insistence on perfection led him to alter his design step by step as he went along."

Various groups continued to pressure the government for return of Utzon. On March 28, the Royal Australian Institute of Architects voted on whether to continue its "Utzon in Charge" campaign. The vote was 369 votes in favor and 283 against. The next day, Lis Utzon, Jørn's wife, telephoned the president of the RAIA and pleaded, "Please do not try to keep Jørn here, he is not a well man."

After several Australian architects turned down the opportunity to replace Utzon, the Government Architect offered it to Peter Hall, a former employee of the NSW Public Works Department, who had recently opened his own architectural practice. Hall said that he would accept it on the condition that he would step down if Utzon decided to accept Hughes's "Basis of Proposal." When the Government Architect agreed to his condition, Hall decided to call Utzon. He was astounded when Utzon accepted his telephone call.

"I will never agree to the demeaning terms of the Basis of Proposal," Utzon told him. "I will return only as Architect-in-Charge when the government needs me because my replacement has failed. I expect you will not be able to finish the job, and the government will have to invite me back on my terms."

Peter Hall accepted the position and joined together with Lionel Todd, to oversee contract documents, and David Littlemore, to supervise construction, forming the firm of Hall, Todd, and Littlemore to work under the supervision of the Government Architect and Davis Hughes, Minister for Public Works.

On April 24, Ove Arup and Jack Zunz flew into Sydney. They drove to Utzon's Palm Beach office and then to his home in an attempt to reconcile with him, but he would not see or speak to them.

On April 28, 1966, Jørn Utzon and his family flew out of Sydney.

* * *

James Bennett finished his social work degree at Sydney University and passed his final exams in December 1966. He looked forward to the graduation ceremony where he would be recognized as the second Aboriginal graduate of the University of Sydney. His advisor smoothed the way for him to work for the New South Wales Department of Social Welfare in its community outreach division.

Before beginning this position, James joined the Federal Council for the Advancement of Aborigines and Torres Strait Islanders (FCAATSI) to work for the passage of a national referendum on the so-called "Aboriginal question." The referendum was a straightforward "Yes" or "No" vote to remove discriminatory language from the 1901 Commonwealth Constitution that excluded Aborigines from being counted in the Australian census and allowed only States to make laws affecting Aborigines. The FCAATSI wanted Aborigines to be counted in the census like all other peoples and the Commonwealth Parliament to be given the power to make laws for Aboriginal people that would supersede those of less progressive states.

The vote was set for May 27, 1967. An effective lobby, composed mostly of white political activists from universities, churches, and the Australian Labor Party joined Aboriginal leaders across Australia to work for passage of the referendum. James worked with Faith Bandler, the campaign director in New South Wales. She effectively lamented in the press and nightly news that it was unjust that the federal government could legislate to build housing for migrants but not Aborigines, could teach English to refugees but not to its own indigenous people, and was prohibited by the Constitution from passing a national law making racial discrimination illegal.

Harvey worked with the Aboriginal Advancement Association in the Gura district to promote a "Yes" vote.

The result of the referendum was amazing. Australian voters, who had a history of rejecting referendums, voted "Yes" by an overwhelming 90.77 percent. This provided a clear mandate to the Federal Government to implement policies to benefit Aboriginal people and give them "a fair go."

* * *

Sam Kee called Archibald on the phone. "Can you stop by for a free lunch with me today or tomorrow? I want to talk to you about a business opportunity that I came up with in San Francisco." He and his wife had recently returned from their first visit to the United States with stops in Hawaii, Los Angeles, and San Francisco.

The Modern Chinese Palace hostess Tam-ho warmly greeted Archibald and showed him to his favorite booth with a view of the Sydney Opera House. Its roof shells gleamed brilliant white in the midday sun. It looks like a large yacht under sail on the harbor, Archibald thought to himself, a truly beautiful piece of architecture.

Sam Kee greeted Archibald, and they ordered their meals. While telling him about his vacation, Sam Kee excused himself three times to greet important customers. Returning to the booth the third time, he abruptly asked, "Archie, would you be willing to talk to Edward and discourage him from joining the army?"

Archibald face indicated his surprise. "He's at uni, isn't he?"

"Yes, but his name was drawn last week in the government's national service ballot. He wants to serve as a soldier. He doesn't seem to care that he'll probably be sent to fight in Vietnam. He won't listen to me."

"Wait a second, Sam, let me understand this," Archibald said. "He's been conscripted in the birthday lottery of twenty year olds? He's not twenty yet, is he?"

"No, but he'll be twenty on April 28, and his name was drawn in the March lottery for boys who turn twenty in the first half of '69. He could apply for a temporary deferment as a university student, but he won't do it."

"Why not?"

"I don't know why! He won't talk to me about it, and he's such a smart mouth!"

"What do you think I can do, Sam?" Archibald asked. "There's no reason why he'd listen to me. I'm not that close to him, really."

Sam Kee wanted to say: You have war and valor written all over your face; he respects you as a warrior. He sees me as a weak person, maybe even anti-Australian, because I've never been a soldier and think this is a stupid, wasteful war. Instead he said:

"He respects you because you've been a soldier. He'll listen to you."

"I talked to him once when he was in high school. He was considering joining the army after graduation. I told him that I agreed with you. He should go to university first."

"I know you did, and I appreciate that, Archie. That's why I want you to talk to him again."

Archibald did not want to talk to Edward. He remembered how he felt at Edward's age, and how he couldn't wait to prove his manhood in the defense of Australia. If Edwards's mind was made up, talking to him would be a frustrating and futile exercise. However, if he begged off, and *Edward was killed!* Sam would never forgive him for not trying. Archibald heard himself saying "Of course, I'll talk to him, Sam."

"Thanks, Archie. Mei-lan and I will invite you and Lin Yee to dinner at our house. Edward may approach you before or after dinner to talk to you about his plans. If he doesn't, you could ask him about it after dinner in a private conversation."

"Do you think I should point out that this is an unpopular war, which many people see as a civil war that we shouldn't be involved in?"

"I've already said that to him, Archie. That angle won't do any good. He sees the protestors as naive and misguided, anti-war pacifists, who don't appreciate the communist threat to Australia. He thinks that China and the Soviet Union want to take over the whole free world. He said we either defeat the communists in Vietnam or there's going to be a domino effect in Southeast Asia that will lead directly to Australia. I think the best thing is to persuade him to stay at university, so when he graduates he can go directly into officer training school and serve as an officer rather than as a conscript."

"Okay, I'll give it my best effort, Sam," Archibald said with an optimistic smile.

After finishing their lunch, Sam Kee said, "Let's go to my office, I have something I want to show you."

From a large cardboard box sitting in the corner of his office, Sam Kee withdrew a white double-pan container. He folded one of the pans over the other and fitted a lip under a corresponding protrusion, so the top pan closed on the bottom pan. With a smile of satisfaction, he handed it to Archibald. "Have you ever seen anything like this?"

"No," Archibald said, opening and closing it. "It's a lightweight container. What's it used for?"

"*For takeaway food!*" Sam Kee said, slapping his side. "I saw it for the first time in San Francisco's Chinatown. It's *doubling* their business! It keeps the hot food hot and cold salads cold, so you can take food home to eat, or eat in your office, or in a park, or *anywhere!*"

He removed nested white cups from the box. "Look at this cup, made from the same disposable polystyrene foam. And this plastic lid snaps tightly around the top of it—see?" He handed it to Archibald, then lifted from the box a see-through bag containing plastic knives, forks, and spoons. "These eating utensils are lightweight too, but strong. With these, you have everything you need to package food and drinks and take it away to eat somewhere. Equally importantly, these are more convenient, hygienic, and well thought out than anything we have here. They are all lightweight and cheap to import. This is going to revolutionize takeaway food, and I have the inside track."

"How's that, Sam?"

"I've got a deal with an American exporter in San Francisco and a Chinese friend here who can import these products. They're made by The Dow Chemical Company, which calls their product Styrofoam. I'm going to start offering takeaway food at both my restaurants as soon as I receive my first shipment. I should do a large volume with downtown office workers. If it takes off like I think it will, I'm going to open several suburban shops at train stations to offer Chinese takeaway food. I won't have any waiters and waitresses, just a kitchen, counter and cash register, and a shelf against the wall for people who want to stand and eat. When other merchants see my success, I'm going to make more money from selling the containers, cups, and plastic utensils. It ought to be a really good business for at least five years, until others get into it."

"This is a great idea, Sam. I've never liked the way that takeaway fish and chips are wrapped in used newspaper and meat pies drip through your fingers as you eat them." He picked up the polystyrene container again. "I can think of all kinds of food that can go into these containers: Shepherd's pie, Italian spaghetti dishes, and Greek moussaka come to mind. This is going to be a bonanza for you."

"For *us*, Archie, if you want to invest."

"I'm *in*—you don't have to ask me twice, Sam. Have you set up a company yet?"

"Not yet, although I've given away thirteen percent to the American exporter and ten percent to the Chinese importer, leaving seventy-seven percent. I want to retain majority ownership, so you can have up to twenty-six percent of the company, if you want."

"Twenty-six percent it is then, Sam." Archibald offered his hand to shake on it. "Thanks for the opportunity."

While shaking Archibald's hand, he said, "This will be *very* good for us, Archie, I'm sure of it. I'll have my solicitor give your solicitor a copy of the draft company agreement. We can decide together on the name of the company, its officers, and board members. Ah, this is going to be great fun."

* * *

On a Saturday afternoon, Harvey sat watching a rugby league match on television with a beer in his hand, when he heard someone running up his drive. He put down the bottle and rose from the couch as the person bounded onto his veranda and rapped on his front door.

The man squinted through the screen door as he banged on it. *"'Arvey, ya in there?"* he said. His eyes had not adjusted to the darkness of the living room, so he could not see Harvey approaching.

"What's the matter, Ronnie?" Harvey asked, opening the door. Katie walked quickly toward them from the kitchen, drying her hands on her apron.

"Paul in bad trouble!" the man said, a bit out of breath. " 'E knife two mates an' the Super call the cops!"

"*Ah, God!*" Katie exclaimed.

"Are they sure it was Paul who did it?" Harvey asked.

"Yeah."

"*Is Paul hurt?*" Katie asked.

"Dunno," Ronnie said.

Harvey asked, "Where is he?"

"Dunno fer sure. Them fight down by Mulugong Creek, over grog or petrol or somethin', an' Paul knife Bruger and Freddie. Bruger cut real bad. 'E might die."

"How long ago?" Harvey asked.

" 'Alf an hour ago or so. Freddie bring up Bruger. 'E bin cut real bad in the stomac'."

Harvey knew he had to find Paul before the police. "When was the p'lice called?"

" 'Bout ten minutes ago. I run over as soon as I 'ear."

"I'm goin' ta find Paul," Harvey said to Katie.

"I go with ya, 'Arvey," Ronnie said.

"No, Ronnie, it's better if I go alone. Stay 'ere with Katie in case Paul comes here." He jumped off the veranda and while running toward his car said, "Tell Paul to put his hands up in the air when the police come an' lay down on the ground."

He drove toward a place along the creek where "no hopers" met. Paul had been drinking or petrol sniffing or both and was bound to be scared and irrational. Harvey feared the police might shoot him if he was holding a knife when they tried to arrest him.

Driving near the creek, he slowed to look for movement in the bush. Seeing none, he turned off the sealed, two-lane road onto an unpaved rutted track that ran through the bush for a hundred yards to a dirt turnaround. There were no parked cars or people around. A few steps from his car, he saw a fresh splatter of blood in the dirt and a trail of two wounded men, dripping blood, walking up the dirt track toward the sealed road. Harvey stood quietly, listening and looking about. The birds were not disturbed. Everything sounded right, almost peaceful.

Harvey followed the blood trail across the turnaround and down a path through the bush to a clearing next to a beautiful stretch of Mulugong Creek. Broken beer and liquor bottles, discarded petrol-sniffing containers, and trash were littered about. There was also evidence of a fight and more blood. Harvey did not think Paul was hiding nearby, but called out anyway. "PAUL, IT'S DAD. COME OUT IF YER 'ERE."

Hearing no response, Harvey walked around the periphery of the clearing closely examining each of four trail heads leading into the bush for evidence of recent foot traffic. He returned to one that was scuffed up as if a person had begun to run. Several yards down the trail, he found a single spot of fresh blood and then a few more.

Harvey continued down the trail. The person had run about sixty yards before slowing to a walk. There were no longer any drops of blood indicating that the walker was not bleeding. Harvey walked quickly down the trail for a while and then stopped, looked around and listened—no unusual sounds or movement. He yelled down the trail.

"PAUL, IT'S DAD, ANSWER BACK IF YA 'EAR ME." He listened. When there was no reply, he cupped his hands and yelled even louder and listened again.

Harvey wondered where Paul was headed.

He's travelin' away from Gura and Murraroo Mission. Maybe these aren't Paul's tracks after all. Who'd help him? He's lost every mate he ever had. I don't know this Bruger, but Freddie's a no-hope druggie. Suddenly, the distant sound of a police siren intruded into his consciousness.

Harvey was too deep in the bush to see the approaching police car. Its siren told him the police were coming down the road from the mission. He expected the police were going to the scene of the fight described by the knifed men. The siren sound traveled down the road, around the curve, and then parallel to the creek. When it turned onto the dirt track, Harvey started down the trail with renewed purpose. Then the police siren stopped.

Further along the trail, the walker's tracks changed back into a run and left the trail to break downhill through the bush. Harvey reckoned that the walker had become a runner again when he heard his last yell and was now fleeing from *him.* Following signs of crushed grasses and broken twigs, Harvey became aware that he was feeling the kind of stress he had not felt since the war. The police were behind him, probably with drawn guns, and a desperate man with a knife, *probably his own son*, perhaps drugged out of his mind, was somewhere in front of him.

The runner crossed the creek and halfway up the slope became a walker again. His tracks led into an orchard and then along its border before reentering the bush. Harvey speculated that the walker had decided he could not risk exposing himself in the orchard. A flock of shrieking galahs rose from the valley alerting Harvey to the location of the person one hundred and fifty yards ahead. He was in the middle of the bush between the creek and the orchard. Harvey reckoned that if the person did not cross the creek again, he could cut him off where the bush narrowed between the creek and the corner of the orchard.

In long easy strides, Harvey ran silently on the grass of the orchard toward its distant corner. He was going to have to cover three hundred yards running downhill in the time it would take the person below to cover half that distance through the bush. Harvey was fifty-five and had not run one hundred yards for a very long time. At one hundred yards, he wanted to stop to catch his breath, but he continued running. After two hundred yards, he had to slow to a brisk walk. Further along, out of breath, he had to stop. Placing his hands on his knees, he drew in deep breaths of air. He could hear the person walking through the thick bush about sixty yards away and slightly in front of him, though he could not see him.

Bent over and careful not to step on anything that would make a noise, Harvey jogged on the grass to the corner of the orchard and entered the bush silently. He paused and seeing no movement in the direction of the approaching person, chose his steps carefully to move stealthily to the center of the bush. He dropped to one knee behind a shrub. In seconds, he saw movement in the distance and then *Paul*. He was holding a knife in his right hand, as Harvey had feared, and was walking directly toward him. For a moment, Harvey thought to take him by surprise and disarm him but was afraid one of them might be injured. He decided instead to stand up and confront his son.

Paul was walking forward while looking back. Harvey stood up, took a step out from behind the shrub and said, "Paul, it's Dad."

"*Ahh!*" Paul exclaimed, jumping back. "Howdya—?" he stopped his own question and stood looking at his father through confused glassy eyes.

Harvey was relieved to see that Paul's body language was non-aggressive: his knife arm was not cocked. "Didn't you hear me yell to ya?"

"No," Paul said with an edge to it.

From the tone of his voice, Harvey knew he was lying. He'd run from me, he thought.

Harvey saw blood on Paul's collar and a deep gash across his cheek. "Yer face is cut, Son. Are you wounded anywhere else?"

Paul raised the hand holding the knife and ran the back of his hand across his cut cheek. He looked at the blood and then bizarrely licked it off the back of his hand. "Did this runnin' in the bush." Then he looked at Harvey with weird eyes. "I ain't goin' to let them catch me alive. *I ain't goin' ta jail!*"

Harvey decided to lie about Bruger's serious wound. "Bruger's goin' ta be orright. Ya just had a fight, Paul. That's all. Ya can say it was self-defense. Give me the knife now, and let's go home." Harvey put out his hand, while purposely standing in place so not to threaten him. "Let's go back."

Paul stepped back, his eyes turned crazed, and he raised the knife. They were ten feet apart. "I *ain't* goin' back! Bruger's Freddie's mate. They *hate* me an' want ta kill me! *I ain't goin' ta jail!* I'd *kill* meself first ta git out of this *fuckin' world!*"

Paul was now in a defensive posture. They stood there looking at each other. Feet apart. Father and son. Harvey did not know what to say.

He's pathetic; a druggie capable of taking his own life and fightin' me. I've failed me own son.

Tears welled up in Harvey's eyes, and a tear ran down his cheek. "I won't try to stop you, Paul." Despondently, Harvey sank to his knees and put his head down.

Paul said nothing. He angled away from Harvey and continued

on his way. Clearing the shrub, his feet were suddenly knocked out from beneath him. From his sitting position, Harvey had sprung sideways and swiped Paul's ankles. As his back hit the ground, Harvey deftly removed the knife from his hand. Paul tried to struggle, but Harvey lay across his chest with his full body weight, pinning both his arms and his torso to the ground. For several minutes, Paul struggled and screamed obscenities. Harvey said nothing. Gradually, he quieted. They lay there for a while longer until Paul agreed to surrender to the police.

Bruger lived, although he had a long, difficult recovery. Burger and Freddie testified against Paul, who was found guilty of aggravated assault with intent to kill. He was sentenced to a five-year prison term.

*　*　*

"*Eddie*, do you know who you look like, mate?" a friend asked.

Edward and his platoon were in a truck and talking about movies on their way to Nui Dat base camp in Phuoc Tuy province, Vietnam.

"No, who?" Edward said.

"Since you've grown that fuzzy wuzzy on your face, you look like Odd Job, the baddie Chinese bloke in *Goldfinger* . . . ya know, that James Bond movie."

They had been in transit for three days. Freed from daily inspection, Edward and other soldiers had gone without shaving.

"Ya really do, mate," another soldier said. Others laughed and nodded their heads in agreement.

"Yeah, I've heard that before," Edward acknowledged. "Odd Job knocked the bejesus out of 007, though, didn't he?"

"Great fight scene inside a vault," said the friend who had originally mentioned *Goldfinger*. He enthusiastically described the fight scene. "Bond can't do shit against him, see. Odd Job throws his bowler hat with this razor-sharp steel brim at him, Bond ducks, and it gets caught between two steel bars. Odd Job goes over to pull it out, and Bond cooks the Chinaman with a live electric cable cut earlier by his hat. Cool."

"Odd Job's a Jap, by the way, not Chinese," Edward said.

"So what? Ya still look like him."

In early January 1970, Edward had been flown with his battalion from the Jungle Training Centre in Queensland to Saigon, Vietnam. After processing, they were being trucked in a convoy the sixty miles to the Australian Task Force base at Nui Dat, located southeast of Saigon. They had been on the road for nearly an hour.

"Are we almost there, Sarge?" Edward asked. "I have to use the dunny."

"Got a way ta go yet. Piss out the side of the truck."

With a mischievous grin and affected sheepish voice, Edward said, "But I have to lay a cable too, Sergeant, sir."

His mates guffawed and so did the sergeant.

"In that case, we'll stop the bloody convoy for your convenience, your lordship," the sergeant laughingly said, "*or* ya could use that bucket over there in the corner."

"I think I'll hold it," Edward said.

When they arrived at the base, Edward urgently asked, "Where's the crapper, Corporal, I have to take a leak."

Two of his mates behind him said almost simultaneously:

"And *lay a cable!*"

Edward was a private in the eighth battalion of the Royal Australian Regiment (8RAR). The Australian Task Force had grown to 8,500 military personnel, who soldiered in three army battalions, flew helicopters and transports in the air force, and crewed ships in the navy. The task force operated under the nominal control of the Americans but retained operational independence to carry out its distinctly Australian approach to counter-insurgency.

After the devastating 1968 Tet Offensive by the Viet Cong and North Vietnamese Army, when they attacked almost every city and major village in South Vietnam, the Australian Task Force operations became increasingly concentrated on the ongoing presence of the Viet Cong in Phuoc Tuy province. In 1969, an attempt by the task force to disrupt the free movements of the Viet Cong was unsuccessful, in part, because of their nearby sanctuary in the Long Hai Hills. In early 1970, the Australian command planned a major assault on the Viet

Cong battalion thought to operate out of the Long Hai Hills.

Edward was ready for combat when he arrived at Nui Dat base camp, so he became impatient with the two weeks of additional "orientation" training the new arrivals had to undergo. By the time he went on his first search and destroy mission in late January, he was anxious to prove himself. However, the mission turned out to be little more than a five-day walk through local villages and along rice paddies. A subsequent two-day patrol also made no contact with the enemy. A promising night ambush proved uneventful. Edward began to lose hope that he would ever fire his M-16 rifle at the enemy.

On February 10, Edward's 8RAR was part of a major assault into the Long Hai Hills. Their objective was to find Viet Cong base camps, training areas, and underground bunkers. Camps were to be destroyed and bunkers blown-up with high explosives. The elusive Viet Cong battalion was to be forced out of its sanctuary and ambushed as its guerilla members tried to escape along egress routes from the hills. After four days of walking through the hot, steamy jungle, Edward's company had found only a small abandoned camp. They burned the three hooches and a cache of rice they found there.

On the fifth day of the operation, around midafternoon, Edward felt his company was about to engage the enemy. They had come upon an area crisscrossed with recently used trails. There were freshly broken branches, small pieces of discarded litter, and other indications that a large force was using the area. The tension in the air was palpable.

The order of march had placed Edward's section of fifteen men behind the point section. The company was walking forward in a flat "V" formation. The captain of the company had attached his command post to Edward's section to be close to the action when it developed. The third section in Edward's platoon followed. The second and third platoons formed the arms of the "V." A mortar platoon followed and provided rear security.

It was hot and muggy. Edward was sweating, his pack was cutting into his shoulders, and his mouth was dry. He wanted to take a drink from his water bottle but did not dare delay the steady movement of the "V" through the dense jungle undergrowth. They were "scrub-bashing" through the "j" or jungle. Trails were avoided because they could be mined and were too easily ambushed. The captain stopped their advance when the point section sergeant radioed that his scout had found a recently cut stump. It had been camouflaged by pulling live ground cover over it and by rubbing dirt into the fresh cut. The point section sergeant came back to strategize with the captain and first platoon lieutenant.

Edward could hear their conversation.

"We're definitely onto somethin', sir," the sergeant said. "A stump can only mean a VC camp or bunker is nearby."

"There's enough fresh signs around here that it could be a company-size facility," the lieutenant said.

The captain had been studying the topography map. "There's a water source for a VC camp in this valley. Move your point ahead very slowly, Sarge, to recon. If you don't see a camp, look for a worn area at an entrance to an underground facility. Don't fire unless fired upon. Bugger out as soon as you see evidence of a camp. If the shit hits the fan and you can't move, then go to ground. We'll get you out. Got it, Sarge?"

"Yes, sir."

"We'll advance with you but at a distance, 'cause I'm not taking the company too far into this valley to be ambushed from the opposite slopes. Hopefully, you'll see their facility and be able to back out. We'll call-in the artillery then and blow them to kingdom come. Okay?"

"Righto, sir."

"Off you go, then."

The sergeant returned to point. After twenty minutes, the captain ordered the formation forward. Everyone was trying to move as quietly as possible. Hand signals only, no talking, five yards apart. Edward was looking down, watching his step, when a *brraaaat*— short burst of small-arms fire—erupted from the right hillside, about a hundred yards ahead. Before he could move, the entire jungle ahead exploded in an incredible crescendo of gunfire. The first section was being hit hard!

Edward took two steps forward while raising his M-16 to his shoulder and placed himself behind a tree. He looked for a target. First section's M-16s were responding and then he heard the throaty sound of their M-60 light machine gun *tuttututtuttutut-tuttuttut-tuttutut*. Australian and Vietnamese screaming and shouting could be heard above the racket. He couldn't see any movement ahead, except falling vegetation that was being cut down by desultory fire. The *zip zip zip zip* of bullets passing by excited him.

His section corporal yelled, "Rifle group right."

Crouching low, Edward ran forward and to the right. His safety was off and his finger was on the trigger. No one was shooting for fear of hitting the Australians in the first section somewhere ahead. Anxious, though not scared, he ran ahead hoping to see a back-clad VC running through the jungle.

BOOM. An explosion behind Edward drove him to the ground.

Shit, that whooshing sound was a RPG (Rocket Propelled Grenade) going by me—*damn* that was close. Feeling lucky, he got up and crouching even lower ran forward. There seemed to be shooting near him now, still he could not see the enemy. He heard an impact explosion behind him.

Mortars! We're in deeper shit than Ned Kelly, he thought to himself. He dropped to one knee behind a clump of bamboo and looked around for the other men in his rifle group and became frightened when he saw only one Aussie soldier in the distance behind him. Was he too far out in front?

The bamboo suddenly exploded into confetti around him, getting into his eyes and mouth and burying him beneath bamboo stalks. For the first time in his short life, Edward heard the terrifying sound of an AK-47 assault rifle being shot directly at *him*, an entirely different sound than one shooting at someone else. Like a lizard, he crawled beneath and through the fallen stalks trying to get away.

I'm goin' to die without even shooting my fuckin' rifle!

A fallen log provided refuge. Bamboo stalks and leaves continued to cascade over him. He prayed that his assailant thought he was dead. There was one more long burst. Edward was scared . . . but also mad as hell. He thought the enemy was walking toward him to finish him off.

Ah fuck it. Edward jumped up through the fallen bamboo while emptying a full magazine in the direction of the unseen enemy and running for a thick tree trunk several yards away. Behind the tree, he jammed in another magazine. *Ya sonofabitching bastard!* He whipped around the tree and shot a long burst in the same direction. Hyperventilating, he returned to the center of the tree trunk and waited for a response. And waited. And waited. He peeked around the tree.

Maybe I hit the bastard, he thought.

A distant yell caught Edward's attention: *"Fong, get the fuck down!"* It was the voice of his corporal, who was lying on the ground and motioning him down.

Edward dropped to one knee, then heard the sound of a speeding locomotive coming directly at him. He dropped flat on the ground. The locomotive roared over him and *karrBOOOMM* hit the ground with a tremendous force further down the valley. The ground shook beneath him.

So that's what artillery sounds like—*cripes!*

The shell rounds started to walk up the valley toward him. He desperately ran from the tree toward his corporal staying as low as possible. The force of an explosion behind him sent him sprawling. He slithered behind a tree and clawed the moist soil to dig a depression for himself. The noise of the explosions was deafening. The ground shook more violently with each shell impact, and the pungent smell of cordite reached his nostrils. Then it was over.

Edward's ears were ringing, and, for a moment, he thought he had lost his hearing. Gradually, the sounds of individual small-arms fire picked up again. An Australian was screaming in great pain behind him.

The corporal ran to Edward and said, "Stay with me this time, dumbo."

Edward was curious to see if he had shot the Viet Cong who had tried to kill him, but instead followed his corporal. They joined their section and worked their way to the right along the slope, shooting at the distant shadows of withdrawing enemy.

"*They're pissin' off!*" an Australian yelled.

They came into an area destroyed by the artillery shelling. There was still some sporadic firing further down the valley, which Edward assumed was the first platoon pursuing whatever was left of the enemy. He looked around and saw that they were standing over a caved-in system of underground tunnels and rooms that had taken at least a couple of direct artillery hits. There had to be VC buried below, he thought.

Further down the slope, someone yelled "*Fire in the hole!*" and a muffled explosion sounded.

The firing had ceased in their area. Soldiers were standing around, spent.

"Don't touch him!" a corporal said to a soldier who was tapping a dead Viet Cong with his rifle barrel.

Shit, look at that, Edward thought, the VC's body is still twitching. It was the first dead enemy he had seen, in fact, the first dead person he had ever seen outside of a funeral home. The VC's body had some blood on it, but he did not look *that dead*. He seemed to be looking serenely at the clouds.

"Got another nog KIA" (killed in action) "over here!" a soldier yelled. "This Charlie is really *fucked* up!"

A crowd was forming, and Edward walked over to see. A soldier in the crowd stumbled away and retched. One look at the body told him why. The partial corpse of a VC was suspended upside-down, ten feet above the ground, caught on a splintered tree trunk, which was doused in his blood. Flies covered the body and swarmed around it.

With ghoulish curiosity, Edward looked in awe at the mangled body. Its eyes were looking directly at him, appealing . . . for what? This poor bugger was walking around thirty minutes ago. About my age. This is *bloody unreeeal*. Crikey—ugh—I'm out of here.

"Break it up, ya morbid bastards," a sergeant said.

The sound of an approaching helicopter drew everyone's attention. It passed directly overhead. Someone said, "Charlie's stonkered; no firing on the dustoff bird." The helicopter hovered and dropped beneath the trees to pick up the wounded.

Edward heard his lieutenant's voice. "Listen up. Charlie could have mines and booby-traps around this complex. There's not much daylight left. Captain says we'll go through this lot in the morning. We're going to bivouac uphill for the night. Let's go and watch your step."

"Second section over here," Edward's corporal called out. All fifteen men walked together up the valley and were assigned positions in a defensive perimeter for the night. The corporal ordered Edward to dig their two-man pit while he set out claymore mines.

Edward took off his shirt and splashed on some mosquito repellent. He picked up his shovel and started digging. He felt strong and was pleased with himself.

I was tested today and came out pretty well. Probably got that son-of-a-bitch who tried to shoot me too. Now I've been shot at, mortared, and lived through an artillery barrage. If anyone asks me, I can honestly say I've been in combat. I wish Dad could see me now, and Uncle Archie too. Uncle Archie . . . tried to talk me into taking a university deferment! I hope he writes me after he gets my Nam photos.

The corporal, a regular army man, came back trailing wires and sat down on the ground next to the pit. He attached the wires to the clacker firing devices for the claymores. Then he lit a cigarette.

"You going to help, Bucky?" Edward asked.

The corporal kept smoking, staring out into the jungle. After a while, he quietly asked, "What happened to you out there today?"

"Whatayamean?" Edward said as he stopped digging.

"Keep diggin', you're goin' ta finish the hole," the corporal said as an order. "Why'd ya take off like that? Did ya forgit yer trainin'?—yer mates?"

"I guess I got kind of excited. I didn't know I got that far ahead of you."

Bucky turned his angry face toward Edward. "Ya never even looked back, ya arsehole! Ya took off like a blasted rabbit. You weren't around when we had to pull back for the artillery. This ain't the fuckin' movies, and you ain't John Wayne. Out here we git killed, see. Yer my responsibility; yer part of *my* team. And I had ta fuckin' find ya. Ya could've got me killed. You *ever* pull that shit on me again, and I'll fuckin' go to town on you. *Ya hear me, Eddie?*"

"Sorry, Bucky, I hear ya," Edward said contritely.

A couple of minutes later, the lieutenant walked up on them as he made his rounds to check preparations for the night. "Can't call you 'cherry' anymore, hey, Eddie?" he said, laughing. "Finally got that action you've wanted, eh?"

Edward smiled uneasily at the lieutenant.

Bucky glumly answered for him. "Yeah, now he's ready for a proper screwin'."

The lieutenant and Bucky discussed his section's preparations for the night, while Edward finished digging the pit. The lieutenant moved on.

Edward set up his Hexi stove to warm his rations. Trying to make amends, he asked, "Can I heat up your 'C' rations, Bucky?"

Bucky dug into his pack, took out two ration packs, and handed them to Edward with a slight grin. "That would be right nice, *love*."

While they were eating, Edward's mates joined them. An old sergeant mate of Bucky came by and asked, "Ya got any of those Marlboros left, mate?"

The sky through the jungle canopy had changed from vivid red and yellow streaks to bright gray, but there was still time for a smoke before lights-out discipline. The men wanted to talk after today's action. They knew that they would soon have to be completely quiet, once it turned dark.

The old sergeant said to Edward and his two mates. "Too bad, you newies were sent up here to get yer arses shot off for nothin'."

Edward and his friends were taken aback by his cynicism. Being a sergeant, they had to be careful what they said. Edward chose a neutral response: "Buying time, Sarge. The peace talks are probably going to fall through."

"The prime minister said he's pulling us out," Bucky said.

"Only if Nixon pulls out the Americans, which may never happen," Edward's university mate said.

"How ya goin' to feel when ya go back an' all yer pretty uni sheila's call ya 'baby killers'?" the sergeant asked.

"Screw them," Edward's friend said.

"I'm all for that," Bucky said. "Ha ha ha."

Edward felt he had to voice his opinion that communism had to be fought. "The longer we stay, the stronger ARVN" (Army of the Republic of Vietnam) "and the PF" (South Vietnamese defense forces) "become to fight the communist after we're gone."

"That's bullshit, mate," the sergeant said, "you've been jerkin' off too much. We trained the PFs, gave them guns, built them pill-boxes, and laid mines around their fuckin' villages. The Viet Cong came in at night, killed a few of them, and they fell apart. Now we're steppin' on our own fuckin' land mines and being shot by our own guns. The same goes for ARVN. They can't fight their way out of a friggin' paper bag."

Edward's third friend said, "If we drive the VC out of the hills, Phuoc Tuy might have a chance."

"As soon as we leave, they'll be right back in here," Bucky said. "The VC have used the Long Hai Hills as the center of resistance since fighting the French in the First Indochina War."

"*Damn*, how can you fight if you feel like that?" Edward asked sincerely.

The sergeant had been getting up as Edward said this. "Hey, I didn't start it. I just fight it. It's a livin'," he said. "You university boys need a reason. To me, it don't mean a thing. I got to get back to my section. G'night, Bucky." He walked away from the "newies" like they meant nothing to him.

By February 18, the Australian command deemed that the Viet Cong battalion was trapped in the hills and arranged an air strike by US B52s. Since the strike was near populated areas, it was necessary to get clearance from the Republic of Vietnam authorities, who had to get permission from the provincial chief, who had to notify the district chiefs. By then, the Viet Cong intelligence network knew. When the Australians pulled back the required safe distance of ten thousand feet (nearly two miles) from the bombing site, the Viet Cong battalion slipped through the gaps in the Australian cordon.

After the B52 strike, Edward's 8RAR returned to search the hills. They discovered several caches that were exposed by the bomb blasts, but no bodies. Australian casualties were light, until on February 28, when two booby-traps killed nine Australians and wounded sixteen. When the operation was over, ARVN was unwilling to occupy the Long Hai Hills. The Viet Cong returned and were still using the hills when Australia pulled its last troops out of Vietnam in December 1972.

Edward served out the remaining ten months of his a one-year term of duty in Vietnam without receiving any injuries. He returned to Australia in early 1971.

* * *

"I'm afraid they're heading for a divorce, Lin Yee," Archibald said as they drove to meet Lydia and Ferenc. "They seem very unhappy with one another lately."

"Let's try to be positive and not speculate, all right Archie," Lin Yee said. "We don't know the depths of their feelings for each other, and they have lovely children to keep them together."

It was a hot sunny day before Christmas in 1972. They were driving to Bronte Beach to picnic with Lydia and Ferenc, whose boy, age eight, and girl, age six, were spending the day with their grandparents, Wilhelmina and Nigel.

"Well . . . I'm not looking forward to seeing them, is what I'm saying," Archibald said. "It's no fun the way they go at each other. They seem to want us to referee their blues."

Lin Yee smiled pleasantly at Archibald. "Talking negatively about them, before we see them, won't put us in the right frame of mind to enjoy ourselves. We should try to be a positive force in their relationship, and I think we are—that's why they keep inviting us. So . . . now, tell me something you like about them."

"My positive-thinking wife. That's what I like about you, Lin Yee—you keep me positive. Okay . . . Mmm. I like the way Ferenc looks at other women."

Without hesitation, Lin Yee said, "And you *don't*?"

"*Me*?" Archibald gave her a feigned look of incredulity. "I'm offended."

"Okay, let's see if you can keep your eyes in your book then, instead of on the young girls walking by on the beach."

Archibald chuckled. "I don't like the way this conversation is going."

As they walked into the park, they saw Lydia seated at a picnic table reading a book while Ferenc was working on the grill. Lydia saw them approaching, laid her book down on the seat, and stood up. After greetings all around, Archibald provided steaks for the grill while Lydia and Lin Yee set the table.

Lin Yee noticed Lydia's book on the seat. "Oh, you're reading *The Female Eunuch*."

"Yes, for the past two months. It's hard to find time to read with two children."

"I haven't read it. It's about women's liberation, isn't it? Do you like it?"

"Well, it's not the kind of book you can like, really, because it's about the oppression of women in contemporary society. It's required reading for my feminist group."

"What's its message or moral?"

"The writer Germaine Greer, an Australian, is a brash, angry anarchist who criticizes the subservient role of women in our male-dominated society. She makes the case that girls are taught rules that subjugate us in later life. It's divided into chapters like 'Work' that says women should be paid the same wages as men if they do the same job. She says society and schools teach women to be submissive and that marriage is legalized slavery, which I can relate to right now."

Overhearing their conversation, Ferenc said, "Don't let Lydia ruin your marriage with that 'eunuch' propaganda, Lin Yee." He flipped one of the steaks on the grill. "See, Archie and I are doing the cooking, and we don't feel castrated."

Archibald opened a cold Foster's beer for himself and another for Ferenc. While handing the beer to Ferenc he asked, "What do you think of Whitlam bringing home the last troops from Vietnam?"

Before he could answer, Lin Yee said, "Hold on, let's not start off talking about *politics!* We've got tickets to see Evonne Goolagong play at the Australian Open next month!"

The four of them were tennis players who often played doubles together at the Maccabi Tennis Club in Paddington.

"She's *amaaazing,*" Lydia gushed. "I'd *love* to see her play. Only nineteen last year when she won both the French Open and Wimbledon. They're calling her the Sunshine Supergirl."

"Indeed, because of her graciousness and sunny, carefree manner," Lin Yee said.

"They're like that, aren't they?" Ferenc said.

Not sure what he meant, the three of them looked at him.

"She's Aborigine, right?" Ferenc said with a questioning look. "At least she looks like one."

"Yes, she is, and it's a wonderful story of realized talent," Lin Yee said to gloss over Ferenc's faux pas. "She's from near Griffith, New South Wales, where her father is a shearer. She was discovered by the tennis coach Vic Edwards, who brought her to live with his family in Sydney where he trained her in his tennis school. She went right into professional tennis after graduating from high school."

"What I want to know is if you have any tickets for us," Ferenc said.

"Yes, I believe we have a couple for you two, if you'll turn those steaks before you cook the life out of them," Archibald said.

"Whoops," Ferenc said. "Who wants a well-done one?"

They busied themselves putting food on their plates in preparation for sitting down to eat.

"What's the latest on the Opera House, Archie?" Lydia asked.

"I walked through the interior a couple of weeks ago. I must say, it's coming along quite nicely."

"But when will it be *done*?" Ferenc asked.

"About six months, mid-1973, they say."

"It was started in the early '60s, wasn't it?" Lin Yee asked.

"No. The competition was in 1956, and Utzon won it in January 1957," Archibald said.

Ferenc said, "Let's see, assuming it opens in mid-1973 . . . That's sixteen and a half years. And way over the cost estimates—thank god the lottery punters are paying for it. An iconic building but what a debacle."

They sat down around the picnic table and began to eat. Ferenc wanted to answer Archibald's initial question. "About bringing the troops back from Vietnam," he said. "I think 'Vietnamization' is a face-saving tactic thought up by 'Tricky Dicky' Nixon and Kissinger to get the US out of Vietnam. They don't have the will to fight any longer and are willing to see South Vietnam go communist. Whitlam is just going along."

"Whitlam isn't *going along!*" Lydia said indignantly. "He's opposed the war for donkey's years. It's in Labor's platform. The US and Australia are being forced out of the war by public opinion—by the war protesters!"

"Oh, by people like you, I presume," Ferenc said.

"Yes, that's right."

"Whitlam's against the war because he's a socialist," Ferenc said.

"He's not a socialist, *Jeez,*" Lydia said. "He's a social-democrat, who believes in a fair go for everyone: eliminating the White Australia Policy completely, equal pay for women, Aboriginal land rights, barring racist sports teams from competing in Australia, especially the South Africans, and—"

"You're comin' on a bit *strong!* You think it *fair* to drop charges against draft resisters and let them out of jail? That's not fair to the soldiers who served, or democratic. How can he make decisions like a dictator?—this isn't Russia."

"It does amaze me," Archibald said, "in the two weeks he's been prime minister, he's made about forty policy decisions like that off his own bat."

"How can he do that?" Ferenc asked.

Lydia said, "It's all legal. He's formed a two-man cabinet with his deputy to run the government until all the electoral results were in, and he could form his government. The governor-general went along with it, and even allowed Whitlam to declare an end to imperial honors given by the Queen. However, that's all behind us now that his ministers have been sworn in."

"He wants to recognize communist China and establish diplomatic relations," Ferenc said. "I think Australia should be fighting the spread of communism, not capitulating."

Lydia gave him a look of exasperation. "We've had twenty-three years of Liberal government and kowtowing to America's paranoia about communism, and look were it's got us—Vietnam! Whitlam is saying there's another way. He intends to trade with China rather than fight them."

"I've lived under communism," Ferenc said, "I know. You can't cajole a totalitarian state. Whitlam is going to be a disaster for Australia—you just watch and see."

There was a break in conversation, with Lydia and Ferenc both angry.

Lin Yee introduced a subject she thought would be less controversial. "How is your term of presidency going with the Paddington Preservation Society, Lydia?"

"It's a lot of work, more than I expected, Lin Yee. We've had a couple of recent successes though. We stopped the widening of Jersey Road and persuaded union workers to walk off the demolition of a row of terrace houses on Glenmore Road, where an apartment building was planned.

"Getting Jack Mundey's Builders' Labourers Federation involved with us was the best thing we ever did. He's working with us to impose work bans on projects that would remove historic buildings. We are assisting other inner city preservation groups too, in The Rocks, Millers Point, Woolloomooloo, and Potts Point. The incredible architecture in our older neighborhoods can never be replaced once it's gone."

"The *only* problem is, Lydia's always gone," Ferenc said.

Lydia's enthusiasm wilted. "He thinks he has to watch the children too often."

Ferenc appealed to Lin Yee and Archibald. "I wouldn't mind if it was just the Paddington Preservation Society, which I agree with, but it's also the Vietnam Moratorium Committee, the Women's Electoral Lobby, and god knows what else."

"The anti-war demonstrations won't be necessary anymore," Lydia said defensively.

"I'd like to see you get back into painting again, Lydia," Ferenc said earnestly. "You have a real talent and could make some money at it. You haven't been in your studio for years. Don't you agree that she has real talent?"

Lin Yee and Archibald agreed, without putting pressure on Lydia.

"After lunch, we're going to lie out on the beach awhile," Ferenc said. "Are you going to join us?"

Archibald did not want to spend more time with Ferenc and Lydia. "I think we'll head back. I shouldn't lie out . . . my scars, you know, sensitive to the sun."

Chapter 8

The Last Melting Pot

Lydia felt terrific as she strode through the streets of Double Bay on a Saturday afternoon. Finally shedding those extra pounds had given her a lighter step and renewed confidence, enough to buy a form-fitting dress. She gave her shopping bag a sassy swing.

Ferenc's going to love this divine little dress on me, she told herself with a sexy laugh—and won't be able to keep his hands off me. I should drop by his office to show it to him. She spun around and headed for his office where he was finishing drawings for an Armstrong Development Company building.

The office door was locked, so she used her key to get into the dark reception room. A lively romantic jazz piece was playing, which she sashayed to as she approached the light emanating from the glass-enclosed drafting room. Two people were too close together. Lydia paused in the shadows. Ferenc pulled the woman toward him and placed his hand on her breast. They kissed, and their bodies entwined. Lydia stormed into the room and swung her bag with all her might. The woman was knocked back against the wall. Lydia slapped Ferenc hard across the face.

"*You're MARRIED!*" she shrieked. "*How COULD YOU?*"

Stunned, Ferenc stared blankly back. Her face contorted, Lydia abruptly turned and bolted for the door, ignoring his calls "*Lydia!* *LYDIA!*"

Ferenc returned home later that afternoon and found Lydia upstairs already dressing for the grand opening gala performance at the Opera House. She halted his advance with an extension of her hand and coldly said, "Don't say a word. This is a *very* important day for my family. I don't want you spoiling it!" Hoping he would get off lightly, again, Ferenc did as told and began to dress.

Nigel's guests had agreed to meet in the forecourt of the Opera House. When Nigel, Wilhelmina, Archibald, and Lin Yee arrived, they saw Lydia and Ferenc talking to Sam Kee, Mei-lan, and Edward. While they were greeting one another, Archibald's guest, James Bennett, joined the group.

"This is a large area, Archie," James said as he shook hands with Archibald. "It's lucky I found you."

"I didn't expect so many people meeting in the forecourt," Archibald said.

Ferenc said, "The forecourt *is* large, because it's meant to be used for outdoor entertainment with spectators sitting on the steps, like an amphitheater."

Looking up the steps toward the gleaming white shells, Lydia said, "It's more imposing and stately now that it's finished. It looks as though the Opera House is sitting on a hill."

"Impressive," James said. "How much did you say it cost, Archie?"

"It looks like the final cost will be around 102 million dollars."

"The first estimated cost was *only* seven million dollars," Ferenc said with a hint of cynicism.

Wilhelmina slipped her arms through those of Nigel's and Archibald's as they walked up the steps. "I'm so proud that my men had a hand in this monumental building."

Standing in front of the shells, Ferenc could not help but lecture. "Utzon designed the ceramic, chevron-shaped, white roof tiles that reflect the sunlight so brilliantly and found Höganäs ceramics factory in Sweden to produce them. Notice the articulation of the underside of the roofs. Those beautiful, strong-looking concrete ribs are structural and actually hold up the shells. These details were important to Utzon. He wanted every part of the Opera House that could be seen to be impressive."

"It's a shame that Utzon has vowed never to visit his creation," Sam Kee said sadly.

"What kind of person makes such a vow and sticks to it?" Lydia asked no one in particular.

"A scorned egomaniac," Nigel answered.

Before entering the Opera Theatre, they paused to take in the spectacle of a boat-filled harbor and the crowds milling around Circular Quay and the Royal Botanical Gardens. Archibald said with a laugh, "If *this* seems festive, imagine what it's going to be like on October 20 when Queen Elizabeth *officially* opens the Sydney Opera House."

Inside the foyer, a prominent group of invitees were mingling. As they circulated among the invitees, Archibald saw James slip away from their party and walk over to a crowd around Prime Minister Gough Whitlam. He returned when the lights blinked, signaling that the performance was about to start.

Archibald led the way to their seats via the angled stairway. Wilhelmina stumbled part way up, but Nigel held her up on his arm. "Oh, dear me," she said, embarrassed. "I don't know what came over me. I-I just felt . . . *odd* there, for a moment."

"Not to worry," Ferenc assured her. "You had, hmmm . . . How do you pronounce v-e-r-t-i-g-o?"

"*Vertigo*," Lydia said pointedly.

"Ah, yes, vertigo. It's the lack of right angles in this area. It does odd things to the sense of balance"—he crossed his eyes comically—"and to the mind."

Wilhelmina chuckled at his silliness. Entering the interior of the Opera Theatre, she said, "Oh, I'm *so* pleased that I waited until everything was completed before seeing it. It's, it's magnificent . . . the inside, the outside . . . everything I hoped for."

"Me too, Mum," Lydia agreed. "Good job, Dad and Archie." She purposely left out mention of Ferenc.

They moved along the row and found their seats.

The conductor entered to applause, Prokofiev's passionate music began, the curtain rose, and "War and Peace" commenced. During the performance, as more and more performers came onto the stage, Wilhelmina grew concerned and whispered into her son's ear, "I've *never* seen such a full stage. I'm afraid someone's going to fall off." She looked at him quizzically, as if to say, How could a brand new facility not accommodate its inaugural opera adequately?

"Don't worry. This is just a particularly large cast," Archibald whispered back and patted her hand. Although he too was surprised by it.

At a post-theater supper at Sam's Modern Chinese Palace restaurant, Archibald said, "James, I saw you walk over to Whitlam's group. Did you get to talk to him?"

"Yes. I just told him that I'm an Aborigine, and he's doing the right thing," James said. "I asked him to keep it up."

"He shook my hand and said, 'I'll keep my election promise. I want my administration to be remembered for delivering justice and equality to the Aboriginal people.' "

Whitlam's government had taken office that year and adopted the United Nations Convention to eliminate all forms of racial discrimination, created a special commission to advance Aboriginal land title, and created an advisory body of Aborigines.

Ferenc was finishing his third vodka-soda when he got Edward's attention and too loudly asked, "Edward, you hate the commies as much as me. Whaddya think of Whitlam signin' a trade agreement with China?"

"I think it will be good for us," Edward said. "China wants our raw materials, but I'm not sure what we'll buy from them. Maybe we'll make them capitalists." He forced a laugh to diffuse Ferenc's intemperance.

"Don't hold your breath," Ferenc said derisively. "I know how *they* work—"

"We have to engage China, Ferenc," Archibald said, "regardless of their politics. We're a little nation on the edge of Asia."

Lydia made a discreet, terse comment to Ferenc, and he snarled something incoherent back under his breath. Infuriated, Lydia abruptly stood and excused herself.

There was an uncomfortable silence. Hunched over his drink, Ferenc felt miserable.

If Lydia leaves me, I'll lose my contracts with Armstrong Development Company. She's angry because I screw around a little. So what! I'm a good father. All blokes do it... well, at least the handsome ones do. This marriage thing and family—it's like a bloody noose!

He turned to Edward. "You know, mate, you're the lucky one. Freeee as a bird! No kids, no naggin' wife, no responsibilities. Enjoy life while ya can, mate." He raised his glass to him.

Embarrassed, Edward said, "You're the lucky one, Ferenc. Attractive wife, beautiful children, and successful architect." He raised his glass to Ferenc, but Ferenc waved him off.

Trying to lighten the mood, Edward launched into a humorous story about his recent attempt to date a woman who wasn't interested in him.

"Oh no, not *another* one of your stories, mate," Ferenc moaned, rose unsteadily, and knocked over his chair as he headed for the men's lavatory.

Ensconced in the ladies lavatory, Lydia was sitting in a stall, head in hands, contemplating her predicament.

What a botch this marriage is. What am I going to do? I have to think of the kids . . . Mom and Dad will help out. But the kids love him. She sighed. Am I being selfish? In spite of his philandering, I think he still loves me. He's better than most Aussie husbands. At least he walks *with* me, not ahead of me! Doesn't hang out with his *mates* all the time. Is that enough? Can I go on living like this, distrusting him?

She blew her nose and stared at her wedding ring.

I deserve better. I *want* better. No, I've had enough of his shit. He'll never change—he's got to go!

She stood up, as though a great burden had been lifted. She dried her eyes in front of the mirror, refreshed her lipstick, and fluffed her hair. Taking a deep breath, she walked out into the restaurant proudly. A faint smile formed on her lips, as she mused, Germaine Greer would be proud of me. Ferenc will blame it on her anyway, and her *Female Eunuch* crap!

Lin Yee welcomed Lydia back to the table with "Are you all right, Lyd?" No one else said anything.

Lydia nodded yes, most assuredly.

* * *

On a sweltering evening at 10:00 p.m. in January 1975, Paul showed up unexpected at Harvey's house. Hearing the door open and slam shut, Harvey came out of the kitchen to see Paul carrying a swag of belongings into his old room.

"Hey, Dad," Paul mumbled. A young pregnant Aboriginal woman was standing inside the front door. Harvey had not seen or heard from Paul since his release from jail more than seven months earlier after serving his five-year sentence.

Harvey and Katie had arrived at the appointed time in the afternoon when Paul was to be released, but found he had been released in the morning with a friend. Paul left a note apologizing for going with his friend to live in Redfern, a largely Aboriginal neighborhood in Sydney.

Hearing her son's voice, Katie rushed in and flung her arms around him and kissed him. "Who this?" she said. "T'at yer baby, Paul?"

"Sally," Paul answered and grunted "yes." Harvey and Katie offered her a seat on the sofa.

"She not stayin' long," Paul said. "Goin' ta her mum in Koorawatha tomorrow." Paul motioned to Sally not to sit down. "We tired an' got ta git some sleep."

Paul and Sally left early the next morning. The following night, both returned after Harvey and Katie had gone to bed. In the morning, Paul walked into the kitchen, scowling and scrounging around for food.

Looking up from his breakfast, Harvey said, "I see Sally come back with ya."

Paul shrugged his shoulders.

"Is everythin' orright, Paul?" Harvey asked.

"Her mum don't want 'er. Threw us out, stupid *cunt!*"

"Don't use that word 'round 'ere," Harvey said.

Sally walked into the kitchen looking tired.

"Mornin', Sally." Harvey checked his watch. "I have ta leave, or I'll be late fer work."

Katie met Harvey at the door to see him off and gave him a kiss goodbye.

Paul quickly left the house after eating without saying where he was going. Sally spent the day helping Katie and gradually revealed her history with Paul. They had met in Redfern when she was visiting a girlfriend. They hit it off right away. She moved into a house with him owned by a couple, who rented rooms to Paul and two other men. Paul earned his money doing odd jobs, but spent too much of it drinking with his mates. He didn't want to get married.

"But maybe he change his mind," Sally said hopefully. "Last night, he say maybe we git married before baby come."

After the evening meal, Harvey asked Paul to take a walk with him in an attempt to draw out his plans, but all he got from him was a shrug or "Don't know." He decided to give him a few days to settle in before asking again. That night Paul and Sally loudly argued in their room. Their arguments became a regular thing every night.

Arriving home from work, Harvey saw Paul sitting alone at their picnic table in the backyard. He opened two bottles of beer and went out, giving Paul one of the bottles and taking a seat opposite him.

After determining that Katie and Sally were visiting a woman friend, talking a bit about the weather, and then how Harvey's day had gone, Harvey brought up what he needed to discuss.

"Are you looking for work in Gura?"

"No."

"Yer gonna have a baby, Paul. Time to settle down an' get a regular job. I'll—"

"Who gonna bloody hire *me?*—fuckin' Abo convict!"

Paul glared at Harvey, his face full of anger. He took a drink from his bottle and stared off into the distance. Harvey didn't say anything, giving him a chance to cool off. Paul's hostility melted into frustration.

"Life is shit, Dad, I don't know. Everythin's confusin'. Don't make no sense, can't win . . ." He began to massage his temple. "I never feel good 'bout nothin' 'cept when I beat someone's brains out or steal somethin'."

Harvey sat speechless. Did he just hear him say that he only feels good when he beats someone's brains out or steal something?—stealing?

"Look Paul, maybe I can get that Aboriginal union fella ta help ya get a job."

Paul said nothing.

Harvey asked, "Will ya go talk to him, if I can get a meetin'?"

Paul nodded yes.

Harvey set up a meeting for the following Monday. As the weekend approached, the arguments between Sally and Paul grew longer and louder. On Saturday night, soon after Paul arrived home glassy-eyed at 10:00 p.m., the inevitable dispute erupted with Sally. Harvey rolled his eyes and tried to ignore it, until it became a shouting match and then he heard a *slap*. Harvey flung open Paul's bedroom door and saw him with his hand in the air and Sally cowering and crying.

"*PAUL!*" Harvey yelled angrily, "*What* ya doin'?"

Paul protested. "I wasn't gonna hit 'er!"

Katie joined Harvey in the doorway. "Ahhh, Paul," she said, horrified and disappointed, "and she pregnant wit' *yer* baby."

"*I don't want 'er!*" Paul shouted, then violently grabbed Sally's arm and swung her around into Harvey's arms. "Here ya take her. *I don't want this fuckin' bitch!*" Paul grabbed the door and swung it against them forcing them out of his room. He locked the door.

"PAUL!" Harvey demanded. "Ya stop this! It's no good fer nobody."

Paul opened the door with his swag over his back. "I'm gettin' out."

Harvey looked at him as he headed for the door.

"Don't leave like this, Paul," Katie said as he went out the door.

Paul did not return or contact them to tell them where he settled. Having no one to help her, Sally stayed on with Katie and Harvey. On March 24, 1975, she gave birth to a healthy girl. Sally wrote a letter to her girlfriend in Redfern to tell her she had a girl, which she had named Elizabeth, and asked her to tell Paul, if she knew where he was.

On June 30, Harvey received a telegram, addressed to him. He eagerly opened it. It was from Constable Linwood at the Redfern police station. It said:

MR. HARVEY HUDSON-*STOP*-UNABLE TO CALL YOU-*STOP*-SON PAUL IN JAIL-*STOP*-CANNOT GIVE DETAILS-*STOP*-PREFER YOU VISIT RATHER THAN CALL.

Harvey made arrangement with his boss for a day off and took the train to Redfern.

On the train, Harvey leafed through the newspaper, trying not to think too much about what trouble Paul might have got himself into. A photo of Frank Sinatra with the article heading "Cranky Frankie" caught his attention. He always liked his song "Come Fly with Me" and started humming it in his head as he read the article. *What*? Harvey shook his head and chuckled as he read that Sinatra had described Australian women journalists as "buck-and-a-half hookers" for asking offending questions about his personal life. Then he refused to apologize. The journalists union joined with the transport workers union and women's liberation groups for a three-day siege of the Boulevard Hotel where he was staying in Sydney. "Unless he can walk on water, he won't be leaving Australia," one union boss said. The transport unions would not refuel his private jet or service any plane, train, bus, or boat he wanted to use. His "Ol' Blue Eyes" tour had to cancel his appearance in Melbourne. He was stuck until he decided to apologize.

By the time Harvey arrived in Redfern, he had resolved to be stern with Paul, but also to let him know that his father could be counted on to help him through this. At the police station, an officer took Harvey to the office of Constable Linwood, who was smiling until he was told that his visitor was Harvey Hudson.

Seeing the upset look on the constable's face, Harvey thought, oh no, what has Paul done now?

In a somber voice, Constable Linwood said, "Is this your son, Mr. Hudson?" He showed him mug shots of Paul from the front and side of his face.

"Yes, that's Paul. What's he done?"

"He was arrested for a burglary. Then he got himself into a fight with several other inmates, who beat him badly. When the jailers intervened on his behalf to save him, he fought them and had to be forcibly subdued. They placed him in solitary confinement." Linwood took a deep breath and said:

"I regret to inform you, Mr. Hudson, that he hung himself in there with his bed sheet."

"Is he dead?" Harvey asked.

"Yes, he is. I'm sorry."

Harvey was dazed for a second, but pulled himself together quickly. "Where's his body?"

"In the morgue. All I need from you is some identification and the address of your funeral home. We will incur the cost to send the body there."

"I'd like to see him—his body."

"There's no need."

"Don't I have ta confirm it's my son? I want to see him."

"This isn't the first time we've had a problem with him. He's from Gura. He's your son all right."

"I still want to see him."

"That's not allowed by our protocol, Mr. Hudson. You can see him at the funeral home."

Having no alternative, Harvey spent the next two hours on the phone making arrangements with a Gura funeral home and filling out forms to release Paul's body.

Three days later, Harvey shuddered as he followed the funeral director, wearing a stiffly starched white coat, down the stairs and into the embalming room. He saw a body covered by a white sheet on a cold metal table.

"Director, can I 'ave some time ta say goodbye to my boy?" he asked.

"Of course, Mr. Hudson."

Harvey reached hesitantly for the sheet and then lifted it to see Paul's face. He gulped.

It's Paul all right, but his face is horribly battered an' nose smashed ta one side. His front teeth are gone. His neck don't show the damage I'd expect from someone who hung himself an' hung fer a while. More injuries on his arms, torso, an' legs. His right arm's broken. These are more injuries than a brawl with other inmates. He's been beaten with something hard that left long bruises on the skin—like a police billy club. My poor boy.

Harvey was sickened and anguished.

What should I do 'bout this? Those bloody bastards! They beat the hell out of him, an' he died in solitary confinement. But what can I do? Who cares?—no one but Katie an' me. Be smart, don't do nothin' stupid. Admit it, ya can't do nothin'. And nothin' goin' ta bring Paul back, anyway.

Harvey shuffled out of the funeral home thanking the director for giving him some time alone with his son.

* * *

"**Eddie what are** you doing here?" Lydia asked, nonplussed.

"Same as you, to help the Vietnamese boat people," Edward said slightly miffed.

"I'm sorry, Eddie, I just embarrassed myself. I think of you as a Buddhist and didn't expect to see you here in a Catholic church."

"Well, here's the reason for that." Eddie put his arm around the white woman standing beside him. "Colleen, this is Lydia Karolyi, who is . . . Let's see . . . sister of Archibald Armstrong, who yo—"

"Colleen!" Lydia said. "Of course—you're engaged to Eddie."

"Yes, I am."

"Oh, I'm so pleased to meet you. I've heard all about you. Most of my family has met you, except me. You were brought up around here in Marrickville, weren't you?

"Yes, I was, although I live and work in the city now. My parents live only a few blocks from here."

"So, Eddie, did Colleen get you interested in helping the Vietnamese boat people?"

"Wrong again, Lydia. I got *her* involved. But *she's* the reason I'm here, 'cause I'm becoming a Catholic."

"A Catholic, *really* . . . How does your father feel about you leaving your Buddhist faith?"

"I told him I'm not giving up my Buddhist beliefs. Like I told Colleen, I'm just adding Jesus to what I already believe." He looked at her lovingly. "I don't feel any conflict in believing in both."

"What's your religious belief, Lydia?" Colleen asked.

"I'm Anglican."

"Well, Colleen's a serious Catholic. I'm becoming a Catholic because she wants a sacramental marriage by her priest in St. Bernardine's Church and wants to bring up the children as Catholics here—and I agree. I have no problem with becoming a Catholic, except it's a lot of work: I'm learning the catechism, taking religious instruction classes, working with a sponsor, and I have to take some kind of a test and go through something called a rite of election."

Colleen laughed quietly to herself.

"All right . . . I'm muckin' up the process a bit here. Somewhere in there, I convert, I'm baptized, and finally, I'm accepted into the Catholic Church. Once we're both Catholics, no worries."

Colleen asked, "Is this your first time at St. Bernardine's, Lydia?"

"Yes. Though I've been making financial contributions to St. Bernardine's to help with resettlement costs and providing services. Now, I'd like to do a bit more by volunteering my time. St. Bernardine's is doing a great job and is nearest to me in Paddington. How did you get involved, Eddie?"

"I fought in the worthless Vietnam War, you'll recall. I don't feel good about it. We left many of those poor buggers who helped us to fend for themselves. They're desperate now to escape firing squads and reeducation death camps."

"They're also escaping religious persecution," Colleen said. "More than ten percent of those escaping are Roman Catholics. They converted under the colonial French, you know, and the Communists are atheists."

"Yeah, that's right," Edward said. "The least we can do when they arrive here in leaky boats and half-starved is to accept them as refugees and help resettle them. Those calling them 'queue jumpers' are a bunch of heartless, irresponsible bastards."

"Thank goodness, there aren't too many of them," Lydia said. "I've been heartened that the majority of people ... well, at least in Paddington, are sympathetic to helping the Vietnamese boat people resettle here and not worrying so much this time about queue jumping. Actually, a relatively small number of the boats are making it here. Most are ending up in refugee camps in countries north of us. I'm pleased that the Fraser government has made a humanitarian commitment to admitting refugees for resettlement. Of course, the Labor Party is supporting Fraser on this one."

"I think Lydia is right, Eddie, you shouldn't be so negative," Colleen said.

"Hold on, she didn't say I was negative. How could I be negative when the Whitlam Labor government passed the Racial Discrimination Act, eliminating the last vestige of the White Australia Policy? It's finally dead now. Then Fraser turns out to support humanitarian policies—it's all good!"

Colleen asked, "Lydia, don't you have two children an—?" She was cutoff by the booming baritone voice of the priest.

"EXCUSE ALL ... EVERYONE! Please move into the meeting room, so we can start."

* * *

"Here it is!" David Bennett said, "I found it."

"Ah let me see it," his wife Mary said, anxiously taking the newspaper from her husband. The heading of the short article was "Bennett to Planning and Records." Mary read the article aloud:

> "'Mr. James Bennett, the former Head of Community Outreach, NSW Department of Social Welfare, has been appointed the Director of Planning and Records, within the same Department, effective immediately. He undertakes the position vacated by Mr. Frank Cummings, who retired after twenty-three years of devoted service.'"

Two weeks later, James Bennett sat in his new office on a Friday afternoon anxiously waiting for the last employee on his fifth floor to leave for the weekend. Tonight, he intended to break the law. He would try to find his adoption and abandonment records. His Division of Planning and Records was the repository for documents from previous social welfare agencies, including the Aborigines Welfare Board abolished in 1969.

He had determined that his records had to be in the Aborigines Welfare Board's corroded file cabinets or in its musty storage boxes. The keys he needed were in the top drawer of his desk. He hoped that this would be the momentous night that he would find the names of his birth parents and answer questions that had bedeviled him for most of his life.

At six o'clock, James put down his pen and wiped his sweaty hands and forehead with his handkerchief. He took the keys out of his desk and walked around the fifth floor. Finding no one working late, he headed for the storage room.

A burglar must feel like this before he commits a crime, James thought. He paused at the storage room and listened ... It was quiet on his floor, but sounds of the cleaning crew emanated from the fourth floor below. He had to be fast. This is it. He put the key into the door, opened it, and quickly slipped inside. Locking the door behind him, he turned on the lights and walked to the area of the room where the Aborigines Welfare Board's records were stored.

There were fifteen file cabinets against one wall. He walked quickly along them looking at the dates on the file drawers, 1969 to the last cabinet date of 1955. His heart sank. This was not going to be easy. A stack of wood file boxes were piled up in the corner of the room, one on top of the other, in four rows. Scanning the boxes, he found a box at the top of a stack dated 1944-45. Thank God, it's not at the bottom, he thought. He carried a chair over to the stack, stood on the chair seat, got the box down, and carried it to a table.

He began going through its contents, flipping hurriedly through yellow-tinged pages one after another looking for adoptions under the name "Bennett." There was no "Bennett" in 1944. He moved into the "Bs" in 1945 and—Eureka!—found "Bennett, David and Mary." His eyes raced down the page. "Hudson, Katherine and Harvey" were his birth parents, Gura, New South Wales.

Overwhelmed, he sat staring at the piece of paper. Hudson, he repeated to himself . . . Katherine and Harvey Hudson of Gura. *My* parents. The name rang a bell, but he didn't know why.

He had to hurry. Placing his records inside his shirt, he put the box back on the stack, turned off the lights and peeked out the door. With the way clear, he locked the door and rushed down the hall to his office thinking Harvey . . . Hudson . . . Harvey Hudson . . . Gura . . . Hold on, Wellington, that solidly built Aboriginal activist I met at Nanima reserve near Wellington! *His* name was Harvey Hudson! A smile formed on his face. God, could that be him? When was that, the Freedom Ride—1965! Harvey Hudson . . . must have been in his 50s then, so he's nearly . . . 70 now. *Good Lord!* He could be *dead!*

He found a NSW mid-western telephone book in his bookcase and looked up "Hudson, Harvey" in Gura. There he was. *He's still alive!*

James looked at his watch, 6:30 p.m., dinner time. He'd be at home, he thought. Unable to contain himself, James impulsively called the telephone number. A man answered.

"Hello."

"Mr. Hudson?" James said, trying to control his emotions.

"Yes."

"My name is James Bennett, I'm a director with the New South Wales Social Welfare Department. I know you are an activist for Aboriginal rights, Mr. Hudson. I'm an Aboriginal activist myself and would like to stop by for a short chat. I'm driving through Gura on my way back to Sydney on Sunday in the early afternoon. I was wondering if I could stop by your house to meet you and have a short chat."

"What about?" Harvey asked. "I'm not too active anymore."

"Could we leave that until I meet you, Mr. Hudson? I'll only take a half-hour of your time. Got to get back to Sydney. Could I stop by around two o'clock?"

"Orright."

All the points of conversation rehearsed during the drive to Gura flew out of James's emotionally overcharged brain when Harvey answered the door. James stood face-to-face with the man he believed to be his birth father.

James said, "Hello, Mr. Hudson?"

"Yes, Mr. Bennett?"

"Yes, sir."

"I think I 'ave seen ya someplace before," Harvey said, shaking his hand. "C'mon in."

"Nanima reserve, Mr. Hudson. The Freedom Ride in '65."

"Yeah—that's it—with Charles Perkins! You were the two Aborigines."

"Yes, sir."

"Well, I'll be. KATIE, Mr. Bennett's 'ere."

Katie walked into the living room from the bedroom with Sally following.

"Ya won't believe it, Katie, but I—" The look on Katie's face stopped Harvey in his tracks. "What's wrong, Katie."

"Wh-What yer first name?" she said to Mr. Bennett.

"James."

Katie fainted.

They rushed to her side to revive her.

Katie came to quickly. "I just knew soon as I saw ya—ya was James. I saw Paul an' Harvey an' me in ya straightaway, all at the same time. Can't ya see it, Harvey?"

"Yeah, I see it now, Katie. I see it now, but I can't believe it after all these years."

*   *   *

Off Shark Island in light wind conditions, Archibald brought his graceful yacht *Pure Poetry* into the wind and told Lin Yee to "Lower the sail," and then yelled "DROP ANCHOR" to Edward who was at the bow of the boat. It was a special day on Sydney Harbour to celebrate his mother's eightieth birthday. First, they would drink to her health, have lunch, and then watch a race in the harbor. Dinner would be in Manly at Sam Kee's newest Modern Chinese Restaurant in an Armstrong building designed by Ferenc.

Archibald and Edward worked together to securely anchor the boat. Lin Yee went below to assist Sam Kee and his helper Colleen organize lunch. Nigel, Wilhelmina, and Mei-lan sat enjoying the view. Lin Yee emerged carrying a tray of glasses. Behind her, Sam Kee carried a platter of hors d'oeuvres, and Colleen carried a bottle of champagne in an ice bucket.

They were anchored to watch Ferenc race his thirty-two-foot Cavalier yacht. Both Archibald and Ferenc were members of the Royal Prince Edward Yacht Club at Point Piper where they kept their sailboats moored. Their club and the Royal Sydney Yacht Squadron jointly ran inshore races on Saturdays for different classes of keelboats.

Archibald opened the bottle of champagne with a good bit of theater and then walked around filling everyone's glass. He raised his glass to make a toast. "Happy eightieth, Mum! May you have many happy returns."

After "Hear, hears" and clinking of glasses, Lin Yee said, "Leave some champagne to toast my nephew, Eddie, because he's just been elected vice president of his Returned Soldiers League club."

"Thanks, Auntie. . . . I'm the first Chinese-Australian ever to serve in such a position at the RSL club, so I'm pret—*oh look!*—there's Ferenc's boat *Gift of Sydney*." Edward pointed at a sailboat among many approaching.

Nigel peered through the binoculars. "Lydia's at the wheel. That won't last much longer when they jockey for the start line. Uh . . . there . . . Ferenc is taking over."

Ferenc's crew was his wife Lydia, sixteen-year-old son Neville, and thirteen-year-old daughter Megan. They all waved as their boat passed by Archibald's. Everyone waved back.

"WE WILL FOLLOW YOU TO MANLY AFTER THE RACE," Ferenc yelled.

Archibald gave him a thumbs-up okay.

Nigel was pleased to see Lydia's family happily working together on their yacht. It had been touch and go for years. When Lydia had asked Ferenc to file a joint application for divorce, he refused. Upset, she forced him out of their house and filed a sole application for divorce. Before Family Law Court, Ferenc asked the court to order a twelve-month separation for the good of their two children. After they worked out his visitation rights and their finances, Lydia agreed. The one-year separation grew into three with neither of them developing a serious relationship—thank God. They started dating again, and after several months she allowed him to move back into the house. They seemed happier now than ever.

The Fongs and Armstrongs began making their choices about which boat would cross the start line first. Wilhelmina, Sam Kee, and Mei-lan went with *Gift of Sydney*. Edward liked the boat that seemed to be darting around most speedily, and Archibald and Nigel chose the boat captained by a well-known winner. Lin Yee and Colleen both chose the sailboat that looked the most streamlined.

The horn sounded indicating five minutes until the start. The boats maneuvered for the best position to cross the line first, often looking as if they were about to collide and somehow avoiding each other at the last moment. There was a lot of shouting between skippers as frustrations mounted. Nigel was the self-appointed timekeeper with his stopwatch. He called out the completion of each minute from four down to one and then every ten seconds and then individual seconds.

The horn sounded the start when Nigel was on the seventh second to go. No one had selected the boat that crossed the starting line first. *Gift of Sydney* was fourth of the nineteen boats in the race. The boats sailed away from Archibald's anchored yacht on a beam reach heading for the first buoy to be rounded in the race course.

Those on Archibald's *Pure Poetry* settled back to enjoy their afternoon on the water with convivial company, delicious food, and plenty to drink.

*　*　*

"James Bennett is one of the organizers of the event for the New South Wales government," Archibald said. "He's reserved a row of seats for us and the Bennetts in the mid-gallery, so we can hear and see Prime Minister Malcolm Fraser well. There's going to be thirteen of us if everyone shows up."

On November 30, 1981, Archibald and Lin Yee had arrived with Lydia and Ferenc to meet their family members in the grand ornate vestibule of the Sydney Town Hall. Nigel, Wilhelmina, and James were talking together when they arrived. David and Mary Bennett walked into the vestibule shortly thereafter and joined them. James handed out programs to everyone.

They were all invitees to hear the prime minister's inaugural address on multiculturalism intended to welcome and inspire the appointees to the Australian Institute of Multicultural Affairs. While waiting for Sam Kee, Mei-lan, Edward and Colleen, Archibald read the program and the purpose of the Institute:

> By an act of the Federal Parliament, the Australian Institute of Multicultural Affairs was enacted to raise awareness within Australia of its diverse cultures, resulting from increased levels of migration, and how they serve to enrich the whole; to promote tolerance, understanding, harmony and mutual esteem among communities and, in so doing, create a cohesive Australian community; and under the direction of its Minister, provide advice to the Commonwealth Government on all matters relating to the objective of equal participation of every person in our multicultural society.

"Well, Dad, I imagine you never expected to hear a speech by a prime minister embracing multiculturalism," Archibald said.

"Especially Fraser. But then I recall years ago, when Calwell said 'Two Wongs don't make a white' that I told you I didn't expect to see the end of the White Australia Policy either. I've lived long enough to have to eat my words, which I do willingly and gratefully."

"You've created multiculturalism within your own family, Dad," Ferenc said.

"I didn't do it," Nigel said. "Lydia and Archibald were the ones that brought you lot into the family."

"You and Mum didn't have a problem with it though, Dad," Lydia said.

"Do I hear you talking about me," Lin Yee said, "and allowing the 'Yellow Peril' into the family?"

"A beautiful Yellow Peril," Nigel said.

"Aah, Dad," Lin Yee said, putting her arm around his and laying her head against his shoulder.

"I'd like to join this conversation," David Bennett said. "Don't you think that immigration and multiculturalism are doing great things for our city? It goes beyond better restaurants. I think the infusion of new blood has greatly improved our economic and cultural development."

Ferenc said, "With our Greek, Italian, Chinese, Vietnamese, and Jewish neighborhoods, I reckon Sydney and Melbourne are nearly as cosmopolitan as London and New York City, though I haven't visited them."

"We may be the last melting pot after America," Nigel said.

The chimes called people to take their seats. Sam Kee, Mei-lan, Edward and Colleen entered the vestibule and joined their group as they moved toward the hall entrance.

After several preliminary speakers. The Prime Minister, the Right Honorable Malcolm Fraser was introduced. He said:

> Mr. Chairman, Councilors, and appointees to the Australian Institute of Multicultural Affairs, distinguished guests, ladies and gentlemen. I greatly welcome the invitation to give the Institute's inaugural lecture because of the opportunity it provides to explore issues important to the future of our country.
>
> Driven by the conviction that Australia must 'populate or perish,' governments in the postwar period mounted a massive program of immigration, a program which was to create one of the world's most diverse populations. The transformation wrought by that program on our society has been immense and dramatic.
>
> The record shows that Australia has, since 1947, set-

tled almost 3.5 million people from more than 100 countries. Together, we have built a nation capable of embracing an ever increasing degree of ethnic and cultural diversity.

But multiculturalism is concerned with far more than the passive toleration of diversity. It sees diversity as a quality to be actively embraced, a source of social wealth and dynamism. It encourages groups to be open and to interact, so that all Australians may learn and benefit from each other's heritages. Multiculturalism is about diversity, not division—it is about interaction not isolation.

I think each of us will have our own perception of the moment when multiculturalism became more than an aspiration. In my own perspective, in terms of substantive governmental action, that moment came with the Commonwealth's acceptance in 1978 of the Report of Post-Arrival Programs and Services to Migrants. The report identified multiculturalism as a key concept in formulating government policies and recognized that Australia was at a critical stage in its development as a multicultural nation. It re-examined existing assumptions and methods, and urged the need for policies and programs to take new directions. What is important above all is to have in place programs and services which work to create and strengthen the fundamentals of a multicultural society.

Ultimately, the responsibility for multiculturalism rests not just on the government but on the community at large. And in the Australian community, over the past decade, multicultural awareness and practice have indeed spread at a growing pace, and ideas and impetus for change continue to flow from individuals, groups and organizations. We must all be responsible.

The 'we' of whom I speak are not only Australians of Anglo-Celtic origins, but all Australians. To a newly arrived group, earlier migrant communities and their children are now as much a part of the established community as are those who can trace their forbears to the First Fleet.

Our reality is that a growing number of Australians share the conviction that for Australia, multiculturalism is an opportunity to be seized, not a threat from which to retreat.

The appointment of the first group of members of the Institute—who are convened here for the first time—is a very real and tangible indication of this. Your appointments are both a recognition of the contribution you have already made, and an expression of confidence in the work you will continue to undertake in promoting multiculturalism.

Australian multiculturalism is a unique achievement. Australia may have stumbled into the multicultural epoch. We were a nation comparatively small in size and insular in outlook. But within a period of time that is short in historical perspective, Australia has been enlarged in capacities, talents and outlook by millions of men and women from every corner of the globe. Let us take strength and confidence from this knowledge and work together to bring the promise of multiculturalism to fruition, that promise of a cohesive nation that draws strength and unique character from its diversity.

Family Tree
of
Principal Fictional Characters

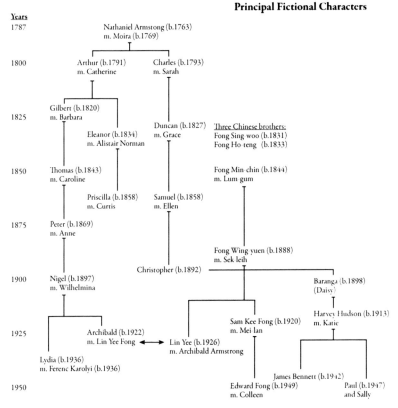

Note: The timeline is approximate and lists only the principal fictional characters. Years of births are shown, but not deaths because they would compromise the story.

FACT OR FICTION?

Because *Gift of Sydney* is a fictional story based on history, the reader may want to know whether some specific part is fact or fiction. By chapter below, I have tried to anticipate readers' questions in this regard.

Chapter 1–CONVICT STAIN

The Aboriginal girl Baranga (Daisy) is an imaginary character. The Benevolent Foundation Orphanage in Bathurst is a made-up name but there were two orphanages in Bathurst in 1903.

There were two managed Aboriginal stations not more than forty miles west of Bathurst where Daisy could have been taken. However, both Warrawindra Aboriginal Station and the nearby town of Barmora are fictitious names. Warrawindra Aboriginal Station is a composite of several stations existing in New South Wales in 1903 where the lives of Aborigines were managed by station managers employed by the NSW Aborigines Protection Board. The description of the station, its policies and management, and its conflicts are offered as typical.

It is true that Sydney streets were illuminated by electric lights replacing gas lamps when the Lady Mayoress threw the switch on July 9, 1904, during a gala event in the Ultimo Power Station.

In 1912, an American Walter Burley Griffin—architect, landscape architect, planner—won the international competition for the city plan design of Canberra, the Federal Capital of Australia. He came to Australia in 1914 to oversee the implementation of his plan and left twenty years later in 1935.

In 1913, Nigel and his mates are "bodysurfing the breakers," which began in the late 1890s. Surfboarding began in 1909 at a few beaches, but really caught on after the famous Hawaiian Olympic swimmer Duke Kahanamoku stayed in and around Freshwater Beach from December 1914 through February 1915 demonstrating surfboard riding techniques to local enthusiasts. For the purposes of my story, I made Kahanamoku's visit two years earlier.

Chapter 2–THE WAR TO END WAR

From the late 1800s, "jack" was used as an euphemism for "anus." It is true that Australian soldiers denigrated their Turkish enemy soldiers by calling them Jacky, Jacko, John, Johnny, and Johnno. These pejorative names had historically been used as racist epithets: Jacky and Jacko for Aborigines and John, Johnny, and Johnno for Chinese.

The Australian Light Horse charge at Beersheba is factual, has been included in several movies, and is often described as the last great cavalry charge of the twentieth century.

Lawrence of Arabia was outside Damascus at the same time as the Australian Light Horse and drove an armored Rolls-Royce, which he called the "Blue Mist."

Chapter 3–THE GREAT DEPRESSION

The historic landmark, The Hotel Bondi, designed by architect E. Lindsay Thompson, was the first large luxury hotel built along the beachfront. However, it was opened in 1920, not 1931, as I have written.

The Murraroo Aborigines Mission, it's Methodist church, and the nearby town of Gura are all fictional. However, the United Aborigines Mission, a Methodist missionary organization, did run missions throughout Australia, including the La Perouse Aborigines Mission south of Sydney on Botany Bay. Their missions in New South Wales were supported by the Aborigines Protection Board and Aborigines Welfare Board. The missionaries and school teachers taught Aborigines their Christian religion and social principles, in part, to facilitate assimilation of light-skinned Aborigines.

Chapter 4–THE SECOND WORLD WAR

The Ninth Division, which the fictional Archibald Armstrong served in, did fight General Rommel, the Desert Fox, in the battle described in Tobruk, Libya. The 14,000 Australian troops called themselves the "Rats of Tobruk" as a badge of honor because Rommel could not defeat them. The division went on to fight in the crucial victory at El Alamein, Egypt, that drove Rommel's Afrika Korps into retreat. The Ninth Division was returned to defend Australia from the Japanese and later was sent to fight in Papua New Guinea as described.

It is true that the military did not accept Aborigines early in the war as recruits, except light-complexioned Aborigines who held a Certificate of Exemption, derisively called a "dog license," issued pursuant to the Aborigines Protection Act, which gave them the same rights as "white" Australians. Later in the war, Aborigines without a Certificate of Exemption could enlist if they passed a doctor's evaluation and verbal test.

On June 1, 1942, three midget Japanese submarines did enter Sydney Harbour and cause the havoc described. A week later, a submarine surfaced off the coast of Bondi Beach and fired ten shells into Sydney with three falling in Bellevue Hill.

Government policy continuing through World War Two allowed the forcible removal of white or black children from their parents for the child's health and welfare when "at risk of significant harm from neglect, abuse, or abandonment." It did not matter if the father or mother was overseas serving Australia during the war. This policy was egregiously applied, however, because most of the children removed (or stolen) from their Aboriginal parents were light-skinned chosen to fulfill the government's policy of assimilation.

Chapter 5–POPULATE OR PERISH

Nigel Armstrong repeats Arthur Calwell's statement "Two Wongs don't make a white" a year earlier than he actually said it, but the remainder of the episode is historically accurate.

It is a fact that the Sydney Opera House was constructed on the peninsula of land that in 1791 was the site of the small brick house built by the first governor of Australia, Arthur Phillip, for his Aboriginal friend, Bennelong, hence the name Bennelong Point.

Chapter 6–CULTURAL CRINGE

The Goossens story is not fiction.

Stage One of the Sydney Opera House was the "podium," which means little to most readers. So, I have referred to Stage One as the concrete foundations and four-story building: basement, ground floor, first floor, and second floor. It is a massive concrete structure that provides the columns on which the three roof shells sit. Within this podium are some 900 rooms, including theaters, music room, rehearsal and recital halls, administrative offices, box offices, conductor's suites, dressing rooms, kitchens and dining rooms, lavatories and lounges, workshops, storage rooms, and mechanical and electric rooms.

The Aboriginal Advancement Association (AAA) is a made-up name. However, the objectives, policies, and programs of the association and the issues it addressed are similar to those of several Aboriginal activist groups at the time.

On March 1, 1961, the name of the client was changed from Sydney Opera House Executive Committee to the Sydney Opera House Trust. For continuity and to avoid confusion, I did not make this name change.

I changed the Department of Local Government to the Department of State Planning because reviewers thought "Local Government" meant the local government of Sydney. The NSW Department of Local Government represents and assists councils and shires throughout New South Wales.

The last Sydney tram service ride was changed from the actual date of February 25, 1961, to November 8, 1962, for the purposes of the story.

Chapter 7–DISSENT AND A FAIR GO

The residents of lovely Duxford Street in Paddington will not find glazed plaster brick plaques with the date of construction and

"NB," for Norman Builders, above their brass doorbell pulls, because it is a fiction for the purposes of the story.

The Freedom Ride as described is historically accurate. The Student Action for Aborigines organization did adopt a nonviolent resistance policy, and American black entertainers did see them off while singing "We Shall Overcome." The students visited Nanima Aboriginal Reserve and did conduct a rather uncomfortable fact-finding survey of living conditions, but the involvement of the Aboriginal Advancement Association is a fiction. Charles Perkins, a creative and tenacious activist for Aboriginal rights was the student organizer and leader of the Freedom Ride and was the first Aboriginal Australian to graduate from university (University of Sydney) in 1966.

It is true that Arup partner Michael Lewis suggested to Jørn Utzon twice that he should retain the large, respected Sydney architectural firm Peddle Thorp & Walker to assist him in the preparation of working drawings and specifications. For fair disclosure, I worked for this firm as a landscape architect and site planner during 1973-75.

Chapter 8–THE LAST MELTING POT

The siege of Frank Sinatra in Sydney for describing Australian women journalists as "buck-and-a-half hookers" is true, but happened in July 1974, not July 1975 as written. Bob Hawke, President of the Australian Council of Trade Unions and future prime minister, negotiated a written apology from Sinatra that allowed him to finish his tour and leave Australia.

The Refugee Resettlement Assembly is a made-up name and there is no St. Bernardine's Catholic Church in Sydney, but several Catholic parishes assisted the Vietnamese boat people to resettle in Marrickville and other communities in the Sydney area.

In 1980, the correct name was Returned Services League not Returned Soldiers League, as I have written it.

Prime Minister Fraser's inaugural address on multiculturalism to the Institute of Multicultural Affairs in on November 30, 1981, is factual. Although it was given in Melbourne, not Sydney.

Multiculturalism is part of the unifying theme of this novel, in part, because years ago I read a policy paper resulting from the 1995 Global Cultural Diversity Conference held in Sydney, Australia (www.unesco.org/most/sydpaper.htm). I was amazed that Australian society could transition in such a short number of years from its exclusionary White Australia Policy to a policy of multiculturalism, and did it relatively smoothly. It illustrated to me the maturation of its democratic society, its institutions, and its people, whose ethos is egalitarianism and giving everyone a fair go.

ACKNOWLEDGEMENTS
AND SOURCES

This novel would not have been written without the indispensable assistance of my wife Judy, a published author (Judith W. Richards), whose love and support were unwavering throughout the years of researching, writing, and reviewing the novel. She was my principal editor and critic, pushing me to rewrite until I could get it right, or at least, better.

As in the first Sydney novel, l am greatly indebted to Nigel Parbury, formerly with the New South Wales Ministry of Aboriginal Affairs and author of *Survival: A History of Aboriginal Life in New South Wales* for saving me from many errors, offering his clear historical perspective, and making suggestions to improve the story.

I am grateful to the following friends who honored me by reading early drafts of part or all of the novel and providing their comments: Australians Rhonda Bell, Eileen Rainey, and Stafford Watts; and Americans John Ryan, Gary Rubens, Pat and Tom Baubonis, and Judy and Stu Searles. My warmest thanks to them all.

Readers should not presume that the reviewers above agree with everything I have written in the novel. The interpretations of historical issues and events, many of them controversial, are entirely mine alone, as are any outright errors.

I thank AuthorSupport for the cover design, illustrations, interior layout formatting, and placing the entire paper book in print-ready form. They also produced the ebook in Mobi and ePub formats. I enjoyed working with them again. And lastly, I thank Aries Books for its continued support.

With a commitment to accuracy, I list below my primary sources of historical information on which this novel is based.

PRIMARY SOURCES

Australian Institute of Aboriginal Studies. *La Perouse: The Place, the People and the Sea, a collection of writing by members of the Aboriginal community*. Canberra: Aboriginal Studies Press, 1987.

Baker, Sidney J. *The Australian Language*. Melbourne: Sun Books, 1976.

Barnard, Loretta, et al., eds. *Australia Through Time*. 10th ed. Sydney: Random House Australia, 2002.

Baume, Michael. *The Sydney Opera House Affair*. Sydney: Thomas Nelson Ltd., 1967.

Beaumont, Joan. *Australia's War 1914-18*. St. Leonards, NSW: Allen & Unwin, 1995.

Bergerud, Eric M. *Touched by Fire: The Land War in the South Pacific*. NY: Viking, 1996.

Bevan, Christopher. *A Kinchela Boy*. Sydney: Bideena Publishing Company, 2009.

Bishop, Bert. *Hell, the Humour, the Heartbreak: a Private's View of World War I*. Kenthurst, NSW, Australia: Kangaroo Press, 1991.

Blainey, Geoffrey. *A Shorter History of Australia*. Sydney: Random House Australia, 2000.

Blake, Barry J. *Australian Aboriginal Languages*. Sydney: Angus & Robertson, 1981.

Calwell, A. A. *Be Just and Fear Not*. Hawthorne, VIC: Philip & O'Neil, 1972.

Chambers, John H. *A Traveller's History of Australia*. Gloucestershire, UK: The Windrush Press, 1999.

Charlton, Peter. *Pozieres 1916: Australians on the Somme*. Australia: Methuen Haynes, 1985.

Choy, Wayson. *Paper Shadows: A Chinatown Childhood*. Ringwood, VIC, Australia: Penguin Books, 2000.

Clark, Manning. *A Short History of Australia*. 4th ed. Ringwood, VIC, Australia: Penguin Books, 1995.

Day, David. *Claiming A Continent: A History of Australia*. Sydney: Angus & Robertson, 1996.

——. *John Curtin: A Life*. Sydney: HarperCollins, 1999.

——. *The Great Betrayal: Britain, Australia and the Onset of the Pacific War, 1939-42*. London: Angus & Robertson, 1988.

Diamond, Jared. *Guns, Germs, and Steel, The Fates of Human Societies*. New York City: W. W. Norton & Company, Inc., 1999.

Drew, Philip. *Sydney Opera House: Jørn Utzon*. London: Phaidon Press Ltd., 2002.

——. *The Masterpiece: Jørn Utzon, A Secret Life*. South Yarra, VIC, Australia: Hardie Grant Books, 1999.

——. *Utzon and the Sydney Opera House*. Annandale, NSW, Australia: Inspire Press, 2000.

Duek-Cohen, E. *Utzon and the Sydney Opera House*. Sydney: Morgan Publications, 1967.

Facey, A. B. *A Fortunate Life*. Ringwood, VIC, Australia: Penguin Books, 1983.

Fitzgerald, Shirley. *Red Tape, Gold Scissors: The Story of Sydney's Chinese*. Sydney: State Library of New South Wales Press in association with the City of Sydney, 1997.

——. *Sydney 1842-1992*. Sydney: Hale & Iremonger, 1992.

Fitzgerald, Shirley and Garry Wotherspoon, eds. *Minorities: Cultural Diversity in Sydney.* Sydney: State Library of New South Wales Press, 1995.

Floyd, Carol and Julia Collingwood. *The Sydney Opera House.* Sydney: New Holland Publishers, 2000.

Fromonot, Françoise. *Jørn Utzon: The Sydney Opera House.* Electa, Milan: Elemond Editori Associati, 1998.

Gilbert, Martin, *Winston Churchill: Road to Victory, 1941-45.* London: Houghton Mifflin, 1986.

Hall, Robert A. *Fighters from the Fringe: Aborigines and Torres Strait Islanders recall the Second World War.* Canberra: Aboriginal Studies Press, 1995.

———. *The Black Diggers: Aborigines and Torres Strait Islanders in the Second World War.* Sydney: Allen and Unwin, 1989.

Harney, W. E. *Tales From the Aborigines.* Sydney: Seal Books, 1995.

Hill, A. J. *Chauvel of the Light Horse: A Biography.* Carlton, VIC: Melbourne University Press, 1978.

Horne, Donald. *The Lucky Country.* Ringwood, VIC, Australia: Penguin Books, 1971.

Idriess, Ion L. *The Desert Column.* Sydney: Angus & Robertson Publishers, 1932.

Jackomos, Alick and Derek Fowell. *Living Aboriginal History of Victoria.* Melbourne: Cambridge University Press, 1991.

James, Lawrence. *Imperial Warrior: Life and Times of Field-Marshal Viscount Allenby.* London: Weidenfeld & Nicolson, 1992.

Jill, Duchess of Hamilton. *First to Damascus: the Australian Light Horse and Lawrence of Arabia.* Sydney: Kangaroo Press, 2002.

Johansen, Midge. *The Penguin Book of Australian Slang.* Castle Hill, NSW: Penguin Books, 1966.

Jones, Peter. *Ove Arup: Masterbuilder of the Twentieth Century.* New Haven, USA: Yale University Press, 2006.

Kelly, Paul. *100 Years: The Australian Story.* Crows Nest, NSW: Allen & Unwin, 2001.

Keneally, Thomas. *The Chant of Jimmie Blacksmith.* Sydney: HarperCollins, 2000.

Laidlaw, Ronald. *Australian History.* Sydney: MacMillan Education, 1991.

Latimer, Jon. *Alamein.* Cambridge: Harvard University Press, 2004.

Lockwood, Douglas. *I, the Aboriginal.* Sydney: Seal Books, 1971

Lydon, Jane. *Many Inventions: The Chinese in the Rocks 1890 -1930.* Melbourne, Australia: Monash Publications in History, 1999.

Maddock, Kenneth. *The Australian Aborigines, A Portrait of Their Society.* Ringwood, VIC, Australia: Penguin Books, 1972.

Messent, David. *Opera House Act One.* Sydney: David Messent Photography, 1997.

Mikami, Yuzo. *Utzon's Sphere: The Sydney Opera House, how it was designed and built.* Tokyo: Shokokuska, 2001.

Moorhouse, Geoffrey. *Sydney.* Sydney: Allen & Unwin, 2000.

Morgan, Sally. *My Place.* Australia: Fremantle Arts Centre, 1987.

Morris, Jan. *Sydney.* London: Penquin Book, 1993.

Nolan, Melanie, current ed. *Australian Dictionary of Biography.* The Australian National University: www.adb.online.anu.edu.au.

Nunn, Judy. *Beneath the Southern Cross.* Sydney: Random House, 2000.

Parbury, Nigel. *Survival: A History of Aboriginal Life in New South Wales.* Sydney: NSW Department of Aboriginal Affairs, 1986 and 2005.

Park, Ruth. *The Harp in the South*. Ringwood, VIC, Australia: Penguin Books, 1975.

Human Rights and Equal Opportunity Commission. (Bringing Them Home Report) *Report of the National Inquiry into the Separation of Aboriginal and Torres Strait Islander Children from Their Families*. Canberra: Commonwealth of Australia, 1997.

Project Gutenberg Australia. *Dictionary of Australian Biography*. See: www.gutenberg.net.au.

Read, Peter. *A Hundred Years War: The Wiradjuri People and the State*. Canberra: Australian National University Press, 1988.

———. *Charles Perkins: A Biography*. Ringwood, VIC, Australia: Penguin Books, 2001.

Read, Peter, ed. *Down There With Me on the Cowra Mission*. Sydney: Pergamon Press, 1984.

Reed, A. H. and A. W. *Aboriginal Words of Australia*. Australia: New Holland Publishers, 1994.

Shaw, A. G. L. and H. D. Nicolson. *An Introduction to Australian History*. Sydney: Angus & Robertson, 1959

State Library of New South Wales. "Historical Records of Australia" series in the Mitchell Library, Sydney.

Turnbull, Lucy Hughes. *Sydney, Biography of a City*. Sydney: Random House Australia, 1999.

Watson, Anne, ed. *Building a Masterpiece: The Sydney Opera House*. Sydney: Powerhouse Publishing, 2006.

Webber, Peter. *Peter Hall, Architect: The Phantom of the Sydney Opera House*. Boorowa, NSW: The Watermark Press, 2012.

Welsh, Frank. *Australia: A New History of the Great Southern Land*. Woodstock, NY: The Overlook Press, 2006.

Weston, Richard. *Utzon: Inspiration, Vision, Architecture*. Hellerup, Denmark: Edition Bløndal, 2002.

Willard, Myra. *History of the White Australia Policy to 1920*. Melbourne, Australia: Melbourne University Press, 1974.

Williamson, Brian C. *Six Bob Trooper*. Sydney, NSW: Tenterfield Star, 1992.

Woolley, Ken. *Reviewing the Performance: The Design of the Sydney Opera House*. Boorowa, NSW: The Watermark Press, 2010.

Wilkes M. O. *A Dictionary of Australian Colloquialisms*. Sydney: Sydney University Press, 1978.

Id Photography

About the Author

D. MANNING RICHARDS has lived and worked in Sydney, Australia, three different times for a total of eight years. He holds Bachelor of Science in Landscape Architecture and Master of City Planning degrees and is an avid amateur historian. His writing of short stories led to his debut novel *Destiny in Sydney* published in 2012, which was the first in a series of novels about Sydney. *Gift of Sydney* is the second. He lives in Virginia with his wife. His most recent information may be found at www.dmanningrichards.com.

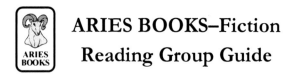

ARIES BOOKS–Fiction
Reading Group Guide

Gift of Sydney

<u>Discussion Points</u>

1. What was the most surprising thing you learned about Sydney or Australia in this novel?

2. Who was your favorite character and why?

3. What was the saddest event and the most uplifting in the novel?

4. Could Harvey and Katie have done something to reverse Paul's slow slide into drugs and self-destruction?

5. Should Lydia have divorced Ferenc?

6. Why was Lin Yee drawn to Archibald?

7. Christopher was a rogue, but what do you think of him as a character in the novel?

8. Did you sense the gradual change in Chinese generations from traditional Chinese values to Australian white values? Over generations, will the minority culture always adopt the values of the majority culture regardless of the country?

9. The author wrote in his Author's Note that he gave a disproportionate number of pages to dramatize the story of the Sydney Opera House. It was obviously an interesting topic for him, was it for you?

10. Did you like or dislike the author's emphasis on action and adventure?

11. Discuss the similarities and differences of Aborigines living with racism in Australia as compared with American Indians and black Americans living in the USA.

12. The storyline mentions time and again that egalitarianism and giving everyone a "fair go" are deeply held values of Australian society. Discuss how these values could have existed at the same time Aborigines, Chinese, and other minorities were mistreated.

13. What are the pluses and minuses of multiculturalism as illustrated in the lives of the characters in the novel?

14. Was there an overriding theme that held the narrative together until the end of the novel?

15. What was your favorite part of the novel and your least favorite? Write it down, sign it, and drop it into a hat for the fun of comparing your choices with others.

Lightning Source UK Ltd.
Milton Keynes UK
UKOW02f2243021014

239588UK00001B/20/P